FOR ALL YOUR ENDEAVOURS

DAVID SHARP

CRANTHORPE
—MILLNER—
PUBLISHERS

First published by Cranthorpe Millner Publishers (2024)

ISBN 978-1-80378-223-2 (Paperback)

www.cranthorpemillner.com

Cranthorpe Millner Publishers

Printed and bound by CPI Group (UK) Ltd
Croydon, CR0 4YY

MIX
Paper | Supporting
responsible forestry
FSC® C013604

For my family

PROLOGUE

Jimmy sat inside the cab of his JCB excavator rolling a cigarette. He looked down the length of the digger arm, at the matted, but obviously curly, hair just visible amongst the deep brown of the peaty mud. The exposed hairy nape of neck extended into broad, rounded shoulder-blades, clothed in a brown tinted, tight, but wrinkled, leather-like skin. If there was more of the body to be found, at present it would stay nestled deep into the bottom of the trench, held fast within the peat and mud. He had no intention of digging further.

He pushed the door right back, so that it latched in the open position. He pulled a flask from his ancient canvas snack-bag, unscrewed the dented tin cup from its top, removed the stopper, then, balancing the cup on the grimy dashboard, he poured a full cup of the dark brown liquid that was supposed to be tea. Having retained the flask for so many years, the tannin on the inside had taken the colour of old teak, giving the liquid a taste of its own. A flavour somewhere between coffee and tea, but with a subtle, nicotine-like aftertaste.

With the engine off, door wide open and the warm rays of sun streaming into the cab, Jimmy relaxed into the natural silence of the open moorland surrounding him. He never had a radio on. He hated the constant chatter, interspersed by the occasional decent music, a radio offered. So, once the ignition was off, the stillness was all but complete, interrupted only by the gentle ticking of the machine cooling down. There was an occasional creak as the hydraulics controlling the digger bucket settled into their own downtime rest period. Jimmy struck a match, lit his roll-up, took a draw on it, inhaled, then, picking at the loose bits of tobacco stuck to his lower lip, he pushed his seat back and put his feet up on the door frame to enjoy his break.

An occasional gentle breeze rippled the stems of sedge, cotton grass and weedy clumps that clothed the ground around his work place. Enough to rustle and move them erratically, as if things crawled between them. Somewhere, very, very high up, Jimmy could hear the almost continual song of a skylark, the sound rising and falling, carried on the wind. Though Jimmy recognised the repetitive song, he'd never seen the bird itself in all the years he'd been working the land. He'd learned to identify the different bird songs that accompanied his long days. The 'poop-poo' of the cuckoo in early summer. The machine gun taps of a woodpecker. The conglomerate chatter of swallows skimming the ground scooping insects. Screaming squadrons of swifts chasing around the sky before disappearing into roofs of old farm buildings up on the moor. But the skylark, well, that was the one that had got away. It always lifted well clear of the ground before it commenced its chorus, by then it was out of Jimmy's sight. But he knew who was singing.

Jimmy was locally renowned. He could scrape a trench to

2

an exact depth or measurement as requested. He could give it a fall in any direction you wished, with a slope in millimetres if need-be, though he preferred inches. He could use the excavator bucket to tap in marker pegs, leaving exactly twenty centimetres standing clear of the ground. Neat enough that you could lay a spirit level across them, watch the bubble hover in the centre of the glass. But watching a skylark, singing on the wing, no chance. Too quick. Too small. Too high and too far. Far outside his sight boundaries. But that didn't stop him loving the sound of its song drifting on the wind.

It was Jimmy's skill with bucket and blade that kept him in high demand and, as today, often contracted for work by Dartmoor Parks Authority. They knew he could be trusted. Left alone with a task to be completed on time, to the agreed budget, no additional scars to be seen. Not a granite marker or waymark cross-post laid flat. No gates left hanging off hinges, broken beyond repair. The moors were in safe hands with Jimmy at the controls.

Jimmy's task for the last week had been digging drainage channels to dry out an area of bog that had caused endless problems for the farmer who leased the land, as well as for hikers and walkers who came this way using the right-of-way for a shortcut onto the high moor. Many an animal had to be roped up, hauled out of the mire. Ponies, sheep, and cattle. After many years of negotiation, it had been agreed to drain this area, and form a proper pond and scrape lower in the valley. This way, one problem solved meant an improved wildlife habitat would've been created. Jimmy had identified the best location for the pond, and the task at the moment was stripping back the sedge and cotton grass to be reused around the newly created wetland. Once finished, the water table would backfill. To be honest, he could've done it in half the time using the big swing-shovel, but the Park Authority were sticklers. They wouldn't let a tracked vehicle come down the old drover's road. It would've caused too much damage to the ancient trackway they'd said. They were probably right. So, the excavator it had to be.

It had been taking out the deep, second slice of the main trench that had brought Jimmy's day to a sudden halt. He was in amongst the wettest part of the mire. He'd put on the wider feet. Pinned them onto the ends of the stabilising legs to stop him from sinking. Laid the wide front bucket to full extent as an extra precaution on this soft surfaced, deep bog and, using the smaller backhoe to slice through the peat, he created individual channels in a herring-bone pattern, connecting up with the long, deep, rift-like valley that had been cut previously to take the surface water away and down the hill.

The moment Jimmy's blade had slid across the soft peat and exposed the deep brown, shiny, leather-like surface, Jimmy had thought it was a suitcase. But, in an instant, he knew what he'd exposed. It was flesh. His first thought was, a pony, calf or a long-dead cow. If he opened it, it was going to smell bad. Really, really bad. With a deft flick of his wrist, he'd lifted the blade a couple of centimetres and cleared the peat around the body. As it cleaved away, the dirty water disappeared, exposing what appeared to be a shoulder, an arm, part of a sloping back. A human back. A shiver had rippled through Jimmy. He'd heard about 'bog bodies', pulled from bogs elsewhere in the country. Sacrificed. Dumped into watery graves thousands of years before. However old it was, however long it had lain there, Jimmy knew one thing for certain. This job wasn't going to finish on time.

Jimmy had grabbed his old builders' trowel, kept in the door pocket for scraping his boots, and jumped from the cab. Stepping across the top of the back-hoe blade so as not to have to get down into the mud, he'd taken a closer look. There were no two-ways about it, it was a body. He could see the curve of a shoulder tapering back toward the arm, the lower part still buried out of sight in the peat. The body was lying face down, left arm drawn back. Using his trowel, he gently peeled back the wet, sticky peat. He could clearly see naked flesh, the shoulders, part of both arms, the top part of a broad back. Flesh a deep, peaty brown, stretched taught. Wrinkled, yet unmistakably skin. As Jimmy crouched and took it all in, the breeze stirred the grass once more, sending a chill across his back, cooling the sweat on his shirt and setting the hairs on the back of his neck standing on end. Just for a second, Jimmy had felt fear. Fear, and sudden deep sadness, from being that close to somebody who'd lain here, face down in the mud, in silent darkness for possibly thousands of years, just waiting to be found.

Back in his cab, Jimmy flicked dregs from the cup and screwed it back onto the flask. It went back into the canvas bag beside the seat. Leaving the door open and, taking one last look around the valley, he turned the key, shattering the silence. Putting rooks to flight from sycamore trees in the bottom field. Jimmy lifted the blade to one side of the recumbent body and took another long, deep gouge to take the water away from where he knew people would have to work. Scraping away with little trowels. Knee-pads embedded in mud. Wire frames marking grid references. Every point of extraction catalogued, photographed for a historical database.

As the water trickled down the new trench, Jimmy gently laid back a section of grassy turf over the exposed leathery skin. He wanted to make sure the foxes, or local crows, didn't cause any harm to the remains. He kicked back his seat, turned off the engine and poured himself another cup of the brown flask liquid. There'd be no more work here for some time. The body had lain there for a long while. The time taken over a cup of tea would make no difference. It didn't matter for the moment. There was no mobile signal up here. He'd have to walk back up the trackway to his van, then drive back almost to Princetown before he could get a decent signal.

Once there, he'd phone Brian Cave, the park ranger, his go-between, and report his find. After that, he'd just have to sit back and watch as the site exploded. Filling with archaeologists, scientists, park officials and the rest. Still, looking on the bright side, they'd find no one better to complete the excavation. With his gentle touch of hand to eye coordination, and his digger already on site, there was still some money to be made from this. Maybe even a picture in the paper or a bit on the telly. There could be exciting, cash-filled times ahead. He'd better wipe the mud off his name, written on the arm of the digger, before he left site, then drop into the Polish car wash with the pickup. On the way home, he'd pop into the Copy House. Get some more cards printed. Yep, busy, busy days ahead.

CHAPTER ONE

Damn was Brian's first thought when he got the call from Jimmy that evening. Damn on many levels.

Firstly, he'd started making the cheese sauce to go with the pasta, it would never work if he stopped stirring now. Secondly, he'd spent months negotiating the drainage plan with farmer Pete Claypole at Whiddons Farm. He was a cantankerous, miserable sod who only ever thought of himself. Coming up with one scheme after another. Anything that would pull in a grant or funding. Anything rather than actually working the land himself.

And thirdly, bloody thirdly, head office would have a field day!

Brian had fought long and hard with superiors to get that mire drained down. Claypole had been mithering on about that bog for four years. Brian couldn't prove it, but he was sure at least two of the cows that had gotten stuck in that mire had probably been driven in by Claypole himself, prior to calling the fire brigade for assistance. The only way Brian was going to get him off his back was to drain it, something the Parks Authority didn't like doing. Any change to the Dartmoor habitat had to be researched, debated, argued and proven. Then, researched again, habitat recorded, costed, funding sought, project risk assessed and, finally, approved at committee level before any work began. This plan had taken two years before the digger work had begun. Now it would grind to a halt. The CEO would blame him. Just for the sake of it. Farmer Claypole would blame him. For not just pulling the body out and sticking it in a skip. And Brian's wife, Chrissie, would blame him, because he'd been left with the simple task of making the dinner, now the sauce was lumpy and the pasta stodgy.

Damn, damn, and treble damn.

Brian thanked Jimmy for the call. Told him to move to the bottom field, continue taking out the pond and scrape, at least the water that drained would have somewhere to go and begin settling out. It would drain the excavation site, and if he was still around over the coming days, whatever the authority decided to do, he'd be on hand to help out. At 5:30 p.m. there was no point telephoning the office. It would wait until the morning. For the moment, the important thing was to get the pasta and ruined sauce into the bin and start again before Chrissie came back downstairs from putting the kids to bed. The last thing he wanted was to give any excuse for yet another earbashing. There'd been far too many of those of late.

Now he had time to think about it he realised, providing of course Jimmy was right, and that what he'd uncovered wasn't just the arse-end of a cow, it was in fact, quite exciting. To his knowledge, during his working life on the moor, there'd never been a bog body found in this part of the world. In recent years ancient, long-forgotten dwellings, villages and ridgeways had been located across the moor. These were being archaeologically excavated and mapped to give a better understanding of how places like Dartmoor developed and became the landscapes they saw today. A collection of roundhouse dwellings had been located close to the main farm buildings at Whiddons. A 'collection of dwellings' was stretching it a bit. Basically, the outlines of a small village had appeared during a drought several years ago.

They'd been spotted from an aircraft that had been specifically looking for shadows and outlines. They'd been plotted, noted, and there was a plan afoot to cut a trial excavation through the area to try and get a complete timeline for the hamlet. Of course, to date there was no funding. If this did turn out to be a bog body and they could prove a connection with the dwellings, this could be the start of a whole new project. Brian had a real buzz of excitement. Could this be a way of getting rid of Claypole? Terminating his lease, which by coincidence only had two more years before renegotiations, then develop the farm as a visitor centre. Have a museum for any artefacts recovered. Build replica roundhouses, and have actors dressed in the role of villagers. School visits, education space, bloody hell, this could be big. This could be huge. To make matters even better, the cheese sauce mark two was creamy, smooth and spot-on. The pasta had bubbled the right length of time and there was the sound of footsteps on the stairs.

The following morning, bang on eight o'clock, Brian put in a call to Alison Graves, Dartmoor Parks Director of Conservation and Archaeology. To be honest, he should be reporting to Steve Clift, the head ranger, but Brian and he didn't get on. Brian would leave it to Alison to move the story further up the pipeline.

"Morning, Ali. You know you've been mapping the shadows of roundhouses at Whiddons Farm? Well, I've something that may interest you."

"I thought you were draining down Claypole's bog, so-to-speak," replied Alison. "Don't tell me you've found some relics, Brian, please, that would be too much to ask."

"Well, don't get too excited, but if Jimmy's right and, wait for it, he only phoned last night, so I haven't had a chance to confirm it. But... he thinks he's unearthed a bog body."

"Are you serious? A bloody bog body! On Dartmoor? Seriously?"

"Well, it may still turn out to be a cow's arse," Brian said, aware of the snorted laugh on the other end of the line. "Jimmy did appear quite positive last night though, almost frothing at the mouth. I've told him to hang fire until we've had a chance to verify, but I flipped a coin as to who to tell first, you or Steve, and you're it. So, what do you reckon? Do you have time to meet me this morning, take a look before we flag it up the line?"

"Well, it's nice to know I was on one side of the coin, Brian, and I'm always glad of a chance to get out of this bloody office. So, the answer is yes, what time?"

"How about 9:30? I suggest you bring your wellies. We can drive down as far as the barns and park there. See you then."

Brian turned off the tarmacked road and down the Whiddons Farm trackway. In his mirror he caught sight of Alison's white 4x4 coming down the road from the opposite direction. At the bottom of the lane, he pulled in beside the barns, pulling up beside Jimmy's beaten-up truck which, unusually, looked remarkably clean. Seconds later, Ali pulled in beside him in her new purchase, all part of her divorce settlement, a Porsche 4x4.

Brian swung out of his Jeep. "Morning, Ali," he said with a broad smile.

"Oh, shut up. It's just a posh motor, stop drooling."

"Ali, I never said a word. I was smiling because I was pleased to see you."

In fact, he was telling the truth, he enjoyed meeting up with Ali. She knew her stuff and was good at it; he liked that. She also had a wicked sense of humour.

"Stop it," said Alison, a hint of frustration in her voice. "You know it does you no good to get excited early in the morning. A car's a car. It's just that some are better than others. Now, which way's the bog? And no jokes. Let's take a look at Jimmy's find."

Alison pulled on a jacket, tucked her hair into a beanie hat and they strolled off in the direction of the valley, the sound of Jimmy's digger in the distance.

"So, what does Claypole think about this find?" asked Alison.

"You've got to be joking? He'll be the last to know until we know for sure what we've got. Whatever his reaction, it'll be a pain in the arse, you can bet on that. He'll either moan we're trying to get out of draining the mire or want to claim some credit. Whatever he does, he'll want to make money out of it. I want to make sure he doesn't make any mileage whatsoever.

As far as he knows, we're heading down to see how the ponds are shaping up. I told Jimmy to say nothing."

When they reached Jimmy, he hadn't been wasting his time.

There was a neat series of herringbone trenches leading out of the mire, connecting to one long, deeper, V-shaped gulley. This ran with a curve down the hill, ending in a shallow, wide scrape, terminating in an even wider, deeper pond. It was now several feet deep, filled with brown, peaty water, the surface covered in drifts of twigs. Brian was impressed. He liked Jimmy's work. He was a craftsman. Jimmy had only been here three days, yet the groundwork was almost complete. If they could sort this bog body business quickly the whole job and associated landscaping could be over. Done and dusted by the end of next week. Brian waved to Jimmy to get his attention. Jimmy laid the bucket down in the bottom of the trench and turned off the engine. He jumped down from the digger.

"Morning, Jimmy," said Brian. "I think you've met Alison; she's been drawing up the site plan with regards the shadows of the settlement. I thought it'd be good for her to join us, to have a look at what you've found. Have you seen Claypole?"

"Nope. Can't imagine he'd make the effort to walk this far from his fireside without a grant. I've not seen hide nor hair and that suits me. Suits me bloody fine."

"So, Jimmy," said Alison, "don't keep us in suspense, where's this bog body then?"

Jimmy led them up the hill, stepping across the network of trickling channels, to the tufted section of turf laid across his friend in the bog. He rolled it back, hearing the intake of breath from his companions.

12

"Bloody hell, Jimmy! It's a body," said Brian.

"Well to be honest, Bri, I did tell you that last night."

"Christ, it's freaky," said Alison. "It's lying there as if it's asleep."

"Well, unless it can hold its breath for a couple of thousand years, I think that's highly unlikely," Brian added flippantly.

"Oh shut up, you know what I mean. Look at the skin, you can see the shape of the shoulder muscle. However long it's been buried here it's just... so well preserved," Alison whispered.

"Why are we whispering?" whispered Brian.

"I don't know, I just think a little reverence for the dead should be in order."

Alison pulled rubber gloves from her coat pocket and gently rolled back the corner of turf cut by Jimmy to cover the corpse. She rolled the turf upwards, exposing the back of the neck. As the nape was exposed, she realised there was hair attached to the base of the skull.

"My God, Brian! It had curly hair."

She looked for a couple of seconds, tempted to touch, then rolled the peaty slab back down to cover the find. When she turned to climb out of the gulley, Brian noticed the glint of tears in her eyes.

"This needs a forensic team down here bloody quick-smart before the body starts to degrade or, worse still, some animal finds it," said Alison.

"Worse still if that animal turns out to be a Claypole," Jimmy added.

"He'll have it up in front of some TV crew and selling

tickets by tonight," replied Brian. "We need to take control of this right now. Jimmy, will you carry on around the pond edges? Make it look like normal routine down here until we can get a team together and hit this site hard with fencing and security before Claypole knows what's happening."

"Not a problem, Bri. Just keep me in the loop, don't fence me out, so to speak. You know I wanna be part of this."

"Not a problem, Jimmy, we owe you that." Brian held out a muddy hand and they shook on it.

Back at the cars they were changing their boots when, much to Brian's annoyance, Pete Claypole came around the corner of the barn.

"Morning, Mr Claypole, not a bad one, is it?" said Brian, holding out his hand in friendship in an attempt to keep things normal.

Claypole took it, gave it a limp handshake. They both knew there was no love lost between them.

"How's it going down there? Hope ain't making a bloody mess," the farmer said gruffly.

"Why don't you pop down and have a look? To be honest, I'm pleased with it so far. Jimmy's cut the drainage channels. Taken out both the pond and the scrape. There's already a couple of feet of water settling..."

"Just as long as tis finished when you said t'would be," interrupted the farmer. "I hope to pull the cattle down off the tops and put em into that field soon as you're done."

"I've already told you, Mr Claypole. It'd make sense to leave that land for six months or more. Let it settle. It needs to finish draining for the grass to return naturally," Brian said, still managing a smile, the corners of his mouth just turned up enough to support the impression.

"All right for you to say, Cave. But I need access to grass and water for the summer. My cattle have been working through the top of the moor right through winter. Now they need a boost for the calves," Claypole said, standing full on to Brian, face to face.

"Do you know, Mr Claypole, we've worked on this project for two years and to be honest with you, I'm sick and bloody tired of it. So, you can stick your poxy cattle in there any time you like. I couldn't give a monkey's arse any longer," Brian replied, smiling broadly.

He held out his hand, took hold of Claypole's before the man realised what was happening, shook it and turned his back on the man.

"Right, Alison, the 'Plume of Feathers' for coffee and a bit of a regroup and catch-up?"

He opened Ali's door for her, watched as she swung her legs in and closed her door, all the while aware of the broad smile across her face. Within minutes, they were driving away in convoy, leaving Claypole standing by the barn, his mouth wide open.

Brian put the coffees down on the table as Alison started to laugh.

"Did you see the look on Claypole's face? God, that was brilliant. I've never seen that man stuck for words, he just stood there dumbfounded. I couldn't believe you kept smiling. Bloody hell, that's made my day. Brilliant, Brian, just bloody brilliant."

"Well, if I can make your day, Ali, it was worth it. I just thought 'what a tosser you really are, mate'. You've no idea that, by morning, the whole field will be fenced, chained and padlocked. I've had it up to here with him. He has me on speed dial, as if I was his personal bloody dogsbody. Well bog body or no, I've had enough of him." Brian sat down opposite her, bending to tuck a folded beer mat under one table leg to stop it rocking.

"So, who goes on the list?" Alison asked, picking up her coffee and taking a sip.

"Well, we have to tell Steve Clift and Chris Wyre for the parks authority, which means Steve will want to bring in his brother Colin from the university in Exeter, which makes sense, really. He's been involved in archaeological digs and investigations across Devon, quite a few on the moors. He knows his stuff and always brings along his best students. Gut feeling is we should leave it at that for now and see who else they decide to bring in. What do you think?"

"I'd go with that to start with," Alison replied. "It's a bit out of my league, really. I'm at my best with artefacts, dating buildings and that sort of thing, digging up an ancient body is a whole different ball game, but I want to be included though, wouldn't want to miss this one."

"I don't know how long we can keep Claypole out of the picture, but the longer the better."

"We might as well order more coffees to celebrate. We can divide up the list and start making calls. Start doing something about getting this body out of the ground before Claypole smells a rat."

The task took longer than they originally thought. One thing everybody agreed on though, was the need to keep it a secret until they knew exactly what they were dealing with. After many phone calls, texts, e-mails, more coffees and eventually a pub lunch, they all came together for eight o'clock the following morning. The convoy arrived on site for 8:45. The pickup truck, with the wire fencing panels, had reversed down the trackway and was offloaded. Many of the panels were up and bolted together by nine o'clock. The area around the barns had turned into a car park. Brian's Jeep and Alison's 4x4 were tucked in close, next to Jimmy's pickup, followed by a DPA Land Rover and a Range Rover belonging to the university team. As a joyous surprise to all, there was, as yet, no sign of Farmer Claypole. The team were busy pulling on wellies and overalls. Getting trays of gloves, tools, wheelbarrows, tarpaulins and ground sheets organised. The team leaders, including Brian, had all looked at the remains hidden under the turf. The leathery, deep brown, slightly wrinkled flesh, tanned by years of submersion in the acidic peaty residue. All agreed it was a bog body. The go-ahead was given for a full excavation.

By 9:15, the fencing truck was on his way back to Plymouth, just as Mrs Claypole came walking down the trackway towards them. Whiddons Farm house itself was tucked into the hillside between the main road and the barns. The barns pre-dated the farm bungalow by hundreds of years. The original farmhouse was nothing but a scar on the landscape to the rear of the barns. Twenty or so years previously, a fire had ripped through the old house. By the time anyone got to a phone and raised the alarm most of the building had been destroyed. What was left had to be razed to the ground. Only the foundation platform remained, used now to park machinery. Within a year, Farmer Claypole had his insurance claim agreed and a new prefab bungalow erected further up the hill. The new location was a better site than the original. Tucked away into a cleft in the hillside, hidden from the worst of the south-westerly weather. Built far enough up the hill to escape the worst of the frosts and high enough to catch the sun, when it chose to come out. In a bad year, it escaped the worst of the snowdrifts. It was a shame the building looked so bloody horrible, but had been passed by the planners, based on the homeless situation of the farmer and his wife. Though staying at the Plume of Feathers with the insurance company picking up the tab was not what Brian had ever thought constituted being homeless.

Brian spotted Mrs Claypole heading their way. He alerted his superior, Steve, who informed the DPA's CEO, Chris Wyre, both of whom looked up and took notice, then passed the buck back to Brian to take care of.

"You might as well tell her what we've found," said Steve, the head ranger. "She's going to find out at some stage, it might as well be now."

Brian walked up the track, meeting her halfway. "Morning, Mrs Claypole," he said brightly. "How are you this morning? Where's your husband today?"

"He's gone Tavy to pick up some geese. Was gwin'on down here? What's with the fence? Pete ain't gonna like having a bloody fence round his field. You'm never said nothin bout a bloody great fence," Mrs Claypole said through gritted teeth. "Pete ain't gonna like it one bit."

"Well, Mrs Claypole I don't think Pete's going to be happy at all, I'm afraid," Brian said, bracing himself for an outburst. "Unfortunately, we've uncovered a body in the process of clearing the bog and so—"

"A body?"

"Yes, that's right. A body," Brian repeated.

"Is it a boy?"

Brian noticed the colour draining from her face, turning her an ashen shade of grey.

"Well, it's too early to say at the moment. That's why we've fenced off the site to carry out a proper excavation."

Brian watched as Mrs Claypole suddenly crumpled, slowly, gently, like a deflating balloon, into a heap in front of his eyes. When she came round, she was surrounded by faces. Brian, a first aider, had immediately gone into action. He had rushed to her side, checking for life signs, putting her into the recovery position and shouting for blankets. Alison joined him as soon as she saw what was happening.

"What happened, Bri?"

"I told her about the body and she collapsed. I never thought she'd be affected in that way. She asked if the body was a boy, then just kind of slumped."

Mrs Claypole was now wide-eyed and trying to sit up. Brian realised she'd simply fainted. The reason for this was yet to be ascertained, but at the moment, with the colour coming back into her cheeks, he was confident that for the time being she was in no immediate danger. He was relieved it wasn't a stroke or a heart attack.

"Mrs Claypole, how are you feeling? You gave us a bit of a

fright there for a minute," said Brian. There was no reply, but her eyes were focussed on him. "Can I help you sit up?"

"Tell this lot to piss off. I'm not dying, I just need air," she said, pulling herself up on the drystone wall into a sitting position.

"OK, everyone, I think Mrs Claypole is OK, she could just use some space," Alison said to those that had gathered. The excitement over, most were happy to go back to the task in hand. Alison stayed, crouched close, holding Mrs Claypole's hand.

"Do it look like a boy?" Mrs Claypole asked again.

"All I can tell you is that the body has signs of curly hair," replied Brian.

Before he could say more, Mrs Claypole started sobbing, little jewels of tears gently trickling down her weathered cheeks, her body shuddering as she wept.

Alison and Brian looked at each other, mystified. "What is it, Mrs Claypole. What's wrong?" Alison asked.

"It's Garry. Tis my son, Garry. I knows it. I been waiting so long. He's been missing over twenty years. He were twenty-two when he disappeared. Lovely curly black hair, he used to moan he wanted it to be straight. I used to ruffle it just to wind him up. Him and Pete never got on. Garry hated him, Pete hated Garry. One day, Garry just never came back from Plymouth. Pete said he was a loser, I should forget about him, but sometime later, up Tavy market, I bumped into the mate he was gwin into Plymouth to meet. According to him, Garry never showed. He's never seen him since. I told Pete. He just told me to shut my mouth and get on with the feeding. He said

Garry buggered off rather than do a day's work. I knew Garry wouldn't have just left me alone with him. Garry knew what a bastard Pete was, we were hoping to save enough money between us to bugger off one day. Just the two of us. Get a flat and a job in Plymouth, leave all this behind... but he just disappeared... just disappeared... left me here alone."

"Why didn't you just leave your husband?" Alison said, feeling an instant bond of sympathy with the woman.

"I couldn't leave here, case Garry came back for me. Now he's never coming back, is he?"

"Listen, Mrs Claypole," Brian said as he helped her to her feet, "there's been a misunderstanding. I'm truly sorry about your son, but I need to tell you, at the moment we think the body we've found is what's known as a bog body. It could've lain there for thousands of years. We think it's connected with the hut circles we've been mapping. It's possibly part of a Bronze Age settlement. I really don't think it's your son. In one way, I'm sorry, but at least it still leaves you with hope."

"Hope," she replied. "Bloody hope. What chance of that? For one moment, when you told me about the body, I was sad. Then in a second, I thought, that's it, now I've found him. I'm free. Now I know I ain't. I be stuck here for the rest of my bloody days, waiting. Just bloody waiting, either for Garry to come home or for that bastard husband of mine to die."

She stood, turned, and walked away up the hill.

"Should we go with her?" said Alison.

"No, I think she'd rather be alone. The colour's come back to her face, and the way she was talking, I'm pretty sure she's OK. Poor woman," Brian said as he watched Mrs Claypole walking up the track. "What a bloody life. Oops, warning, there's a CEO coming up behind you."

"So, what was all that about then, Brian?" said Chris Wyre, as he strode towards them. "All looked a touch dramatic."

"Well to be honest, sir, we're not quite certain. Mrs Claypole fainted when we told her about our find. She thought we may have found her long lost son Garry, who disappeared about twenty years ago. Disappeared suddenly and without trace."

"Bloody hell. Garry! Garry! You couldn't make it up, could you? No wonder he left home," Wyre commented. "You put her straight about our body, I hope."

"Yes. But it didn't make her any happier." Brian watched Mrs Claypole reach the top of the track, then on toward her lonely home on the hill.

By now, the team were organised. There was a group around the body, gently scraping back the peat. There was a photographer from the university taking shots of everything. Another group taking buckets of mud away down to the, by now, nearly-full pond. Here they'd set up mesh tables and frames. They were washing the soil, looking for artefacts. Seed pods, acorns, anything to set a timeline for the internment.

"Just an idea, Brian," said Chris Wyre, "but I reckon you should contact the police. I'm sure they must have some system in place for reporting bodies, even ancient ones."

"Good point," replied Brian.

That was something he hadn't even considered. The mindset had been about an ancient bog body, but it was still a body. So the authorities should be notified. The annoying thing was, he'd have to go up the main road as far as the layby to make the call, but it had to be done. The only other option was to go up to the farmhouse and use the landline. He didn't like that idea in the slightest.

"Not wanting to be funny, sir, but it's probably best if you contact them. For one, you're, in fact, the senior representative here and secondly, your car is at the back of the pack. We'd have to move everybody to get my motor out."

"Valid point, Brian," said Wyre. "How far do I have to go to get a mobile signal?"

"I have to go anyway, Chris," said Steve. "I have to be in Okehampton after lunch at a meeting. If you follow me, I can show you where you can catch a signal."

With that, they strode off through the gate and up the track.

Brian crossed to where Alison was standing.

"So, what's happening here?" he asked Alison, who was leaning against the drystone wall overlooking the bog and the group of overall-clothed folk, working diligently around the body.

"Well as much as I'd love to be in amongst it, it's weird, but I think I'd rather leave the dig to the others. I'm OK with normal excavations, looking for archaeological remains, bits of old buildings, tools, artefacts, I've even found bones before, but yesterday... I can't explain it. There was just something freaky and sad about that body. I was looking at the skin, and for a while was really excited by the find, but the moment I saw the curly hair on the back of the head and realised it had actually been a person it just turned my stomach. Daft, isn't it?"

"No, not really. I think it's a perfectly natural response. We're used to ancient things looking, well, ancient. Even I was shocked to see that skin stretched across the shoulder. It was bloody weird."

"Then, I reckon, let's just stand back here in the sunshine, try to maintain an air of overall authority and leave them all too it," Alison said, leaning back against the warming stonework.

Colin Clift, Professor of Archaeology from the university in Exeter, was crouched on his knees in the trench, glasses perched on the end of his nose. He was gently peeling the mud from around the edges of the body, attempting to leave some attached to the skin. The mud he was cutting away was collected into buckets to be taken to the pond for sieving. The plan was to excavate the outline of the body, leaving the final cleansing till last, so as not to expose the flesh to the elements until the last moment. The acidic nature of the body's resting place, the closed, anaerobic conditions it had been held in, was what had preserved its flesh in such perfect condition. Once immersed and under the surface, the body would have sunk, but not to the bottom. The density of the mire would have held it in suspension until, bit by bit, the peat settled and formed around the body, holding it close, protecting it. Sealing it in, acting like insulation and suspension. Over the years the body would have absorbed the brown colouring from the peaty mixture it was encased in and that, acting like pickling fluid, would have preserved the corpse in its entirety.

Professor Clift had seen the remains of one of the most famous UK bog bodies, Lindow Man. Lindow Man had been found whilst a company were digging peat in Cheshire, at

Lindow Moss. The body had been interred over two thousand years before machinery dredged him up in an undignified, unceremonious fashion, dumping his remains onto the conveyor belt. The professor couldn't believe his luck when the call had come in the previous day. He had been called upon many times to carry out research or run digs on the moor. It provided the university with practical work for archaeology students. It had also given him a lucrative additional source of income over the years. It was accepted by his bosses at the university, who saw it as a vital local link, as a great example to their board of trustees of 'southwest partnership working'. It also formed the lifeblood of many of his archaeological papers and lectures for the university, and now this. This body could provide lecture material all the way to retirement, followed by book tours. Indeed, this could be a boost to his whole pension plan. Colin climbed out of the trench carefully, not wanting to drop anything onto the partially-exposed body now appearing in the bottom of the damp trench.

"Alex," the professor called to a student jogging past with an empty bucket. "Could you pop to the car, bring down the gazebo? I think now the sun's got up we could do with shade for us and the body."

Alex trotted up toward the carpark. At that point, Colin noticed Chris Wyre on his way, heading in their direction. As Colin walked back to his trench, he passed Brian and Alison, still leaning against the wall in the, by now, warm sunshine. "Heads up, people, chief exec on the way," he murmured as he passed. The couple separated without giving a glance up the track. Alison headed toward the dig alongside the professor and crouched on the edge of the gulley, where she took a great interest in the goings-on in the depth of the trench. Brian made a beeline for Jimmy working his digger. Jimmy turned off the engine as he saw him approach.

"What's happening then?" Jimmy said, pulling out his tobacco pouch, taking the opportunity to roll a cigarette.

"Well, the professor's team have cleaned round most of the body, it looks to be virtually complete," Brian replied, while turning his head slightly to see where Wyre was. Sadly, he appeared to be making a beeline for his location. "The plan is to leave the body with a covering of peat, removing enough to be sure they're lifting a body, not just a lump of mud. They hope to slide a board under it, take the thing away to the lab for final exposure, thereby reducing the risk of environmental contamination."

Just then, they were joined by Chris Wyre. "Morning, Jimmy, bloody good job so far. Once this has all grown over and the pond weed's gotten hold it's going to prove to be a proper wildlife haven. I'm thinking about the installation of a hide for the 'twitchers'. Well done."

"I think we should congratulate Jimmy on his discovery of the body as well," said Brian.

"Well, yes, of course," Wyre said, "I was coming to that." He gave Brian one of those looks. "Thanks for keeping it quiet, Jimmy. We didn't want all and sundry turning up with cameras, all after a bloody selfie with the stiff in the trench. If you're happy to stay on site for the time being, we'll obviously settle up at the end of the job. Now, need to have a quick word, Bri." He led Brian away with a hand on his shoulder.

"Right," Wyre said brusquely. "I've been in touch with the police at Exeter. They say it falls under Plymouth jurisdiction, so I've called them. It took a bloody lifetime to find the right person to talk to. Anybody would think they've never had a two-thousand-year-old body reported before. Anyway, they've given us permission to continue with the excavation, but not permission to remove the body until they've sent their forensic pathologist to confirm our find, and confirm it's ancient, not recent."

"What's the forensic pathologist's role in this then, sir?"

"Well, it'll be the pathologist's job to inspect the corpse. Observe and identify, if possible, the pathological process, injury or even disease – sometimes known as the mechanism of death – that may have directly or indirectly lead to the individual's death," Wyre said with an air of authority.

"Well... I'm impressed, sir. How did you know all that?"

"I googled it in the car."

"So, when is this liable to happen?" Brian said, pleased that Wyre appeared to be in a good mood. "I think the professor was hoping to pull the body out by the end of the day so as not to leave it exposed overnight."

"Well, there's the joy. The duty officer put me in touch with the pathology department at the hospital, they put me straight through to the pathologist. A chap called Benjamin Landy. Who, I have to say, was chuffed to bits to have, and I quote, 'something weird to inspect'. His words, not mine. He's on his way as we speak, should be here within the hour. If all goes to plan the professor should have his wish and we can wrap this up and all be home for tea."

"That's brilliant, sir. I'd better go and pass on the news, tell them they've time to stop for lunch."

"Well I've got calls to make back to the office. My plan is, head back up to the layby, make the calls and meet the pathologist there, then bring him down with me. We're running out of space in the parking area, he can leave his car and jump into mine. You're in charge till we get back."

Brian walked across to where the team and Alison were working. Alison saw him approaching and climbed out of the gulley, holding out her hands for assistance as she did so. Brian willingly obliged.

"So, what did the bossman have to say?" she said, only then realising they still had hold of each other's hands. They both realised and let go.

"Well, it's for the ears of all the team really," he said, turning to look down onto the backs of the group, crouched under the pergola in slightly spooky, green-tinted shade. "Professor. Sorry to interrupt, can I have everyone's attention for a moment?"

All eyes turned toward him. The professor raised his glasses to a position on top of his head. Nestled into the thinning hair like a pair of owl eyes in a nest.

"I've spoken with Chris Wyre, he's had a conversation with the police," Brian continued, aware all ears were now listening intently. "The police are happy for you to continue your excavation, but will not allow us to remove the body or any artefacts from site until their pathologist arrives to verify the body is, in fact, ancient."

"Well, that's just ridiculous," retorted the professor, standing bolt upright under the awning, so that for a moment his head actually disappeared from view. He bobbed back down and out from underneath it. "Of course it's ancient. What do they think we are, simpletons? I've been doing this for bloody years, I don't need a second opinion."

"If you let me finish, Professor. The reporting of a body is a police matter, whatever the age of internment. It's a legal requirement for the discovery of any body. The parks authority had a duty to report this find. The police say they have to send their pathologist to certify the facts as they are and," he added quickly, aware the professor was about to explode again. "The pathologist in question is on his way out to the site to get it done as soon as possible. So, if it's OK with you, we've time for a quick lunchbreak. By the time we've all had a break the man will be here. He'll take one look, tick his box, then we can all continue with what we're doing and hopefully get this body out of the mud before dark."

"Well... if he's on his way, we might as well take a break," the professor replied with a note of disgruntlement. "Right, everybody, get tarpaulin over this area to retain as much moisture as we can."

Brian turned to Alison. "Flask of tea in my truck if you don't mind sharing a cup?" He smiled.

Having drunk tea and chatted for twenty minutes, they'd just got out and started back toward the trackway when Wyre's car came down the road. Brian and Alison turned back to meet the occupants, Chris Wyre, and the man getting out of the passenger door heaving a large leather satchel over his shoulder, who they presumed must be the pathologist.

"Just in time, you two," said Wyre, as the two men strode

toward them. "This is the forensic pathologist, Benjamin Landy. Benjamin, this is Brian Cave, Area Ranger for this side of the moor, and this is Alison Grave, Director of Conservation & Archaeology."

The newcomer held out his hand. "Benjamin Landy, everybody calls me 'Rover'," he said with a smile. "As in Land Rover... Landy... Rover... I know, it's not very funny but it's been with me for years."

Brian shook his hand. Rover wasn't what he'd envisaged. Though, to be honest, he'd never met a pathologist before. The man was younger than he'd expected. Probably about forty, not much more. He'd long dark hair, tied in a shaggy, rasta-style ponytail. He sported a huge, silver, circular earring-type plug in his left ear, through which daylight could be seen. Wearing baggy multi pocketed black trousers and a short-sleeved denim shirt, he clearly displayed tribal-like, deep black, full arm length tattoos, that looked both bold and striking. Without a doubt, the guy was truly not what Brian was expecting at all.

"Welcome to Whiddons Farm," Brian said. "Let's take you down and introduce you—"

"To the body?" Rover asked.

"Well, I was going to say introduce you to the team," Brian laughed. "But I suppose it would be a good idea to show you the body. I should warn you, the professor in charge of the dig, Professor Clift, was a touch disgruntled when we told him you were on the way and you'd have to verify the existence and state of the body. He felt he knew what he was talking about and didn't need verification."

"That's not a problem, I'm sure we'll get on fine. It's water off a duck's back to me. It's my job to go to any scene of crime and confirm there's a body, not a bag of rubbish. Confirm the body is, in fact, deceased, not just in desperate need of an ambulance, then try to identify cause of death and, if possible, also the time. I don't doubt for a moment that what you guys have found is a genuine bog body. The fact that you found him a couple of days ago with his face in the mud and he hasn't moved since does hint at the fact that an ambulance will not be needed. So, I don't expect to take too long to verify the body as deceased. Having said that, I'm fascinated by this whole situation. I've never had anything like this on my doorstep. If I can stick around without pissing anyone off then I've booked myself out for the day so, point me at the professor and let's get this show on the road."

The professor and team were gathered around the depth of the gulley, shaded by the green pergola. They all turned, as if by a single command, as Brian and his group approached. The professor stepped out of the trench as they got closer. His face held no sign of friendship.

"Professor Clift," Rover quickly said, holding out his hand. "I am so pleased to meet you. I'm Benjamin Landy. Plymouth and Derriford area forensic pathologist at your service. I've read so many of your papers and followed much of your work. I'd always hoped to meet you. What a pleasure this is for me. What a great, great pleasure."

Rover took the professor's hand without waiting for it to be proffered and shook it enthusiastically whilst smiling broadly.

"I understand you've found a bog body? How splendid. Please, do show me your find." Rover took the professor by the arm and led him back towards the trench.

Brian and Alison looked at each other with just a hint of a smile, both recognising they'd just seen the ultimate in scene stealing, with not a breath of wind left in the professor's sails. Rover and the professor jumped down into the trench and Colin called for the rest of the team to clear the site and make some space, which they duly did.

"Right," said the professor. "Well, here's our corpse, at present we don't know the gender of it. As you can see, we've left a covering of peat over the outer surface of the body but we've been down to the skin in many places, then re-covered it in the peat, just so we could ensure the whole body was complete. Amazingly, it appears to be, on the whole, a complete body, there doesn't appear to be too much damage, normally these bodies tend to be either damaged in discovery, or damaged by length of time or material they've been immersed in. In this case, I suspect by the nature and consistency of the material the body's been contained by, much of the body, despite a small amount of contraction of the body frame, probably caused by degradation of the inner organs, appears to be in an excellent state of preservation. There's an element of skin shrinkage and tanning from the peat, but all in all it's almost perfect."

Rover had been doing his job whilst the professor had been educating him on the corpse. He'd noted the position and depth, by the metre-measuring stick the team had placed in the ground as part of their site survey. He'd also noted and recorded the approximate size of the body. He'd acknowledged the fact that the corpse was definitely deceased, but at present there was no way of being able to discover cause or time of death. This was going to have to wait until the body was fully exposed in the lab theatre. He just had to find a way to persuade the professor it should come to his lab in Plymouth, not be transported to the university laboratories in Exeter.

"Professor. If I may, I've a suggestion to make. I'd very much like to observe both the way you work and the final uncovering of the body. I realise you're nearly at the point where you can lift the body for removal. My problem is, if you lift it and take it to Exeter, it falls outside my jurisdiction and comes under the team at Exeter's Wonford Hospital. Then I go back to my day job. This means I'll miss out on the opportunity of working with you which would, to my mind, be a travesty."

Beside the trench, crouched to view under the pergola, Brian and Alison listened with admiration as Rover quite obviously turned this meeting to his advantage, continuing to butter-up the professor in his attempt to get this all to fall in his direction.

"It would be a bloody shame if I lost the chance of watching you at work," Rover continued. "I think you'll agree this is probably a once in a life time opportunity, if not for you then certainly for me."

"Well yes, quite," the professor replied. "What do you have in mind?"

"My idea is quite simple really, Professor, or might I call you Christopher?" Rover said with a broad smile.

"By all means, Benjamin," the professor smiled back.

"Well, my idea is this: If I assist you lifting the body, I can order a vehicle to come and collect it directly from here. We'd remove it to my lab at Derriford, where we could work on the corpse together, that way saving a long, possibly damaging road journey over the moors to Exeter. It would then stay within my jurisdiction, which means I'd give you my undivided assistance and make my entire theatre at your disposal. Obviously, any knowledge gained during the unveiling process would all be made over to you, but it would be a great, great privilege to work with you on this. What do you say, Christopher?" With that he held out his hand.

As if under a spell the professor took it, shook it and said, "Benjamin, I think that sounds like an admirable plan, welcome to the team."

By five o'clock that evening, the mortuary ambulance had made its slow, sedate drive up the farm track on its way back to Plymouth, with a couple of slightly freaked out paramedics in the front seat. They'd both transported accident victims, injured people, even, sadly, transported the deceased before. But there was something about the lump of 'thing', curled up in the back of the ambulance covered in an outer layer of smelly, peaty, mud, which was in turn covered in damp blankets. It resembled something from a horror movie. It lay on a body board, curled in a humped foetal position. Sex as yet unknown. Age unknown. Cause of death unknown. The body had been found slumped forward, on its knees, face down as though forced into the mud with its arms pulled back behind. The way the body was bent and the arms crossed, it gave the impression of the wrists being tied. However, at this moment in time the lower part of the arms including the wrists were still encased in mud. Further work in the laboratory would tell the whole tale.

Professor Clift and Rover followed in the professor's car.

They were followed just as closely by Chris Wyre, who wanted to see this thing through to completion. As the rest of the group were packing up, Jimmy was loading his lunch bag and tools into the back of his truck. Out of the corner of his eye he saw Pete Claypole striding down the track. Even from that far away he carried a storm about him. Jimmy crossed to where Brian and Alison were standing talking.

"Brian, heads up, mate, trouble coming down the road in the form of Claypole."

"Oh bugger, I thought we'd get away before he got back. OK, it's my shout." Brian headed off to meet the farmer before he could get down in amongst the students and members of the team, all gathered by the cars.

"Evening, Mr Claypole..." was as far as Brian's greeting got before the farmer exploded in his face.

"You bastard, Cave," the farmer roared, loud enough to draw attention from the rest of the group. "My wife's in bloody bits up at the house. What's this shit about you finding a bloody body in that field? You stuck it there, you bastard, just to piss me off and stop the drainage going ahead. Why'd you bloody tell her it was her son? How dare you, how dare you?"

With that, he swung a fist wildly towards Brian's face. But Brian had been watching the man and could see his anger, he knew where it was going to end. As the man swung at him in a state of fury, Brian stood braced. He stepped back and to one side, and the fist missed by a mile. The momentum carried the raging man onward. As his body slid past Brian's shoulder, Brian wrapped an arm around the man's neck and with his other hand, grabbed the flying fist and pulled it up the middle of the farmer's back, sidestepped with his foot and tripped Claypole up, dropping him onto his knees into the muddy grass of the track.

"Now I'm only going to say this once, Claypole," Brian said quietly into his ear. "Before I let you up, you'll stay there quietly and listen to what I have to say."

Claypole tried to twist away from Brian's grasp but Brian increased the pressure upward on the man's fist, locked fast, twisted up behind his back. The farmer stopped his struggle.

"As I was saying, Mr Claypole," Brian continued. "We've found a body. It's what's known as a bog body. It could've been there for thousands of years. At no time did I tell your wife it was your son, in fact, quite the opposite. It was she who told us she thought it was Garry and we made no bones about it. We told her what I've just told you; it's an ancient bog body, though to be honest, from what I know of you it could still turn out to be a distant relative."

"It's true, Mr Claypole," said Alison, who'd joined the pair. "Your wife came to us with the suggestion it could be your son, we specifically told her it wasn't."

"Enough," Claypole said through gritted teeth. "Let me up."

Brian relaxed his grip on the man and went to help him to his feet, but Claypole shook him off.

"Bugger off, I don't need your bloody help," the farmer said, pushing himself up to his feet. "And lost or not lost, he was never my son, he was hers." The man turned his back on them and strode off up the track.

"Are you OK, Brian?" Alison said with concern. "I saw him

swing at you and ran as fast as I could. What happened? What did he say?"

Brian relayed the conversation.

"Bloody hell, the man's a complete fruitcake, Brian. You'd better try and steer clear of him for a while, he's the sort of bloke who'll come out with a shotgun."

"Well cheers for that advice. I wasn't planning on getting too social with the guy any way," Brian said with a laugh.

"Everything OK?" Jimmy said as he reached where they stood. "I was coming to give you a hand but you seemed to have it all under control. I figured an ex-Royal Marine wouldn't need a digger driver, except maybe to bury the bugger," he said with a smile.

"Well cheers for your support, Jimmy. Somehow, I managed."

"What was it all about then?" the digger driver asked.

Brian outlined the various conversations that led to the altercation. The morning chat with Mrs Claypole. Her fainting. Her story about Garry, the subsequent incident with her husband.

"We tried to explain to them both that the body we've found is ancient, but something got lost in translation," Brian said.

"Ah, Garry," Jimmy replied.

"OK, so what do you know about Garry then?" said Brian.

"Well, it's only what I've heard over the years. In the pub or what the missus picked up on the grapevine, so to speak," continued Jimmy, pleased to have something to say that the other two didn't know about. "As you know, the Claypoles took over this farm at least forty years ago, they been ruining it bit by bit ever since. Garry was born soon after they moved here. Most people just thought it was the result of the joy of moving out onto the moor," Jimmy said with a smile. "But it didn't take long before stories started to spread about fighting and arguing. Mrs C' turning up at the shops with a black eye, etcetera. It didn't take many steps before folk were reckoning the kid weren't his, what with the little 'uns black curly hair and all and the both of them with straight brown hair. Most folk reckon that was what pissed him off."

Jimmy ran his tongue down the side of his cigarette paper and finished rolling his hasty cigarette.

"Then," he continued, "One day, must be twenty-odd years ago now, Garry just buggered off. Can't say as I blame him. T'was about the same time the old farmhouse burnt down, can't remember exactly, might have been before, don't know… anyway, it was about then. Yep, he just upped and buggered off."

Brian interrupted. "Mrs Claypole said he disappeared, rather than buggered off."

"Well yes, that's what she said," Jimmy continued. "She weren't gonna go round telling folk her boy had upped and left was she? No, she even went to the police, said he were missing. Put posters up an all, he never appeared. Police never found him, though to be honest, I don't reckon they looked too hard. Anyway, after a while it all just went quiet. Her being always miserable and him being a right bastard. Been like that for years. To be honest, most folk were bloody surprised they stuck together this long."

Brian and Alison regrouped by the cars. One by one, the parking area had emptied and the team had almost departed. The university team, minus the professor, would be returning the following morning to continue sieving through the mud that had surrounded the body. Jimmy would return to continue finishing off around the main pool. Alison and Brian would have to be there to keep an eye on proceedings. They just hoped the Claypoles stayed out of the picture.

"I don't know about you, but I fancy a drink, do you want to stop in at the Plume on the way home?" said Brian, hopefully.

"Well, maybe just a small one. We're driving, and as you know, I always like to act responsibly," replied Alison with a sly smile as she slid into the driving seat, and in a very obvious and exaggerated way, swung her legs in and closed the door.

CHAPTER TWO

Having transported the body to the pathology lab the previous afternoon, it had been decided there was no time for any work to take place by the time the inbound paperwork was completed, which turned out to be harder than expected. There didn't appear to be any boxes to tick that said: ancient bog body, eventually, in homage to 'Lindow Man', 'Dartmoor Man' was tagged and stored in the mortuary chiller room, ready for the following morning. The body sat slumped on the trolley, encased in a coating of mud and peat, this meant there was no way it would slide into a storage cabinet. Chris Wyre had arrived when they were bringing in the gurney with the body laid upon it, keen to be involved until they'd stepped into the operating theatre, whereupon it all came home to him. This was actually about dissecting a person. It didn't matter what age it was, it was human. Wishing them well and asking to be kept in the loop, he'd made a hasty retreat.

Professor Clift and Rover, who were the last of the team to leave, had shared a coffee in the hospital canteen that evening. Rover allowed the man to regale him with the benefits of his years of studying archaeology.

"I can't wait to strip that peat layer off, get to see the person underneath," the professor had said. "We can learn so much about who this body really was, when it lived, how it lived. Even better, if we can pin the body down to the era of the roundhouse settlement that used to inhabit that landscape, we can close the circle. From an educational point of view, this could be huge."

"Where do you hope the body fits with the settlements history?" Rover had asked.

"Well, this will be the interesting thing. I'm convinced, having the arms pinned back the way they are, that our body has its hands tied. If that's the case there's a good chance it will have been a sacrificial offering. Now, if we can date the body and find artefacts within the shadows of the round house settlement that we can date and correlate with our body, then we build a story of this village and its development throughout history. If it turns out to be Neolithic it will not surprise me one bit. During the Neolithic Era, the act of death became something of great importance. Sacrifice was a powerful tool for encouraging support from the gods. It could be the spring that forms the bog where our body was found, had greater significance when the round houses were occupied. It's just an incredible opportunity to build an entire picture of this period in our county's history."

"Then I think we should make an early start tomorrow, don't you?" Rover had suggested. They'd shaken hands and called it a day.

†

Rover flicked the lights on in theatre at 7:30 the next morning. The professor was due at eight o'clock. Rover planned to have everything ready to go the moment the university team arrived. The gurney and its corpse had been brought into the operating room. It stood beside the table. Rover would await the professor and his assistants to help transfer the body to the table. It was, after all, a heavy, awkward object, partially covered in peat, its lower extremities nestling in mud. The removal of peat was going to be a messy business, but the stainless-steel mortuary table was made for jobs like these. It had sluicing facilities and suction pipes; he didn't foresee any problems.

Rover had discussed the day's operation with his immediate superiors. Persuading them that being involved in this process could not only be a valuable experience from an educational point of view, but valuable as a partnership. Being linked to this project equally, working with a prestigious university, any archaeological discoveries would for ever be associated with the hospital pathology department. That would help in future funding bids or budget allocations.

Professor Clift and three assistants arrived bang on eight o'clock. The professor's job would be to continue cleaning the body. The assistant's job would be the collection of peat and mud from the stainless-steel table, and the placement of the material into plastic bins. It may hold clues to help determine the age of the body and date of its internment.

Rover's task was to assist the professor, whilst allowing said professor to think he was in charge of the process. The professor decided the unveiling should start at the shoulder area. As far as Rover was concerned, he'd no preference where they started. In effect, his role was spectator and student of the master, he wanted to be part of this unrobing. When the professor started cleaning back the peat layer around the base of the neck, Rover watched with the open eyes of a pathologist and the wide eyes of a student. The first thing Rover noticed, as the layer was picked at with a small trowel then washed away using a soft brush, was the dark, possibly black curly hair visible at the nape of the neck. Extending upward into the peat layer still covering the skull, it looked like it had been washed that morning.

"Is that normal?" Rover asked the professor.

"Is what normal?"

"Well, the hair! I mean, a bog body with what looks like a full head of curly hair. Is that normal after all these years?"

"To be honest, Benjamin, we've no normal to go by. As yet, no precedent has ever been set. All the bog bodies found to date had their own characteristics, they have all been different. Some have just been sections of a body, and those where the majority of the corpse has been found intact have all been buried in different situations. When you talk about hair, the 'Arden Woman', found in Denmark in the 1940's, had lain in the ground for two thousand years. She'd got a full head of blonde hair tied into a pair of pigtails, both coiled into a hairstyle like a doughnut on top of her head. She was wearing a small bonnet to protect the hair. Then again, from the Jutland peninsula, 'Graubelle Man' was discovered in the 1950's. He'd been interred in mud for a couple of thousand years. Not only did he have a full head of hair, but his hands and fingers were so well preserved they took his finger prints."

"Did the police manage to find any outstanding warrants?" Rover asked with a smile.

"I'm sorry?" Colin said seriously, looking up from his task for the first time in thirty minutes.

"Nothing, Professor, I'm sorry. It was a flippant comment, ignore me."

"Oh... I see. Fingerprints, outstanding warrants, I see what you mean." The professor laughed. "Well knowing the efficiency of the Danes, I expect they checked."

There was something about that mass of hair that drew everybody's attention. Whilst two of the university grads had been clearing peaty mud from the feet area, the professor, Rover and the other assistant couldn't switch their focus from cleaning the hair and the bulk of the head, a task that was revealing a complete head of hair so far. Whether by natural colouring or by intake of the colouration of the peat, the hair did indeed appear to be jet black.

"What's your gut instinct, Colin, as to the sex of our corpse?" Rover asked. Though he'd already made up his mind based on muscle texture of the shoulders and upper torso.

"Well, I think we have to await the clearing of the mud from the obvious areas at the front, but looking at the muscle structure and the short curly hair I'd say male."

Although when discovered, the body had been slumped forward as if it had died on its knees, then the corpse fell forward, its face buried in the mud; the body was now lying on the table on its left side in an almost foetal position. It was only possible at the moment to reveal just over two thirds of the body. Within that area it was still possible to reveal almost all of the hair and clean the right-hand side of the head and face. The body's right ear was flattened against the skull, probably due to compression of material around the body. As the professor worked away gently cleaning the side of the face, he gave a sharp intake of breath.

"My god," the professor muttered, almost too quietly to be heard, but loud enough to draw instant attention.

"What is it?" Rover asked.

"Well, our bog body has tribal markings or tattoos on the side of its face," the professor whispered.

"Is that unusual?"

"Well, in this detail, it's not common from this time period, I can tell you. You have to remember, the further back you go, the more primitive the tools. There've been ancient bodies found with tattoos, but normally from a later period than I was expecting our body to be from. I mean, the Celts were tattoo masters, but they were normally artistic interpretations. Geometric shapes, religious symbols, mazes etcetera, but I have to say, I've never seen anything quite like this."

Rover leant in to inspect the area the professor was sponging clean. Rover was used to working with dead bodies. They came in all shapes and sizes, all stages of decomposition, and he was used to the smells that emanated from a corpse. But there was something instantly primeval about the fungally-impregnated peaty air that permeated Rover's cotton face mask, invading his nostrils. For a moment this took his breath away; he regained composure rapidly, focussing his eyes on the shapes appearing. He could see patterns in the brown, weathered skin of the right cheek. The shapes seemed random, geometric in form. He had to admit, he knew nothing about tattoos from this far back in ancient times.

His own inkwork had been chosen from a book of New Zealand Māori artwork he'd looked through in the tattoo parlour, though both he and the tattooist who'd completed the inking added adaptations and additions. On closer inspection, he wasn't impressed with the artwork on show on the right cheek. But his own artwork was just that, artwork for display when he wanted it to be. These markings probably had huge meaning or symbolism to the person lying on the table. The symbols may have denoted his tribe. They may have denoted gods, they may just have been the best he could manage on a wet winter's day, in his hut, with the village tattooist using a piece of sharpened bone and a wet mix of wood ash for ink. They'd never know. Rover hoped that whoever this person was lying on the slab hadn't paid good money for the inkwork.

The dark lines marking the ingrained skin appeared in two rows neatly down the middle of the right cheek. Starting just below the closed, peat-filled eye, and ending just above the lower edge of the chin. The shapes varied in form, but were all of a similar size. There were representations of arrowheads or right-angle symbols, a half or crescent moon and, lower down, a full moon. Whatever they were, they looked precise. They must have meant something to the individual or to the tribe he belonged to. *It does look religious, although,* Rover thought, *it could just be the corpse's birthday tattooed on the face.* For the moment, it was a complete mystery.

One of the students was taking a complete photographic inventory of the symbols, the hair and the full visible side of the corpses head. At the moment, only one side of the face was clear of mud. The professor made the decision the face was less important than trying to find out what was going on with the hands. The team went back to uncovering the rest of the shoulders and the twisted-back arms, following these down to the wrists, thereby hoping to solve the mystery of where the hands lay and if they were indeed tied.

There was a complicated mass of mud gathered around where both wrists appeared to cross. It would have to be picked apart with great care. Meanwhile, the assistant sponging down mud from the shoulders and back of the body made another discovery. Across the middle of the shoulder blades was a straight tattooed line. Rover and the professor stopped work on the lower arm area to take a look. Rover realised this mark, though uniform and straight, was not, in fact, a tattoo, but a scar. On inspection, once sponged away, it was possible to see the dirt was actually nestling inside an indentation. Twenty centimetres in length, a uniform few millimetres in depth throughout its entire length. The indentation had been made with some kind of blade and made with some force.

"So, Benjamin, from the viewpoint of a forensic pathologist, what do you think caused the scar?" the professor asked.

"Well, a quick guess would lead me to think a short sword, but if it was then it was blunt."

"Interesting you should think that, those are my thoughts exactly. Without a doubt, the weapon has caused a laceration. Looks precise. Not deep. Obviously, the body's been absorbing peaty fluids over the lifetime of the internment, the edges of the wound have puckered and swollen, but it's not deep. If it had been deep then, as the swelling built up along the edge of the wound, it would've opened up like a ravine. Although the blade's left a mark, that's even in depth throughout its length, it's not deep. If we're talking about this being a sacrifice then I could quite imagine a sacrificial sword that came out for special occasions, but not the sort of thing you'd normally sharpen on a regular basis, as opposed to a sword for fighting. If it was made of bronze, then the earlier Bronze Age technology was very simple, they hadn't developed the fine art that was later to come out of the smithy, where they folded and doubled the metal where the edge was to be formed. This gave them a greater ability to make a toughened cutting edge that could be honed to a sharp edge. So, at first glance we both think it was a blade, but neither of us are impressed with the workmanship."

The debate over weaponry came to an abrupt halt when the professor noticed that his whittling away at the wrist mud pack had revealed thin strapping materialising from the slime enclosing the ends of the arms. All attention was now drawn to this spot.

"It would appear the wrists are bound by strapping. It goes round the wrists several times and the lower part of the arms," the professor said. "It looks to be a strap no more than twenty millimetres wide, possibly leather. It's a job to tell because of the mud still attached to it. We'll tell once it's cleaned." The professor put two of his assistants on the sponging of the mud to expose the strapping.

"Right," continued Colin, "whilst our young assistants finish tidying the strapping and wrists let's determine the sex. Would you give me a helping hand, Ben? I think if we clear the chest area, we'll be able to tell whether this corpse is male or female. At present, trying to clear the groin area is going to be a delicate business." He handed Rover one of the small, toy-like, round-ended trowels and the pair lent themselves to the task of clearance.

"We obviously need to proceed with great care," Colin said. "I think a gentle paring away of the worst of the mud followed by a sponge down and we should know if it's a Jack or a Jill."

Rover followed the professor's lead, picking away at the pieces of peaty mud still stuck to the body. Working slowly, carefully and diligently was the very nature of Rover's day job. You had to be forever observant. Looking for anything that could be classed as unusual or pertinent to cause of death. Even signs of anything that may be symptomatic of some abuse to a body that could, over a significant period of time, be shown to have influenced or directly caused a death. Rover had many tools to aid him in this task, but a miniature, round-nosed builders' trowel was, at present, not one of them. He and the professor quickly realised that either the body was a very flat-chested woman, or it was indeed male.

Rover stepped back to allow the professor to sponge down the flesh. Each swipe of the sponge revealed more of the brown, leather like, slightly crinkled skin. The whole corpse began to look more human. As the almost-certainly-male cadaver lay there on the slab, still folded in the foetal position, Rover took stock using a clinical eye.

The body definitely looked male.

At present, half the face was unmasked. It looked to be a strong-featured man in his twenties or early thirties. It had short black curly hair. It had tattoos or tribal markings on at least the right side of its face. The body appeared naked. Death had occurred with hands pulled back and tied behind with a leather strap used as restraint. It would therefore appear the body had been murdered. It may even have been an unwilling participant in a sacrifice. There was a definite scar across the shoulder blades, cut at about the same time as, or just prior to, death. This was identified by the fact that the peat extended into the skin via the open wound.

As yet, they'd come across no other sign of trauma, so it was probable that the cause of death would be drowning, brought about by the face or entire body being pushed down into the mire. Only a full autopsy would reveal the content of lungs and stomach. Rover suspected the professor would probably not allow this kind of forensic intrusion to take place this early in the unveiling of the corpse, or in their professional relationship. By now, the professor was picking gently away toward the groin of the corpse, a delicate task that made the observer wince. It was obvious there was no hair across the chest, so either this man was younger than he looked or, he may have been shaved before death.

The professor called a halt for coffee. Rover checked the clock, and realised it was 11:30. Three and a half hours had ticked by almost in silence. Just the sounds of little trowels scraping away, the occasional burst of conversation, and the sounds of dustpans and brushes scooping the peat debris into bins for storage. Rover phoned through to the canteen for takeaway coffees and the professor dispatched an assistant to collect them. Stephen Mace, the professor's cameraman, clicked away, taking close-ups of all the areas requiring detail.

Stephen had taken photographic records for Professor Clift before. He'd been fortunate to work on digs previously. To be amongst 'The Chosen Ones' was a sought-after position at the university. If you performed well, did the job, kept your head down, your degree with a first was almost a forgone conclusion. Stephen wanted to ensure this record of the Dartmoor bog body was a comprehensive collection of digital prints, covering not only the extraction of the corpse but the whole unveiling of the cadaver. The big reveal.

At the moment, Stephen was documenting the wrists and bindings used, attempting to record just how it had been done. The strapping appeared one complete length, wrapped round both wrists and up the lower part of the arms. It was possible to see the strap had been pulled so tight that the skin had folded over the edges in places. It had swollen with the intake of moisture over the years since internment. It was possible to see that because of the absorption of fluid into the material of the strap, the different layers of binding had virtually grown into each other. It was hard to tell which direction each strand went. The other problem was getting a clear shot of the knot that tied the strap in place. Stephen thought the body's arms must have been forced backwards and upwards because the lump, obviously the knot, was on the inside of the wrists. For the moment, this semi-hidden location was causing a problem, and he was trying to get the area completely clean and photographed.

Stephen had a brainwave. He hated using the flash in enclosed situations, like this underarm area. It produced so much glare that details often flared out. He grabbed one of the shiny alloy trays the pathology department used for sterile instruments and placed it on the table next to the lower torso. Using his lens cap to prop up one end of the tray he found he could bounce diffused light up and under the lower part of the arms, illuminating the entire area. He set about getting the camera down low on the table, angled upwards, where he managed to shoot off several shots of the strapping and some good close-ups of the whole knot area. He removed the camera and reviewed the shots. The joy of working in digital was you could zoom in on the object within the photograph and choose to keep that zoom, then save or return to the original. It was whilst he was in zoom mode on the strapping that he noticed the writing.

Engraved into the strap, he could clearly see, in neat, small, capital letters with just the slightest hint of gold colouring, the wording.

HYAM &

Stephen, a third-year archaeology student, instantly realised the significance of what he'd found. This form of lettering was certainly not around in the period everybody believed the body to be from. The strap was therefore definitely not from the distant past. It was very unlikely somebody had found an ancient bog body, tied it up and thrown it in a bog on Dartmoor.

Somehow, this must be a semi-modern corpse.

Stephen's mouth went dry. He wished he hadn't seen what

he'd just seen. He looked again at the photographs. He tucked the camera back under the body and shot more photos, hoping they'd show something different; it would've been just a trick of the light. But it was not to be. Even without macro you couldn't mistake those symbols.

HYAM &

Stephen was going to have to break the news to the professor.

"Professor," he said quietly. "We've a problem."

"Oh damn. What's gone wrong now?"

"Well, there's nothing wrong with the camera, Professor. In fact, this is the one time I wished the camera lied. But I appear to have found some inscription on the strapping."

"But that's brilliant, Stephen." the professor said, putting down his coffee cup and heading back to the table. "What is it? Does it look like religious wording or symbols? This could be very important."

"Actually, Professor, it looks like part of a maker's name," Stephen said, watching the colour drain from the professor's face as the man's eyes focused on the zoomed photograph.

"My God... My God! What the bloody hell do we have on this table?" the professor whispered through half closed lips. "I just don't understand."

By now Rover and the assistants were all at the table.

"May I?" Rover asked, taking the camera from Stephen, who, funnily enough, appeared to be quite happy to pass it on.

"That, Professor," Rover said, staring at the image displayed, "that, I fear, is the mark of a bespoke tailor. My father used to have suits made by a tailor in London in the 1960's. They had a similar system of stamping a logo on the belt. Not this one, obviously, but I don't think it could be anything else. It would seem the rest of the name is tucked under the next piece of strap; we won't know who they are until we disentangle the binding."

"But I don't understand," the professor said meekly. "I don't see how a strap made by a bespoke tailor ended up wrapped around the wrists of an ancient bog body and buried in the middle of Dartmoor. I just don't understand."

Rover looked at him and realised he was a man in a state of shock. Blind to the facts before him. The professor had turned white as a sheet and appeared to have aged over the last few minutes. Rover saw that this intelligent, studious man genuinely couldn't take in, or didn't wish to acknowledge, the blindingly obvious reality of Stephen's photographic evidence. His great archaeological find of the century, the find of his career even, wasn't, in fact, an ancient bog body.

"Sadly, Professor, I hate to break it you, but it would seem to me that our label, 'Dartmoor Man' is drastically wrong. Your bog body would appear to be a much more recent murder victim. Unfortunately, it's now my task to try and find out who it is. What killed him? When did it happen and why? To start that process, I'm afraid it's time for everybody to down tools and for me to contact the police."

CHAPTER THREE

Detective Inspector David Lancaster was almost asleep at his desk when the telephone raised him from semi-slumber. That was the thing about his new office and its big windows. It wasn't bad enough that from his window the only thing he could see was either the traffic jammed up outside or the horrendous monstrosity of the shopping mall across the road. Just to compound his misery, when confined to office during winter months, and despite double glazing, it was bloody freezing all down his left side. During the sunny days of spring and summer it was roasting. Today it wasn't only roasting, but he was bored. The team had put a case to bed two weeks ago, now they were doing the paperwork. Dotting the I's, crossing the T's. Cross-referencing statements, evidence bags and labels. Checking staff reports, then getting them all in chronological order prior to a court case. Yes, there were 'minions' who'd do the work, but the last thing anybody wanted was to get tripped up by some smart-arsed defence barrister in a suit who noticed a discrepancy in reporting.

DI Lancaster's first reaction when the duty officer on switchboard called was 'it's a wind-up'! Somebody reporting a bog body, that wasn't a bog body, but was a real body.

But wind-up or not, if it got him away from the greenhouse windows and the view of the mall for an hour, it was too good an opportunity to miss. He handed the last of the paper trail to his sergeant, Marie Vidêt. He'd have to check it once she'd finished. He knew the old saying 'the buck stops here'. Vidêt was good, and Lancaster did trust her to finish the work, but at the end of the day it was his balls on the line when he stood in the box in court.

Having checked details with the duty officer, he realised he recognised the name of the caller. He'd worked with the pathologist a year ago on another case, his first murder. It had come in as a suicide, but didn't smell right. After detailed forensic work by Landy, in the lab and at the scene, it became obvious the woman had, in fact, been murdered. Once all the evidence had been gathered, it didn't take long before a case was made against the ex-husband. He was arrested, charged and found guilty at Plymouth Crown Court. Lancaster remembered Landy, or Rover, as everybody called him. He'd been a touch on the wacky side. A scruffy set of curls tied in some kind of ponytail. Arms covered in tattoos and a whacking great hole in his earlobe, plugged with a silver disk. He hadn't been what Lancaster was expecting as a forensic pathologist, but then Lancaster had just been newly appointed as a detective inspector, having just moved from robbery to murder.

As usual, driving from town out to the hospital was a nightmare. By the time Lancaster reached the pathology department it had gone two o'clock. He realised he'd again missed lunch. Lancaster pressed the intercom. The door was opened by the unmistakable form of Benjamin Landy, AKA

Rover.

"Afternoon, Mr Landy," said Lancaster, extending his hand in greeting. "DI Lancaster, Plymouth CID."

"Hiya, David. I remember you from the suicide that never was. Please, call me Rover."

The two walked into the path lab where Lancaster was faced with an unusual sight. In the centre of the room was the large, stainless steel operating table, brightly lit from above by the overhead gantry. In the centre of the table lay what appeared to be a partly-exposed human body that looked like it was emerging from a lump of mud. The whole body was stained or coloured brown with irregular areas of muddy skin exposed. The human aspect of the cadaver then morphed into a muddy brown mess like some partly finished Damian Hurst work of art arising from a brown blob of clay.

"Well," the detective said, trying to think of something to say next that wouldn't be a cliché but failing badly. "What do we have here then?"

"I think it's probably best if I start from the beginning, also, I should introduce you to Professor Colin Clift from the university at Exeter," Rover started. The professor nodded a polite greeting, but offered nothing more in the way of information, so Rover filled the DI in with everything he knew so far about the original finding and reporting of the suspected bog body and his involvement in the work to date.

"So, what leads you to think this body isn't, in fact, ancient?" Lancaster said, having listened to what Rover had to say.

"Well, one of the other members of the team, Stephen

Mace, while shooting photos for record keeping, spotted something wasn't right."

"And where's he now?"

"We sent the students to the restaurant for a drink. Once they realised we'd been sponging down and cleaning out the orifices of a real person, they all turned a funny shade of green and asked to be excused," Rover added with a smile. "But I have the camera and can show you what the problem is."

Rover pulled up the pictures onto the touchscreen in the lab. He'd taken the opportunity, whilst Stephen was out of the room, to download all the images from the camera onto the lab's hard drive so they could be seen on the screen.

"This is where the bog body theory becomes debunked," Rover said as he pulled up the image of the logo. "As you can see, the strapping used to bind the wrists and lower arms has a maker's mark on it. I've taken the liberty to cut the next section of strap, and that's given me access to the rest of the inscription. It now reads: Hyam & Son."

"This isn't some kind of ancient text then?" Lancaster asked with a slight smile.

"Well, there is a possibility we've found the first piece of work ever recorded of a Jewish tailor and his son manufacturing sacrificial wrist bands during the Neolithic period. But somehow, I don't think so," Rover replied, without taking his eyes off the image on the screen.

"Is that a presumption then? The whole Jewish tailor idea?" the DI asked.

"Actually, no. Once I'd uncovered the rest of the logo, I googled it. They still exist. According to Companies House they've been Hyam & Son since the 1960's. The father, Abraham Hyam, died several years ago. The son runs the business in the same building it's been based in for just over a hundred years. Number 44 Glasshouse Street, Soho, London."

"You don't get paid a bonus for doing my job as well as your own," Lancaster quipped, "and I hope the students aren't all exchanging selfies of the body whilst quaffing coffee."

"We thought of that, the professor's forbidden any contact with regards the body until further notice under the threat of a failed degree."

"So, what do you make of these markings on the face?" the detective asked.

"Well, for the moment, I'd say tribal. They look like some sort of symbolic collection of shapes. It might be worth posting close-ups onto the Tattooist group Facebook page, see if anybody recognises the work or the shapes. What I'd like to do though, with your permission, is finish cleaning the body so we can see if there are markings on the other cheek, or, in fact, any other markings elsewhere on the body."

"I don't think we'll have a problem with that. At the end of the day, we need to see the whole body anyway, so it needs to be done. It may be a good idea to keep the mud you remove for analysis; it may help with dating the body's immersion."

"Already on it," the pathologist replied. "Everything's been saved and labelled. Also, at the site another team's sieving all the mud that was surrounding the body, collecting any objects, seeds etcetera. At the moment, they still think they're working on the location of a bog body."

"Well that's bloody handy. Let's just hope nobody's told

them anything different."

"Unlikely. There's no signal out there, the only landline is in the farmhouse. Let's just say, he's not a friendly farmer. I can't see anybody popping in to use it and coming out alive."

"Brilliant. So, what next? Well, to start with, I'll get my sergeant out here to take statements from you. I know the body's been dead for a while, but we'll still need a complete record of who found what, saw what and in which order. Just out of interest, you're confident it's male?"

"Actually, don't quote me on that. I don't think there's much doubt, but I won't know for certain until I've cleared the last of the mud from the groin area. Professor, would you be willing to help with that? Your skills would be greatly appreciated. Once we've done, I'll give you a final analysis of the sex, but not before."

"Fair enough," the DI replied, acknowledging the other man's professionalism. "So my plan is this: I'll get my 'oppo' out here 'toot sweet'. Between us, we can get statements done whilst you carry on picking away at its bits. By the time we're done with the rest of the team here, then hopefully you should be able to give me a conclusive answer."

Detective Sergeant Marie Vidêt arrived within twenty minutes. Which, although prompt, did annoy Lancaster just a touch. It meant she must have hit all the lights on green. Between the detectives, it didn't take long to get the details down from the team at the lab. Lancaster took possession of the camera. He didn't want images cropping up until he was in full control of the facts. By the time they were finished, the professor and Rover had made a definitive call. It was male.

"OK, so evidence is gathering," said the DI. "What can you tell me about this skin colouration, Rover? Is it genuine or something to do with the peat?"

"Well up until a couple of hours ago I was happy the skin colouring was down to being entombed in a swamp for thousands of years, but discovering that logo on the strap puts us in a whole new ball game. Until we narrow down a date for internment I wouldn't like to say. I mean, it's a fact that being under the surface of a peat-based material will allow the acidic liquid to permeate the epidermic layer, starting a dyeing process, if you'll excuse the pun. But if our body's only been in the ground for a couple of years it could actually be the guy's skin tone. I'll need a bit of time, but I think we should be able to give you age, height, hair colour and hopefully some kind of nationality by tomorrow. If I can take a small drilling from his teeth and get a sample fast-tracked through isotope analysis, that should give us a definitive place of origin."

"Good. So we're on our way to when. The next big thing is who?"

"If you don't mind a suggestion?" Rover offered. "Contact Hyam's in Soho. If they're anything like my dad's old tailor they kept handwritten records of their items and who buys them. It's a prestige thing. They like to be able to refer back and tell you 'Lord So-and-so' bought this and 'Sir Somebody' had that. I'll crack on and disentangle the strapping from the wrists. We've plenty of photographic records of it in situ, so it serves no purpose leaving it there. It makes more sense to extract it, see if there are any other reference numbers stamped on the back. It could save a lot of time."

"Cheers for that, Rover. If I can leave you with that task then, Frenchy? But before you tackle that, I think we should drive out across the moor and head that lot off at the pass before they all bugger off back to Exeter."

"Who's 'Frenchy'? Rover asked quizzically.

"That will be me," Marie Vidêt proffered, an unmistakable Gaelic lilt to her voice. "I am originally from Brittany in France, but my colleagues in Plymouth have a lack of originality when it comes to handing out names."

"So what do they call you then?" Rover asked Lancaster.

"Sir, if they want to stay employed."

†

It was late afternoon by the time Lancaster and Vidêt arrived at Whiddons Farm. They could see people in the bottom field under a green canopy. They headed down the stony trackway between a pair of beautifully-crafted dry-stone walls. Lancaster often came out onto the moors walking; the walling always amazed him. He couldn't fathom out how they'd ever been put in place without the aid of some kind of big digger.

Marie Vidêt also enjoyed being out in the sun. Out of the office and out of Plymouth. She'd driven across the moor before but had never stopped and got out of her car. There was never enough time and never anyone to show her the places to go. The area had a touch of fear about it. Back home in Brittany there was moorland, but much smaller, just gorse and heather covered hill tops. This place, this Dartmoor, was so big she felt lost whenever she was out there. It looked barren, lifeless, yet her DI was strolling down the track as if he knew what he was doing, confident in himself and his own ability. She appreciated that in a man. By the time the officers reached the bottom of the track they'd been noticed. A guy wearing the green shirt and logo of a Dartmoor ranger was heading toward the gate in the metal, slightly out-of-place fencing to meet them.

"Afternoon," the green man said. "I'm afraid the footpath's closed, there's a notice at the top of the track. You must have missed it."

DI Lancaster held up his warrant card. DS Vidêt did likewise.

"Detective Inspector Lancaster and Detective Sergeant Vidêt, Plymouth CID. We need to have a word with everyone if we may, and you are?"

"Brian Cave, Local Area Dartmoor Ranger. Is this with regards to our bog body? Because it's been taken to Derriford Hospital, yesterday, by your pathologist."

"It certainly is to do with your find, but rather than repeat myself, can we just gather everyone around in one spot, please?" the DI said with authority. "Let's make it over there by the digger in the sunshine. We detectives don't get to see it very often, sunshine, that is, not diggers." With that, the detectives strolled through the gate and onto the site, leaving Brian following in their wake.

Once Brian got everyone's attention and they were all gathered together, Lancaster gave them the facts, with as little detail as possible.

"Ladies and gentlemen. Unfortunately, there's a problem

with your discovery of a bog body. It turns out it isn't actually ancient. It appears to be a murder victim. Dumped into the mire probably no earlier than the 1960's." At this, there was an audible, mass intake of breath from the whole group, and from the guy that was sitting in the yellow JCB a loud exclamation of "Bugger!"

"But what...?" Brian started to say.

"I am not at liberty to divulge any details at this moment in time," Lancaster continued, aware that he sounded like a TV script. "But believe me, it's not a bog body. All I can tell you is, you've uncovered the body of a young male, at present, age unknown. He was murdered and his naked body was pushed into the bog, until your man here with the digger uncovered him."

"My God," Alison said, looking shocked and almost on the verge of tears. She looked at Brian who was obviously thinking the same as she. He gave a slight shake of his head and a look that said 'not yet'.

Lancaster wasn't finished. "I know there's no mobile signal out here, but I'm quite sure that some of you folks will have taken shots and selfies with the corpse. I'm afraid my sergeant's going to have to see all your phones and we'll need you to delete any shots you have on hard drives. Then, we need you to hand over your SIM cards. You'll get them all back. However, for the time being there are aspects of this guy's internment that we need to keep out of the public domain if we wish to have any chance of finding the person or persons who murdered this young man." There were murmurings of dissent rippling through the group, Lancaster nipped them in the bud.

"Listen," he said loudly, holding his hand up to get their attention. "Listen! I know you people can't live without your phones for ten minutes. That's why I intend to give them back straight away. You know you can all pick up another SIM on any street corner or supermarket, but that guy you people have diligently lifted from this bog, he never even got to see the mobile phone invented. He's lain here under the soil for years. Now, thanks to you, he's been found. With your help and support, we intend to reunite him with his family, and catch the bastard who did it. I don't want this guy's mother or father to have waited years to find their boy and the first they know about it is a photo of a shrivelled face dug up from a swamp. So please, guys, help us out with this."

That final heartfelt plea turned the dissidents within the group. One by one they started to step up to the front. The DI got them organised into a line and Vidêt started the process of taking names and addresses, putting SIMs into tagged evidence bags. She also delegated one of the senior students to start collecting all the tubs with finds in and taking them up to their car for analysis. Lancaster was keen to get a look at the location of the internment. Both Brian and Alison were keen to show him. Once the three of them were away from the group, Brian was the first to speak.

"DI Lancaster," Brian started, "I think there's something you should know. When we first discovered the body all we knew was that it was a body, and it appeared to have black curly hair. We happened to tell Mrs Claypole, the farmer's wife, about it. She went white as a sheet and promptly fainted. When she came round, she told us she thought it might be the body of her son Garry. He also had black curly hair. He disappeared over twenty years ago; of course, at the time we were under the impression we were dealing with some ancient bog body and we told her as much, but it did shake her up quite badly."

"And later that day Pete Claypole, her husband," Alison added, "was so angry about us finding a body that he got into a fight with Brian about it. It got as far as Claypole throwing a punch."

"Did you report this to anybody?" Lancaster asked.

"Well... why would we? As I said, we were under the impression the body was ancient," Brian replied. "Anyway, as for her lost son, she informed the police at the time of his disappearance and nothing happened."

Lancaster took a look at the site where the body had been. He quickly realised there was no evidence to be gained from further inspection. The whole place had been turned over. Dug through, drained, trampled and trashed. The university team had got a detailed collection of photos he could access. Having observed protocol, got his shoes dirty and looked at the site, he turned his back on it.

"I'll need to take statements from both of you," he said. "If there's anything else you can add to the story, now's the time."

"Well, the best man for that," Brian added, "is Jimmy, the digger driver. He's lived here for years. He and his wife seem to know most of what goes on around this side of the moor."

Jimmy was parking the digger up and dropping the jacks when they approached.

"I figured you'd wanna word at some point," Jimmy said

as the detective introduced himself again. "So, what you want to know? I dug a ditch, I found a body. If it had bin me what done it, I wouldn't have dug the bugger up, would I?"

"Let's start again, shall we?" Lancaster said. "Can we just stick to the facts and cut out the wisecracks. The days getting on and I want to be home for dinner. All I want to know from you at the moment is information about the Claypole's missing son, Garry."

"Oh bugger. Is that who you reckon tis then?"

"Well, let's not speculate at the moment," Lancaster said quickly. "It's my job to gather information, then try to make some sense of it. Mr Cave tells me if there is one person around here that can fill in local detail, it's you. So can you tell me what the word is on the missing Garry?"

Jimmy told the DI everything he knew. A lot of which, he pointed out, was just local speculation. Lancaster knew that, in this part of the world, there was a lot of fact hidden within fiction.

"Thank you, Jimmy, you've been very helpful," Lancaster said. "Can I ask that you keep this conversation to yourself? I don't want to pre-empt any stage of this enquiry."

"I can keep my mouth shut," Jimmy said. The DI shook the man's outstretched hand. Which again, in this part of the world, meant a lot.

The two detectives, along with Brian and Alison, stood by the gate at the entrance to the trackway.

"So, what happens now? Can we continue working?" Brian asked Lancaster.

"In normal circumstances I'd have a team here, the place

would be crawling with forensics. But honestly, this crime happened a long time ago. The place has been trashed as regards any evidence. We've statements from everyone apart from you two. My sergeant will take those in a moment. We've got the plastic tubs from the excavation, if there's anything worth knowing from the site it's in those tubs. I haven't got a problem releasing the site back to you to continue with whatever you had planned."

"Thank you. At least Jimmy can finish grading the area. Then we can claim to have met the end of our contract and complete the whole pond and wetland area. But I've a feeling this place is going to acquire a different claim to fame."

Once DS Vidêt had taken statements from Brian and Alison, they said their goodbyes and made their way up the hill to the car. Lancaster outlined to his sergeant what he'd been told about the Claypole family and its missing son, Garry. For the time being, Lancaster was going to let that one simmer on the back burner. He felt it was important to get back to base and set up a case board and timeline and look at the missing person records to extract whatever data he could about the missing Garry, before returning to the farm for a chat, with what could be, according to Brian, a very volatile family. It was also important to eat. Having missed lunch, he was starving. He could never concentrate on an empty stomach.

Heading back toward the city, Lancaster's mobile came back in range and pinged, several times. As Vidêt was driving, Lancaster checked his messages. Two weren't important, but one was from Rover at the lab. Lancaster hit the call button.

"Evening, DI Lancaster," the cheery voice of Rover came

over the phone. "Thought you might be home by now having dinner."

"Fat chance, but it's next on our list. What have you got for us then?"

"Well I can confirm our man is definitely that, a male. Despite years under soggy ground, I would say that in life he was quite well endowed. Approximately 1.6 or 1.7 meters, that's his height, not his penis length, by the way. I can also confirm the hair is natural. Black and curly. From initial teeth dentin analysis, I'd say he was in his early twenties when he died. I'm waiting for results of other dental tests, however, I'm hopeful of finding out where our man originated."

"I know I have heard of this before, refresh my memory on how you can do this, in layman's terms."

"Well at present what we've done is just a tooth dentin analysis. As I said, this gives us a good shout at the body's age when death occurred. The thing about isotope analysis is it can measure certain elements stored within the material of the tooth; this can then be measured against a whole database of previously stored analytical records that will help us identify where this guy originally came from."

"Brilliant, thanks for that. What about cause of death?"

"Obviously, I'm yet to open him up, but best guess is going to be drowning. His mouth and throat were full of sphagnum moss. I've picked it all out now, most of it's so well preserved I'm pretty confident we can use it for carbon dating. We should then be able to work out when he died. The moss grows on the surface so it wouldn't have seeped in. I imagine he took in a mouthful of the stuff as he was pushed through and under the surface. There's something else, but at the moment it won't help at all."

"Go on, try me," Lancaster said.

"Well, there's something wrong with the skull and face. I can't put my finger on it, but it appears to be misshapen. I've worked on many dead bodies... it's my job. But this one just has something different about the skull shape. I think it has more to tell us yet."

"OK, Rover, cheers for that. We're on our way back to base to get everything written up. I can tell you that we think we may have picked up information that may help to ID the victim, but we need to keep it to ourselves for the moment."

"So the sooner I can get you results, the better. As soon as I have them, I'll give you a bell."

"Cheers, Rover." Lancaster rang off.

It was late by the time Lancaster and Vidêt finished marking up the whiteboard.

They had photos of the location of the find. They had photos of the bog body that never was. They even had photos of the yellow JCB taken from one of the student's cameras. Somebody obviously had a thing about diggers. They also had a surprising number of photos of the female team members' bottoms, taken from one of the male team members' cameras. They had a complete timeline from Jimmy making the first discovery through to verification of the find by the professor and the true verification of the find by Rover. They also had every detail with regards the body since, including close-ups of the strapping, knots and logo continuing right up to the time they'd arrived at the lab. On a second board they'd started a 'Possible Who' record. On this they'd all the details that they had on the corpse. Sex, height, age, hair colour and photos of the mysterious tribal markings.

DS Vidêt had gone back through the records and located the original missing person's report from over twenty years ago on Garry Claypole. It had been noted by the constable who covered the initial interview with the mother, Mrs Florence Claypole, 'that there was no love lost between father and son'. Reading between the lines, Vidêt got the distinct impression the investigating officer at the time, a man who records showed had retired several years ago, was of opinion that Garry had enough of being bullied by his miserable father. That, one day, when old enough to make up his own mind, he had just walked out. There was certainly a strong hint from some of the comments about the volatile father, following his approach for an interview with regards his son. It also appeared from the dates on various records of actions taken, that the investigation had been closed early.

For DS Vidêt, this all struck a familiar chord. There'd been no love lost between her and her own father, Jean-Luc, a coastal fisherman in Benodet, Brittany. He was a tough man and hard to get along with. There was his way in life and no other. There could be no dissent within the family. You toed the line or faced the penalties. As a child this meant a leather strap as punishment. She often wondered what her mother had faced. But to be honest, her mother seldom spoke and struggled to show affection to either her or her elder brother, Raymonde. She could easily see how Garry had come of age and one day just walked out on his miserable life and miserable father. After all, that was why she now lived in England.

Lancaster and Vidêt went to a local Indian restaurant to eat following their long day. It would not have been Vidêt's choice, but it was late. She was hungry. Lancaster was buying.

"So what are your thoughts, Marie?" asked Lancaster, using her first name, which was unusual.

Her first thought, whilst adding mango chutney to her plate in the hopes of giving it more flavour, was to wonder why they couldn't have gone somewhere nice to eat. Her second thought was that she wasn't drawn to the first name idea.

"Well, sir," she replied, whilst thinking. "My gut feeling, as you would say? From what we have heard about Mr Claypole and his temper, and given the age, height, hair colour and location of the body it would make the missing son Garry a very strong candidate. If your new friend Rover gives an approximate date for death and it matches the timeline for Garry Claypole's disappearance, then it would certainly warrant deeper investigation than it was originally given. It could be that he never walked out. In fact, it could well be he's been at the farm all the time," she said, crunching a chunk of poppadum, then sluicing it down with a mouthful of lager.

"I quite agree the body statistics at the moment do make a match for Garry," Lancaster replied. "From all we've heard about Pete Claypole he sounds, given the state of the relationship with his family, capable of murdering his own son, though maybe during an argument or something. The problem I have with that theory is why Claypole would then spend the best part of two years seeking permission to drain down the one piece of ground that he should, by rights, never want anybody to go near, let alone put in a man with a bloody great big digger."

Vidêt thought for a second whilst swallowing another mouthful of lager.

"Then maybe it was the wife? Everybody talks about fiery Mr Claypole. Maybe the wife was the one stuck in the middle? One day she just flipped and that was that. She then goes on a crusade about her missing son. Calling the police, sticking up posters over Dartmoor. Everyone feels sorry for her."

"Actually, DS Vidêt, that's not a bad shout. I was thinking along the same lines. It's as good a place as any to make a start. We've all been made wary of Farmer Claypole and we all feel sorry for her. I think whatever happens, while we wait for a better timescale and area of origin for our body, there's certainly enough going on here for us to go and have a chat with them in the morning, see what we can stir up. Eat up, we may need to make an early start and catch them during breakfast."

†

It was 7:30 the following morning when the two detectives turned off the tarmac road and down the track towards the Claypole's bungalow. Down by the barns, Lancaster could see Jimmy's pickup truck. Obviously another early starter.

Lancaster and Vidêt approached the front door of the farmhouse. An already-open door led into a dark, lean-to porch filled with smelly, damp coats, work boots, wellies and the like. A dirty-looking shotgun leant in one corner, a pair of dead rabbits hung from a hook screwed into the wooden beam of the ceiling. Lancaster rapped on the inner door and waited. The door opened. A scruffy, unshaven man in a woollen tartan overshirt and dirty jeans stood in his socks facing them. His demeanour was unwelcoming.

"What you want?" the unshaven face said gruffly. "If you're with the bloody university people you'm in the wrong place. Them's all down the track, bottom of the hill."

Lancaster held up his warrant card to the unshaven face. "DI Lancaster and DS Vidêt, Plymouth CID," he announced. "Are you Mr Pete Claypole?"

"I am," the face replied.

"If that's the case, we wonder if we could come in and have a chat about your missing son, Garry," Lancaster said, whilst watching for the other man's reaction. There didn't appear to be one.

"You'm having a bloody laugh, ain't ya?" the face replied, but with no change of facial expression. "Twenty-one years. Twenty-one bloody years. You'm didn't give a bugger then, so why now?" the face continued. Same face, same flat, unwelcoming monotone. "What you'm wanna go draggin it all up again for now after all this bloody time? Is this bloody Cave put you'm up to this, the bastard?"

"Actually, Mr Claypole, no. If we could come in for a chat we could explain," Lancaster said, quietly and as politely as he could.

The face, and the scruffy man attached to it, turned and walked into the farmhouse, leaving the door open. Lancaster and Vidêt followed in the man's wake, aware of walking through a distinct, invisible haze of body odour as they did so.

They entered a large kitchen with a Range to one side, from which the heat could be felt from the doorway, above which hung a wooden rack covered with washing, including another three identical shirts to the one the man was currently wearing. These appeared to be slightly cleaner. Only slightly. In the centre of the room was a large wooden table. They presumed there was a table, as something should be holding up the piles of papers, letters, clothes, cups and plates that would otherwise be just hanging, suspended in midair.

"May we sit?" Lancaster asked, then wondered where.

"No, you may not," the farmer replied. "Just say your piece and bugger off."

We'd like to ask a few questions about your son's disappearance," Lancaster said. Again, politely.

"He was a bloody waste of space. Idle, brainless, useless, a bloody pain in the arse. You know, when he pissed-off, I didn't notice any difference. I still had to do all the work. My missus just got more bloody miserable, but I'd already got used to that. Spending her time walkin round with a face like a bloody wet weekend. Where's this all goin, anyway?"

"Well," Lancaster started, leaning back against the kitchen worktop and regretting it as his hands touched the slightly sticky surface. "Mr Claypole," he continued, standing up straight again, "as you're probably aware, the university team were thought to have discovered an ancient bog body on your land whilst draining the mire in your field."

"Bloody waste of time," Claypole said gruffly, "it's just a bloody scam by the parks to get out of doin it. Tha's what that is, they got my missus wound up good an proper just to piss me off an all."

"As I was saying, Mr Claypole. They thought they'd found an ancient bog body, but it turns out it isn't."

There was total silence from the farmer, so Lancaster continued.

"What they have, in fact, discovered," he said, still watching for some significant sign from the other man, "turns out to be the naked body of a young man. In his early twenties, of stocky build, between five or six foot in height. The young man had black curly hair. We suspect he was forced into the bog, face first, until he died." Still the same facial expression from the other man. Not a twitch.

"We've gone back through the original missing person's report for Garry that you lodged..." was as far as Lancaster got before the other man interrupted him.

"I never lodged nothin, I never reported him missing. I didn't give a shit. It was her, his bloody mother, what told police he'd gone missing, stupid cow. I couldn't care less. I was glad to see the back of him, wasn't even my bloody son, he was hers from some other bloke. One night stand she said, lying bitch, one minute up against a wall, more like. I had to put up with him though, the bastard. She wouldn't even tell me who the father was, I had to just put up with him. Well I didn't have to put up with him and his shiny bloody black curly hair anymore..."

Claypole's voice trailed off midsentence and Lancaster noticed a change in the man's demeanour. He looked surprised, the colour gone from his face. Lancaster realised the man was no longer looking at him, but past him, as if he'd just drifted away to another place. It was then he heard a double click. It was a sound he recognised instantly and the hair on the back of his head stood up on end. He turned slowly and DS Vidêt did the same. They both saw the scruffy lady with the swept back grey hair and greasy Barbour jacket standing in the open doorway. They also saw the two black holes that marked the ends of both barrels of a shotgun held in her hands. At present, they were both pointing directly at Pete Claypole.

"You killed him, you miserable bastard," she said to Pete. "I bloody well known all along. You bastard."

"Mrs Claypole... I presume you're Mrs Claypole?" Lancaster said calmly.

"Of course I'm Mrs bloody Claypole," the woman said, not taking her eyes of her husband. "You think I'd let any other bastard kill him? I've put up with this stinking pile of shit for years, for the last twenty of those, I just been waiting to be sure my boy weren't coming back. I knew if he didn't it would be cause he was dead. He'd never have just left me with this bastard. Now I know he ain't coming back, this scumbag killed him, always jealous cos he weren't his boy. Treated him like shit. All day, every bloody day, right from when he were a bairn."

Lancaster stayed calm and kept his voice relaxed, level.

"Please, Mrs Claypole. This isn't justice for Garry. If your husband's guilty of killing your son, he needs to be tried for it. If he's guilty, he'll spend the rest of his life in prison. That would be justice. Killing him lets him off the hook and it still won't bring Garry back."

"It's too late now. To be honest I don't give a shit bout'

justice. I put up with him for forty-odd years the mean, vicious bastard. There ain't never gonna be any justice for him treating me and Garry so bad for all those bloody years. I just wanna see him dead. Now step to your left, boy. I don't wanna hurt you, but I'm gonna do this."

"You stupid bitch," Claypole said.

"Claypole, shut your mouth," Lancaster said harshly to the man, without turning to look at him. "Please, Mrs Claypole. Please don't do this."

"Listen to me, you stupid woman," Claypole said.

"Mr Claypole, shut up," Lancaster said. "Please... Mrs Claypole," he said to her, gently.

The next few seconds happened in a flash, but in slow motion. A dark shape rose up behind Mrs Claypole. In an instant, the barrels of the shotgun flicked upwards as another hand grabbed them. The gun exploded in a flash of light and a roar of sound in the confined space of the kitchen, bringing down two great chunks of the ceiling, filling the air with plaster dust and the smell of gunpowder. In that same instance, Mrs Claypole dropped to her knees as the backs of her legs were knocked from under her. At the same time, the gun was taken from her hands and flung backwards to land on the floor of the porch where Alison neatly picked it up, cracked open the barrels and stepped back out of sight.

Brian knelt at Mrs Claypole's back. He held her wrapped in his arms, one of her arms twisted up behind her, the other folded across her chest. One of his arms was just around her throat, exerting just enough pressure to let her know that he was in charge, but not enough to hurt the woman.

78

"Everyone all right?" Brian looked up and said in a steady voice.

"What the bloody hell were you thinking, you idiot?" Lancaster said as the dust began to settle and the air began to clear. Finally letting his anger at the situation rise to the surface. "You could've got us all killed, you bloody idiot, why the hell didn't you just leave it to us?"

"Actually," Brian replied calmly, without raising his voice, "I did fourteen years in the Royal Marines. Three tours of duty in Afghanistan and trained and operated as a brigadier's close protection officer in Kabul. I know how to read a situation. I can promise you, she was getting ready to unload both barrels. There was no chance, you wouldn't have got to her in time. Although it was that piece of shit she was after you would've got caught in the crossfire and at this range so would your DS."

With that he stood slowly and raised Mrs Claypole to her feet.

"DS Vidêt, put the cuffs on her and take her out to the car please," Lancaster said to his sergeant, only then noticing how pale she looked. "Are you OK?" he asked, suddenly concerned.

"Yes," she replied, but added nothing else. She stepped forward and took control of Mrs Claypole, who was quite silent. Withdrawn. Shrunken in size.

Lancaster turned to Pete Claypole, who for the first time looked shaken. "Pete Claypole, I am arresting you on suspicion of the murder of—"

"No... no, you don't understand. I'm tryin to tell you. Bloody Garry ain't dead. I can prove it," the farmer said.

The room went silent.

"What do you mean, you can prove it?" Lancaster asked.

"In my desk, in me box," he said rapidly. "I got letters from him, loads of em."

In the doorway both DS Vidêt and Mrs Claypole stopped in their tracks and turned around.

"What do you mean you'm got bloody letters?" Mrs Claypole said.

"He wrote you, I got his letters. When I picked up the mail from the box up the lane I always took em and hid em," said Pete Claypole with no hint of irony. Just matter of fact.

"You really are a bastard," Lancaster said. "Show me, and if anything else comes out of that desk that isn't a letter, I'll drop you where you stand without missing a beat."

Pete Claypole crossed the room to the big wooden desk in the corner. With a swipe of his arm, he cleared the papers and plaster debris from its top and opened the lid. In the back was a tin box. He reached for it, but Lancaster was on it before he had a chance.

"I'm on it," Lancaster said, taking the old biscuit tin up and out of his reach before he could touch it. The DI opened it. There, filling the space within, were bundles of different coloured envelopes. Some quite obviously Christmas cards covered in glitter. Some birthday cards, others just simple letters. All addressed to Mrs Claypole. At a glance the dates were all over ten years ago. Nothing new, but certainly if they were written by Garry, then they were written after the interment of their dead body.

"Mrs Claypole, would you recognise your son's handwriting?" Lancaster asked.

"Course I'd bloody recognise my boy's writin."

Mrs Claypole, led by Vidêt, crossed to where Lancaster stood. Pete Claypole backed away, sitting down on the only clear chair. Mrs Claypole looked at the first letter and cried gentle tears.

"It's Garry's writin," she sobbed. "All these years you'm known. All these bloody years." She turned to Lancaster. "Can I av'em?"

"Not yet, Florence," Lancaster said quietly. "But once we've checked all the dates you can. I'll make sure of that, personally." With that, Vidêt led her from the room.

"What'll happen to her?" Pete Claypole asked.

"She'll be charged with attempted murder," Lancaster replied.

"Her wouldn't a done it. Bloody gun only went off when Cave grabbed a hold of her. If he hadn't stuck his nose in twud amount to nothing. She didn't mean for nuthin, her were just riled. Twas my fault for leavin cartridges in, see. Her thought twas empty, I don't wanna press no charges."

"Well for the time being we'll take her into custody for questioning regarding all of this," Lancaster said. "And for everyone's sake, I reckon it'll be best to keep you two apart until we work out just what's going on here. We'll need you to come down to Charles Cross Police Station to make a statement at some point later today, the sooner you do that the better. I need to get everything you know and everything you think you know down on paper. Is that clear?"

"Course tis," Claypole said.

DI Lancaster stepped out into the fresh air and leaned his

back against the short garden wall. He could see the small, grey-haired Mrs Claypole, sitting quietly in the rear seat of his car. Her head laid against the head rest, her eyes closed. For the moment there was no sign of Marie. She appeared from behind the car, she'd been bent double being sick into the flower bed and was now wiping her mouth with a tissue.

"Are you OK?" Lancaster asked.

"Yes, I'm fine," she replied, tucking the tissue up her sleeve. "Just feeling stupid."

"Anybody would think you hadn't been shot at before," Lancaster said, putting his hand on her shoulder. "Honest, Marie, don't feel bloody stupid. That was a close call. I'm bloody angry with myself for not coming with backup, we knew he was volatile and had a shotgun, but having seen it stood in the porch I crossed it off my mind. I shouldn't have done. I should have taken charge of it there and then, put it in the car till we were ready to go."

"But it was just a routine inquiry about a missing person, sir," Vidêt replied. "Nobody would have expected it to escalate so quickly. Anyway, he was not the one holding the gun. Neither of us expected a crazy lady." At this last comment she started to laugh then, within moments, the laugh had turned into tears. "I'm sorry, sir, I don't know what is wrong with me," she said, pulling another tissue from her pocket and dabbing at her eyes.

"Listen, DS Vidêt. It's your first time in the firing line. You're in shock. Just take a little stroll down the lane in the sunshine and have a sit on the wall and cry. Then, when you're ready, come back and we can deal with Mrs Claypole, OK?"

"Thank you," Vidêt said, and walked off towards the track.

Lancaster turned and looked for Brian. He was beside a Porsche 4x4 hugging Alison, with the shotgun lying on the floor next to them. One of Brian's feet was on it, making sure it went nowhere. Lancaster approached them, his feet crunching on the gravel alerting them to his presence. They broke off their embrace and turned to look at him.

"Listen, Mr Cave," Lancaster said, "I apologise for shouting. I should thank you for your help. To be honest, my superiors would be pissed off that a civilian had got involved even if it was to save my bacon."

"Two civilians, actually," Brian replied. "Alison played her part to a tee."

"Well yes, exactly, thank you, Mrs Grave," Lancaster continued. "But how did you both know what was happening in the house?"

Brian spoke. "I needed to speak to Claypole about finishing the bottom field. But the last time the two of us had a conversation it ended with Claypole throwing a punch. When Ali and I turned down the drive and saw your car parked outside the farmhouse, we thought it was the ideal opportunity to have a conversation, with you as witness and referee. When I got to the porch door it was wide open, I could hear the way the conversation was going. To start with I didn't want to interrupt. Then, as soon as I heard the shotgun being cocked, I knew we had to act. The rest of it just fell into place."

"What made you realise she was serious?"

Brian smiled. "You haven't known them as long as I have. I'm surprised he lasted this long. It's the first time I'd seen her with the shotgun though, but I've no bloody doubt she was going to do it."

"Well thanks again, both of you. If I may, I think I should take the gun, don't you?"

Brian picked it up and passed it to him.

"So what will happen to her now?" Brian asked.

"Funnily enough... I don't really know. She was facing a charge of attempted murder, but Claypole says he doesn't want to press charges. He's adamant she wouldn't have gone through with it, just wanted to frighten him. He says she'd never used the gun before and didn't know he'd left the cartridges in. The only reason the gun went off was you grabbing hold of it, so he's blaming you," Lancaster said with a smile. "So, to be honest, although we all have a pretty good idea what nearly happened, and I don't think it could have happened to a nicer bloke, it didn't happen. So it could get complicated. I may have no charges to lay on her at all, but we're going to take her in for a chat and a cup of tea anyway."

Once Vidêt returned to the car, Lancaster took the wheel and the three of them drove back into Plymouth. Throughout the journey Mrs Claypole was silent. Once in the interview room, little changed in her demeanour. She wasn't the woman they'd both stared at with hate in her eyes and holding a double-barrelled shotgun an hour before. She was a grey-haired, scruffy, sad, diminished individual who smelt faintly of cow manure, sitting on a hard chair without a clue what to do next.

Lancaster made the decision that enough time had been spent down this line of enquiry. There were other things they needed to be doing. This action needed to be closed.

"Mrs Claypole," he started. "I'm going to speak and I want you to listen carefully and not interrupt. Does that sound clear?"

There was a nod from the woman sitting opposite.

"I've decided that you didn't know that the shotgun was loaded. That you'd no intention whatsoever of harming your husband." Mrs Claypole started to speak, but Lancaster put his hand up and stopped her. "I believe you just wanted to frighten your husband. So therefore, I cannot charge you with attempted murder which, if found proven in a court of law, would undoubtedly lead to a long prison sentence. Do you understand? Please just nod if this sounds correct." Mrs Claypole looked a little confused but nodded her agreement. "If I cannot charge you with attempted murder, then all I'm prepared to do is give you a very good telling off about the handling of a shotgun. Is that clear?" Mrs Claypole nodded, but with just a hint of a smile. "Bearing in mind the state of affairs between you and your husband, I'm suggesting that you stay away from Whiddons Farm for the time being. Do I still make myself clear?" At this point Mrs Claypole, like a child at school, raised her hand to indicate she had something to say.

"I ain't got nowhere else to go," she said sadly.

Lancaster held up his hand again and continued, "With your permission I'd like to contact a friend of mine, Kate, who runs a women's refuge here in the city. She looks after women who've lived with abusive husbands or partners and who want a fresh start. It's a safe house, a warm house. There'll be other women there. Some with children. I think it would be a very good place for you to get your breath back until we can give you back the letters from Garry. Whilst we have them, we may be able to track him down for you."

The light came back into Mrs Claypole's eyes. She'd almost forgotten the letters. Forgotten the knowledge that in fact her son was not actually dead but, out there somewhere. And still alive. There was a world outside of Whiddons Farm and this was the time to start exploring it.

"I'd like that," was all she could say.

"Marie, would you get Mrs Claypole a nice cup of tea and a few biscuits from the canteen? I'll make a couple of phone calls."

Back at his desk, he found he'd missed calls from Rover. He dealt with his call to Kate at the refuge first. He felt it more important to make arrangements for the living. Then he called Rover to discuss the dead.

"Good morning, DI Lancaster," the cheery voice said. "Have you had a busy morning? I've tried to ring you several times but alas, to no avail."

Lancaster drew a breath, then decided there was too much to tell so he wouldn't bother. "It's been a touch busy, mate. What have you got for us?"

"Well confirmation of some previous thoughts and some interesting new finds. I can confirm that cause of death was asphyxiation by intake of foreign bodies, in that the oesophagus and trachea—"

"Layman's terms please, Rover."

There was a laugh from the other end of the line. "Philistine. Well mouth, nose cavity and most of his throat were full of duck weed and a mass of sphagnum moss. There's no sign of any of this within the lungs. My feeling is, his head was forced into the surface of the bog. In his panic, with his final gasp, he inhaled debris, the moss and loose duck weed from the surface. They were too solid to penetrate through to the lungs, so it clogged the whole breathing system. He tried swallowing, but just ran out of air as he was pushed under the surface. He didn't drown. In fact, as water did get into the mouth the moss acted as a sponge, absorbing it, clogging up the throat even more... but he definitely died. We did an initial report on the carbon dating of the sphagnum. I can tell you he was pushed under the surface about twenty years ago, storing the moss in his windpipe for us to find later. So, how does all this fit with your possible identification of the victim?"

"We've pursued that line of enquiry. It's not our corpse. What else have you found?"

"Well. Pin back your ears." Accompanied by the sound of a drum roll on a desk, Rover announced, "Our corpse was from North Africa..."

"What?"

"Ah, that surprised you, didn't it?" Rover's delight was evident in his voice. "Our man came from North Africa. I can't narrow it down exactly at the moment, but best guess would be Morocco or Algeria. So, you're looking at a North African, with tribal markings who has his belts made in Soho and likes walking naked on Dartmoor."

"Maybe he was doing the Ten Tors and got lost," Lancaster said.

"Very droll, Inspector, very droll."

"So the skin colour isn't down to the ingress of peaty fluids. It's natural."

"Well, yes and no. Without a doubt over the twenty years the body's been under the surface, it will have absorbed some of the acidic brown water. But the skin tone already had a starting point."

"Look, I'm sending over one of our artists. He should be with you in about thirty minutes, if that's OK? If I can't track this guy down via missing persons then I'll have to post a picture at some stage, and to be honest we can't really take a snapshot of our man. His face has been submerged too long. I need something that looks more like he would've done before he went in the water. He can also do a better job of showing the facial markings. My feeling is they must be unique. Somebody out there must have missed him. I don't mean to be funny, but there aren't that many dark-skinned North Africans wandering around down here in Devon, there would've been even less twenty years ago."

"How did you get on with contacting the tailor in London?" Rover asked.

"We've yet to follow that up. We've been a bit preoccupied going down this other line of enquiry, but we've got to the end of that one. Soho will be our next stop."

"Nice," Rover said. "I should put that on expenses," he added with a laugh. "Well, I can tell you the belt is unusual. I've unwrapped the whole strap from the body. It's a normal length belt, but is unusual in design. At either end its normal belt width, then about three inches in from either end the leather's been cut lengthwise as part of its design and becomes three separate strips. It would've been expensive to make, the belt's a back and front section stitched together along its full length. From the state of the stitching at one end it appears the buckle has been torn off. Along the rear of the belt at that end, I've found an embossed number '42', could be a maker's number. Anyway, I've taken a selection of pictures of it, I'll send them to you now. I'll email the rest of my report tomorrow morning. I've got a fatal RTA stiff on the table to deal with who may well have been drinking. I'll get back to you in the morning, OK?"

"Cheers, Rover, good luck with your stiff," Lancaster said, hanging up the phone.

Vidêt, at the desk next to him, looked at him quizzically at that last comment. Lancaster ignored the look.

"Can you take Mrs Claypole to this address for me please, Marie?" he asked, handing her directions to the refuge. "It's not the place a man's face is welcome, especially a male policeman. Kate Barrow, who runs the place will be waiting for you. She owes me favours, but she'd help us out regardless. See Florence in, get her settled then get back here ASAP, we've updating to do. In the meantime, I'll call the Soho tailor and try to source this belt."

"Will do," she replied. "Can I just say, sir… it's a good shout. The right thing for Mrs Claypole. She will be safe away from the farm, it will give her time to think. It's the right thing to do." She turned and left the office.

"Well let's hope my superiors agree with you on that one," Lancaster said to himself quietly as he picked up the phone.

The call to Hyam & Son was easier than expected, but then he'd never dealt with bespoke tailors before so had no standard by which to measure them. He was impressed, nevertheless. He described the belt, told them of the logo and gave them the number Rover had found. The gentleman he was speaking to immediately said, "Ah, the Bermuda Belt."

"The Bermuda Belt?"

"Yes, sir," the gentleman continued. "It was a belt made many years ago, specifically for the waist of a pair of Bermuda shorts. The belt was a 'fashion item'. The shorts, their accompanying waistcoat and a fine cotton pin stripe jacket that went over the ensemble were part of a range we made some years ago. The design was off the shelf, but each sale was a made-to-measure garment. The logo is applied to all our belts and shoes and a matching label is stitched into each of our garments. As for the number you have found, number 42? Well, if I remember rightly, we only ever made fifty of those belts and they were never sold separately, only with the shorts. We never want any range or item to become commonplace. All our sales are written down in a log book so I can easily track down who the garment was purchased by if that would help."

"I would be very grateful for any help you can give."

"If you could give me an email address, I can send you whatever details I can locate," the gentleman replied.

"Could you?"

"Oh yes, sir. We're quite modern here, you know," the man replied, with what Lancaster thought was a note of humour.

By the time Vidêt returned from her role of taxi driver and nursemaid, Lancaster had updated and redrawn the white board, one of his special needs for an in-depth enquiry. Garry Claypole had now become a section of his own, down one narrow left-hand side of the board. At the top, smack bang in the centre, were details of the body. Below this, a selection of various photographs that were or could be relevant, including the tribal markings. Below this were the details known:

Victim: North African Descent
Age: 20 – 23
Height: 1.6m – 1.7m
Build: Stocky
Hair: Black/Curly
Tribal Markings
Death by asphyxiation

"North African!" Vidêt said surprised. "Well, as you would say, 'that's a bent ball'."

"A curveball," Lancaster corrected as Vidêt looked at him quizzically. "The saying is 'a curveball'. It's American and yes, you're right. I didn't see that one coming. Listen, Marie, it's been a tough day. We've taken care of Florence, for the moment at least, until I can work out what we do with her. We won't get Rover's report until the morning. The Jewish tailor guy is emailing me sometime in the morning and the police artist has gone to see Rover and the body. He won't have a likeness until sometime during the morning either. I think it's time we called it a day and had an early night for a change. Then we can start again fresh in the morning."

They packed up. Turned the lights out and went their separate ways, which was a small relief for Vidêt. She couldn't face another curry night.

CHAPTER FOUR

Lancaster's phone rang as he was walking into his flat.

Seeing the name on the screen was his boss, DCI Craven, he felt an instant twinge of guilt that he was getting home early. Admittedly, the first time in about six months, but there was still guilt. He quickly stepped back outside the door to where there were sounds of traffic before hitting 'accept'.

"Evening, sir," Lancaster said, checking his watch to make sure it was. Just...

"So who the bloody hell is Alex White?" the man said. Detective Chief Inspector Craven didn't sound angry which was a relief. The tone of voice was more 'what now?'.

"Sorry, sir, not with you?" Lancaster was racking his brains, but couldn't place the name at all.

"You've not seen this afternoon's *Herald*?"

"Sorry, sir, no. It's been a busy day." Lancaster still wasn't sure where this was going, but he had a feeling it wasn't going to go his way.

"Front page, this afternoon's *Herald*. Big picture. 'Dartmoor bog body', which I have to say looks a touch gross. The heading then says 'Bog Body Not Ancient'. It continues with the details: '...it turns out to be a murder victim found at Whiddons Farm', blah-de-bloody-blah. 'Plymouth CID are investigating' and so on and ends by crediting 'University archaeology student, Alex White'."

"Bugger."

"My thoughts exactly, Bomber." Still one of the few people who used his nickname. "It had to come out sooner or later, but I thought you had all the students covered and gagged."

"So did I, sir. I have to say, I've no idea who this person is." Lancaster thought quickly. "But it could be one of the students we do know about, using a false name to get his picture published in the paper. Give it another ten minutes and the nationals will pick up the story as well. He could just be after making a quick buck and a name for himself. I will find him though and I'll bloody roast him."

"Please do so. Wouldn't want him to think he'd got off scot-free, the cheeky bugger. Still, as I said, it's out there now, so brace yourself. Are you OK with it?"

"Yes, sir. We're thinking of publishing an artist's impression of our man anyway. So it could work in our favour if I can get our artist to polish up his artwork quickly, then when the national press do find me, I can use them to work for us. I think we call it 'partnership working'."

"Partnership working with the media my ass, I don't think so, Bomber. Oh hang on, a pig just flew past my office window!" The man laughed at his own joke. "Well anyway, give me a shout if you need any extra support. You know I'm stuck with this crime commissioner seminar, it's a bloody nightmare. If I have to look at another bloody croissant I intend to retire. Anyway, I'll leave you to it, just keep me in the loop. Give me a call with an update this time tomorrow. When those on high call me up, I like to at least sound as if I know what's going on. Cheers, Bomber." With that, the man rang off.

Lancaster texted Vidêt to warn her about the *Herald*.

Vidêt's text came back. 'Alex White?'

Lancaster texted: 'Talk tomorrow'.

The following morning, having gone through all the names they had from the university team they could find no Alex White. However, a call to Professor Clift cleared the matter up. Alex White had been there on day one for the first part of the excavation, but due to other commitments he'd dropped out of the team at the end of the first day. Yes, he'd had his phone with him and probably took photos. Sadly no, he hadn't been told about the media ban. So the cat was out of the bag and wouldn't go back in.

Lancaster put Vidêt onto the task of gleaning as much information as possible from the pile of letters and cards from Garry Claypole. What he wanted was a timeline. Also, if possible, details about where the guy had gone. He was determined to give Florence Claypole some closure on her missing son. There was something ticking away in the back of his mind. When he had a moment to sit back and think, he was sure that ticking would materialise into something tangible.

Lancaster put in a call to the *Herald*'s news desk and set up a meeting for later that morning with a reporter he'd worked with before. He buzzed down to the police artist and had the guy bring up the impression. When it arrived it was good, but sad. In the mortuary, the body the team had been carefully cleaning had skin that had taken on a peaty, stained, mottled patina. The flesh had developed an exaggerated, wrinkled look. Like an old suitcase, or if you'd stayed in the bath too long. The face had been misshapen, squashed by the weight of the surrounding mass pressing down on him for the last twenty years. But thanks to the artist, the face now took on all the characteristics of a good-looking, young, North African guy. The skin golden, olive brown. Taut, unblemished. The only thing marring the good looks were the strange tribal markings on the right-hand side of the face. Somewhere in the world there was a father and mother wondering where their boy was. Wondering why he hadn't come home, or called.

How did this boy come to be here? In a Dartmoor bog? What had he done to deserve that? Why was there no record of his disappearance? And the biggest questions of all, who murdered him, and why?

When the front desk phoned through to tell him that a Pete Claypole was on the line, he was reluctant to take the call. Claypole had been in the office the previous afternoon, briefly. One of the PCs had taken a statement from him with regards when he'd last seen Garry. How long had he been hiding the letters, etcetera. He'd been so matter-of-fact about the whole thing. He couldn't see what the fuss was all about. After all, he'd only kept back some old letters. As far as Lancaster was concerned, that was all he wanted from the man. In answer to Claypole's question about where his wife was, it had been very easy to just say that 'she was still helping with enquiries'. However, he felt answering the man's call was unavoidable. He had it put through.

"Mr Claypole. What can I do for you, sir?" Lancaster said,

remaining civil.

"I thought you said you'm not chargin my missus with anything?' came the monotone voice at the other end of the line.

"We aren't," Lancaster replied. Not certain, but he felt sure he noticed the smell of sheep shit and stale body odour seeping from the phone.

"Then where is her? She never come home last night."

"She's chosen to stay elsewhere for the time being, Mr Claypole. I'm sure she'll be in contact when she wishes to, maybe she'll write?" the DI said with relish, and with amusement at the irony of Pete Claypole phoning to report his wife as a missing person.

"Well who's gonna help with the bloody sheep then?" the voice said gruffly.

Lancaster took a deep breath and swallowed his first reply.

"I'm sorry, Mr Claypole, I can't answer that question. You might just have to look after the sheep yourself for the time being. You have a nice day." Lancaster rang off. He felt guilty that he'd gained an inordinate amount of pleasure from that little interchange. *But then, a little pleasure goes a long way in this job*, he thought, and he was due some.

Rover's report landed on his desk next; it clarified everything the pathologist had told him. There was nothing new for the whiteboard, but he logged its arrival.

The email from Hyam & Son, however, was a completely different kettle of fish and threw an unusual spanner in the works. It was accompanied with a scan of an invoice.

The sales book entry for Bermuda Belt (No.42) showed

96

it had been purchased as part of a 'complete ensemble' suit comprising of:

1 Tailored, linen-lined Bermuda shorts with accompanying belt, double pocketed in a light grey with pin-stripe.

2 x Plain white, short sleeved single pocket, linen shirts.

1 Double-pocketed pinstripe waistcoat with tortoise shell buttons to match.

1 light grey, triple-pocketed, pinstripe jacket to match.(It is noted that no tie had been requested)

The sale was a made to measure. It was completed and delivered to a Hyam's regular customer, Sir Philip Stottard of Dolphin Court, Pimlico, London.

What made Lancaster's heart skip a beat though, was that according to the date of sale of the Bermuda ensemble recorded in the Hyam register, it put it firmly at twenty-two years ago. So, the belt couldn't have been more than a year or eighteen months old when it was used to tie the wrists of Dartmoor Man.

A quick search showed there'd be very little chance of an interview with Sir Philip Stottard. His ashes had been scattered across a grouse moor from a helicopter on the family estate in Scotland some ten years ago. Or so his *Times* obituary said, so it must be true.

According to the internet, Sir Philip Stottard attended Eton, followed by an Oxford education. This was an established family of the landed gentry having been involved over several generations in banking and stock trading. After Oxford, Sir

Philip spent many years in the foreign office, though there were few details as to what he'd actually been doing whilst he was there. He'd advised various prime ministers and members of government, regarding world finance and trade. All this whilst still managing to maintain a tight grip over the workings of the family business. He retired from his role early at the ripe old age of sixty with a huge payout and pension package, but had promptly died a year later from a sudden heart attack. Sir Philip Stottard left behind a wife, Lady Pamela Stottard, and two sons, Philip and Peter, now both grown up and running the family firm and its estates and assorted properties.

There were homes in Scotland, London, the South of France, Bermuda and... South Devon.

Lancaster sat up in his seat. He googled again. Lady Pamela Stottard. The South Devon Estate.

Lady Pamela appeared to be considerably younger than her late husband. She was still alive and now, if it was to be believed, in her 'early fifties' and... was a local magistrate. Lancaster didn't recognise the name. The South Devon Estate was a small estate, located at Boldean Saint Martin, near Totnes in the South Hams. The gardens of Boldean Manor were open to the public under the local branch of a national scheme, opening gardens to raise money for charity. Lancaster searched again. Lady Stottard was not in the *Times* rich list. Something had gone wrong somewhere down the line.

Probably death duties, he thought.

She'd been dropped from the list too far back for Lancaster to be bothered finding a date. He didn't have the time now, but this family deserved more research.

Lancaster had that feeling again. The hairs on the back of his head had pricked up. He knew there was some mileage to be had from this new information. There had to be a connection between the purchase of the belt by a member of this family, who happened to have a home in the South Hams, and, it being used as a restraint prior to murder. Maybe the belt had gone to a charity shop and been picked up there by the assailant. Maybe it had been given to a member of staff as a gift or had been taken by them, and that they were the murderer, or knew the murderer. Harder to believe, but still needing to be written into the equation. One of the family may, in fact, be the murderer, though Lancaster couldn't see how that would fit with their North African friend in the morgue.

That was as far as Lancaster got before the reporter from the *Herald* had arrived. He called Vidêt and they headed for the interview room, on the way he filled her in on the Stottard revelations. It didn't take long to get the reporter onside. The DI gave a fair amount of credit to Professor Clift and the team from Exeter, thereby saving them any embarrassment over the body's misidentification. He made mention of their assistance in uncovering, with great care, a body originally thought to be ancient, but quickly identified as being a murder victim, interred over twenty years ago. Lancaster gave the reporter a copy of the artist impression for publication with the heading, 'Do You Know This Man?'

Lancaster didn't know if the man was local or brought here just for his murder. However, there was no harm in having the picture out there in the public domain. It might stir up something. Lancaster couldn't help thinking that the location of the body, the location of the country retreat of the person who purchased the belt used to tie the man's wrists, and the date of purchase of the belt, all had to be connected in some way. Lancaster realised there was only one way to find these things out, but that would need to be run past DCI Craven later in the day. Contacting an acting magistrate who was also a Lady and asking if their knighted, deceased husband or another member of the family had murdered a North African servant or whatever was frowned upon in the upper circles of the police establishment. He'd have to ask permission before making that phone call.

Vidêt appeared with Garry Claypole's letters. She'd read through most of them.

It appeared he'd started writing within weeks of departing the farm. He was open to his mother about where he'd gone and why. His relationship with his father was intolerable. He obviously, at that time, had no idea Pete Claypole was not actually his real father. He'd an obvious dislike of the farm, its lifestyle, the work and its location, and the difficulties of getting into Plymouth with a reluctant father for your transportation needs or the other option, an infrequent bus. It seemed Garry had made a few friends at secondary school. These had consolidated whilst on day release to college. One of these friends had found work and had moved to Torquay to a house share and invited Garry to join him. He'd moved there the same day he left the farm. Immediately, he walked into a job in a factory in Torquay. Over the following years there were regular updates to his mother. Never long letters, just simple lines telling her of his new life, promotions, changes of address and relationships.

He often asked about her and why she didn't reply though, unsurprisingly, he never asked about his father. Then, some seven years ago, he'd stopped writing and given up hope of seeing her again. During the last three years of letters and cards, the boy had settled down. All mail had come from the same address in Torquay. Lancaster had Vidêt make enquiries with the Torbay electoral register. Garry Claypole appeared to be the head of the only Claypole family in Torbay. Still living at the last address he'd written from, along with his wife and two children.

"I think, Vidêt, at the moment your time would be well spent making a return visit to the refuge. As it's evident these letters have nothing at all to do with our dead body, I've got no reason to hang on to them. I think they'd be better off in the hands of Mrs Claypole. You can pass on Garry's address and telephone number; the rest is up to her. I suspect she'll want to get in touch. I'm sure Kate will advise her or act as a go-between. You may like to tell Florence her husband's been in touch, he wants to know when she plans to come home and, I quote, 'feed the bloody sheep'.

The next call came as Lancaster was leaning back in his chair, tucking into a chorizo and salad wrap, a rare lunch break and time spent looking out of his 'greenhouse' window. He was trying to think what the hell the architect of the shopping mall across the road had actually been thinking when he decided that sticking a collection of bloody great giant ice-cream wafers or waffles on the gable end of the building would constitute an improvement. The call was from a journalist from the *Daily*

101

Sun. Lancaster thought about telling them to bugger off, but he knew this would only make things worse. It would be better to attempt to get the facts straight right from the start, though he knew it wouldn't matter. They'd put their own twist on the story whether he gave them the truth or not. Lancaster gave them the facts he'd given the *Herald*. He checked his watch; the local paper wouldn't be out yet and he wanted to give them a chance to get the story out first.

"Can you give me a fax number, mate?" Lancaster said in a helpful tone. "I can get the police artist to send you through an up-to-date copy of the latest drawing."

"Can't you just email us a photo of the bod'?"

"I don't think even the *Sun* would want to post a picture of a face that had spent the last twenty-odd years under water in a bog, mate. Take it from me, it doesn't look good. Ideally, we want somebody to recognise our man. I don't want people phoning up and wasting my time."

The reporter passed on the fax number to Lancaster, in return, he promised to get the police art department to send over a copy of the facial likeness ASAP. Lancaster then planned to wait until the *Herald* was out in print before that fax went off, he owed them that much at least. Lancaster checked his watch. The afternoon was ticking by. He decided it might be worth trying a call to Craven. The call went to answerphone, so Lancaster left the man a brief message asking Craven to call when free. DCI Craven was free within two minutes of leaving the message.

"Bomber, you rang?" the cheery voice of Craven came over the phone. "Just an update, or problems?"

102

"A bit of both really, sir," Lancaster replied. He updated the DCI on the situation with the Claypole's, grateful his boss concurred with his decision not to prosecute. Craven saw it though as less as an act of humanity, and more of one of practicality. Next, Lancaster told him about his contacts and conversations with the representatives from the newspapers. Again, Craven was pleased and supportive. It was always key to try and keep the media on-side. It was even more important to keep the local paper working with you.

Then it was time for Lancaster to flag up the knight of the realm situation and his wish to contact the family. After which there was a very long silence from the other end of the line.

"Are you still there, sir?"

DCI Craven was still on the phone, thinking this through before framing a reply. He'd had dealings with Lady Stottard. She appeared straight enough. To be honest, he wondered what, other than money, she could ever have in common with Sir Philip. Craven had met the man once in the presence of the Devon & Cornwall Chief Constable, not long after he'd moved down from London as a newly-promoted DCI. Stottard had mocked and ridiculed him, subtly but noticeably, mainly for his London accent, but there was something nasty about the man. He'd not been able to put a finger on it, but Craven had felt it was personal.

"You're certain about the connection here, Bomber?"

"Well, sir. There can be no doubt from the records of Hyam & Son that Sir Phillip purchased the clothes and belt twenty odd years ago. What happened after that is anyone's guess. So, if nothing else, we need to find out how the belt went from being in their possession to being used as a restraint on our corpse. There may be a simple reason, they may have sent it to a charity shop or given it to a member of staff. If we can at least rule the family out of the picture then we can start to follow the route the belt went to end up where it did."

There was another long silence. Lancaster waited. He heard the other man exhale a long, stored-up breath before replying.

"I don't think you've any option but to follow this as far as you can, Bomber. If, in the future, it turns out that there's a connection, any connection at all, and we haven't followed it, someone will have our balls on a plate for breakfast. But tread very lightly, Bomber, my son, you tread very, very carefully. Lady Pamela Stottard's a working magistrate. A friend of the new police and crime commissioner. If murmurs are correct, and I do say murmurs, with a capital M, she's seeing a chap at the moment who's flagged up as being the new high sheriff of Devon. So she's mixing in high places, very bloody high. So high, Bomber, you'd get a nose bleed. So, make sure you know what you want to ask her and be sure you know what you hope to achieve before you even make an appointment. Then put on a clean shirt and tie. You smile, be nice and be polite. She'll smell an accusation before you even fart it. Do I make myself absolutely clear?"

"Indeed you do, sir. Very much so. I just want to cross them off my list, that's all."

"I understand, Bomber. Like I said, son, you just go steady. I haven't told you this, but don't be surprised if you find the whole family are part of the funny handshake, rolled-up trouser leg brigade. You know what I mean, don't you, so just be extra careful."

"Indeed I do, sir. I will tread very, very carefully."

"Right, keep me in the loop." Then he was gone.

Craven was right, of course. He needed to work out what he wanted from this interview before he telephoned her office. He pulled a sheet of paper from his desk. He hated working from a list. He worked better on his feet, making it up as he went along. Off the cuff. Spur of the moment, reacting to the state of play. That's how he was going to do this. He'd two questions planned and he'd react accordingly on what answers they provoked. After all, these people weren't suspects, just pieces of a bigger puzzle. Lancaster wanted to get all the straight-sided bits in place before he set about filling in the middle, bringing the picture to life. *Right, let's do this,* Lancaster thought. He tracked down the number for Lady Pamela's office and rang. He felt completely deflated, when told by an office secretary, that Lady Stottard was out of the country until Friday. Two days away. But she'd be driving straight to the Totnes estate as soon as her flight touched down, in readiness for a magistrate court that was due to be sitting the following Tuesday.

Lancaster left his mobile number and asked for Her Ladyship to call him at her earliest convenience on a matter of some urgency. So, two days before he could move this enquiry forward. Well, at least by now the *Herald* would be out so he could send off the fax with the artist impression of their dead man and hope the *Daily Sun* hadn't already made something up and posted their own picture. Vidêt walked in as Lancaster was hitting the send button and at the same time working out his next move. Who said men couldn't multitask?

"So, how was Florence?" Lancaster said. "Settled in OK?"

"Yes, sir, she's become the house nanny. When I arrived, she was sat on the floor of the playroom surrounded by children, reading them a story. I think they thought she was making up the voice and the accent."

"Was she pleased to get the letters?"

"Almost in tears. Kate said she'll sit with her when she reads them. She also has the contact details and will make the call for her if that's what she wants to do. Florence wanted me to say thank you for finding her a place to stay. She's realised her life would've ended at the same time as her husband's if she had pulled that trigger, even though she really wanted to. She's asked if we could contact Brian and say thank you to him as well."

"All in a day's work, really," Lancaster said, retrieving the artist's impression from the fax machine. "But it's better when there's a happy ending, for somebody at least."

"So what do we do now, sir?"

"Well, I plan to phone Brian straight away, cross Florence's request off my list. In the meantime, give the *Herald* a call. I know it's early, find out if they've had any tugs following the picture release. If nothing comes back following those calls then I think we may be done for the day. First thing in the morning I've a treat for you, well, to be honest, it could be a treat for us both. Lady Stottard's gardens are open to the public tomorrow and I think we should visit as members of the public. I fancy a bit of a snoop round, get a feel for the place before we go and chat with the lady herself. She won't be back till Friday so we don't have to worry about bumping into her.

It would be nice to have a wander, maybe casually have a chat with any staff around."

Just then, the phone rang.

"Rover, what can I do for you mate?" Lancaster said.

"Just thought I'd give you a quick update," the cheery voice said at the end of the line. "I've been sending out pictures of the markings from our boy's face onto various tattoo chat rooms and websites, obviously without telling them anything about where we got them. The weird thing is, absolutely nobody has seen anything like them. I mean, if the body had been ancient then I would have expected there to be nothing out there to match. But now we know it's modern, I thought there must be something out there in tattoo land that rang a bell, but not a bloody sausage. One of my tattoo mates did say the closest he could match to were some old masonic lodge symbols. Apparently, they're big on cycles of the moon and stuff, they do go all mystical at the lodge."

There was that tingle up the neck again. The second time the Masons had been mentioned in one day. In this game you didn't like to believe in coincidences. There's a family who might have owned a belt used to tie up a murder victim. This family are purported to be in the masonic lodge, now the signs on the body's face could be masonic symbols. When they come this close together there was no such thing as a coincidence, it was just evidence building.

"Cheers for that, Rover, keep in touch."

With Vidêt having nothing to report from the *Herald* and no reply from the *Sun*, it was time to call it a day and regroup in the morning. Lancaster was tired. It had been a thinking kind of day. He always found those days trying, inspiring but still tiring.

CHAPTER FIVE

The drive across to Totnes the following morning was a complete contrast. The sun was shining. The countryside looked stunning in early summer greenery. Across the fields the first lambs of the year were already fattening. It really was a joy to be out of the office for the morning. Vidêt sat back and enjoyed the ride. Lancaster had chosen to drive, Vidêt happy to let him. After all, he was the boss.

The countryside in this part of the world was a giant, large-scale version of her own home in Brittany. There were many rivers, tributaries and estuaries. Rolling hillsides covered in woodland and as a backdrop, constant glimpses through gaps between trees of the wilds of Dartmoor. Its grey-green patchwork of grass, bracken and yellow flowered gorse dotted with cattle, sheep and ponies. She'd been to Totnes before by train. It was a wacky place. It was the only place she'd ever been where she'd seen a vicar with a dog collar, a Buddhist wearing a saffron robe and an obvious, dress-wearing transvestite, complete with hairy legs and chin stubble. All sitting outside a streetside café, drinking tea, eating cake. Completely delightful, quaint and so very British.

Lancaster bypassed the centre, heading into the wooded,

river cleft hillsides to the east of town. The satnav indicated a left turn, taking them through a wide gateway delineated by a pair of stone gate pillars. To the left of the open gates as they drove in, following the yellow 'Garden Open' signs, was a large two-storey gatehouse set back from the road at an angle, but with a double door in its gable end. A reminder of times when whoever lived in the house had the job of guarding and opening the gates for arrivals or departures. Lancaster drove down the tree-lined drive following the yellow signs to the parking area, some way back from the manor house. There weren't many cars in the carpark, but then it was still early. They parked, locked up and walked into the woodland garden, paying the lady on the gate as they passed.

The nostrils were instantly assailed by perfumed air. The scent of rhododendrons, flowering cherries and viburnums. They walked down the shrub-lined woodland walk, leading to formal gardens around the manor house, seen in glimpses through the trees. They caught the different smells of early summer. Bluebells forming a carpet under the woodland canopy, the subtle scent of late magnolias, the herbal waft from the first flowers of wild garlic forming clumps among the bluebells. Walking along the hardcore pathway led them through woodland to an 'out-of-office' experience for both detectives. Lancaster had another twinge of guilt at the enjoyment he was getting from this morning.

"Do you have gardens like this in Brittany, Marie?"

"Yes, we have some. But they are mainly found around the châteaux owned by the British," Vidêt said with a laugh. "French owners don't tend to like having the public wandering around their homes and gardens, unless it's some of the much larger houses down in the Loire Valley. They need the money for the upkeep. We have only just accepted the idea of trying to save our national heritage and properties and to value the tourist money they bring in. Don't forget, it wasn't all that long ago that the French public kicked out many of their ruling class and burnt many châteaux to the ground. It's taken a long time for people to realise that we need to preserve some of these places to remind us of why we had a revolution in the first place."

Lancaster laughed. "I never thought of it like that. We British tend to be much more forgiving. We like to sponsor the homes of the upper classes so we've something to moan about from time to time. Then we like to have a wander round their homes and gardens every now and then, just to remind them we're paying for them to live there. For some reason, we have, over the years, developed a collective obsession for anything to do with plants and gardens and the stately homes that own them."

Vidêt laughed at that.

Lancaster realised this was really the first time he and Vidêt had actually had a normal conversation, other than talking shop. Even when they ate at a restaurant, it was talk about the day's events or what they were going to do next. It was also the first time he'd heard her laugh and seen the way her eyes had glinted as she talked of France. It was funny the way the 'job', police work, dominated their entire working relationship. He was well aware of the comings and goings of other teams in the crime office. Always some kind of drinking session, bowling tournament or party being planned. They shared their social lives outside of the workplace. Lancaster always shied away from that. Besides, he hated bowling. He was also selfishly aware Vidêt disliked it also.

Lancaster and Vidêt emerged from the cover of the trees and entered the main gardens, via an archway in a long, red brick wall. Their tickets were checked, which Lancaster thought was taking security just a touch too far for a three quid ticket. The pair wandered among the flower beds and roses. They were walking beside the windows of the main house. Lancaster took the opportunity to peer inside, somewhat surprised to see a gentleman sitting in a chair, a blanket over his legs, watching a large screen TV, who turned as he realised that Lancaster was watching him and casually flicked two fingers up, before returning his gaze toward the TV. Lancaster laughed out loud at the simple gesture and backed away from the window to leave the man in peace. Around the corner from the windows were the walled kitchen gardens, which were entered through yet another door set into a wall that was nearly ten feet tall. They walked between beds holding young vegetable plants, arranged in rigid, orderly rows. There were majestic tepees made up of hundreds of bamboo canes all meeting at the top. They had been planted with runner bean plants, striving to climb the strings tied around them. There were beds filled with cut flower plants and areas where pots filled with bedding plants, stood outside the greenhouses in preparation for being dotted around the grounds.

At one point, Lancaster spotted a member of staff watering in one of the greenhouses and nodded to Vidêt, it was time for a chat. Lancaster, followed by his sergeant, entered the greenhouse and started looking closely at the plants, reading labels, touching leaves, pointing things out to his partner. Eventually, they reached the spot where the gardener was watering a selection of large evergreen plants in expensive terracotta pots.

"Some stunning plants in here," Lancaster said to the man. "You're doing a marvellous job with them; they look well cared for."

"Tis what them pay me to do," the man said without turning. "But makes it worthwhile when you'm turn out a good-looking plant. Glossy foliage, plenty of strong flower buds all set for the season."

"Do you supply all the plants for the main house?"

"We do," the man replied. "Manor house and gatehouse and two holiday cottages as well. Not just pot plants, mind, us also do bedding plants for the gardens and cut the grass twice a week. Us supply the house with veg and cut flowers right throughout year, well almost, us do struggle a touch during winter, but us do our best."

"I think I spotted one of the family through one of the windows just now," Lancaster said with a smile. "An elderly chap, bless him, who stuck two fingers up at me when he caught me peering in through the glass."

The man in green overalls laughed. "That'd be Mr Jenks. He ain't family though he's a resident. Place is a retirement home now. Them's all got posh flats but them all retired. Ain't bin lived in by the family since before Sir Philip died. No, Lady Pamela lives down in the gatehouse, rest is rented out now by the boys. Us don't see much of em these days. Them's either up the smoke or up Scotland making money. Still, can't complain. Truth be told, if 'em weren't making money us'd all be out of a job wouldn't us?" With that, the green-overalled man laughed loudly.

"So, Lady Stottard doesn't live in the manor house then?" Lancaster asked casually.

"Thas what I said. To be honest, her was moved down the gatehouse before the old man died. Them had a fallin out sort of and they split up. Shame twas, caused a right rip up, bad blood, arguments. Bugger, I can tell you this much, us all had ta keep our heads down." The man was in full flow now. "After that, twasn't long afor the old man died. Sad twas, I always liked him. Always had time for a chat, always wanted a walk round the grounds, see what was up and growin. Took proper interest he did. I mean Her Ladyship, her takes interest in the cut flower, them ave to be right or there's hell to pay, but Sir Philip, well he took interest in everything."

"Have you worked here long?"

"Started as a boy, fresh from school. Took over running the kitchen garden and the greenhouses and such from father when he retired, some twenty odd year ago. Bin 'ere ever since."

"I expect you get quite a lot of casual labour from Totnes during the growing season? I've seen lots of hippy types and travellers down in the town on market days. I expect they come in handy for a bit of cash in hand from time to time?"

"We've had a few over the years. Some of em bin handy, keen to learn, know their way round the tools. T'others is a waste of space. Them start but ain't keen on turnin up every day. Can't rely on em, see."

"I've got a friend in Dorset who grows organic veg," Lancaster said. "He says the same thing, if you get a good one, you're keen to keep them, but they don't always stay long. He reckoned some of the best he had working for him were some North African guys from a refugee programme. Algerians and Moroccans mainly. Bloody good workers they were. Have you had any of them working up here?"

"Ha," the gardener said. "He was bloody lucky, your mate, if he found one that wanted to work."

"What do you mean? Haven't you had much luck with them?"

"Never worked with one to be honest," the gardener replied, rolling up the hosepipe. "Come across one once though. Waste of bloody space. Anyway gotta get on, bin nice chattin. Hope you'm enjoy the garden." With that, the man went through a door that said 'Private' and disappeared into the back of the main house.

"Bugger," Lancaster said. "Thought we were about to get somewhere then."

The two officers continued strolling until the heavy weight of guilt got too much for Lancaster. Realising it wasn't likely the gardener was going to reappear and chat some more, he decided this jolly had to end. As the two made their way down the drive they realised what a come down it would've been, moving from the large house up the drive to end up in the gatehouse beside the road. Lancaster drove through the gate and headed back towards Plymouth. A few miles to the west of Totnes, Lancaster headed off towards the rounded slopes of Dartmoor, seen stretching across the horizon from left to right, topped off by a bright blue sky.

"I've had a thought, Marie. We don't have much back at the office other than wait for the phone to ring about the article in the papers. I've got to confess, I've got brain blockage at the moment. I need to get this interview with Lady Stottard done to see what it clears from the pile. Annoyingly I can't think past it, so, whilst we are out and about and nobody's started chasing us, I thought we'd cut across the moor, revisit the farm and the site of the murder. With a bit of peace and quiet we might get a feel for why the place was chosen."

"Sounds good to me," Vidêt replied. "Can we pick up lunch along the way? I am starving."

"I think we can do better than that, Marie. How about a pub lunch somewhere, on me?"

For Vidêt, the drive across the moor was a joy. Having somebody else doing the driving meant she had time to take in the wide landscapes around her. The countryside was beautiful. This part of Dartmoor, the southern slopes, was completely different to the parts she'd visited. They passed through villages, some no more than four or five houses and a church. How did people originally come to be living out here in the middle of nowhere? It looked idyllic now, very touristy, but when these places were first built there would've been nothing for miles around apart from sheep.

On the lower slopes, the countryside was varied, a collection of farm fields, dry-stone walls and mixed woodland. The stroboscopic effect of the sunlight flashing through the tree branches was intoxicating, mesmerising yet comforting, something quite primeval. The road climbed ever higher until they were crossing the high moors. The countryside changed once again. Fewer walls, more open wild spaces, bright yellow gorse flowers highlighting the skyline. The dappled greens of new bracken blowing in the breeze. Here and there, shaggy-coated Dartmoor ponies crisscrossed the road, dicing with death, accompanied by the traditional sheep, still bundled in their tatty winter coats prior to summer shearing.

Lancaster came to the junction at Dartmeet and took a turning, signed, 'Tea room.'

Vidêt was disappointed. Although she'd come to like the national drink, she'd also grown to love its real ale. The full-bodied flavour of it was something she'd had in mind when the DI had suggested a pub lunch. After all, she wasn't driving. In France, when you asked for a beer, what you actually got was some form of lager.

Lancaster turned into the car-park of the rustic tea room. They chose a picnic bench in the sunshine overlooking the river. Lancaster went inside, returning with menus.

"Although this is classified as a working lunch, I'm picking up the tab. It might look odd handing in a receipt from the Dartmeet tea rooms," Lancaster said with a smile. They chose and Lancaster went in to order, returning with an orange juice for himself and half a pint of Dartmoor Ale for her, which put a smile back on her face.

"While we wait for the food to arrive, what are your thoughts about our murder?" Lancaster said, sipping his juice.

"Well, sir, I am certain it's not a spontaneous act. The fact that the murder was almost ritualistic makes me believe it was calculated, premeditated. Nobody decides to kill someone and then thinks, I know, I will drive this victim across Dartmoor and push him in a bog. Whoever did it knew about that place before they set off."

"Agree. Carry on."

"Well, if we had not already disproved it, Farmer Claypole fitted the bill perfectly. Motive, knowledge of site etcetera. But as there has been nobody else farming that land in all the years our body has been buried there, then we can discount the Claypoles."

"Can we?" Lancaster said with a quizzical, challenging note to his voice.

"My God," Vidêt said after a moment's thought. "Of course, why did I not think of it before. Garry? My God. I was so busy feeling sorry for him and his mother it had never entered my head. Of course, he disappeared the same time as the murder, of course, of course. We don't know the motive, but certainly he had the knowledge and capability. Working around the farm he would have been strong enough to do it. He would know when his parents were away so he would not be surprised whilst committing the murder. Then he just walked away, moved to Torquay. Of course."

"He kept in touch with his mother," Lancaster said. "He wasn't to know his father was hiding the post. He thought if he kept in touch with mum then should the body pop to the surface, she'd be sure to mention it. Then after years of writing, getting no reply, no bad news. He figured he was in the clear, so he just stopped writing."

"And now we have an address for him and we know he's

still around. Is it worth giving him a visit?"

"Not yet. I don't want him to know we have him in the frame. What we need to find out first is, did he have a connection with the Stottards? If not, how did he get the belt from them and what his motive was? I think we can safely leave him in peace for now. If his mother's been in touch, she'll have told him about the nice policemen and how they'd helped her get back in touch. I'm hoping he'll be put at ease."

"What do we do next? Do you still think we should visit the site of our murder?"

This last comment caused raised eyebrows and a look of surprise from the young waitress who'd arrived with plates of food. So much so, Lancaster felt it necessary to show his warrant card and tell her they were talking shop. The young lady headed back to the restaurant, no doubt eager to tell everyone what she'd just heard.

"I think we should still go to the farm," Lancaster replied. "It was hard to get a good feel for the site when we were last there. There were too many people milling about to imagine what the killer was doing choosing a location such as that to do the deed. It's a strange place at the best of times, there had to be a reason our murderer chose the spot. At the moment my only thought is that Garry's the only person that fits the bill. For him, it was home turf."

"I could kick me. I should have thought of him sooner."

Lancaster was too busy laughing to reply.

"Why is that so funny?" she asked, staring at him.

"I just love your translation of our phrases. The phrase is, I could kick myself."

"That is what I said! Myself, I, me, myself. It means the same thing. It is not funny," she replied, with a definite French lilt to her voice. Something that always happened when she barked in anger.

"I know, I apologise. I shouldn't make fun of you, Marie. You've mastered English very well, you're almost a local."

"Now you make fun of me again," she laughed.

They finished lunch. Lancaster went and paid, aware of whispers and stares from the staff behind the counter. Still, they probably didn't get to hear the word 'murder' being uttered in a conversation very often. He was glad they'd spiced up their day. The detectives continued across the moors. Half an hour later, they were turning down the farm drive. They were surprised to see both Brian and Alison's cars parked up side by side. Her Porsche with its black tinted windows looking a little out of place down this old rugged track. Lancaster and Vidêt walked towards the fields at the bottom, the glint of water in the new pond very noticeable. Through the gateway at the bottom of the stone-bedded track stood Jimmy's JCB. No sign of Jimmy or his truck. It appeared work was finished. The fencing gone. The landscape, though still freshly scarred by the works carried out, was already beginning to revert to normal.

The rooks had returned to the sycamore trees in the valley, 'cawing' back and forth. Above the rustling sounds of leaves on the trees, there was a tinkling noise of trickling water coming from the drainage gullies. These now filled with rough stone and hardcore, across which a pair of pied wagtails dipped and darted, after the flies and insects that were settling. A pair of mallard ducks, one male, one female, paddled serenely across the surface of the new pond, filled now with clear water. The surface crisscrossed by water striders, the long-legged insects skimming across its upper plane. An idyllic oasis of calm. It was hard to believe that just over twenty years ago two people stood here. One bound, frightened and helpless; the other cold, intent on murder.

"I can only think of Garry Claypole doing this," Lancaster said quietly. "Pete Claypole wouldn't have dug up the only place where he knew the body would be found. Unless, of course, he secretly knew what Garry had done, and was determined to get the body dug up knowing he could prove that he himself didn't do it. Sooner or later, he knew we'd connect Garry moving to Torquay and the timing of the murder. Florence was so convinced the body was her son, she fainted and nearly killed her husband. I don't think she had anything to do with it. It took her forty-odd years to build up the courage to pick up that shotgun. As for a casual stranger wandering down here to commit a murder, I just don't see it. There'd be no other reason for anybody coming down here, even knowing of the bog's existence."

"Well, that's not strictly true," Brian's voice said from behind them.

"Where did you spring from?" Lancaster said, turning to see both Brian and Alison standing in the gateway.

"We were up in the barn when you arrived," Brian said, hastily adding, "Alison and I were checking it out as a possible location for some outreach work for schools. Just an idea at the moment, of course."

Lancaster decided not to pursue this line of questioning. By the look on Alison's face, it was probably more than a bit of outreach they'd been investigating in the barn, but it was none of his business. Well, not for the moment anyway.

"What did you mean by 'not strictly true', Brian?" Lancaster asked.

"Well up until a few years ago, there'd been a series of letterboxes hidden down here. So loads of people over the last twenty-odd years would've been down that trackway and into this field. They would've clocked the box, then carried on up the track and out onto the open moorland. They used to do a loop that took in about ten boxes, ending with the stamp from behind the bar in the Plume of Feathers."

"What do you mean? 'Letterboxes'. In a field? I don't understand?" Vidêt asked.

"It's an old Dartmoor tradition," Lancaster replied. "All across the moor people hide boxes. Plastic sandwich boxes, metal tins. Inside these would be a rubber stamp with some kind of picture or emblem cut into them, alongside a tin with an old-fashioned inkpad inside. The idea is you pick up clues and map references for these boxes, then use your map reading skills and your ability to solve riddles etc. to track down their hiding place. Then you open the box, use the stamp and ink pad to mark your own visitors' book, or a blank postcard. You write the date on it and add it to your collection. Then you sign the visitors' book that's in the letterbox. Some people carry their own ink stamp and mark the book with their own symbol. You put the box back into its hiding place, then move on to the next."

"But why?" Vidêt asked, looking perplexed.

"Well, it's just a test of skill really," Lancaster replied. "Skill and endurance. Some of the boxes are a long way out on the moor, you have to be a hardened walker to clock some of them."

"But why?" Vidêt asked again.

"It's a way of getting people out of their homes," Brian suggested. "Getting them out of their cars, away from the telly and onto the moor. Most people who come onto Dartmoor, park up in one of the parking areas. They have a picnic, walk the dog and that's it. They never get further than a few feet from the road. Letterboxing's just another way to encourage folk to go further out, enjoy the whole moorland experience. It teaches them how to read a map at the same time."

Vidêt didn't look convinced, but nobody could be bothered to try and make her see the fun in it.

"So you're saying that there were boxes here for years?" Lancaster said. "So why'd they disappear?"

"Mainly because Pete Claypole frightened them off," Brian replied. "He used to shout at them. Tell them to get off his land. It isn't his land, he leases it from the park authority. He doesn't own it and we make the rules. Even so, bit by bit, people got fed up complaining to us about the miserable old bastard, eventually the boxes just got moved."

"But twenty-odd years ago, the boxes were still in use?"

"As far as I know. I wasn't here then, but I've a couple of books about letterboxing and at least one of them mentions 'Whiddons Mire'. Part of the fun of this one was you had to watch your step, you could end up waist deep in the bog before you'd got your stamp."

"Well, I can't think our dead body was a letterboxer murdered for his rubber stamp. But it does show that other people could've known the location, and that it could be deep. That opens it to a wider audience. Shame really. Every time we think we have it in a nutshell, something keeps making it difficult. Why doesn't anybody just go for a simple murder?"

"Did I overhear right," Brian said, "you're thinking it could have been Garry?"

"Forget you heard that! It's just one of many avenues we have to follow up. I'd much rather you ignored it. OK?"

"Lips are sealed. Well, we're heading off now unless you need us for anything?"

"No, you're OK. We're calling it quits now, anyway.

"Can I just ask," Brian said, "what's happened to Mrs Claypole? I know you said she wasn't going to be charged with anything, but she hasn't returned?"

Lancaster explained briefly what had happened, but didn't go into detail. It was time Florence had some life to herself. She should be able to have some secrets about where she was and what her plans were, if any. If there was a chance that Garry was to be implicated in this murder then she was going to lose him all over again. A few days of peace was not too much to give her. They got back to the cars and said their goodbyes. The two detectives reversed out and turned up the drive. Lancaster had a quick look in his rearview mirror and smiled as he noticed the other two both getting into Alison's car. *There is something going on there,* he thought, *but it's not about the case in hand.* The detectives returned to the office, where they added more items to the whiteboard, all of them with question marks beside them.

They checked for messages from the item in the paper only to find nothing. There was disappointment at the *Sun* having put back their showing of the facial reconstruction by a day due to a terrorist incident in London which stole most of the pages.

"Right, Vidêt," Lancaster said. "This is frustrating me now. I hate not having an immediate avenue to go down, whether it leads anywhere or not. I need to eat a decent meal and think, so, you name the restaurant. I'll pay."

This was an offer Vidêt couldn't refuse. She chose a Greek restaurant on the Barbican, the ancient port of Plymouth, one of the only areas that didn't get bombed during the war. It still held character. Many old buildings, cobbled streets and alleyways. It was a lively area filled not only with tourists, but many locals frequented its cafés and bars. They chose to walk from the office. It was a nice afternoon, promising to produce a lovely evening. The ten-minute stroll would help boost the appetite.

On the way to the restaurant Lancaster received a call from Rover.

"Rover, what can I do for you?"

"Afternoon, Inspector Lancaster," Rover said respectfully. "Something you may find of interest, but adding nothing to your enquiry. You know I said I was interested in the shape of the head? Well I couldn't be sure if the changes to the shape were down to pressure of the peat layer over the years so I had an X-ray done of the skull. It turns out our man was given a bloody great whack across the right-hand side of his face some time before he went under the water. He was hit with enough force to shatter the cheek bone and split the jaw in two places. I'd imagine that would certainly have rendered him unconscious. When his head was stuffed unceremoniously under the surface his last full gasp was filled with the intake of moss and duck weed. He wasn't killed by the blow, though. Cause of death still remains asphyxiation due to weed intake clogging his ability to breathe."

"Cheers, Rover. You're right, it doesn't add anything to the enquiry, but it helps to flesh out the bigger picture. Whoever committed the murder appears to be somebody obviously strong and pretty cold-hearted. It takes a special kind of person to strip a man naked, take him to the moors, tie his wrists, wade him into a bog then smash the side of his face in and push him under the surface. It's not a casual act, it's calculated and cruel. Just out of interest, any idea what the murder weapon may have been?"

"It's interesting you should ask that, Inspector."

"Not really, Rover. I'm a detective. It's the sort of question I'm meant to ask."

"Good point. Well looking at the face and the way the cheek bones have been shattered it wasn't a sharp or rounded instrument. There doesn't appear to be a point of impact. The blow's been struck across a wide area. My best guess is a spade or a shovel, something with a flat surface area."

Lancaster thought it would certainly be the sort of implement you'd readily find around the farm. Was it used by Garry?

"OK, cheers for that, Rover. I'll let you know when we've something firm to tell you. For the time being, just keep the bod in the chiller until we find an owner."

Lancaster rang off and told Vidêt what Rover had found.

"Let's wait till we have some food in front of us before we discuss what to make of it," Lancaster said.

Sitting in the restaurant with a chilled glass of pale pink rosé each and a full Greek mezze for two spread out on the table, the pair waded into the selection. Helping themselves to olives, tzatziki, meatballs, stuffed vine leaves, delicious zucchini fritters. It didn't take long to settle down and drop out of office mode.

"OK then, Marie," Lancaster said, taking a sip of the chilled wine. "What do we think about this murder weapon? Does it bring anything else to the case?"

"Well not really, sir. If we are thinking our murderer is young Garry, then it changes nothing. It gives us a possible murder weapon in the farm yard. What is interesting is, when we found the victim was African, my first thought was it could be racially motivated? But I just do not imagine an African visiting Plymouth, deciding to go for a walk on the moors down an unmarked track. Unless you already know of it, of course. There, an angry Garry makes him take his clothes off and hits him with a spade? It doesn't make sense. I think whoever did this knew the victim. Maybe they both knew each other? If that is the case, how does Garry get to know a North African, when by all accounts he hardly ever left the farm?"

"Valid point," Lancaster replied. "So, first thing in the morning contact the city college. Find out if they had any

North African students studying with them twenty-one years ago, but don't mention Garry to them. I know it's a long shot, but if we don't ask, we won't know, and if they say yes, then get down there with the artist impression."

"What do you hope to get from Lady Stottard?

"Well I'm not expecting a signed confession. But I need to know what connection her husband had with the clothes from Hyam's and, where they went after he used them. If all our time lines are correct then her husband purchased the clothes, yet within eighteen months the belt was being used by our murderer. Now I know the rich like to change their clothes as a regular thing, but the rest of the suit is no good without the belt. So, what happened to make Sir Philip get rid of them? That's what I hope to get from Lady Stottard." Lancaster munched his way through another stuffed, rolled vine leaf and thought for a second. "I think we mustn't try to rush this enquiry. Our victim's lain there for a long time. We can take time over this. I think we get our interview with Lady Pamela out of the way before we go after Garry."

Vidêt sipped at her wine, appetite replete. That's the way with a full mezze. When it arrives your mouth waters, you can't wait to begin. Then, halfway through you start to fill up. She'd never been able to clear a whole selection, she was glad she'd been able to share it. She finished her glass, raised her hand to attract service and ordered another. After all, the boss was paying.

CHAPTER SIX

The following morning, Vidêt had a long conversation with a helpful lady in admissions at the city college. Mrs Stacey had, apparently, 'been there for years'. According to her, although they did have foreign language students studying at the college, learning English as part of the city's refugee and asylum seeker programme, and many had indeed come from the Southern Mediterranean and North African regions. They didn't have any twenty years ago. They did, however, have some French students twenty-odd years ago. As if to pre-empt Vidêt's next question, no, none of them were North African. They were all white and from Paris, part of an exchange with another college. But as DI Lancaster had said the previous evening, it could have been a lead. It had been followed and crossed off; even that took them closer to a conclusion.

When Marie Vidêt arrived in England, she was on loan to the Metropolitan Police in London. She felt very much a 'fish out of water', as the saying went.

She'd been a detective with the Police Nationale in Brest, Brittany. They'd begun an investigation that had started off small, but developed into a major league investigation into a drug smuggling gang, operating out of the Caribbean via various ports and harbours throughout Northern France. The gang were recruited from companies engaged in chandlery work, sail makers, winding gear etcetera. It had taken a long time to work out exactly how the gang had operated, but eventually the story emerged. They were using sailing yachts involved in cross ocean racing, using a network of berths in small marinas around the coast, bringing in reasonable amounts of drugs, mainly cocaine. This was transferred to other yachts that plied backwards and forwards throughout the channel ports, regular, recognised 'yachters'. This final move was made once the gang thought the coast was clear. The drugs were often stashed aboard the boats without the owners even knowing, sometimes attached to the outside of the hull. Removed once it reached safe harbour. The Metropolitan Police had become involved as two of the key players were Londoners based in Kent. They had been identified through an Interpol investigation, flagged up by the European Drug Enforcement Agency.

Vidêt, with her Breton coastline knowledge and excellent use of English, was conscripted to act as liaison in London. There was belief locally, within the ranks of her colleagues, that turning down an offer of a romantic liaison with her commanding officer in Brest could have been another reason for her posting abroad. Vidêt never saw it as a punishment, she was happy to go. On many levels it felt like a good idea. She was keen to see policing in different countries. Keen to leave Brest and its complications and desperate to leave Brittany. She was at the time, still living at home, well, most of the time. She tried to stay at the base dormitory whenever she could. Having chosen to join the police, an organisation her father loathed and despised, she then had to suffer continuous comments and snide remarks from him. Moving from the Police Municipale, working locally in the coastal districts around Benodet, to working with the Police Nationale out of Brest, was, as far as her father was concerned, the final straw. Much to Marie's joy, he'd stopped speaking to her. With her now being in the police, he'd also, quite sensibly, stopped hitting her. This was also a blessing, but tinged with regret. There was part of her, in fact, quite a big part of her that wished that one day he'd lose his temper again and attack her, so she could arrest him and take pleasure in locking him up.

Once she'd settled into London and been accepted within the Met, through her knowledge of the boats, harbours, ports and tidal vagaries of the Breton coast, she'd made herself invaluable to the whole investigation. She revelled in the new tactics, techniques and investigation routes being used. The shared databases being cross-referenced by different departments, the combining and sharing of personnel when extra force was needed. Back home in France, the inter-department, inter-police force rivalries often defeated an investigation, leading to many members of the force living in deep frustration. Not being able to get through the various roadblocks, obstacles and difficulties inflicted on them whenever an investigation crossed over boundaries between forces. In recent times, even the head of a French regional drugs investigation branch had been arrested, charged with actually being involved with drugs trafficking, along with several of his senior officers. Here, in the UK, there were still conflicts between regional forces, but seldom to the same degree as back home in France.

Once the case had been brought to a conclusion and Marie had assisted in giving evidence, it became possible, in fact necessary, to continue using her knowledge as a source of information to tackle other cross-channel crime syndicates. These had come to light during the course of the original investigation, operating on both sides of the channel. Slowly but surely, she became indispensable. Following some movement of paperwork, Detective Marie Vidêt transferred to the British police force. For some reason, her time with the Met didn't last long. She sought a transfer to another area, ending up in Plymouth under the Devon & Cornwall regional police force banner. She arrived in Plymouth as a detective constable, but was rapidly promoted to detective sergeant and assigned to work under DI Lancaster. A promotion and assignment she wholeheartedly agreed with.

As a boss, she liked and respected Lancaster. Although, there were times when she couldn't understand his way of thinking and struggled to understand his humour. He was meticulous in his work, something she appreciated. He turned over every leaf. Inspected it, replaced it if not regarded as relevant. But not before he'd noted it down and recorded its location, just in case he needed it again someday. If he turned over a leaf and thought it was relevant, then it was noted down, recorded and stored on the whiteboard until he could stick some more leaves to it. 'Never discount anything until you've investigated it, no matter how small. And never act on anything until you're sure it will have a result' was his mantra. Vidêt liked this approach. It gave her time to learn, time to understand how the picture was built. She'd already realised there were others within the local CID that thought his way was too slow. He never liked working with a big team, only called in extra resources when he felt it was warranted. However, he got results. That annoyed them, but did gain their respect. Not friendship, but respect.

That was what he was now doing with Garry Claypole.

DI Lancaster had obviously put Garry into the picture early on in the investigation. At least once they had turned over the leaf that was Pete Claypole. Inspected it, dealt with it, recorded it, reacted and moved on. Lancaster had spotted Garry from the corner of his investigative eye. The timing of Garry's departure from the farm was too much of a coincidence to be ignored. Vidêt was annoyed with herself for not picking up on it straight away. She'd fallen into the trap of seeing herself in this young man's shoes, feeling sorry for him. She was just glad he'd escaped an abusive father and made a new life for himself in Torquay. *Merde!*

When she returned to her desk Lancaster was grabbing his coat, getting ready to leave.

"Right, Marie, coat and notebook. I've had a call from Lady Stottard's PA. Her plane got in early, she's home, intrigued and wants to see us before lunch. After that, she's busy until the middle of next week. You can tell me about the city college en route."

Vidêt drove whilst Lancaster sat going through his notes. As they drove, she filled him in on her conversation with the college.

"OK. When we get back make a side note on the board," Lancaster said. "We always need to show where the investigation's gone and what conclusions we make. We need to prove we've covered every avenue in case anybody ever asks."

"I also checked with Kate. Florence has been in touch with her son, they have plans to meet up. Kate is taking her to Torquay next week. According to Kate, she made the first contact, then handed it over to Florence. She says the conversation was brief. Florence told Garry she had left her husband, told him his father had hidden all of his letters, and that she had never known he had written to her. He was keen to meet, but not until next week. That means he won't know anything about the finding of the body until then, that gives us some breathing space."

"Well done, Marie, was Kate OK?"

"Yes. She sends her regards, I obviously told her nothing at all about our thoughts on Garry."

"Brilliant."

The rest of the journey continued in relative silence as Lancaster worked his way through the notes he'd made over the last few days, adding new scribbles in the margins as he did so, making sure of the timeline of events so far. He wanted to ensure he'd missed nothing. No side street or undetected alleyway that would have solved this murder earlier. He was fully aware that Lady Stottard was a magistrate, an active one at that. He'd done his research and knew her views on police incompetence. If he made a wrong move, asked a question with a potential hidden twist, he was sure she'd react and the interview would turn against him. If it did, she'd be moving her thoughts up the line and DCI Craven would be on the phone and on his case. He was also aware this was an avenue he had to go down; a leaf to turn before there was any chance of eliminating the family from the enquiry. The facts were simple. Her husband, Sir Philip, had purchased a suit of clothes, delivered to their London home. Shortly after, the belt from that suit had been used in a serious crime. Not raising this point with the family was not an option, full stop.

Vidêt turned the car in through the gates to Boldean Manor and pulled into the parking area. Lancaster put all the notes back into the folder and slid it into his slim-fit briefcase.

"Marie, would you be able to memorize the bulk of this interview?" Lancaster asked. "Obviously, if it gets too long and complicated then make brief notes and as soon as we've gone up the road a bit we can stop and make a full account. I want Lady Stottard to be at ease with talking to us, she may clam up if you're scribbling in your notebook."

"Understand, sir, not a problem. I could set up my phone to record, if I keep it in my pocket the recording might not be brilliant, but it's worth a try."

"OK that's good, just make sure she's not aware."

They crossed the drive to the imposing doorway of the gatehouse, as Vidêt reached up for the ornate bell pull beside the door, it opened.

Lancaster had his warrant card out and on display, he held it up to the lady in the doorway.

"Good morning," he said politely. "DI Lancaster and DS Vidêt, Plymouth CID, we've an appointment to see Lady Pamela Stottard. We're a little early, we weren't sure how bad the traffic was going to be."

"You're speaking to her," the lady in the doorway replied.

"Early is never an issue. Late always is. Do come in." She waved them both inside.

Lancaster was taken by surprise. He'd looked Lady Stottard up the day before to get an insight into what he was letting himself in for. This lady looked nothing like the photos he'd found. These had shown a local magistrate looking very officious, formal, efficient and slightly frumpy. Two years previously, she'd attempted to get herself elected as the Devon and Cornwall Police & Crime Commissioner, but had been narrowly pipped at the post by yet another forceful and prominent lady. There were photos of the two ladies, Lady Stottard congratulating her rival, wishing her well. The lady who'd just opened the door, now walking in front, leading them into a spacious lounge area, was a stunning-looking woman with long dark hair. Definitely a country woman. Wearing dark blue jeans, simple shoes, a loose-fitting, sharp-collared shirt tucked in at the waist. Her hair tied back by a wide, deep blue hairband and, despite the fact that they were indoors, across the top of her head, sitting on the hairband, were a pair of designer sunglasses. Her media profile said Lady Pamela was in her 'early fifties'. Lancaster had the impression she'd been in her early fifties for several years, but still looked good on it.

"Would you care for coffee?" she asked. "I was planning on having one."

"Well if you're sure it's not a problem, we'd both love one, thank you."

She rang a bell beside the fireplace, the lounge door opened and a young woman appeared.

"Coffee for three please, Krista. We'll take it on the patio."

She walked to the double glass doors and swung them open with a flourish, then walked out to the patio overlooking a small but florific garden surrounded by trees.

"So," Lady Stottard said, sitting down on a cushioned wicker chair, motioning for the detectives to do likewise. "I am intrigued, Detective Inspector. My PA said you wished to have information regarding the family tailor! A subject I have absolutely no knowledge of at all. I didn't know we had one. I've made enquiries about you DI Lancaster. I'm sure you wouldn't be here wasting either my time, or your own, without good reason. So, intrigued as I am, why don't you enlighten me as to what it is you are actually after?"

Lancaster unzipped his briefcase and removed a sheet of A4, which he handed to Lady Stottard.

"Lady Stottard. This is a copy of an invoice from the tailoring company Hyam & Sons of Soho, London. It shows that twenty-two years ago, your husband, Sir Philip, purchased a bespoke suit of clothes that included a distinctive leather belt. We are at the moment trying to trace the whereabouts of either that suit or, better still, knowledge of the belt itself. Of course, with Sir Philip now deceased, you became our next port of call."

Lady Stottard reached across and took the sheet of paper, studying it intently. Just then Krista appeared with cups and accoutrements for coffee which she set about pouring.

"That's OK, Krista, I can manage," Lady Stottard said, waving the woman away. She stood up and walked to the edge of the patio. Still looking at the invoice in her hand. She lowered the sheet of paper and stared momentarily out into the garden before returning to the table.

"Coffee?" she asked, lifting the pot.

"Thank you." Lancaster watched as the woman poured the steaming liquid into the three cups on the tray.

"Hot milk?" she asked, picking up the silver milk jug.

"Yes please, for both of us." Lancaster was reluctant to speak further until he'd had a response from Her Ladyship. He'd recognised the signs of somebody, deep in thought, racking past information files for something. He waited patiently as the woman passed the cups around then retook her seat, neatly crossed her legs and took a sip from her cup. She replaced the cup on the table and picked up the invoice once more. After looking at it for a short while, she spoke.

"May I ask, why this information is relevant to any enquiry you're involved in?"

"At this stage, Your Ladysh—" Lancaster said, and was cut short by the woman.

"Please, just call me Pamela. Actually, I am never quite certain if I am at liberty to still use the term lady anymore since my husband's death. I don't normally correct others when they use it. I have found it doesn't hurt to bandy the title around some days."

"Well, as I was saying, Pamela, at this stage I'm not at liberty to divulge much about the case we're working on. I can tell you, an item that's part of that invoice has turned up as part of a current investigation. We're keen to find out how it went from your husband's clothing collection and ended up where it's been found."

"Well, for God's sake, Detective Inspector, this suit was purchased over twenty years ago, according to this invoice. An item of clothing from it could have ended up virtually anywhere since then. In fact, it's a sign of a good tailor that any of it has survived this long."

"The problem is, Pamela, the item in question arrived at the location, within a year to eighteen months of its purchase and delivery to your home in Dolphin Court."

"I am presuming then, the fact that Plymouth CID are involved and not a London-based force, that the item of clothing found must have been located here in Devon?"

"Correct," Lancaster replied, impressed with her speed of supposition.

"You don't give much away do you? But what you're saying is, my husband purchased these items as stated on this invoice, at the date stated, and then, as if by magic, quite soon thereafter, part of the suit became separated from the rest, ending up here in Devon, where it's been used for over twenty years until it came to light in your current investigation. Is that correct?"

"Correct," Lancaster replied.

Lady Pamela put her cup down. With the A4 sheet still in her hand, she stood and walked to the patio balustrade, looking at the document. She lifted her eyes from the page to the garden, momentarily lost in thought. Lancaster looked sideways at Vidêt and put his finger to his lips, the universal sign for silence. He was aware something had been triggered by showing the invoice. Lady Pamela was working out what to say next. It definitely meant something to her, but what? When she turned towards them, Lancaster thought the sunlight caught a glint of tears in the woman's eyes.

"No disrespect meant, DS Vidêt," she said, "but may I speak with you alone, DI Lancaster, just for a moment?"

Lancaster thought for only a second before turning to Vidêt. "If you wouldn't mind, Sergeant, would you wait in the car for me? If I need you I'll call, OK"? His voice made it sound like a request, but his eyes were saying 'go'. Vidêt got up and headed for the door. Before she reached it, Lady Pamela spoke.

"DS Vidêt? Thank you," the woman said with a smile.

When they were alone, Lady Stottard sat down.

"What do you know of this family's recent history, DI Lancaster?"

"Only what I gleaned from a quick Google. I know the family has homes in various parts of the world. I know you have two sons who run the family business since your husband's death some ten years ago. I know you're an active local magistrate. Beyond that, I'm afraid I know very little." Lancaster was lying, he'd done better research than that, but felt he needed to keep some knowledge to himself.

Lady Stottard laughed. "I suspect you know far more than you're letting on, Inspector. You forget, I've done my homework too. Nevertheless, I must take you at your word." She thought for a moment before continuing. "The period when this invoice was issued was a very painful one for me. My husband and I were estranged at the time. He was living in the apartment at Dolphin Court, I was living here at the manor." Again, a long pause before she spoke again. "I don't know why I feel so sensitive about this issue. After all, these days it's commonplace, but the reason we were estranged was that I'd found out my husband was homosexual. He apparently had been throughout all our married years; well, all of his life, really. It wasn't as if we got married and then he suddenly became one. When we married he was obviously what they called, 'a closet gay'. Frankly, I should have known from the start, but when we first met in the sixties, he was fresh out of Eton, they all sounded camp and effeminate. I just presumed it was down to too much debagging and casual 'rumpy-pumpy' in the dorms. I mean, it wasn't as if we didn't have plenty of sex, the two of us. After all, we begat two sons, but there you are. When I eventually found out what was going on when he was supposed to be at his club, I was disgusted. I was horrified at the thought that I'd been sharing his body with other men. I walked out there and then, took the boys with me. We became resident here at the manor. I made it quite clear our married life was over and that the manor would be my home. He could have the rest and that was that. Obviously, back then, even though homosexuality had been declared legal, there was still a huge stigma attached to it. Philip's business interests would have been damaged if the knowledge had been made public or, as they say, 'outed'. After all, he wasn't just any old Tom, Dick or Harry, he was a peer of the realm. To this day, the facts of his homosexuality are known only to a select few. Now you're a member of that elite club, Inspector."

"I presume what you're saying is, during the period of the issue of this invoice you were apart and that you have no knowledge of this suit."

"Ah, you presume too much, Inspector. The answer is yes,

and no. You are correct that at the time of this purchase we were separated. As for knowledge of the suit there are some things I can tell you. For a start, he wouldn't have been seen dead wearing Bermuda shorts. He would never, ever have purchased a suit for himself from Hyam's without a tie. So, at a guess, I would imagine my husband purchased this outfit for one of his rent boys."

For a moment, Lancaster was shocked. Why would a peer of the realm, a very rich peer at that, have need of rent boys?

"I have to ask, did you ever see or meet any of your husbands... male friends?"

"How quaint, male friends. Well, I met several of his friends, but I have no idea and do not wish to know if any of them were my husband's lovers. So no, Inspector. If what you're asking is, did I know any of his 'bed buddies', then it's a definite no."

"If I can ask one more question, Pamela? Did Sir Philip ever have any North African friends that you were aware of?"

"Not that I'm aware of Inspector, but then I spent twenty-odd years being married to a homosexual and I never noticed that either."

"Well, thank you so much for your time, Lady Pamela. I'm very grateful for your candour. Should you by any chance come up with a theory as to how an item of your husband's clothing came to be separated from its suit, ending up down here in Devon, please do contact me." With that, he handed over one of his cards and shook her offered hand. "And thanks again for giving me so much of your time, and for the delicious coffee."

"It was a pleasure. And if I think of anything I will of course be in touch."

Lancaster returned to the car to find a sleeping sergeant behind the wheel. *Who could blame her*, he thought. "Right, let's go, Marie, the first layby you spot, pull in and let's regroup."

Vidêt had just reversed out of the parking bay when Lancaster spotted Lady Stottard coming out of the gatehouse door, waving at them. He motioned to Vidêt to pull back in to the parking space.

"Did you want us?" he asked.

"It's occurred to me, when I said I laid claim to the manor house, that wasn't, in fact, the end of the story. Philip did, in fact, turn up here just after I'd moved to our house in France. He telephoned me from Boldene, livid with me for taking the boys away from London. He threatened to write them and I out of his will if I didn't give up the manor house and let him have access to the boys. Initially, of course, I refused. I threatened to fight him in the courts and bring up his lack of fidelity, bring to light his indiscretions had all been with men. He, of course, brought it to my attention that this would destroy his reputation within the banking fraternity, which would, in turn, threaten our financial existence in its entirety. We agreed to disagree, but both agreed that fighting was futile and could, in fact, be bloody expensive. Eventually, during the course of all this Philip and I agreed, well, I was forced to agree, that for financial security it would be best if I had the manor, but used it as my own source of income. By moving myself into the gatehouse and having the main house converted into flats and apartments to bring in my money. Again, to be honest, I'd always hated the draughty old place. It was a bloody nightmare to keep warm, so we agreed that Philip would fund the refurbishments. The boys would have an inheritance from his business and a job with the firm when they left school. I would shut up and stay down here in Devon. That was fine by me, but whilst the boys and I were in France I know Philip was down here on a regular basis, meeting with planners and architects. So there is, of course, a distinct possibility that he may have been accompanied on some of those visits, if you get my drift. Though, of course, I have no idea either way. I just thought you should have that information for your file."

"Well, thank you for that, it may give a time period for the item to have been lost or detached, but if nothing else it does all help put flesh on the bones of the picture I'm trying to fill in."

"Look, I have to ask, even I see the papers and I know for a fact that you're not working two cases at once. Given that you specifically mention a North African connection I have to ask the obvious question: Does this item of clothing have any relevance to the artist's impression of a quite obviously African face that you posted in the local paper?"

"Lady Stottard, as a magistrate you must understand the meaning of confidentiality. My problem is, which again I'm sure as a magistrate you'll understand, is that directly or indirectly, your family may be involved in the case I'm working on. With that in mind, it's not possible for me to discuss any aspect with you at the moment. I'm sorry, you've been very helpful, but I just cannot offer any more."

Lady Stottard looked at Lancaster for a moment then smiled.

"I admire your stance, DI Lancaster, in the face of an acting magistrate and lady of the realm," she said quietly, but still with a smile. "I'm greatly impressed. I look forward to seeing where this enquiry takes you, hopefully we'll meet again." She slipped a card into his hand. "Please, this is my personal mobile, call me if you have further questions."

"I'm sure we will." He slipped the card into his pocket. "And thanks again for your candid assistance."

As Lancaster went to get back in the car a thought struck him, and he reached into his case and pulled out the close-up photo of the facial markings from the victims face.

"Pamela, may I just show you a picture of some symbols and ask if you might recognise them?"

Lady Stottard looked at the photo, turned it around and looked at it again.

"DI Lancaster, I am not a stupid individual, but then I'm sure you already know that. I have to say that I do not recognise the symbols or signs on this photograph, but I do recognise the markings as those that were on the face of the man in your artist's impression. So, quite obviously, your enquiry with me has to relate to this."

"Well, you may draw whatever conclusion you wish, Pamela, but would I be wrong to think that these looked anything like a masonic symbol?"

"Ah, I see where you're going with this now, but for your information, even though my husband was a member, I certainly was not. Yes, I know there's a resemblance to some symbols, the moon, for example, but I have no idea what the rest of it means at all."

"Well, thank you anyway. I'm sure we'll meet again."

Lancaster got back into the car.

The two detectives drove towards Totnes. Within a mile, they pulled into a layby and turned off the ignition. Lancaster had the first word.

"Marie, I hope you've not got a problem with me asking you to leave us back there?"

"Not at all, sir," Her tone said otherwise. She'd felt belittled by her boss agreeing to reduce her to the subordinate role of being just a driver. She had to confess, she'd also felt just a little hurt by his actions.

Lancaster noted the tone, but chose not to pick up on it, hoping his explanation would suffice.

"I was fully aware that the moment we showed Lady Stottard that invoice we'd triggered something. It was important she had the chance to tell us whatever she knew. The moment she asked you to leave I knew it was going to be personal. I trust her enough as a magistrate to know that what she had to say wasn't going be detrimental to our case or cause us any legal problems down the line. Not only that, the fact we both complied with her request has helped to gain trust and get her on our side. I'm sorry if you felt aggrieved about this, but it was my decision and I'll abide by it. If you'd like to get your notebook out, I'll tell you exactly what she told me."

Vidêt felt a little silly. What he was saying was obvious, her boss had yet again used his instinct to great effect. He'd won significant kudos with an important person and there could be more to come. She got out her notebook and started writing. Lancaster gave her all the detail of the conversation, including the piece about Sir Philip being back in the vicinity around the same time as the murder.

"May I ask, sir, do you think the husband could be in the frame for this?"

"You should know me by now. At this moment in time, Marie, I rule nothing out. But to be honest, if you are a knight of the realm, you could get someone to do it for you. If it turns out to be a rent boy, why bring him down here to kill him? Bodies like our man turn up every week in London and nobody ever misses them. It's sad, but true. If Sir Philip had wanted some ex-lover murdered, why not do it in the city where nobody really cares? Why bother to bring him down here, where the body of a black person would stand out a mile? If he didn't want it done in London, why not in Scotland where they own thousands of acres of moorland, nobody ever goes digging up there in case they disturb the grouse. No, I won't rule him out yet, but he's not high on my list. Anyway, he's dead. So we know where to find him if we do put him in the frame."

"So do we still go after Garry Claypole?"

"I think when we get back to the office, the first thing you can do is contact your very helpful lady at the city college. Find out what Garry was actually studying whilst there. And if there was any day release with his course."

"What is day release?"

"Well, depending on what the students are studying, some go out on day release, working for an employer in the field. For example, an engineering student might get day release down in the dockyard, or a student studying to be a vet would get day release with, well, a vet."

"I know this will sound stupid, but what you are hoping to find out about Garry from this?"

"Well somehow we have to find a link between Garry and our victim. I can't imagine our victim wandered onto the farm and Garry just killed him. By all accounts, he hardly left the farm until the day he walked out, apart from attending college. So, if we decide Garry's our man, we have to find a way for the two of them to have met. Now, if he was studying bricklaying or carpentry, he may have got day release with a construction company. They may have worked at the manor. If he was studying agriculture, which is hard to believe bearing in mind he appeared to hate the farm, but, if he was, he may have worked for the manor estate on day release. It's just another avenue, Marie, another leaf. It may lead nowhere, but we need to turn it, and check it out, agreed?"

"Agreed." She liked this man. She liked the way he worked. He was methodical.

They were just about to leave the layby when Lancaster's mobile rang. It was Rover.

"Rover, what's new?"

"Just more flesh for the bones of our victim. It's taken a while for the results to come back. Full analysis of debris from our victim's throat shows it also contained pollen, sycamore pollen, to be exact. It must have been lying on the surface of the moss when he inhaled. Some got encased among the sphagnum and was preserved, almost as well as the day it was deposited, about this time of year, twenty-one years ago as we originally thought. But without a doubt, depending on how good a season it was back then, maybe April or May, when the sycamore was in flower, that's when the deed was done. There's a clump of sycamore trees below the boggy field. There was a rookery setting up nests last time we were there. I'd imagine their predecessors sat in those same trees and watched our man choking to death, then saw our murderer walk away. It's a shame they're not parrots, maybe they could have told us who did it."

"Sadly, Rover, life's never that easy, that's why they need people like us."

"Well you have a nice day, Inspector, missing you already," Rover said in a fake American accent.

You see, thought Lancaster staring out of the window, watching the countryside passing by, *all these little pieces matter. They colour the picture. The complete landscape.* He now had several theories going round in his head. He was going to have to put them in some kind of order before deciding which one to follow next.

Firstly, Garry Claypole. Right place at the right time. An angry young man who knew the land and timing needed to execute his plan. If indeed it was a plan. All they had to do was try and find a connection with him, the victim and the belt.

Secondly, Sir Philip Stottard. They needed to find out when he was at the manor with the planners. If it was April or May, that would put him in the right county at the right time. He would've had access to the belt, but could they find a link with the victim and the location? It could have been a lover that had worn out his welcome and wouldn't go quietly.

And thirdly, yes indeed, thirdly, Lady Pamela. If she was living at the manor at the time, could she have taken revenge on her husband by eliminating a lover? This one couldn't be discounted, but at the moment felt least likely. She'd have to lure the victim away from her husband. He would surely have noticed him go missing? What would be her connection to the location? It felt least likely, but was not ruled out just yet.

Lancaster pulled his mobile out and hunted in his pocket for the card Lady Stottard had handed him. He keyed in the number.

"Well that's a coincidence, Inspector, I was just putting your number into my phone and it rang. I wasn't expecting a call this soon," the woman said.

"I have another question for you, if you don't mind."

"Go on then, ask away."

"I know it's a long time ago, but you said your husband returned to the manor shortly after you took the boys off to France. Is there any chance you can remember what time of year it was when you left for France?"

"It's a question I can answer quite easily. It was either the end of January or early February. I know this because the boys had only just returned to school following the Christmas break. I had an altercation with the boy's headmaster following my request to remove them both. I reminded him we paid him for his service. I then had to pick them up and bring them home before we left for France. I also remember, only too clearly, when we got down there, France I mean, the villa was absolutely freezing. We had to get the agent to get the boiler fired up and the heating on. We were walking around with coats on for the first couple of days. Now I come to think of it, we must have been there more like eight months, rather than six, because by the time we returned a lot of the conversion work on the manor was well under way. We had the start of autumn foliage in the park."

"Thank you, Pamela, that's very helpful. I'll be in touch if I need anything further from you."

Lancaster went back to watching the scenery go by. Just before they reached the main junction for Totnes, Lancaster had a thought.

"Take a left at the roundabout, Marie, I think we should drive by Garry's home. It won't take us long. I think it'd be good to see the lie of the land before we interview him."

He fished out the address and keyed it into the satnav. The address was the north-east end of Torbay. Where the poor rubbed against the well-off. Lancaster had thought Torbay was a well-heeled, affluent, seaside town until he'd worked a case here some years ago with local CID. Down on the sea front there were the usual shops and tourist paraphernalia and, in the harbour, a yacht marina with some good-looking boats moored up during the summer. The town boasted a casino, discos, clubs, large hotels and twice as many small ones, but there was an underlying current of poverty. When you dug beneath the surface you discovered an underbelly of low paid and unemployed. The tourist industry in the West Country had always been, by the nature of the weather, a seasonal affair. This meant short term contracts for many, low salaries for most. With a wealth of caravan parks, holiday villages, chalet lets, B&B and hotels all chasing the same pot of tourists, all struggling to keep going twelve months of the year, there were many unemployed living in the back streets. Many housed in cheap hotels, paid for by the benefits system. This 'cheek-by-jowl' existence often led to substance misuse and degradation of one sort or another. There was no short supply of this in Torbay.

With this in mind, Lancaster was pleasantly surprised when they turned into the road called out by the satnav and drove down a tree-lined street. Curving gently towards the east, a mix of semis and detached houses strung out down either side. Most of which had neat, tidy gardens and a selection of decent cars parked on the road or in private drives. Number 22, Babbacombe Crescent, Garry's address, was a detached, four-bedroom house with a tidy front garden. Down one side, a clean tarmac drive, accessed through a well-defined gateway with substantial gate pillars. There was no sign of life as far as they could see. No car in the drive, no open windows or doors. For a moment, Lancaster had a horrible thought. Maybe there was another reason Garry told his mother he couldn't see her till next week. He'd gone. Only time would tell. There was no point panicking yet. The two detectives continued to the far end of the road where a mini-roundabout allowed them to re-join the main road towards Babbacombe.

"When you get to the roundabout, swing right round, we can go back down for another look."

When they were getting ready for their turn at the roundabout, a green, long-wheelbase pickup truck swung in from the main road and turned down the crescent. Lancaster spotted something to do with tree surgery written along the side as it passed down their right-hand side. Lancaster had a feeling as the truck disappeared in the rearview mirror.

"When you've gone round and back into the road, pull in, park up and hang on."

Vidêt did as she was told, pulling into a parking space just inside the crescent. Lancaster jumped out, crossed the road, walked casually down the street then stopped at a 'For Sale' sign at a house just down the road. He made a show of using his camera phone to shoot a couple of photos, then he turned and appeared to be looking at his pictures whilst holding the camera pointing down the street towards number 22. Vidêt saw him pop the camera back in his pocket before looking again at the house for sale. Using his biro, he appeared to be making notes on a scrap of paper. He turned on his heels and walked back up the street until he was well past where Vidêt was parked. She watched in the rearview mirror as Lancaster re-crossed the road and walked back down the pavement, then jumped back into the car.

"Well the good news is, Garry hasn't left the building."

"Are you sure?"

Lancaster just looked at her and smiled. "Oh. Marie, ye of little faith," was his only comment. "Right, let's head for home." Vidêt pulled away down the crescent. As they drove past number 22 she had a casual look sideways, but saw no sign of any vehicle either in the street or on the drive. She didn't want to ask how he knew, but after a moment she could resist no longer.

"Did you actually see him going into the house then, sir?" she asked, knowing the moment she did the answer would come back in the affirmative.

"I saw a person get out of the pickup truck. I am presuming

he works for K.T. Turner, the tree surgeons, as that was the name on the truck that dropped him off. It was just a hunch when that truck went past and it was worth a punt, purely chance really that it went past when it did. They dropped a guy off at number 22. He went in carrying a chainsaw and a load of gear. I presume he works for them and wasn't just getting a lift, the fact that his name wasn't on the truck makes me believe he's an employee, not the owner. They must have finished a job early as it's only lunchtime, but then they could have started at seven o'clock and finished early for the weekend, it being Friday. The guy that went into the house went in too casually to be a stranger. He went straight to the garage, opened it, stashed his gear before going to the front door and walking straight in. So I don't think he was going there to do a chainsaw job. He looked to be late thirties early forties. Slightly balding, but a chunky guy, I'd say that puts him in the right age range. He told the guy in the truck he'd see him down the pub later so I'd imagine he was local, which corresponds to what we know of Garry having lived in the same house for years. I took a couple of pictures of him before he disappeared, so will cross reference them with the last pictures we have of Garry back in the office. To be honest, Vidêt, I can honestly say I'm pretty sure that Garry Claypole is in the house."

"So... that's quite sure then."

Lancaster laughed. "Marie, just drive us home."

Once back in the office, Lancaster got Vidêt to type up the notes following the interview with Lady Stottard. Again, Lancaster wasn't keen to put this new information on the board. He felt it best to keep Stottard's name out of anybody's gaze for the time being. He was aware the masonic lodge was entrenched within the police force, almost certainly present here in the office. He didn't want messages being bandied about with regards the Stottard family until he knew one way or another if they were involved, other than being the supplier of the belt used to truss the victim.

Lancaster decided it was time to bite the bullet, make contact with Garry Claypole, while he knew he was at home. He got out the file, located the number, dialled and waited.

"Hello?" came the simple reply.

"Good afternoon, am I speaking to Mr Garry Claypole?" Lancaster said, hoping the other man didn't just ring off.

"Yes, mate, what can I do for you?"

"My name's Detective Inspector Lancaster of Plymouth CID, I know your mother, Florence,"

"Aaah, yep, Mum told me about you. You're the bloke who got her away from the farm. Thanks for that. My dad was a bastard, she'd never have got away unless somebody helped her. Sounds like you guys turned up just at the right time. Kate Barrow tells me she was about to take a shotgun to him! Would've been the right thing to do, but then she'd have been banged up for that, so fair play to you, mate, nick of time, thank you."

"I understand you and Mum are meeting up next week?"

"Yes, not till midweek, though. I work for a tree surgeon, we've got a contract to finish by Tuesday. I can't let the guys down and drop out, so we plan to meet up next Wednesday when I can take the day off."

"Well, as you're so busy, I wonder, could you spare me a

little of your time? Hopefully first thing in the morning if possible. We could come to you by nine o'clock? Won't take long, but there are a few things I just want to get clear before I sign all this business at the farm off. Just some loose ends to the paper work really, would that be OK?"

"Yes of course, mate, not a problem. I'll have the coffee on for 9.00."

"I'm very grateful, Mr Claypole, nine o'clock it is. Look forward to seeing you."

Lancaster sat back, looking out of the window at the mall opposite. It sat square on to his window. To his mind, maybe not to others, but to his mind, it had always looked a bloody mess. The building looked as if it had been designed by school children from six different schools, as if they all won and got a bit built. He found looking at it a huge distraction. Distracted or not, he couldn't help thinking, staring at the monstrosity, that either Garry Claypole was a very, very, cool customer or he'd absolutely no idea that a body had been dredged up at the farm. Lancaster had been waiting to hear a gap in the conversation. Some tell-tale sign that Garry had been taken aback, caught by surprise. But he sounded almost pleased to have heard from him. He was going to pop the kettle on. Lancaster had to confess; it didn't sound like the voice of a murderer. Bugger.

It was while he sat staring out of the window, contemplating how he was going to handle the next day's interview that his desk phone went. He answered it just as Vidêt entered the room.

"It would appear we've had a bite regarding our photo.

She's coming through on line two in just a second and I'll put it on speaker phone."

The phone rang twice before Lancaster pressed the answer button. "Good afternoon, Detective Inspector Lancaster of Plymouth CID here. How can I help you?"

"Good afternoon, Detective Inspector, my name is Helena Mehemet. I am the mother of Abdul Mehemet." The lady spoke with a deep, rich, French accent. "I think you have been placing pictures of my son in your papers."

It was Lancaster's turn to be taken aback. This was of course just what he'd hoped would happen when he'd placed the artists impression in the paper. Having it actually happen was still a shock; it was seldom a plan actually succeeded.

"Good afternoon, Mrs Mehemet." He got no further before he was interrupted.

"It is Madame Mehemet, Detective Inspector. I am a French citizen and I am phoning you from the South of France."

"Madame Mehemet, may I ask, exactly what you know at this moment in time about our investigation?"

"I know very little, Inspector. I have a friend visiting London at the moment, she has seen a photograph in the newspaper called '*Sun*'. She contacted me, sent me a photo by her phone. It looks very much like my boy, Abdul, but he never had tattoos on his face. Why would he do that? He was such a pretty boy. Why do they do these things, Inspector, eh? I can never understand. I have looked up the article on the internet, they say you have found a body, but you would like to know if anybody knows this man. Well, I know this man; he is Abdul. My son. What I cannot find out from the newspaper is, is he the body you have found or is he just involved in some other way?"

Lancaster thought for only a second before replying. "I am very sorry to tell you, madame, but the photo is the face of the body we have found."

"But I do not understand, Inspector! The photo makes Abdul look so young, he has not changed much since I last saw him when he went away to work in England over twenty years ago. I have his photograph here on my dresser. How can this be, Inspector? I do not understand?"

Lancaster thought again for a moment. *There is no other way to do this, she has to be told.*

"Madame Mehemet, there is no easy way to say this to save you more pain. Sadly, we've found what may be your son's body. It's been hidden for over twenty years and has only just been discovered. We had an artist draw a representation of the face of the body as it was when he was hidden twenty-one years ago. That's the face you've seen."

There was a silence on the other end of the line, Lancaster let it sit there for a moment before talking again.

"I am so sorry, Madame, are you still there?"

"Yes, Inspector, I am still here. It is a shock to me, though in my heart I have known for years that he was dead. I just felt it somehow. He went to work in England and never came home. I knew he would take a while to settle into a new job, a new country. I kept waiting for him to call, but nothing. The worst thing about the waiting was that when he left he never told us where he was going to work, it was going to be a surprise. Once he got there he would take photos and send them to us. When

158

I started to worry I had nowhere to go to ask if he was all right."

"Madame, may I pass you over to my sergeant who speaks fluent French? Would you please give us your address and we will contact your local police force and ask them to come and visit and get a DNA sample from you. It's just a simple swipe inside your mouth, then we can get that sent straight to us. We can compare the DNA with that of our body and see if they match, does that make sense, Madame?"

"Oui, Inspector, but I can travel to England for the test if you wish."

"Madame, you may come to England for nothing, it may not be your boy. Let's find out first, before you journey here."

"You are very kind, Inspector, but I am already sure. But I will do as you ask."

"I'm putting my sergeant on the line, madame, and we will speak again soon." He put his hand over the phone. "We need her address, contact details and ask if she can scan in a copy of the photo she has." He took his hand away and stepped aside to let Vidêt have more space. Lancaster stood and stared out of the window again, thinking, *How does this affect the case?* Not at all until it could be proven that this body was Abdul, but then he had a name. But this was further on than they'd been yesterday. Lancaster listened to Vidêt talking on the phone. It seemed odd to hear her chatting in her native language, though he'd always known she was French. It sounded strange, she was after all, fluent, and had dropped back into its use immediately. He'd no idea what she was talking about; it was a jumble of sounds. Vidêt was making notes as she spoke and Lancaster could see that, whether she realised it or not, she was jotting down notes in French. After a while, he heard a phrase he recognised.

"Au revoir, Madame." She put down the receiver.

"Well that confirms many things we already knew," she said, turning to Lancaster, speaking with a much stronger accent than he'd heard from her in a long while. "Madame Mehemet is what is unkindly known in France as a 'pied noir', a 'black foot'. Madame Mehemet is Algerian by birth, but married a French citizen, a soldier. He was originally Algerian. When she was very young, she gave birth to Abdul; she was seventeen, but had married her husband a short time before. He was in the French army and was among the last native French-Algerian troops to hang on there after French rule was finished. Like many others, they became persecuted in their own land, but he left the army when his time was up. Later, they all moved back to France where they returned to the home of her husband's family who had already moved to the South of France many years previously. Madame still lives there but she is now alone, her husband died nearly ten years ago."

"You've an address for her, I presume?"

"But of course, she lives in the small city of Narbonne, near the Mediterranean. I have the address, do you want me to contact the police in Narbonne? Explain the situation and get somebody round there to take a DNA sample?"

"If you would, Marie, I'd be grateful. If they can express post the samples by courier and get them directly to us here, we can check the paperwork and give them straight to Rover for analysis."

"I presume we already know if we can get DNA from the

body as it stands?"

"Rover said we can get it from teeth. I suspect he already has it on file, just waiting for us to ask."

Vidêt went off to make phone calls, pleased to make use of her French language, looking forward to being able to contact the French police in Narbonne with some weight and authority behind her. She felt she'd just regained some importance following the events of the morning with Lady Stottard.

Lancaster was going through his notes and came across what he was looking for. He knew there was a connection ticking in the back of his head. He pulled out his phone, hunted through his pocket for the card he'd been given, keyed in the number and hit call. The number rang three times before it was picked up.

"Detective Inspector Lancaster," the voice on the other end said. "What can I do for you this time?"

"Good afternoon, Lady Stottard."

"I won't tell you again, Inspector, it's Pamela."

"Sorry, Pamela, I just had a quick question. You mentioned you had a property in the South of France, may I ask where? It may seem silly but I like to colour in the picture, flesh out the bones of the story for my own peace of mind."

"Inspector, you and I both know that's rubbish, you need to know for some other reason. I don't need to know what that reason is, Inspector, but let's not beat about the bush and fanny about with this colouring in nonsense. Our chateaux is outside the village of Salles-d'Aude, just inland from the Med. We still have it, you must come down and see it, maybe a little break for the summer, Inspector?"

"I don't actually know much about the South of France, Pamela," Lancaster said with a certain honesty. "Where's the nearest city to Salles-d'Aude?"

"That would be Narbonne, Inspector, and good news, there is an airport at nearby Carcassonne."

"Well that's good to know, Pamela, I'll get back to you about the holiday though."

"Oh, Inspector, you're a very nice man, but you're a terrible liar, bye." She rang off.

Lancaster didn't believe in coincidence. Narbonne and Salles-d'Aude were the key to this boy being here in Devon and the links just kept forming. The link he had to make though was with Garry Claypole. How on earth did a farmer's son from the depths of Dartmoor, get to meet a young North African guy? There was going to be a twist in this somewhere.

Lancaster googled Salles-d'Aude. Once on the screen, he google-earthed and strolled around its streets. It looked a peaceful little hamlet. The houses, roofed in the classic red, half-rounded tiles of the Mediterranean regions. There were rural properties on the fringe, occasional tractors parked in the drive. On the whole, it appeared that most of the properties around the outer fringes of the town were gated. A peer over the garden walls via satellite photos showed swimming pools tucked away within walled enclosures. Looking at them, the pools bright blue, the roofs lit by Mediterranean sunshine, then comparing them with the shopping mall across the street, he felt the urge for a continental holiday. He just might take Pamela up on her offer once this case was closed. First, though, he had to close it, tomorrow could be a key moment in doing just that.

CHAPTER SEVEN

The following morning, Lancaster and Vidêt were on the road early. Well, early for a Saturday. Vidêt was driving; she liked that. Lancaster sat reading his notes. He liked to refresh his head with a case. He wanted to keep a flow going from day to day if possible. Otherwise, gaps materialised and needed filling later. Lancaster knew that, amongst his colleagues, he was regarded with some ridicule, but he didn't mind really. He enjoyed the fact that, because of the way he worked, other officers got themselves assigned to other teams. To be honest, that suited him fine. DCI Craven still had faith in him, that was all that mattered. That's why he got the weird cases, the ones with a twist. He couldn't understand why other officers in the squad shied away from jobs like this. They liked open and shut cases, simple. Start, investigate, arrest, close, move on. Other DIs at the station did a good job, but they sent people out to do their ground work. Used up manpower, it was boring, but they did get the job done. Lancaster didn't mind those jobs, but cases like this, Dartmoor Man, well they gave him a buzz, stimulated the juices, kept him thinking. He lived for cases like these, something that needed to be picked through. Slowly.

He also enjoyed working with Vidêt. She was an odd

one, like him. Something about her French attitude helped their relationship tick. She was a bit 'standoffish', but didn't interrupt. She kept her eyes and ears open, picked up bits that Lancaster missed. Never had to be told something twice, always acted when asked. Marie also liked things organised, she appreciated Lancaster's use of the whiteboard. She liked order. Liked lists. Understood his way of working, the way he rearranged all the pieces, filled in the gaps until they had the perfect picture of a crime. She had a long way to go before she could be allowed to roam out and about on her own, but she was coming along nicely. He wouldn't have found out so much detail from Madame Mehemet without Marie's use of her native tongue putting her at her ease.

According to Vidêt, Madame Mehemet was a child bride to her army man. Both greatly in love, but their parents were not happy about the marriage. Her husband didn't care. He married her anyway. Madame had never seen her parents or family since that day. Although he was Algerian born, his family were French nationals. When he finished his service in the army, they returned to his family home in France. Things were tough to begin with, but his family softened to her over the years, they had a very long and happy marriage together. Whilst they were living at Narbonne, Abdul left school early, but was always employed. He secured employment working in hotels and restaurants. He'd been employed virtually since the day he left school. Madame had no idea what sort of job her son was heading for in England. It was going to be a surprise for them, she knew he was very excited about the move. Abdul had met someone who'd arranged the job and the money was going to be very good. He was planning to send them photos once he settled. They'd never seen their son again. They'd been to the police in Narbonne, but they could find nothing. Abdul had just disappeared. With no details of his new English friend, his address, or the new job, they had nowhere to search in England. They were desperate, but over time they gave up hope. Madame Mehemet believed the disappearance of their son was a contributing factor in her husband's death. After Abdul disappeared, her husband became depressed, permanently sad. She felt he had died of a broken heart.

The two detectives arrived outside Garry Claypole's house at exactly nine o'clock. The door was opened to them before they knocked and Garry Claypole welcomed them in with a firm handshake and a warm smile. From the start, this wasn't going the way Lancaster thought it would.

"I've got coffee on," Garry said, leading them through to a large, modern kitchen-diner. "My wife Janice will be back soon, she's just dropped the boys down for football training."

"Where do they train, down with United?" Lancaster said, keeping the conversation lowkey.

"I wish," Garry said with a laugh, pouring coffees from a large coffee pot. "No, the boys train with school. They're both in the school team. They've got a match this afternoon so they have them in for a warm up and a pep talk. We drive'm bloody miles, still, that's what parenting is about. Milk and sugar?"

"Milk for both, no sugar, cheers. So, I expect you're looking forward to seeing Mum next week? It's been a long while."

Garry Claypole slid their cups across the worktop, indicating for them to take a seat on the stools at the counter, he one side, the detectives on the other.

"It never occurred to me that Mum wasn't getting my letters," he said quietly. "I always knew the bloke was a complete bastard, I never thought he would've been that cruel. I thought he'd just be glad to see the back of me. What a spiteful bastard. Honest, I never thought he'd do that. After a while, I just thought Mum was disappointed in me for leaving. We used to joke about saving up money, running away together. I just knew my life was always going to be crap if I stayed. Mum was always trying to get between me and him to stop the fights. I just thought it would be easier all round if I stepped out of the picture. When Pete, my mate at college, said he was moving to Torquay it sounded like he was moving to the South of France or something. When he said he had a spare room I just thought, bugger it, I'm off. I managed to get a job straight away. It was only a warehouse job, but it was miles away from the bloody farm, better still, I got paid. Do you know, when I was in my early twenties, Dad still only gave me pocket money, never a wage. I worked a seven-day week apart from college days. My mates all thought it was a bloody joke, well, except for Pete, he was the one who said I should just tell him to stuff it. But then that was easier said than done. Have you seen my dad when he's angry? It was just easier to walk away."

"Has your mum told you how we came to be at the farm the day she tried to shoot your dad?" Lancaster asked, wanting the interview back where he needed it to be.

"Actually, no. She said she didn't know what came over her. She found the shotgun in her hands and Dad in the kitchen. She says you were there and tried to talk her out of it, but some bloke called Brian stepped in, took the gun away. She can't remember much else until she was sitting in your office. You said she wouldn't be charged with anything. She still doesn't really understand why she was let off the hook, but she loves it at the hostel. Kate, the woman who runs the place, says Mum's in her element, loves having the kids around. Mum says she hasn't got a clue what she's going to do now, but Janice and I have already decided she can move in here. We've a spare room, that's another reason we didn't want to see her till next week. We've decorated the room and moved some furniture around so it'll be better for her. Of course, if she doesn't want to then we haven't got a plan B, so we can stick with plan A for now and see where that takes us. The boys can't wait to meet her."

"I'm sure she'll love it here in a proper home, Garry," Lancaster said.

"So, what did actually happen? Did Dad call you or something? Was Brian one of your guys?"

"Actually, Garry, we went there to see your mum and dad about a different matter." Lancaster was trying to keep eye contact with Garry, watching for any sign that he knew what that 'different matter' was.

"Whilst we were talking to your dad in the kitchen, your mum overheard part of the conversation. The conversation was about a body we'd found at the farm. Your mother thought the body was you. That your father had actually murdered you all those years ago and that's why she'd heard nothing from you. It was then she got your dad's gun. Whilst I was trying to talk your mother into putting the gun away another gentleman who'd been outside the door, Brian Cave, a park ranger, heard what was going on, stepped in and took it out of her hands. Unfortunately, whilst he was doing this, the gun went off. Luckily, it was pointing up into the ceiling, it buggered the ceiling, but nobody was harmed."

"Bloody hell! What a shocker. It's like a bloody soap script, you couldn't make this stuff up could you. Wow! Wait till I tell Janice. So how come you chose not to charge my mum with anything?"

Lancaster had been watching Garry the whole time he'd been telling the story of the kitchen drama. There'd been just a look of incredulity, but nothing else to show he even cared what the 'different matter' was. He hadn't even asked the obvious question, 'What body?' He was more interested in the story from his mum's perspective.

"It's complicated, Garry. From my point of view your mother hadn't hurt anyone. I felt she'd probably suffered enough over the years. The gun wouldn't have gone off if Brian hadn't grabbed it, so we'll never know if she intended to kill your father or just frighten him. In the end, I decided there'd be no charges."

"Well I want to thank you for that," Garry said, holding out his hand across the counter.

Lancaster shook it. He'd still seen no sign of any flinch in Garry's expression.

"More coffee? Thanks for coming to tell me all this. As I say, Mum doesn't appear to remember much at all. She just said she tried to kill my father and you stopped her."

"There was another matter I wanted to run by you, Garry." He'd decided there was no more time left for beating around

168

the bush. Time to drop the 'body bomb' into the room. Pulling the artist's impression from the folder on the counter, he slid it across the surface towards Garry, "Do you, by any chance, recognise this face?"

"Bloody hell! Frightening. No, why? Should I know him? Where's he from?"

"Well his body was found in one of your dad's fields Garry," Lancaster replied, all the time watching Garry's reaction. "I just wondered if you might have come across him at some stage?"

"Well I haven't been there for over twenty years, so it's not likely I would've seen him, is it? Was he a walker or with the Ten Tors crowd? Not being funny, but he doesn't look like your average moor walker does he? So if you found his body, how did he die? Natural causes or something? Did my dad find him? Is that why you were out there?"

Lancaster, watching Garry the whole time, had seen no trace of recognition whatsoever. Not a flicker crossed his face. Either this man was very good at the poker face or he was genuine.

"Sadly, Garry, the man had been murdered."

"Bloody hell! So where was he found then? Oh bloody hell, do you think my dad did it? Is that why you went to see him? Bloody hell!"

"Well yes and no, Garry. When we first found the body, your mother thought it may be yours. That's why we were there, to ask your father what he knew about your disappearance. He showed us the stack of hidden letters to prove the body couldn't be you."

"But hang on a minute," Garry said looking at the picture

in front of him. "How the hell could you have ever thought this was me? This bloke's nearly black, though funnily enough, he does have hair a bit like me, but that's all."

"Well, that's where the problem lay. The body we found was buried in Whiddons Bog. To start with, everyone thought the dark skin was caused by the peat in the water. The body was buried there over twenty years ago. In fact it was the hair that made people think it could've been you."

"Bloody hell... Poor Mum. So, he could've been buried there when I was still at the farm. How was he murdered? Shotgun, was it?"

"No, in fact he was asphyxiated." Lancaster felt there was little point holding back the facts, well most of them, anyway. "His head was pushed into the moss, he filled his airways with it till he choked. Then his body was pushed under and it sank. It stayed there until it was dredged up by accident."

"Bugger! Well I can tell you I would've remembered him if I'd seen him. I mean, you wouldn't forget that face in a hurry, would you? We used to have a lot of walkers mind, mainly letter-boxers because there was a box some scouts had put down in the bottom field. They'd stashed it in the back wall, to be honest, it was dodgy, really. You had to either work your way round the bog or use the grass clumps as stepping stones to get to it. Many's the time some walker would come up through the old trackway, shit high up to his waist because he went the wrong way. But your man here, I've never seen this bloke before. Poor bugger, lying there all that time. At least I escaped. Tell you what, though, I do remember seeing some black guys once, they were with a school from Bristol. I know because it was written on the side of the minibus they'd arrived in. Dad gave them a bollocking for parking down by the barns without asking permission, miserable git. They were training for the Ten Tors, I remember thinking they looked a bit exotic out there on the moor with all the kit and all. But honest, I couldn't tell if this bloke was one of them or not."

Just then, Garry's wife arrived. They all said their hellos, introductions made, more coffee offered and declined by the two detectives. Lancaster had decided this interview had probably gone far enough. In fact, about as far as it could go. He just couldn't see Garry being a cold-blooded murderer. The man appeared genuinely amazed at the story Lancaster had told. He'd interviewed enough criminals to realise this man didn't know anything about their victim. Garry was an intelligent guy, but Lancaster was convinced the man couldn't have put on that show of ignorance just for them. As far as he was concerned, this line of enquiry was, annoyingly, at an end. Lancaster wished Garry and Janice all the best with their future life with Florence, and promised they'd return during the summer to see how they were all getting along. Though Lancaster was doubtful he'd be popping back for a social call.

Once back in the car, waving goodbye to the Claypoles who were standing on the doorstep like a couple of old friends, Lancaster told Marie to drive up the road and find the first place to stop. A parking place materialized and she swung straight in. Lancaster started the conversation.

"Right, what are your thoughts?"

"He didn't do it."

"Based on...?"

"Body language, sir. I watched him all the time you were talking to him. Not once did I see him stall for time. He was confident. Surprised. Genuinely thankful to you for saving his mother. I felt, right through the interview, it was the first time he had heard about the body. He was truly surprised, sad when he heard the body had been lying there all that time. He didn't do it. If you prove me wrong, I will eat snails. I hate snails."

"Well, Marie, as much as I'd love to see you eat snails, I have to agree with you. For all the same reasons. I just don't think he could've been that good an actor."

"So, what do you think we do now?"

"Well, I think we head back to base. I've a couple of ideas, but we need to be at base to action them. I reckon we can be done for lunchtime and call it a day."

The two detectives drove back to Plymouth amid a series of brief conversations regarding the weather, scenery, the case, before Vidêt remembered a question that had come to mind during the course of the interview with Garry. She'd not wanted to broach the subject at the time for fear of looking stupid.

"Sir, a question? What is the Ten Tours?"

"Ah, the Ten Tors. Every year groups of school kids, special schools, disabled schools, boy scouts, girl guides, army cadets and cadets from all the other services, all have a two-day orienteering session with an overnight camp on Dartmoor. They're all going against the clock and using map reading skills to find the quickest route across the moor, but they all have to visit ten tors. The tors are the stone outcrops and high points across Dartmoor. There are loads of them. Each year the organisers choose ten different tors to make up that year's course. Which route they choose can make the difference between being first or last. That's the Ten Tors.

"I see. So is there any point in trying to track down the school from Bristol Garry mentioned?"

"Not for the moment, Marie, if our boy was part of any team or school and went missing there'd have been a missing person case back then." Lancaster thought for a moment. "But, I tell you what, there's another coincidence there. The Ten Tors is always carried out during May, not far off our time of year for his murder, considering the sycamore pollen. I tell you what we could do, go online and find a contact for the Ten Tors. The military help organise it, based at Okehampton Camp. They keep meticulous records. Get them to look up what schools were present during the two years either side of our man's interment. There can't have been many schools from Bristol that attended. So, in actual fact, Marie, well done, good shout. There's just a chance that our boy had actually got himself an adult place at some kind of special school. Perhaps he was working there. His age would say he wasn't a student, but whatever, you know the score. As it was your shout, I'll leave it to you."

"Thank you, sir," she said, unsure whether it had been a good suggestion or not. Time would tell.

Back at the office, Vidêt typed up the notes from their session with Garry. It wasn't much and didn't take them any further towards solving the case. Once she'd finished, Lancaster had one more task for her.

"Before we call it a day, Marie, can you use your language

skills and put a call in to Madame Mehemet? See if our friends from Narbonne forensic have been to her yet? Also, while you have her on the phone, see if you can find out about the places her son worked around Narbonne. Ask if she remembers who it was back when he disappeared that she spoke to in the Narbonne police, or any dates she can remember. If we can't find out why this boy was down here in Devon from here, then maybe we need to be following his trail from Narbonne. We need to start from the beginning, so to speak. We've been trying to work backwards from today, from the discovery of his body to the time before this boy died. The problem we have is there's a twenty-one-year gap between now and then. We need to be searching from twenty-one or twenty-two years ago and working our way forward. If the DNA results come back as positive, and I think sadly they will, then we now know more about our boy. We know he was born in Algeria and spent his formative years there, which corroborates Rover's findings from dental analysis. We also know he spent his teenage years in the South of France working in Narbonne. Coincidentally, very close to Stottard's summer retreat. You know I don't like coincidence, especially when it involves a murder. Then there were only a few years, maybe only months, between him leaving his mother's house in France and being murdered on the moor. We know exactly where he's been for the last twenty-one years. It's before that we need to fill in details. My gut feeling is he was brought from France to England for a reason. That reason got him killed. We have to start right back at the beginning, find out what enticed this young man out of his home town. What was he promised? What was this job he wanted to keep a secret? Why did he think it was going to pay well? You get Madame on the phone and I'll get us more coffee."

"Are you thinking he could have got involved with smuggling drugs?"

"Who knows, Marie, it's very possible. It's a story that crops up often enough. It must be the same in France. Boy leaves school, gets low paid work, sees no prospects, then he's offered the chance to make big money. Once they're in there's no escape. He's no other trade; the only way he can keep up the lifestyle is get in deeper. It's sad, but so often happens. Anyway, to start with, let's get hold of Madame Mehemet."

When Lancaster returned with coffees, Vidêt was in full flow, gabbling away in French to, he presumed, Madame Mehemet. The conversation flew back and forth between the two. Lancaster appreciated the skill she was showing. Then realised that, in fact, all she was doing was talking in her native language. Her greatest skill was actually managing to spend every day speaking English.

Something she does very well, Lancaster thought.

Lancaster had almost finished his latte before Vidêt said goodbye. She popped the lid off of her cup and took a drink, turned her nose up and put the cup back down again.

"So, our colleagues from the forensics team at Narbonne have visited Madame, I will phone them to make sure they courier the package straight to us ASAP. She has given me the names of three of the places that her son worked, one hotel and two restaurants. She thinks there was another place where he did casual work in between but she has no idea where that was. She cannot remember the names of anybody at the

Narbonne Office d'Police Judiciaire, but she does still have a crime number for her missing son. That may help us track down somebody who can find the paperwork. It may get difficult though, we must make sure we do not, as you would say, 'ruff up any feathers'. The French police do not take kindly to anybody suggesting they have made a mistake. They like to guard their backs against accusation of malpractice. If that accusation came from another police force from another country, you have poked the hornet nest with a very big stick. The regional French police forces would suddenly unite and become friends."

"DS Vidêt," Lancaster said, with a smile. "When you say 'we' must tread carefully, I think you misunderstand what's going on here. The 'we', is 'you'. I see no point having a French national in my team, then not let them handle the French side of the enquiry. When you contact the forensic team, make sure that the package is heading direct to us, then talk to people in the Narbonne police office. They already know we've a body that may be French and on their missing persons list. Give them the crime number reference as a casual matter of fact, just to let them know that we know his disappearance was recorded. If you can get anybody chatting, just mention the names of the hotel and the restaurants, see if it flags anything up on their local wavelength. No... on second thoughts, hold onto those names for the time being. We may want to make enquiries in other places for information about all three of them. That should keep you going for a minute or two. I know I said we'd be finished by lunch but it looks like I was wrong, are you OK with that?"

"It's OK by me." She was actually enjoying playing a vital role for a change, not just a driver. She punched in the number for the Office d'Police Judiciaire, Narbonne. Two hours later, she put the phone down. Her throat was dry, she was hungry. It was gone two o'clock. She'd missed breakfast and lunch, her stomach rumbled in revolt at its emptiness.

Lancaster hadn't been idle. He knew that to others, his organising and list making appeared anal. For Lancaster, it was the way he worked. Many years previously, before joining the police, he'd been diagnosed with dyspraxia; a developmental motor coordination disorder. He'd known he was different right from school days. Amongst the annoying problems dyspraxia gave to the young Lancaster were brain-to-motor difficulties, making simple tasks like holding a pencil the right way or doing up shoe laces virtually impossible. It didn't matter how many times the teacher hit him across the knuckles with a ruler, it didn't help him hold the pencil. Probably the worse coordination effect for Lancaster had been the inability to catch things. Balls, apples, virtually anything thrown in his direction ended up on the floor. This made him the last to be chosen for any team game at school. It was to be expected really, Lancaster could see the problem clearly. When choosing your team for a cricket match, the last person you'd add would be the guy who couldn't bat and couldn't catch. This put him on the sidelines. He'd always struggled to fit in with the crowd. Always saw things slightly different to others. He'd a tendency to say things straight out without thinking of possible consequence, whereas others would shy away from stating the obvious for fear of offending anyone. As a child, Lancaster's dyspraxia was never recognised, people weren't so quick to hang labels on kids back then. Easier to call them thick, troublesome. Get them to stand in the corner or move them into isolation rather than sort the problem and integrate them back into the class. Lancaster spent much of his education sitting in rooms on his own with a teaching assistant working his way through lessons. During the undiagnosed years, Lancaster had worked out a series of avoidance techniques. Solving the inability to tie a shoelace by spending a while tying them in a loose knot and bow. Tight enough to keep the shoe on, loose enough that you could treat them like a slip-on. Now he chose his own shoes, they were slip-ons. He rarely wore a tie, all shirts were open necked and went over the head, no time for struggling with buttons.

Lancaster knew from text books that dyspraxia was on the autistism spectrum, but over the formative years of life he managed to perfect so many avoidance tricks that few people now noticed. He was just 'odd'. Sometimes with a capital 'O', often with two capital 'D's, but he didn't care. He was now, almost, his own boss and had developed his technique of organising the whole case into lists:

Who?
Why?
When?
How?
Possible.
Checked.

This had stood him in good stead. His boss understood that Lancaster was meticulous in approach. He could infuriate the hell out of fellow officers but, left to his own devices, he always got there in the end. To date, he'd never failed to put a case to bed.

So whilst Vidêt had been engaged in calls to France, Lancaster had reorganised the board yet again, but not before taking a photo of it with his phone, something else he liked to do. For the moment, all the Claypoles were on the board in name only, denoted with 'D/E'. Dead End.

Vidêt arrived as Lancaster put down the marker pen.

"Right, what's the news? It's nice to know the French police work on a Saturday."

"In France, you plan your day off to coincide with your local market day, it's tradition. In Narbonne, it's obviously not a Saturday." Vidêt opened her notes, a habit she'd picked up from her boss. "I have checked with the forensic team. The samples went with 'International Courier Services' first thing this morning. It's a road system not air, so dependent on catching a ferry it should be arriving sometime tomorrow, Sunday, so we may have to miss church."

"A joke, Marie? You're turning British. If they get to a ferry terminal on the coast by tonight they'll be lucky. If they do, they'll not be docking until after breakfast. I can get the desk sergeant to sign for it and give me a call, but I reckon they'll catch a ferry in the morning. That'll mean they get in just after three tomorrow, so either way I think we can have the day off while we wait. I've given Rover a shout, warned him it's on the way. It's just going to be a case of cross-referencing and wait and see. Any luck with the crime number for the missing Abdul with your friends in Narbonne?"

"You may be surprised to hear this, but the answer is yes. I spoke with a sergeant. He tracked down the paper file, it pre-dated their computer system. He actually had some memory of the case; he remembered Madame Mehemet coming in to the station every five minutes asking if there was any news. He said they had nothing to go on. One day the boy was there, next he had gone. The family said he had gone to England for a job, but they had no names, addresses and no contact details. They were asked where he had managed to find out about the job but they had no answer for that either. The officer I spoke with said they did, in fact, visit the places the boy had worked. Back then, in Narbonne, there was a lot of hatred for the police. At the time, there was racial tension in the south; lots of migrants from Algeria and Morocco. People were not inclined to talk much. Those that did said they knew nothing about Abdul being offered another job in England. He had just stopped coming to work. So the police had nowhere else to look. They had two unidentified bodies during that period, but both of them were white males, and in the end it just got filed and forgotten. He did remember one thing out of the ordinary though, the staff at the hotel the boy worked at were not all that forthcoming about Abdul. At first they claimed not to know him, then they admitted he had worked at the hotel, but only part time. The police got nowhere with it. They had no reason to follow it further."

"And we have the name of the hotel?"

"It's the one Madame told us about. Les Hotel des

Anglaise."

"Are you OK doing a little more before we go for lunch?"

"But of course, sir, especially if you are paying for lunch."

"Fair enough. See if you can find anything about that hotel especially from the late 1990s. If you can't find anything online, try your police friends at Narbonne again. See if they know anything, I just have a hunch that their unhelpfulness when the enquiry team went there is no coincidence. Maybe they'd something going on they didn't want the police to find out about."

"Aah. Running drugs from the hotel and Abdul got involved as a runner. Why didn't the police pick up on that?"

"Because they weren't looking, Marie. They were looking for a young guy who'd gone to work in UK. What was so special in that?"

Vidêt went straight to her laptop, punched in Les Hotel des Anglaise, Narbonne, and began sifting through the information that came to light. Two minutes later, Lancaster arrived at her desk.

"Just had a thought, Marie, keep digging around for anything to do with the hotel. I want a complete fact file on my desk within the hour, if you can manage it. Don't contact the local police at all. I think we back off from talking with them now unless we really need to."

Vidêt smiled. "You mean to say, sir, you do not trust the French police?"

"I wouldn't go that far, Marie, not in general terms. But if this is about drugs then my experience is that it tends to spread the money around. The police don't appear immune.

Corruptions rife. If you pay your defenders of the law a pittance you always run the risk of some of them turning a blind eye, or worse. Now I don't know enough about the force in Narbonne, the questions we've asked so far have been about a missing person. But if this becomes anything more sinister there may be other people who want it all kept quiet. I think at this stage, the fewer people who know what we're thinking the better, don't you agree?"

"Indeed I do, sir."

Just inside the hour, as asked for, Vidêt arrived with a slip file of notes and internet cut-and-paste information. A fact file on Les Hotel des Anglaise.

The hotel was built in the early 1900s, just prior to the First World War. The name chosen to mimic a similar hotel in Nice, the English-adopted watering hole along the coast to the east. The hotel had only just got going before the war broke out and it suffered as a consequence. Only the really rich continued to holiday abroad as if nothing was happening on the Western Front. Those that did still holiday stayed around Nice and Monte Carlo and seldom ventured further than their hotel terrace. Between the wars, the hotel had a renaissance and began gathering a fan base of its own with the 'nouveau-rich'. Those who wished to be like the clientele in Nice, but limited wealth would not permit it. It turned its basement into a casino and the place became a closed shop with only members being admitted.

During the Second World War it became the home of the German officers and Gestapo. The basement casino became used for other more macabre retreats, many of which were terminal. It took a long time after the war for the hotel to regain any sort of trade. Its use by the Germans during the occupation left it marked, physically and mentally in the minds of the local population. It wasn't until the 1960s that it started trading again with any confidence, gaining support from English returners and those new to holidaying abroad. Those that wanted foreign adventure, but with the comforts of an understanding hotel concierge who spoke English and didn't shrug his shoulders at them. Since then it had changed hands several times. During the 1980s it had been purchased and owned by a consortium, 'Leisure World European'. They held hotels in their portfolio throughout Europe.

"Well done, Marie. One other thing, see if Companies House has any detail on the consortium, 'Leisure World European'. It would be useful to know who the directors or owners are."

Vidêt returned wearing a smug look, or a smile. It was often difficult to tell the difference. She put a sheet of paper down on the desk, slid it to Lancaster who picked it up and studied the names. There were several he recognised. The first was Sir Peter Styles, his name had cropped up before in Lancaster's research. Styles had read the eulogy at Sir Philip's funeral. The two names on the board of directors that raised an eyebrow were Philip and Peter Stottard.

"Right, Marie, time to eat. I need to think. What's it to be, somewhere for late lunch or somewhere for early dinner?"

Twenty-five minutes later they were sitting in the little French restaurant on the Barbican quayside looking at menus. They both went for the 'Salade Nicoise' as a starter.

Then Lancaster went for the 'steak frites' whilst Vidêt chose the 'Parmentier maison'. They were both hungry. Lancaster couldn't think on an empty stomach. Whilst they waited for the starters to arrive, they sipped at glasses of chilled Chardonnay. They were, after all, off duty.

"Right, Marie, your thoughts?"

"Well the wine is good, though just a little dry for my pallet." She smiled.

"Two jokes in one day, Marie, you'll be supporting Plymouth Argyle next."

"I don't think even I could manage to raise that much humour, sir. My thoughts are that you were right. The idea of starting at the beginning and finding our way back to today was simple, but accurate. We have already learned more about our victim by going to his home town than we ever had before. I also think there is some kind of link with young Abdul working at the hotel just before he disappeared. That and the fact that even the local police thought the staff at the hotel acted a bit off. But I have another thought if you wish to hear it, sir?"

"Go on."

"Well, I don't think we will get anything more from the Narbonne police, not unless you want to be more direct with our approach. But I also agree, I do not think they can be trusted. If we think there may be a drugs connection, then they will possibly be on the take. I think the only way we are going to track Abdul's movements... is for us to go there and ask around ourselves. What do you think?"

Lancaster sat sipping his wine, watching a fishing boat

come through the lock gate into Barbican harbour. The salads arrived. He waited for the waitress to leave before responding.

"I have to say, Marie, we're both on the same wavelength. My problem is working out how to persuade the boss that we're not just off on a jolly." He saw the look of non-comprehension on her face. "It means wasting your time... doing something just for the fun of it. What I have to do is make a case with the boss as to why it's good use of police funds and time. We can't do that until we have positive ID for the victim. We have to wait for the sample to arrive in the morning. If it tallies with Rover's DNA sample, then we've a genuine reason to pursue this case on foreign soil. Until then, we eat and wait."

"In the meantime, sir, would you like me to find out about flight times and accommodation in Narbonne?"

"I think that'd be a good shout, Marie. Could you do that over the weekend?"

Vidêt smiled, nodded and fed another forkful of salad into her mouth.

†

Sunday morning, slightly later than he would have normally been out and about, Lancaster was returning from a mid-morning run up and around the Hoe and back when the duty desk officer called. There was a delivery for him.

So, he thought, *they must've made the overnight ferry.* He put in a call to Rover who'd been briefed the day before. He'd make his way to the lab and meet Lancaster there to finish off the sample test. Time would now tell. An hour later, Rover opened the door at the lab for Lancaster and set about the analysis.

"What's the timescale, Rover?"

"Well I'm using a fast track method invented in the states. I'm expecting results before the end of the day, probably within the next four hours. If you want to head off, I'll give you a call as soon as I have something."

Lancaster returned to his flat, opened the bi-folds onto his balcony and went out into the sunshine with a cup of tea and his French phrase book, settling down into the recliner to while away a few hours in the sun. He was halfway through his cup of tea when his phone went. One glance told him it was Vidêt.

"Marie, what a glorious day. You should be doing something relaxing," Lancaster said, putting down his now empty cup. "What can I do for you?"

"I thought you should know, if we get the go-ahead, we can get a flight from Bristol on Wednesday. Gets us to Beziers, east of Narbonne, in under two hours. Failing that, the next flight is not until Friday. I have made enquiries at a hotel near the city centre. They have vacancies all week for two single rooms. I have checked out car hire from Hertz at Beziers, they will not have a problem getting us a car on either day. I figured one day to get down there, settle in, go into the centre and sniff around. The problem is there are no direct return flights until the Friday. That gives us all day Thursday to finish whatever sniffing we have to do. Oh, as a bonus, I have found out where the Stottard family retreat is, we have to travel almost past it on the road from the airport to Narbonne."

"Well done, Marie, excellent work." He was genuinely

impressed.

"I have put together a fact file and prices for you to show the boss if he needs to see it," she said. "I think everything is there."

"Well, my news is the DNA arrived a couple of hours ago. Rover's in the lab as we speak. Before close of play today we'll know either way. Bring the file in tomorrow, in the meantime keep your fingers crossed and relax, it's Sunday."

Lancaster had settled into picking out phrases that might come in handy from his 'Penguin French Phrase Book' when his mobile rang again. Rover.

"Rover, what's the news?"

"Simple, really. Sadly, he's his mother's son, and it would appear his name is Abdul."

†

7:30 Monday morning. Lancaster was being driven up the A38 by Vidêt. He gazed out of the window as the Devon scenery passed them by. He'd been born and raised in Plymouth. Devon was his home. He looked out at the rolling, grass-covered hillsides, imagining the shire horses that had walked these same fields for generations, followed by steam engines, then tractors. In all those years there'd been death, probably murder, somewhere across this landscape. The murder of Abdul was no different. Except this young North African had apparently come here in good faith, and died here, on his patch. Admittedly before his time, but still on his patch. Fate had brought his body to the surface on his shift. Lancaster wouldn't stop until the boy had been laid to rest, the culprit identified, if not brought to justice. If that culprit was still alive, then justice would be done.

Lancaster had contacted his boss the evening before, asked to see him on a matter of some urgency that he didn't want to discuss over the telephone. DCI Craven trusted that Lancaster wasn't wasting his time so agreed to meet. He couldn't get away from the police commissioner's seminar in Exeter he was hosting. The meet was to be breakfast at eight o'clock at the DCI's hotel. Lancaster and Vidêt arrived in the foyer with five minutes to spare. Lancaster settled Vidêt in the lounge with a coffee and told her he'd be meeting the boss alone. She nodded her acceptance; she knew this was going to be an important meeting and a leap of faith on DCI Craven's behalf if the trip was to be sanctioned. They certainly wouldn't want any eavesdropping from a third party to complicate the decision making.

Craven arrived, on the dot at eight o'clock. He wouldn't talk shop until breakfast was on the table and invited Lancaster to the buffet to fill their plates. Lancaster felt it would be churlish to refuse. Added to that, he was starving. He felt a touch of guilt at the thought of Vidêt sat in the lounge with her coffee. With that light touch of conscience, he put together a selection of croissants, pain au chocolate, a small pot of jam, one of marmalade, and asked the waiter to take it to her out in the lounge. It made him feel better. The two men filled their plates with an English breakfast montage and returned to a table in the corner by the window where they couldn't be overheard.

"Shall we eat this before we talk shop?" Craven suggested.

"I've had these 'working' meals before. You end up eating nothing and I've a long bloody day ahead of me, smiling and being gracious. You'd be surprised how much energy that takes."

Lancaster agreed and both men tucked in with only the minimum of chitchat between mouthfuls. It didn't take long to clear their plates. Lancaster pulled the file out of his briefcase and placed it on the table, but Craven held up a finger and stopped him.

"Not finished yet. Pop up to the counter and fill a plate with brown toast and all the trimmings I'll be all ears as I munch, OK?" Craven said, pulling out his phone and checking messages.

On Lancaster's return, complete with a toast feast fit for a king, Craven put his phone away and picked up the butter knife.

"Right, Bomber, I'm all yours," he said, buttering the first slice.

Lancaster took a deep breath, wished himself luck, then briefed his boss on where the case was now. The victim, now named, was a French citizen. The mother of the boy had been the one to identify him. At this moment in time the mother hadn't been informed of the results of the DNA test proving positive. The victim was North African originally, but his family now lived in France where the boy, Abdul, had gone to school. On leaving school, he'd been working prior to leaving France to start a new, well-paid job in the UK. As for suspects, all the Claypole family were now out of the picture completely.

"At some stage, Bomber," Craven said, chewing on his

second slice of toast, "I suspect you're going to tell me why this meeting became important."

Lancaster took a quick look around the room to ensure that no one was in earshot. Craven noticed the meaning behind the look.

"Oh bugger it, Bomber," he said, taking a look around them. "This is about the bloody Stottards, isn't it?"

"Sadly, sir, yes. Look, you know as well as I what we think about coincidence. You taught me it seldom exists. For the moment let's just call them the Ss. Well, Mr S owned the belt that tied the victim. The Ss happen to own a home not more than twenty miles from where the victim was buried, ten miles as the crow flies. The Ss happen to own another home no more than twenty miles from where the victim lived in France. It's a bloody great place surrounded on all sides by vineyards and high walls. One of the places the boy worked, in fact, the very last place in France he was known to have worked, a hotel, happens to be owned by a consortium, of whom the Ss are directors and major shareholders. According to his mother, it was whilst her son worked at that place that he was offered the chance to go to England, to work for a very nice pay packet but he had to keep it secret. Now call me suspicious sir, but that's too many coincidences that we already know don't exist for it to be, well... a coincidence."

"I agree. What are your theories?"

"Well, it wouldn't be the first time a company decided to turn to crime to boost its coffers tax free. The South of France is renowned for the influx of drugs into Europe. In fact, six months ago one of the heads of a regional drugs squad in the

South of France got busted along with several members of his team for assisting in the smuggling and distribution of the stuff."

"OK. So where are you going with this then, Bomber?"

Lancaster took another deep breath, there was no going back. "Well, sir, I want to go down to Narbonne and have a sniff around before we involve the French police. If drugs are involved, it's pointless us flagging it up over the phone or the internet. I would imagine the local police will have a hand in it somewhere. So I want to go down, ask a few discreet questions." At this point, Craven laughed out loud.

"Bomber, my son, you're bloody special needs, boy. I'm not being funny, but you wouldn't know discreet if it came up and bit you on the bloody arse. As far as I know, your knowledge of the French language was about bloody nil, so the thought of you blundering about, trying to blend in is farcical."

Lancaster didn't feel hurt by these comments. He knew them to be fact. He also knew his boss had just played right into his hands. He struck whilst the iron was still hot.

"Well that brings me to my other request, sir. I want to take DS Vidêt along with me. She'll do all the talking. I'll give her the questions and do the thinking."

Craven sat chewing his third piece of toast whilst chewing over what Lancaster had suggested. It was a big ask bearing in mind the state of police funding at the moment. Anything that looked like waste would have to have a bloody good explanation. However, there was another thought ticking away at the back of his mind. He'd never liked Lord Stottard, and a couple of times during other enquiries there'd been murmurs about the

Stottard fortune. But the whole family had been guarded by a legion of lawyers for years. Initially, he remembered companies complaining of bullying prior to takeover. Then there were tax evasion suggestions, rumours about Sir Philip's lifestyle, and wealth. Since his death ten years ago, the murmurs had ceased, but the fortune was still there, now controlled by the two sons. It was a dangerous line of enquiry. Only the previous year he'd been part of the interview panel, drawn up to find the latest Devon & Cornwall Police & Crime Commissioner. One of the candidates shortlisted turned out to be Lady Pamela Stottard. Luckily for Craven, the panel made a unanimous decision to put her in second place, thereby letting him off the hook. But if there was any fire smouldering under the surface of the Stottard family seat, it was time to release the smoke and bring it to burn. Craven sat for a moment finishing his toast. He liked Lancaster. Yes, he was bloody weird. He wasn't one of the boys, but he always got results. He finished his mouthful of toast. Took one more look around then voiced his decision.

"This is how it's going to go, Bomber, and listen carefully." Craven leant forward in his seat, speaking directly into Lancaster's face. "I'll cover the cost of a three day jolly down into France for the two of you, but keep it cheap as chips, my son. Go Ryanair and sit on the bloody wing if you can, don't take anything bigger than hand luggage. Book one room with single beds, just don't piss about with Frenchie, you get my drift? Let her do the talking, trust her, she knows her stuff. She's better than sergeant material, but we had to downgrade her to get her so don't waste her skills in her own bloody homeland. Do not bandy the S name about down there unless absolutely necessary. Do I make myself clear? Find out what you can about this boy and find out why he came here. If somebody offers up the S family then follow it, but, I repeat, do not flag them up to the locals. Is that clear?"

"Yes, sir, and thank you for your trust."

"Bomber, it's a murder investigation. I don't take kindly to people making mischief in my space and thinking they're getting away with it. I want you to crack this one, my son, no matter who's guilty. But, and I repeat, BUT, if you go down to the South of France and bugger this up; piss off our French friends? I'll hang you out to dry. If this goes the way you think it will, then at some stage we have to involve somebody in French police on a senior level. If we're talking drug running between the two countries then we can't sit on it or sort it alone. So you're going to have go very carefully, I don't expect this to become an international conflict. I like you, Lancaster. but for my own future, I'll hang you on the line if I have to. Is that clear?"

"Yes. sir. I'll leave you to get on with your day and will keep you posted."

"Be sure you do, Bomber, just be bloody sure you do. Now bugger off before I change my mind." DCI Craven went back to tackling his last piece of toast with a thoughtful expression on his face.

†

Two days later, the detectives were lifting off from Bristol Airport. The 13:55 for Beziers. It had been overcast and cloudy all the way to the airport. By the time they'd parked in Silver Zone and jumped on the bus to departures, it had begun to rain for the first time in two weeks. *So, that's summer over,* Lancaster thought, *and it's not even the end of May.*

As soon as the flight cleared cloud above the airport the sun streamed in through the window and did so for the whole flight, though Vidêt didn't see it. She was asleep almost as soon as the wheels folded up into place, so Lancaster enjoyed the flight alone. Once they'd crossed the English Channel, clouds cleared and Lancaster watched with joy as the French countryside passed below them. As promised, and right on time, the creaking, whooshing noise alerted him to the fact that the ailerons had shifted as the plane set up for landing. On cue, the pilot's voice came over the speakers, announcing arrival at the Airport de Beziers Cap d'Agde. The weather was clear, sunny, temperature a steady nineteen degrees centigrade.

Vidêt woke as the wheels cranked down. By the time the plane landed, she was wide awake. Thirty minutes later, they were outside the airport, walking across a hot tarmacked carpark in search of the car hire office. Lancaster already felt overdressed. He needed some shorts if he was going to blend in; he'd also be needing sunglasses. His were sitting on the dashboard of the car in the Bristol Airport carpark. Twenty minutes later, with Vidêt at the wheel they were heading west along the A9 en route from Beziers to Narbonne and their hotel, along with the awkwardness that was going to be a shared double room, though they had at least stipulated twin beds. Speeding down the main road for Narbonne, they saw signs for Salles-d'Aude. Vidêt asked if Lancaster wanted to check out the Stottard chateaux. Lancaster had already decided he wanted to make base camp at the hotel then regroup before setting out on any research. Apart from that, he stood out too much. He needed to shower, change and drink tea before forming a plan of campaign. As the flight back home on Friday wasn't until late afternoon, 'Chateaux Stottard' would wait for the return journey.

CHAPTER EIGHT

The detectives checked into their hotel within an hour of leaving the airport. The journey had been incident free and faster than Lancaster had thought it would be. What he couldn't have realised was that the journey, once they'd left the outskirts of Beziers, would be travelled through a landscape of rolling vineyards, acres of them. Regimental rows of fresh, green vine leaves wandered side by side across the flat lands and low hills to either side of the road, advertising the wine to come.

Having found their hotel with ease – directed straight to the door by the onboard satnav, parking in the underground carpark below the hotel – they were pleased to find that checking in had been a simple, painless, easy affair. Nobody appeared concerned at the fact that two people of the opposite sex, with different surnames were sharing a room together, because, obviously, this was France. Luckily, the hotel receptionist didn't ask for their passports either, or the ability to remain incognito would have been blown out of the water from the word go. They were also relieved when they got to their room to find their request for a double room with twin beds had been observed. In fact, they'd a nice, neat, well-furnished room with a wide balcony overlooking a square with restaurants, cafés and bars around the sides. Groups of tables and chairs filled with afternoon drinkers and conversationalists, sitting around in the warm sunshine exchanging pleasantries, doing business.

Lancaster, ever the gentleman, gave Vidêt the chance to use the shower first whilst he opened the complimentary chilled water, poured himself a glass and retired to the balcony to sample some sunshine and give her space and privacy. She hadn't actually shown any sign of finding the sharing of the room difficult or embarrassing. Lancaster sat on the balcony and went through his notes. He'd started a new notebook especially for this trip, he'd not wanted to bring any of their previous notes with them for obvious reasons. In his pad were the simple facts and details of the case. Dates, addresses, places of work etcetera. Having arrived at the hotel via the front door, located on the other side of the hotel in the next street, Lancaster was pleased that their balcony at the rear overlooked this lovely, busy, tree-lined square. It had a classic French look, but then he supposed it would have been odd if it hadn't.

It was whilst he was looking out, enjoying the warmth, admiring the scenery that he noticed, through the trees, the building on the far side of the square. A large, gothic-style hotel with a grand façade set off by a pair of very large potted trees to either side of the equally grand front entrance. The building rose to four stories, topped by four, matching, blue slated, conical roofed little towers. The front wall was broken with regimented, stone mullioned windows, organised symmetrically across its grey stone walls, each fronted by an ornate wrought-iron balcony, behind which troughs of flowers spilled between vertical railings, giving colour to the otherwise drab exterior. Above the open double entrance doors and curving up and across the front of this great gothic edifice, standing out from the stonework in relief form, was the gold embossed lettering that spelt out the words 'Les Hotel des Anglaise'.

Lancaster laughed inwardly. He was overlooking the hotel that was the last working place for Abdul. This was DS Vidêt. Showing she knew how to book a good hotel. Lancaster stood and went through the balcony doors back into the room, a big smile on his face. At that moment, Vidêt came from the bathroom with one towel wrapped around her head, another wrapped around her body. The twisted knot of the towel around her body, tied and tucked into her cleavage. Lancaster turned his head immediately and apologised.

"I'm so sorry, Marie," he said, but still, his gaze now averted, he couldn't help remembering the little droplets of water that clung to her upper body, the tan line that showed where she was used to being covered up in the UK. "That was bad timing. I'll go onto the balcony out of your way," he continued, turning for the door.

"Sir, do you not swim?"

"Sorry?" Lancaster replied as he turned half way and looked at her sideways, which felt a little awkward and made him look silly.

"I thought you said you went often to your gym and swam."

"Well, yes I do," Lancaster said, now looking her full in the face. That way he could avert his eyes from the rest of Marie's body, more of which was visible than he'd ever seen before. Vidêt, normally clad in trousers, shirt and jacket, turned up for work looking every bit the masculine detective.

"Well then, if you swim, you must have seen people dressed in a towel before. I do not mean to step out of line, sir, but we need to work together, as part of this we need to be grown up about what happens day-to-day. In an ideal world, we would have had separate rooms. We do not have that financial luxury. We must make the best of it and be professional. Personally, I do not intend spending three days in France, in this sunshine, not showering for fear of offending you. We are both adults and have both seen it all before, so likewise, I do not intend to hide every time you wish to shower, we just need to do our jobs and get over it... sir."

Lancaster felt he'd been told off and initially felt annoyed, being spoken down to by his sergeant, but then he couldn't help but smile.

"You are, of course. quite right. Marie, I was just taken by surprise for a moment. We've neither of us been in this position before. But you're right, we must remain professional. I apologise for my lapse, it won't happen again, and thank you for putting me straight. Now, is the bathroom free?"

A short time later, Lancaster emerged from his turn in the bathroom, for the most part almost fully dressed. The room was empty. He saw through the sheer curtains, clustered around the balcony doors, fluttering slightly in the afternoon breeze that Vidêt was out on the balcony. Lancaster finished drying, hunted through his bag and pulled on a thin, short sleeved shirt. Stuffed his dirty laundry into the side pocket of the case. Ran a comb through his hair and stepped through the curtain onto the balcony.

Lancaster thought immediately, *the next three days were going to be tougher than he'd ever imagined.*

Vidêt was sitting on one of the balcony chairs, wearing a short, flowery patterned dress from the bottom of which emerged a pair of long, brown, tanned legs. On her feet a pair of elegant flipflops, with the over the feet straps decorated with small jewel-like beads. Around one ankle was a silver chain and across the side of her left foot, a delicate Celtic motif tattoo. Vidêt's toenails were neatly painted a delicate shade of pink, matching her fingernails. When these had been seen as standalone items in the office back in Plymouth, they didn't look to be overtly sexual in any way. At no stage in the office had he ever given a thought to the fact that, lurking beneath the socks in the workday shoes, the toes would be matching. As she turned to acknowledge his arrival, he noticed the chain around her neck. Saw the way the little cleft musical note pendant hanging from it, nestled into the tanned top of her breasts. The pendant matched the earrings she was wearing. Her now dry, short, black hair showed them off to perfection. Her eyes were hidden behind the large lenses of the dark glasses she'd been wearing since they'd exited the plane several hours ago. Lancaster reached for the bottled water and topped up his glass as a distraction, to help refocus his mind on the job in hand.

He'd been married for a year when his wife had been killed in a head-on collision with another car. The other car was driving along the wrong side of the dual carriageway on the approach to Plymouth. The driver was drunk. He hit his wife's car at a combined speed of some one hundred and forty miles an hour. Both drivers, apparently. died instantly, so would have known little about it, but the pain they'd left behind had been immense. Lancaster had felt great sadness at the sudden loss of his wife, soulmate and confidant, but he'd also felt great anger. Anger that the other man had died. He would have seriously liked the opportunity to have kicked him to death for his crime and stupidity. There was also anger that his wife had gone, just like that. No goodbye. No chance to kiss, to laugh, to touch. Just gone. In the blink of an eye. The last time he spoke to her, they both said they were leaving their respective places of work and would meet back at home. Their little ramshackle cottage at Wembury, with a view out to sea and more decorating to be done than they'd ever imagined to have in their lives. But they loved it and loved sharing a home.

His wife had understood his 'special needs', they'd made fun of them together. She'd laughed at his avoidance techniques. His lack of shoe laces. His inability to do simple maths without a pencil and paper. But though she laughed she'd always been supportive and understanding. She laughed with him, not at him. He'd loved her for that. He'd also loved her for being beautiful and funny, so it was hard to be angry with her for dying. There was nowhere else to focus his anger so he just carried that anger around for a long time until, little by little, bit by bit, it faded. He realised he still missed her, but life was moving on. Four years had passed. 'It's time you met someone else, Bomber,' his friends would say. The friends who all had partners and who one by one had moved on with their lives. Had children, moved house, stopped calling.

He'd had the occasional meeting of bodies with the odd woman here and there, normally after a drunken night out. But he couldn't imagine settling down with another woman. He'd sold their beautiful little seaside cottage soon after. He saw no point owning it anymore if they weren't going to work on it together. She would've laughed at how much he actually got when the final price was set. He'd used the money to purchase the brand-new flat overlooking the inner harbour at Millbay and the Brittany Ferries terminal. The flat was bland, modern, functional. Simply furnished but warm. It had a balcony that looked over the docks and even during the winter it would catch the sun and stay warm. It was a nice place to sit, watch the boats and people come and go. But it was just the place he went to when he wasn't at work. It held his music collection, sound system and little else apart from the obvious furniture that he needed to live. The bed, the settee, a chair, the flat screen television, and the fitted kitchen. It wasn't really a home, it was where he lived.

It must have been something about this new location, the hotel room, the sun, the warmth, the scenery that had made him look at his working partner in a different light. It was dangerous and not a good idea. He needed to get a grip and stay professional.

"Well done for getting this location, Marie. How did you manage to get us a room overlooking Les Hotel des Anglaise?"

"I google-mapped the Hotel des Anglaise, then looked around for a nearby hotel. Then I found this one shared the square, though if I am truthful, I hadn't realised just how good a view we would have."

"Well, it's pretty damned good, Marie, though just looking at it's not going to help us. I think what I want to do first though is make like a tourist and walk around the centre for a while. I want to try and put myself in our boy's shoes, see the city with a different set of eyes. How does that sound to you?"

"I think it's a good idea, sir, may I make a suggestion?"

"Of course, and I think whilst we are here you should call me David, or it may appear just a little odd to anyone who hears you calling me sir."

"Well... David." Vidêt said, with a slight exaggeration and accent. "If we go along the canal the two restaurants that Abdul worked at are in the centre of the town, the Place de l'Hôtel de Ville. We can check them out then eat in the square. Then we can stroll back towards base and check out the hotel across the road."

"That sounds fine to me. Let's make a start with some shopping. I'll need a pair of shorts before morning or I'm likely to fade away to nothing. And I need sunglasses. You appear to have left mine in the car in Bristol," he said with a smile.

They picked up a street guide from reception and headed out into the late afternoon sunshine. Walking across the square, under the wide spreading plane trees, they strolled down small cobbled side streets, opening onto a paved walkway running alongside a canal, where joggers and cyclists shared space and tourist boats made their way along its course. The pair crossed over the canal, via the Pont des Marchands, a sturdy, fine-looking bridge. The bridge not only crossed the canal, but housed a range of shops. In one, Lancaster purchased a pair of shorts, a pair of rope-soled espadrilles (without laces) and sunglasses ready for the morning.

The pair reached the Place de l'Hôtel de Ville with bustling restaurant tables spilling out onto the square. Each restaurant marking its turf with a different style of sunshade. They initially circumnavigated the square, wandering around the perimeter. In the centre of the square was a sunken, rectangular area containing an unearthed section of the original Roman road, the 'Via Domitia' that once crossed this space. It soon became apparent that neither of the businesses Abdul had worked for still existed. This was no great surprise to Vidêt, she'd been unable to locate either of the restaurants when she researched them. It didn't surprise Lancaster either. Abdul had wandered these streets and alleyways over twenty years ago, it was inevitable things would've changed.

The pair chose a menu they liked and were seated by the waiter. The late afternoon sun was the guiding aspect of their choice, more so than the food on offer. They were looking for a place in the sun for an evening, 'à table, à plein air'. Having chosen from the menu, ordered a bottle of the house wine to accompany it when it arrived, they'd also ordered a Ricard each as an aperitif, delighting in the cloudiness formed as iced water was added. The waiter left the bottle beside them should they need to top up.

"Cheers," Lancaster said, raising his glass to Marie.

"À votre santé," she replied.

"So, looking around at the staff working the square, I don't see anybody anywhere near old enough to have even known Abdul let alone worked with him. We may get some joy if we go inside and speak with management but we'll have to be very casual about any enquiries."

"I think you're right about the young staff. When I go in to use the loo, I will ask about the two restaurants that have changed hands. I'll ask under the pretence that a friend had a holiday here years ago and mentioned them. There is a chance they may know somebody who was working there at the time."

The waiter arrived with their main course just as Vidêt's mobile rang. She automatically picked it up and hit the receive button.

"DS Vidêt, allo," she said, reaching for bread from the basket.

"DS Vidêt, bonjour, it is Madame Mehemet," the voice on the other end of the line said. "I am sorry to trouble you so late in the day, but I wondered if the sample I gave had reached you yet and if so when I would possibly know the results?"

Vidêt looked across at Lancaster, raising her hand to get his attention, pointing at her phone.

"Ah, bonsoir Madame Mehemet, good evening to you," Vidêt replied, raising her eyebrows toward Lancaster. "Yes, Madame, the sample arrived and is with the pathology department, we are awaiting the results. I am sorry, it was remiss of me not to have let you know, but we have been very busy."

"Oh that is not a problem, my phone call was not a reprimand, DS Vidêt, just a question that was all. Abdul has been missing over twenty years, a few days will make little difference to me now. But I do have news for you. I did not think of it when Abdul first went missing, I don't know why, but now I have been busy going through his old photographs from school days. I managed to track down a boy who went to school with him, then worked with him at the restaurant Les Maison Domitia before Abdul left. The restaurant is no longer there, but Christopher lives here in Narbonne and would like to speak with you. May I pass on your number or would you like to call him, but... I am sorry, DS Vidêt, I can hear you are eating, shall I call you at a better time?"

Just then above the sounds of cutlery, the chink of glasses and the voices of fellow diners came the sound of bells chiming the hour. Melodic, rhythmic, clear, being rung from a bell tower to the north of the square.

"But are you here in Narbonne? I hear the hour bells from the city square. I don't understand, why are you here?"

"Just one moment, Madame." Vidêt quickly put her hand over the phone and turned to Lancaster who was listening to her side of the call. "I'm sorry, sir, Madame has heard the bells and knows we are here in Narbonne. She has found someone who worked with Abdul and he wants to speak with us. She knows we are here, shall I tell her we will go and see her? It could be worth our while bringing her into our secret visit."

Lancaster had little time to think. For the moment, their cover was blown. He needed to nip this in the bud before Madame told anyone else. He couldn't believe they'd been in Narbonne no more than a few hours and already somebody knew they were there. What a simple, stupid mistake answering the phone had been. They'd made the mistake of relaxing; it had proved wrong.

"Tell her to tell no one that we are here. Ask if we can come to her home at 8:30 in the morning to explain. Just make sure she understands to tell no one of our visit. We'll explain all to her in the morning."

Vidêt finished her call with Madame and turned the phone off. She looked embarrassed and anxious.

"I'm sorry, sir," she said, looking at Lancaster. "That was a stupid thing to do, I just didn't think."

"It's done now. It was a simple mistake, we relaxed, took our eye off the ball for a moment. Let's not do it again though. Anyway, it may work in our favour. I'll have to tell her our body is her son. It seems right as we're here in her home town. I think you're right, we have to bring her at least halfway into our confidence. It may certainly help to meet Abdul's friend, Christopher."

The pair finished their meal with no more mention of the case, just conversation about the delights of the city at night. It had been at least six years since Lancaster had been out of the UK, a brief holiday in Spain with some friends. He found he liked this new adventure. He loved the fact that it was nearly nine o'clock in the evening and he was eating outside without a coat. He loved the food, chilled wine, scenery and stunning buildings around the square. He loved the sounds around him, the melodic voices chatting in French; loved the ambience and the company of an attractive female beside him to share the meal and conversation.

He'd also just decided he'd probably drunk enough. He topped up his wine glass with water. After their meal they ordered coffees. Vidêt went inside the restaurant to 'powder her nose'. When she returned, she informed Lancaster she'd chatted with the manager about Les Maison Domitia. She'd claimed her parents had once visited the town and had a wonderful meal there. The manager knew little about it, other than it had gone bust following the financial crash of 2008.

Lancaster paid and the pair strolled back out of the square. They crossed the same bridge, then walked down the canal side in the direction of their hotel, the evening still warm but with just a slight chill in the wisp of a breeze.

"Why would anyone want to leave here and travel to work in the UK? At home, we were all surprised that the weather was warm when we left, but as usual it had just started to rain. It's beautiful here; there must be work here the same as you would find anywhere but the joy is that when you've finished work, you still have a warm evening to go out in and plenty of places to eat. What more could you want than the chance to stroll along this canal of an evening, the sound of the swifts screaming over the water; they must have offered Abdul some serious money for him to want to leave."

"The difference is, sir... sorry, David, that Abdul was North African and we are talking about the 1980s and '90s. There was a lot of racism here then. Not just usual white, black racism, but the anger of a country that spent years trying to colonise northern Africa, mainly Algeria. We wanted access to oil and minerals. In the '40s and '50s the British had Egypt, Tunisia, and influence in Libya, Iraq and Kuwait. All France wanted was to hang onto a bit of North Africa. We'd been there for over a hundred years. But when we started to lose so many of our soldiers, engineers and their families to separatists' bombs, then finally we were forced to withdraw. Anybody that arrived here from that area was looked down upon, ostracised. By the '90s it was better but even then, a young man with African looks such as Abdul? He would have struggled to get work if there were French people that wanted the job. We know Abdul was working in the restaurant and hotel trade, we don't know what he was doing? He was probably a washer-up in the kitchens or maybe chopping vegetables, but he would have struggled to be front of house, not unless he was very, very good. I suspect he saw the UK as some kind of 'promised land'. A place where all races and colours mixed and there was work and money for everyone. He was wrong, of course; it was a dream, a myth. At the time there was just as much racial tension in the UK as the South of France. It just had a better accent."

They continued along the canal side, their footsteps on the cobbles drowned out from time to time by the screaming squadrons of swifts hurtling along the waterway, scooping insects on the wing before shooting back into the sky, ready to line up for another run.

They reached the square where their hotel was based, the place now quite busy. Lancaster had a feeling this would've been a nicer place to eat rather than the touristy main square. Maybe tomorrow night they'd find a table here instead. They crossed the square to Les Hotel des Anglaise which, by night, looked stunning. The raised lettering and motif on the hotel façade, up-lit, shining golden in the late evening twilight. The lights within the hotel illuminated every window, making the building come alive. Lancaster and Vidêt walked up the steps and through the open, glazed doors. Inside to the left was a large and ornate lounge with leather furniture, potted palms, dark, antique woodwork around the walls and a long bar with stools to the front. To the right of the entrance doorway an equally ornate, red carpeted staircase wound upwards. To the right of this again, a pair of leather padded, brass studded doors above which was an illuminated sign saying 'Casino'. In front of these doors stood a large, well-suited gentleman, a piece of wire wrapped around one ear, a small microphone curling around one side of his face. He looked like a deterrent to trouble. Directly in front of the detectives was the hotel reception desk with a smartly dressed young man behind it. At attention and ready to greet them. Lancaster strolled with a confident air, straight up to the counter.

"Good evening," Lancaster said in his best English voice, no hint of a Plymouth accent slipping out. "We aren't guests here, but is it possible to get a drink at the bar?"

"Of course, sir, the hotel bar is open to the public, resident or not."

"Thank you." They strolled across to the bar and slid onto a couple of stools. "May we both have a cognac on ice please? Just a very small dash of soda."

"Certainly, sir, would you like it here at the bar or in the lounge?"

"I think we'll take it in the lounge. Thank you."

They wandered into the lounge, choosing two leather armchairs side by side, a small table in front for their drinks. More importantly, with a good view across the room to the casino doors and their guardian.

"I know it's a casino," Vidêt said, "but I can't help thinking the guy on the door is a bit overkill for the job in hand, don't you?"

"He looks a bit like Odd Job. I wouldn't like to try and arrest him."

The waiter arrived. He placed little paper mats on the table and set the glasses down. Next to them he placed a dish of olives, attached to this, a silver pot of sticks to spike them. Alongside this he set another silver tray with a folded till receipt neatly resting upon it. "Enjoy your drinks, sir, madame," he said.

He was about to walk away when Lancaster asked, "Excuse me, we've just noticed the casino." Lancaster nodded in Odd Job's direction. "Is it open to non-residents?"

"I'm afraid not, sir, it is members only. You join by filling in forms and giving references. The management would let you know if you had been accepted. Would you like me to fetch the manager, he can get the forms for you?"

"No thank you, we're only here for a couple of days, it wouldn't be worth the trouble. But thank you anyway."

Lancaster slipped the waiter a small tip. The man thanked him, then left them to their drinks.

"So, if we cannot get into the casino what more can we find out... David?" Vidêt said with a smile.

"Well... Marie..." Lancaster said, echoing her exaggerated use of Christian name. "We can learn a lot just by observation. For a start, there's nothing unusual about a private members club in itself, but putting somebody the size of Odd Job over there does rather look like they are making a statement, and on cue we have some action."

As they watched, two young men approached the casino doors. The waiting doorman stepped forward to block their way. Both men reached into their jacket pockets and pulled some kind of card out which they showed to Odd Job. He expertly sidestepped, opened the door for them, closed it as they passed through. Lancaster turned to Vidêt and saw that she'd obviously seen what he had as well. The last man through the door had patted the other man's bottom as they passed through.

"Again, nothing unusual in that either. Shall we have another drink?" Lancaster asked, and without waiting for a reply, waved his hand in the air towards the barman, then pointed at their empty glasses in the universal sign for a refill. When the barman approached with fresh drinks, Lancaster asked him about the casino.

"We may be back here during the summer, staying longer next time, is it possible to apply for membership on-line or do we have to do it the old-fashioned way?"

"I'm afraid it's part of the custom of the casino, sir, it must be done whilst you are here," the barman replied.

"And is it just a gentleman's club or are ladies welcome also?" Vidêt asked, watching the man's face as he replied.

"Oh we're not quite that old fashioned, Madame. Both sexes may join, with or without a partner. Enjoy your drinks, sir, madam." He left them alone once more.

The pair spent a good thirty minutes watching the comings and goings through the casino door. At no time did they see anything that made them think the place could be a nest of drug dealers or den of iniquity. Yes, there was something odd about the guarded doorway, but then, back home in Plymouth, in the club district of Union Street there wasn't a single club or bar that didn't have a couple of bruisers standing at the doors watching for trouble. Lancaster realised there was nothing that could be gained from sitting here getting slowly smashed. He made the decision to call it a day.

Once back in their room, Lancaster took the precaution of wedging the armchair under the door handle just to slow down anyone who decided to pay them a visit during the night. Both Lancaster and Vidêt had had enough dealings with drugs to know that if that was what was going on down here then there could indeed be an element of danger. Serious danger, violence, and no fear of the police whatsoever, especially foreign, incognito police. Vidêt had slipped off her shoes and gone onto the balcony for some air before turning in, Lancaster followed. They were on the second floor. A quick look over the side showed the floor below them had no balconies and there were no drain pipes or plants to gain a foothold that he could see. He felt they were safe where they were. Vidêt was leaning against the railing looking out across the darkening square, the breeze ruffling the hem of her skirt. She had one leg tucked to the back of the other, the points of her toes extended and touching the floor.

In the light coming from their room, Lancaster could see the muscles on the back of her lower leg highlighted, still see the pale pink tone of her nail varnish. The lighting picked out and glinted on the silver ankle chain with the miniature padlock. That, in turn, drew your eye to the subtle and delicate tattoo across her foot. As she leant forward onto the railing, her arms folded, the movement tightened the dress around her body and displayed the curve of her back and the tanned calves

213

glistened slightly in the light. Lancaster decided it was time for a quick, cold, shower before bed. Asking Vidêt if she minded him leaping into the bathroom first and getting the answer 'no', that was exactly what he did. Returning from the bathroom a short time later in his pyjamas, feeling just a touch chilly after his shower, he jumped straight into bed just as Vidêt headed for her turn in the bathroom. By the time she returned and climbed into her bed, Lancaster's ardour had cooled, replaced by gentle snoring. It'd been a long day finished off with too much alcohol. Vidêt turned out the light, pulled the duvet over herself and was soon snoring gently in harmony.

The detectives woke early, an event triggered by the alarm on Vidêt's phone. She was first into the shower while Lancaster turned over for another doze. He was aware of a slightly fuzzy head, a touch of blurriness with the eyes. No sooner had he dropped back off to sleep than Vidêt was back, wrapped this time in the complimentary bathrobe found hanging on the back of the bathroom door. Lancaster emerged twenty minutes later, having showered and shaved. He found it embarrassing to be sharing a bathroom with a relative stranger, so when he re-emerged, he was pleased to see the room was empty. Vidêt was, again, already sitting on the balcony catching the morning sun. He pulled on his new shorts, added a clean short-sleeved shirt and joined her.

"Morning, Marie. Sleep well?" An obvious opening gambit, but he used it anyway.

"Very well thank you, sir... sorry, David. We have time to grab breakfast before we have to meet Madame Mehemet."

Lancaster was annoyed at himself. Too keen to rush out

onto the balcony to see what his partner was wearing this morning. He was relieved to see that today she'd dressed down. Wearing knee length, neat, denim shorts, tucked into which was a fresh white T shirt with buttoned turn-ups to the short sleeves. Keeping the dark glasses of yesterday back over her eyes, but a smile on her face. Lancaster tucked his notebook into the side pocket of his shorts, slipped his feet into the new espadrilles and they went for breakfast.

Vidêt had plotted the route to the Mehemet house using the street map obtained the previous day. After a continental breakfast of croissants, coffee and masses of jam, the pair set off. The walk took them in the opposite direction to the previous night, but still alongside the canal on the Quai Dillon. After fifteen minutes, the pair cut back into the shopping streets on the western side of the canal, then turned down a side street until they reached Madame Mehemet's. The address given brought them to a double wooden doorway beside which were two bell buttons, one for 'Lavias, F' the other for 'Mehemet, J'. Vidêt pressed the second one and waited. Seconds later, the unmistakable voice of Madame Mehemet came through the speaker grill.

"Allo?"

"Madame Mehemet, it is Marie."

There was a buzz and click as the door unlocked. They climbed the stairs to the second floor. Madame was already standing on the landing looking down at them.

"Bonjour, Madame," Lancaster said, holding out his hand. "Je m'appelle David Lancaster, eh ici mon ami, Marie Vidêt," Lancaster continued, pointing at Vidêt with his other hand.

"Now it's down to you, Marie, unless Madame wants to speak in English, you'll have to be the translator."

Madame Mehemet smiled and shook Lancaster's hand.

"That is not a problem, Detective Lancaster, I am happy to speak in English. If it gets too difficult Marie can translate. Please, come in." She waved them both into her apartment. "Would you like coffee? I have some made. Then you can give me an explanation of why you are here, though I fear I already know the answer."

Madame poured coffee, served black, in large bowls, but at least they had handles. They seated themselves in her large lounge. The doors to her balcony were open. There, a pair of brightly coloured finches sang from a large, oriental-looking cage hanging on a hook from a beam in the ceiling, outside, in the morning sunshine. The apartment was large, grand, finely furnished, with typical dark wood furniture throughout. The darkness was lifted by an abundance of plants. Potted ferns, small palms and large vases of flowers neatly displayed and arranged. The three of them sat in grand leather chairs. Lancaster decided to bite the bullet, get the worst part over and done with immediately.

"Madame, sadly, I have to tell you that the body that we've found in England is that of your son, Abdul. The DNA sample you supplied made a complete match. I'm very sorry to have to bring you this news."

After a brief moments silence, Madame spoke.

"Detective Lancaster, do you have children?"

"Sadly not," Lancaster replied with a tinge of sadness. His wife had been expecting their first child when she'd been killed.

It had been early days in the pregnancy but, nevertheless, it would've been their child.

"Well, Detective Lancaster, when you have a child, especially if you are the mother, you live a new life through the child. You have hopes and wishes. You hope as I did with Abdul, that the world they grow up in will be a better one than the one you lived through. That they have better chances. Better opportunities. A better chance to achieve in life, to be happy. That was all we ever wanted for Abdul, his father and I, so when he said he had been offered a new job, a new life in England we were thrilled for him. It would be a great adventure. A chance to escape the problems we had at the time here in France. When we heard nothing from him, I knew something was wrong. It was not like him not to call to let me know he had arrived safe, that all was well. One evening, as I sat on the balcony after work, I felt a cold shiver. A deep sadness, a darkness that overwhelmed me, I sat and cried. My husband came out to me and asked what was wrong. "I just said, 'It is Abdul, he's dead'. Of course, my husband was having none of that and tried to tell me everything was alright, but I knew. I think that was the day he died. He was trying to tell me he was gone. Calling for me from somewhere. You will think me a silly old lady but I knew I was right inspector. So you see, what you are telling me is nothing that I did not already know. It has just put my mind at rest to know that he has been found and I can bring him home. Can I ask how he died?"

Lancaster knew there was no easy way round this, she had to be told, but not all of it. Not yet.

"Madame, I'm sorry to have to tell you. Your son was

murdered. He died probably within months of arriving in the UK, at most, within the very first year."

"How did he die, Inspector?" she asked, looking him straight in the eyes.

"He was drowned, Madame. Knocked unconscious and he drowned," Lancaster replied, looking straight back at her. He was being as honest as he could without giving her the details. They were not necessary. "I'm so very sorry, Madame, that this happened to your son in our country, but I'm determined to find the person or persons who are responsible and bring them to justice."

"Why has it taken so long to find his body though? I cannot understand this."

"His body was buried, Madame," Lancaster replied. Not strictly true, but close enough, he felt. "He was discovered purely by chance as some digging was being carried out where he'd been hidden. A farmer was having a pond dug, the digger uncovered the body. Otherwise we may never have found him. Our forensic pathologist worked to identify your son's body, which is how we came to publish an artist's impression in our newspapers. Then you saw it. If you hadn't then we would have known nothing about Abdul."

Madame stood up and walked out onto the balcony. She stopped by the birdcage, opened a box of seed and slid out the little container from the side of the cage. The birds started chirping in unison at the prospect of being fed, jumping from perch to perch in anticipation. Madame poured a little of the seed into the pot and returned it, much to the bird's delight. She stood talking quietly to the birds, then somewhere to the east of them, as the crow flies, there came the melodic tones of the hour clock in the city square ringing out nine a.m. This triggered a question in Madame's mind and she returned to the room.

"Inspector Lancaster, although I am very grateful to you both for coming all this way to bring me this news, and put my mind at rest. And, I do feel better hearing it straight from you and not being told over the telephone. But I must think to myself, there is another reason why you have travelled all the way to my home. Will I be told what that is?"

Lancaster realised that in fact he'd just got over the easy part of their conversation, there was a limit to how much he could disclose at this stage. He didn't want her to have too much detail. Too many ideas and secrets. He needed to keep as many cards close to his chest as possible so as little leaked out until he was sure of what he was dealing with down here.

"Madame, I take you into my confidence. I also ask that you tell no one that we have been here. No one at all for the moment, is that OK with you?"

"I understand, Inspector, but why?"

"Both myself and Sergeant Vidêt, Marie, are here as civilians, not as representatives of the British police. We're incognito whilst we are here, though my boss knows we're here and supports what we've come to do."

"And what, exactly, is that?"

"We believe whatever persuaded your son to leave France, whatever this job was, was what got him killed. We strongly believe whoever arranged for him to take up this job was probably involved in his murder. But, whatever and whoever

219

that was, it all started here in Narbonne. The connection is here. So it was important we came here to find out for ourselves as much as possible about his days just before he left. But we've some doubts about how helpful the local police would be if we reopened a case they'd taken little interest in. We've very little time; we fly back tomorrow evening, but visiting you was always part of the plan while we were here. It's just come earlier than I planned, which is why I ask for your secrecy in this matter until we're back home."

"So it is lucky I have found Christopher then. He wanted to telephone you in England, but now you can speak in person."

Lancaster realised that although speaking with Christopher would be helpful, it was yet another person who knew who they were and why they were here. Another risk, but one he knew must be taken if this trip was to be worthwhile, if it helped fill in the bigger picture.

"Madame, would it be possible for you to telephone Christopher? Could you ask if we could meet today? It's important we do this as soon as possible, before anybody finds out we're here and it all becomes official."

"But of course. I can do it right this minute." She turned and picked up the telephone on the table and within seconds was talking with the man himself. After a moments conversation she put her hand over the receiver and asked, "Can you meet him at ten thirty?"

Lancaster checked his watch, then nodded acceptance.

Madame continued talking on the phone for a moment before saying goodbye.

"Bon, Christopher will meet you both at the Café La Place,

in the Place d'Republic at ten thirty. He will be at an outside table waiting for you."

"Thank you, Madame, we must go then. We don't wish to be late, but many thanks for your assistance in this and again, I can only repeat how sorry we are that England hadn't been a safer place for your son to visit."

"May I ask, would you both join me here this evening for dinner? I so seldom get the opportunity to speak in English. It would be a joy for me to have you here, and preparing a meal would go some way to saying thank you for what you are trying to do, and for bringing me the news. Even though it is hard to hear, it is good to know that somebody is trying to put things right. Please say yes."

Lancaster looked at Marie who gave him a nod. "We would be delighted, Madame, on one condition: we don't talk about the case. Our secret is now known by two people, it could be more by the end of the day. We could be getting ourselves into trouble, so the less we say to as few people as possible the better. Agreed?"

"Agreed. Shall we say eight p.m.?"

Having said goodbye, the detectives made their way back to the canal. The river was busy now, small boats and canal tourists churning the water in both directions. The day had warmed. Lancaster was glad he'd purchased the shorts and espadrilles. The walk from Madame Mehemet's home to the Place d'Republic took them thirty minutes. A scenic journey along shady, cobbled streets, through picturesque courtyards and squares. They entered the Place d'Republic square from the cobbled side street that ran next to the old unfinished cathedral walls.

At this time of the morning, slightly off the main tourist routes, the square was busy, but mainly with locals. People frequented the cafés for morning coffee, in the shade of the huge plane tree that stood centre stage in the middle of the square, casting dappled, shady cover over almost the entire space. As the two of them entered and stood looking around for the right café – there were three to choose from – they spotted a man sitting alone at a group of tables. They guessed this was their man, Christopher. He looked to be in his forties, dark skin, a mass of curly hair. He sported a neatly trimmed curly beard. The other giveaway was that he was the only person in the square who was waving at them.

"Good morning, detectives," the man said as he stood to greet them with an outstretched hand. "I am so pleased to meet you both."

"Can we get something straight right from the start?" Lancaster said, with a smile, but quickly, whilst still holding onto the man's outstretched hand. "While we're both in France we're not detectives, we're just tourists. We're not meant to be here and you must tell no one about our visit, is that understood?"

"But why?"

"It doesn't matter why, Christopher. You just have to trust us and say nothing of this meeting, is that understood? Otherwise we both walk away."

"I will say nothing," the man said, looking serious. "Madame Mehemet has told me you think you have found my friend, Abdul. He is dead, is this true?"

Lancaster nodded. "I can confirm that a body we've found in England is Abdul. We've confirmed a DNA crossmatch with his mother. There's no doubt, it's him."

"Then this meeting will remain our secret. But I need coffee." Christopher waved to the waiter. "What will you drink, my friends?"

They ordered coffees and waited till the waiter had left. "So Christopher, what can you tell us about Abdul and where he worked before he left for the job in England?"

"There is lots to tell, but it covered too short a time. He should still be here now."

Christopher told them that he and Abdul had been friends in secondary school. They'd hung out at weekends and holidays. They played football in the park. Abdul wearing his Chelsea T-shirt. Although, like Abdul, Christopher was also of North African descent, also from Algeria. Whereas, the Mehemet family were Christians, Christopher's family were Muslim. Devout Muslim. Yet, Abdul never had a problem with that. In fact, sometimes, when Christopher came out of the mosque after Friday prayers, Abdul would be there sitting on the bench outside with the football, bouncing it on the ground, waiting for him. When Abdul left school, he went straight into a job helping in the kitchen of a restaurant in the main square, Les Maison Domitia. Abdul loved it. Worked hard and was well liked by the staff and the manager. He learnt quickly and could help with many of the jobs in the kitchen, even prepping food ready for the chef, Maurice. Later, when Christopher needed extra cash, Abdul put in a good word for him and got him a job, clearing tables and washing up. He was a good friend, Christopher liked him. He liked him a lot. At this point, conversation stopped as the waiter returned with their coffees, as soon as he'd left Christopher continued.

"After about a year working at the restaurant, Abdul started to stay behind after work. This was quite late at night, sometimes after midnight. He said Maurice was training him in the kitchen, helping him learn about being a chef. Sometimes I would say that I would wait for him but he always said no, I was to go home, that he would meet me the next day. We would go to the park and play football. I was jealous of his new friendship with Chef Maurice. I hated the fact that he would spend time with him and not with me, it upset me greatly."

Christopher stopped and drank some of his coffee. Lancaster's intuition was telling him that more revelations were on the brink of spilling from Christopher's lips. He was holding back from giving them something he'd kept secret for many years, giving him more time wouldn't hurt one little bit.

Christopher looked around him checking the coast was clear. He nearly spoke, then changed his mind, picked up his cup once more to take a sip. Some coffee froth stayed on his upper lip, he dabbed at it with his serviette. Then, looking around one more time, he came to a decision.

"You asked me to trust you, my friend! What I tell you must stay here with we three." Lancaster nodded, as did Vidêt.

"My problem was that I loved Abdul. I had fallen in love with him when we were at school. He was one year older than I, well not quite, but almost. I looked up to him. I admired him, respected him, and this turned to love. It was whilst I was with him that I realised that I was a homosexual, a gay. I do not know what you know of the ways of the Muslim religion but if my parents had ever found out they would possibly have had me killed. My father in particular, he would have never allowed me to bring such shame into his house. At best I would have been banished, but truly... I think he would rather that I died."

"Did Abdul know how you felt?" Lancaster asked quietly.

Christopher smiled. "Yes. One night, in my frustration, I told him. He just smiled and kissed me. He wrapped me in his arms for a moment and said he understood. He said he felt the same about me, but it was too dangerous, we would both get into trouble. He said once he had saved some money and got a better job, he would rent a place of his own, we could be together in secret. I said I was jealous of the time he spent with Maurice, I felt left out. He laughed and said that Maurice was part of his plan to make more money. You see, Maurice was also homosexual, well, he was bisexual. He was married with three children. He was respected, so he kept his sexuality a secret, he was paying Abdul for sex after work. Abdul was saving the money in a secret place so his parents would not find out. I said to him what he was doing was wrong and could be dangerous, but he just laughed at me and said he was OK, that he knew what he was doing."

"How long did his relationship with Maurice continue?"

"It went on for over two years. He worked with Maurice at the restaurant for nearly two years until Maurice landed the job as head chef at Les Hotel des Anglaise. When he left the restaurant, he took Abdul with him as his assistant. I was still clearing tables and washing dishes at Les Maison. Abdul had left me behind, he had changed. I still loved him, but I didn't respect him any longer. I think the tables had turned with Maurice; I think Abdul was either just asking for more money or maybe actually blackmailing Maurice. By the time they both left for the hotel, Abdul had new clothes, was staying late every night and we seldom played football anymore. He was always sleeping late, saying he was too tired. I got angry and said I thought we were going to be together, he kissed me, said it would all happen in good time, we needed to keep our love a secret for a little longer. I felt abandoned, lonely, I could tell no one else about how I felt. I was just so sad."

"Do you know if Abdul was still seeing Maurice when he disappeared?" Lancaster asked.

"I am sure of it. Abdul started spending money. He had new clothes, a new scooter, but he said he still did not have enough money to rent an apartment. He said Maurice had become a member of a private casino in the basement of the hotel, he would take Abdul there at night after work. Whenever Maurice won at the tables, he would give Abdul a share. I warned Abdul to look after himself. He was always looking tired and unwell. Some days, I would go to his house to call for him, but Madame Mehemet would say he had not got in till very late and was still asleep."

"Do you think Madame knew what was going on?" Lancaster asked.

Christopher laughed. "Not Madame, she is a lovely lady, but as you English would say 'there was always sunshine coming from Abdul's bottom'. She was so proud of him, working so hard. If only she had known what he was doing to get his money? It would have broken her heart. He even tried to get me to go to the casino one night. He smiled at me, tapped his nose and said, 'you may enjoy yourself'. I did not want to get involved with him and Maurice so I left and decided not to see Abdul again." Christopher stopped and sipped his now-cold coffee. "I tried to go out with girls, to try and forget about him, but it was no good, I preferred the touch and the body of a man. Women did little for me."

"Did you ever suspect there may be something else going on in the casino?"

Christopher laughed again. He looked around at the other people at the tables under the giant parasols and, making the judgment that all were out of earshot, he replied, "My friend, I know there was more to that club. I am sure it was a gay bar. A gay casino where local gays were meeting foreign tourists... I think... I think Abdul had become a male prostitute. I do not think he was the only one, I will speak no more of it... It saddens me too much."

"One last thing," Lancaster said. "Did Abdul ever use drugs?"

"No, well not that I ever knew. He had changed a lot, of course, but I just put that down to all the late nights and not enough sleep, why? Is that how he died?"

"No, it wasn't, it was just something I needed to ask. One other thing, what did you think had happened to Abdul when he disappeared?"

"I just thought he had moved to England and left us all behind. I was angry for a long time for him just leaving me here. I had no way of knowing where he was living. I waited, like Madame, for him to contact me, then I just got on with my life. But I have never forgotten him. When Madame Mehemet found me and told me what had happened, at first I was happy... happy that he had not forgotten me... he just could not tell me he was dead. Then, when she said you were looking for information about him, I knew I had to tell you what he was like and how he had been changed before he disappeared. You must find out what happened to him. He must be laid to rest here at home with no stain marking his passing, just justice."

"Do you happen to know if Maurice is still at the hotel?"

"No, he is retired now. But he still lives here in Narbonne," Christopher replied.

The two detectives looked at each other and Marie nodded to Lancaster. They both knew where they should go next. Christopher used his phone to track down an address for Maurice and gave it to Lancaster. The three shook hands, then went their separate ways, having first promised that they'd let Christopher know what had happened to his friend and when he was finally coming home. Lancaster had made the decision it would be better to contact Maurice using the telephone in their room at the hotel, rather than give away their mobile numbers. The call would be delicate, Vidêt would make it. It would be ideal if they could arrange a meeting but it was a long shot. The man may still have kept his homosexuality a secret even in this day and age of openness and inclusivity. There were still prejudices. If he'd kept his other life a secret before, why would he come-out now? After all, he had a wife and children, all grown up by now. It would be a tough thing for him to break the news to the whole family.

The midday melodic bells were ringing out their tuneful refrain as they chimed lunch for the French who worked around the Place de l'Hôtel de Ville. The pair walked across the square and down the side street that led to the Pont des Marchands. They crossed the canal and worked their way back to their hotel in the square. Back at the hotel Lancaster unlatched the balcony doors. They went out into the sunshine and settled onto the chairs.

"OK, let's see where we are with this. Did you manage to make enough notes from those conversations for us to be able to fill it all in when we get home?"

Vidêt read back a summary of what she had gotten down. It appeared she'd managed to cover virtually all the conversation verbatim. Lancaster was impressed with the detail.

"Brilliant, Marie," he said, with a hint of true admiration. "Next, I need you to telephone Maurice Durand. It could be an awkward moment for him, and you. If you get through to his wife, I should just call it a wrong number. I think the best way to get to him is just tell him you're a friend of Abdul Mehemet, see where it takes you. He may tell you to bugger off and put the phone down. But if he's involved in any way, he must at least be intrigued by your call after so much time has passed. But I'll leave it to you, it's your shout."

"Do you think he may be involved?"

"Well there's something going on, at least in the past. Something about that private casino. I can't get my head around it, but it worries me. At the time Abdul was being taken down into that club was just short of the time he came to the UK. I said back in England, we needed to go back to the beginning of Abdul's life to know how he ended up where he did. Today we've started to fill in those gaps. Our chef, Maurice, plays a part in that picture and I want to know just how much of a part."

A few minutes later, Vidêt was dialling the number. It rang several times before a rasping, breathless, male voice answered in French.

"Allo?" the voice said. Nothing more.

Vidêt spoke quickly in clear, clipped French. She asked if the man was Maurice, and a slightly gruff and breathless voice confirmed that it was. She announced her name was Marie and she knew of Abdul Mehemet.

A clever turn of phrase, thought Lancaster.

She didn't wait for a response, but then asked would it be possible to meet with him as she had news for him about Abdul. It was important to tell him face to face. She told him there was very little time as she had to fly back to the UK the next day. The voice on the other end of the phone didn't respond immediately, so Marie asked if he was still there then said again it was important to see him. After a few moments the voice reappeared on the other end of the line, again the man sounded breathless, almost tearful, and gave Marie his address. He said he was at home and asked if she could come and visit straight away. Marie replied to say that they'd be there within the hour. The call was terminated from the other end.

Vidêt relayed all this to Lancaster. They opened the town map and found where the man lived. It was in a suburb of Narbonne called La Mayole, to the south of the city, just where the city broke out into the flood plain, becoming rich agricultural land. They'd need to retrieve the car from the carpark and drive, it was too far to walk and anyway, Lancaster wanted to get there under their own steam. It was, after all, the only element of this meeting that he could control. Vidêt decided she'd change from the shorts into something a little better for an interview so started to undress. Lancaster grabbed the desk writing pad from the room and went onto the balcony. He sat at the table and wrote a quick note, which he then popped into a hotel envelope and sealed with a lick and a firm thumb. Vidêt reappeared on the balcony wearing a pair of light blue denim jeans and a short-sleeved blouse, a different pair of leather sandals on her feet. Lancaster agreed with the clothing change, himself opting for jeans, but kept the same shirt and the espadrilles.

"Right, are you ready for this? I'm not sure how deep we're getting in here, Marie, so say now if you're not happy with this meeting?"

"Sir, it's fine. I trust we keep each other's backs covered. We can play it by ear, but when we get there just tell me what you want to ask him. I can judge from his reply where to go next and when I get as far as I can, I will tell you then translate. Somehow, from his voice, I don't think we are heading to see the Godfather. This man sounds old and frail."

Lancaster was thinking, *at the end of the Godfather's life he was old and frail, but still having people killed.*

As the pair headed for the front door of the hotel Lancaster dropped the keys into reception and handed over the envelope he'd sealed, giving the receptionist a quick message and a fifty euro note as he did so. With Vidêt at the wheel, it took no more than thirty minutes to get out to the suburbs of La Mayole. The area was fertile, flood plain farmland, cut through by drainage channels, similar to the Somerset Levels in the UK. As if to echo this similarity, herons and little egrets were everywhere, those close to the road breaking into flight as they passed, to land again with feet in the water as soon as the car moved on. Here and there, corn fields were accompanied with rows of vines, turning green leaves to the sun, soaking it up in a photosynthesis frenzy. They passed large nurseries, acres of poly-tunnels. Beside them, fields laid out with row upon row of lettuce plants. Green and red leafy rosettes, neatly spaced and weed free. It was down the driveway towards one of these plastic covered conglomerations that the satnav directed them. No sooner had they done so, Lancaster told Vidêt to pull in and park up. Lancaster got out of the car and stood listening. He didn't like this. They were now well away from the populated part of the city and all was quiet, apart from the distant rumble of traffic speeding along the nearby A9, en route for Carcasonne in the west or Béziers to the east. Vidêt got out and stood listening as well.

"Are you thinking what I am thinking?" she asked.

"Only if you're thinking that this would be the ideal place to grow masses of dope. You're sure this is the right place?"

"The computer says yes," Vidêt replied.

Lancaster laughed at her turn of phrase. "Maurice did say he lived at his daughter's farm; I suppose you could call this a farm."

They got back into the car and drove slowly up the track until they reached a concrete yard. Vidêt turned the car around, parking it on the lane facing back the way they'd come in case they needed to make a quick exit. They got out and left the car unlocked and, taking the keys with them, walked toward the only house of any sorts that they could see. A long chalet, the sort you stay in at a holiday park. Before they got to it, a yapping mongrel came flying from a hiding place under the deck at the front of the building and ran around them just out of reach, barking in a high-pitched row that Lancaster wished would stop.

A voice from inside the open front door yelled, 'Sylvy, tais-toi!"

With that, Lancaster got his wish, the little dog disappeared back into its hiding place under the veranda. Lancaster was nervous about this location. If it was a working nursery, where were all the staff? *Most worrying of all,* he thought, *if it's a working nursery and the tunnels are filled with dope... where are all the guards?* There was no other option though, this had to be seen through. He turned quickly to Vidêt before they mounted the wooden steps to the front door.

"If this goes tit's up, get to the car and get the fuck out of here, understood? Get out and raise the alarm, is that understood?" Vidêt nodded her acceptance, though she had no intention of carrying it out unless they were both in the car.

They approached the front door. Lancaster reached up to knock, but a voice from the inside called out, "Entrez, Marie."

Vidêt touched Lancaster's arm and gave him a look that said hold back. Lancaster wasn't sure about this, but in a second Vidêt had slipped past and strode through the open door.

"Bonjour, Monsieur Durand, je suis Marie Vidêt, et voici

mon ami David," she said with a confident, breezy attitude. "Comment ça va?"

Lancaster stepped inside the door but stayed in the doorway where he could see out into the yard and into the room. He put his hand up to acknowledge the man, saying in a gruff sounding voice, "Bonjour, Monsieur, ça va?"

The man inside, whom they presumed was in fact Maurice Durand, was not a well man. The reason he'd not greeted them at the door became obvious as soon as their eyes adjusted to the darkness in the room. Maurice Durand sat on a large sheepskin rug, in a large, sturdy armchair. To one side of the chair stood two large metal cylinders that appeared to contain oxygen. From one of these, plastic tubes extended around the back of the armchair, curled, snake-like, over the man's shoulders, reaching up to join a piece of medical tubing that disappeared up either nostril. Maurice's feet were resting on a foot rest, kicked out from the bottom of the chair, or at least one foot was. The other didn't appear to exist. It was a job to tell quite where the left leg stopped as it was partially hidden by a blanket, but it didn't seem to exist below the knee. The man's face was gaunt. His eyes sunken, skin wrinkled and yellow, interspersed by grey and black blotches, making him look a bit like a toad. From where Lancaster stood in the doorway, he could hear the rhythmic click of some piece of kit behind the chair that was assisting the man's breathing. Every time Lancaster heard the man's rasping inhalations they were accompanied by a double click and a slight hiss from behind the chair. Lancaster thought this interview had come in the nick of time; *Maurice didn't look like he was going to be long for this world.*

"Marie, I think I can leave this to you but feed back to me from time to time. I'll keep watch on the yard from here. If I say move, we go."

Vidêt moved across the room and shook the man's limp, yellow hand. A compassionate gesture that brought a brief smile to the man's face.

"Abdul, que s'est-il passé?" the man said.

Vidêt sat on a stool beside the man's chair and broke into a steady stream of French. At one point Maurice had tears in his eyes, but it didn't appear there was enough life left in those eyes for him to break into a full tearful flow. Vidêt continued talking, with occasional interruptions from Maurice. Maurice looked saddened by the news he'd been given. He'd visibly shrunk in his chair since they arrived. Marie reached out her hand to hold his. Lancaster wished he'd an understanding of the language. He'd no doubt she was in control of this situation, but he felt so left out, this frustrated him no end.

Vidêt and Maurice chatted for almost an hour. Once, Vidêt stopped to pour the man water from a jug on the table beside the chair. Lancaster had settled into his position against the doorframe when, from the corner of one eye, he saw movement from across the yard. From the gable end of one building two men appeared, both big and looking in the direction of the car. They started to walk towards it when one of them spotted Lancaster standing in the open doorway. They turned in his direction, making a beeline towards the doorway.

"Brace yourself, Marie, we've company coming." He quickly turned to block the doorway and meet the men face on.

Vidêt spoke quickly to Maurice and stood to join Lancaster. By the time she was in the doorway the two men were coming up the steps with a purpose.

"Qui êtes-vous," the first man said, then shouted, "Maurice, ça va?"

"Oui Stefan, oui, ça va, ça va bien mes amis, pas de problème," Maurice said through a rasping breath requiring multiple clicks from the apparatus.

"Oui, nous sommes amis des Maurice, pas de problème mes amis," Vidêt said through a smile, holding out a hand for a greeting.

Stefan took the hand and shook it then reached across toward Lancaster who quickly forced a smile and raised his hand, but braced in case it was a trick to get in close. They shook hands and Vidêt stepped aside to allow the man to peer inside at the old man, as if for confirmation that he was, in fact, there. The man gave a wave to Maurice and the two men had a quick conversation before Stefan pulled back from the doorway and with a wave to Lancaster and Vidêt, went down the steps and across the yard to disappear into one of the tunnels. Lancaster felt his heart rate coming back down, but with a shiver of sweat trickling between his shoulder blades. He felt they'd pushed their luck far enough; it was time to go.

"Do you have enough?" he asked of Vidêt.

"As you would say, we have flesh for the bones."

The two detectives said their goodbyes and both shook Maurice's clammy, yellow, outstretched hand. As Vidêt shook the man's hand the old man put his other hand over hers and gave it a firm and fond shake. *There is no doubt,* Lancaster thought, *there is a tear in the eye of this aged man.* Lancaster, although feeling slightly guilty, couldn't wait to find out what had been said. They returned to the car and Vidêt got behind the wheel, when Lancaster turned to clip in his seatbelt, he noticed a tear in her eye.

"Are you OK, Marie?"

"Yes," she replied putting the car into gear and pulling away down the track. "But can we wait until we're back in our room before we go over it all, I need a drink."

They drove back into the centre of the city in virtual silence, enjoying the breeze that came in through the open windows. There'd been a stuffy hospital smell about Maurice's room and it hadn't been to their liking. They reached the hotel without incident. Lancaster picked up the key to their room from reception and retrieved the envelope he'd deposited. He also asked for two brandies with ice and some savoury snacks to be sent up to their room. They'd missed lunch. The pair walked into their room and opened up the doors to the balcony. Vidêt went straight into the bathroom and Lancaster had no sooner got out onto the balcony when room service arrived with the drinks and a selection of olives, small chunks of tomato, filled, doughy bread and a big bowl of salty, handmade crisps. Lancaster took them out onto the balcony and settled into one of the chairs in the sunshine, took a first sip of the cold brandy and threw an olive into his mouth. Outside the balcony, the squadrons of swifts screamed across the sky, diving out of the clouds, skimming across the tops of trees in the square, scooping up unseen insects by the beakful with every flypast. Down in the square, under the tree cover, out of sight of the birds above, the tables were still full of late lunch clientele and early drinkers. He popped another olive in his mouth and grabbed a handful of the crisps just as Vidêt rejoined him and took the other chair. She took a couple of sips from the chilled brandy and grabbed a couple of olives before pulling on her dark glasses again and sitting back.

"So, what did he have to say?"

"Although what he told me helps fill in more of the general picture, I think you may be disappointed with the content, but I will tell you as best I can, then commit it to paper."

Vidêt went on to recount the conversation with Maurice with as much detail as she could remember.

Yes, Maurice was gay, always had been, despite his attempt at marriage to give an air of normality to his visible life, even having two children, who he loved, by the way. Yes, he and Abdul were lovers during the late 1990s. Yes, Abdul blackmailed him from almost the very beginning; although he started by just saying that if he stayed late at the restaurant he would want paying. Then he said he wanted overtime rates, then he just asked outright for money otherwise he would have to tell his parents, even the owner of the restaurant about what was going on. But, by then, Maurice loved the boy and didn't mind paying him. They planned to get a flat together as a secret rendezvous. He'd asked Marie several times about Abdul and how he was. Eventually she could hold off no longer and had told him they'd found his body. That he'd been murdered.

Maurice had asked the obvious questions. Who and why? She'd told him they couldn't give more information at this stage. He'd asked if he'd still been with 'm'Lord'; when she'd asked who he meant he became bitter. Apparently, there was an English lord who'd frequented the casino. He'd taken a shine to Abdul not long after they'd both moved to work at Les Hotel des Anglaise. Maurice had worked hard to persuade the owners to take Abdul on as well as him, when he'd been offered the head chef job there. He knew he didn't dare leave Abdul behind. He was sure he'd soon have moved on to be with somebody else. Then he wouldn't be able to keep his mouth shut and Maurice's secret would be out. Everybody now says being gay was legal back then, why were you so worried? But if you'd kept a secret all those years it was almost impossible to 'come out', as they say. So Maurice felt trapped by the situation.

He'd become a member of the private casino, his biggest mistake. Biggest mistake by far. He was encouraged to join and bring his friend Abdul; initially Maurice had a lot of luck, he won big several times, felt confident at the tables and the wheel. Then, one night, every throw of the dice went against him. Every choice on the wheel bounced into the wrong slot, every card took him over the number. It was a disaster; by the end of that night he was thousands of francs in debt to the house. The manager said it would be fine, he was a good customer and a good chef. He would be taken care of. The next day, one of the owners of the club asked to see him. Maurice only knew him by sight, but he did know the man was an English lord. Everyone knew him as m'Lord. He said the debt could be paid off bit by bit. They didn't need to make a formal arrangement, they were all members, friends. But a debt was a debt, after all. Maurice was relieved and agreed. But then he'd go to the casino and win twice and lose three. The debt was never going to be cleared. It was only a matter of time before his wife found out how much he'd lost and how deep in debt he was. Then, one evening, m'Lord had asked to see him. Maurice was scared, but had to go, m'Lord offered him a way out. He said if he gave up Abdul, his debt would be cleared. Maurice, sadly, didn't have to think for long. He loved Abdul and hoped that sometime later they'd be together again. But he needed desperately to get out of debt. M'Lord had taken to the boy and wanted him for himself, but he wasn't prepared to compete for affections in the normal way. He bought Abdul. For release of a debt. Like bartering for a slave. He wanted him for his own plaything and would stop at nothing to get him, so the deal was done. Vidêt had shown him a picture on her phone of Sir Philip, the one from the obituary. He'd recognised him immediately. Later, when Maurice had told Abdul the terrible news and how devastated he felt about betraying him, Abdul had been excited to think that 'm'Lord' wanted him. Maurice had said they could still meet in secret, but Abdul had laughed in his face. He said why would he want to 'sleep with a chef' when he could 'be with a lord'.

The next day, Abdul stopped coming to work. Maurice heard he'd moved to m'Lord's house in the country among the vineyards. Maurice had been broken-hearted and broken financially, although his debt had been written off, he'd still lost all his savings and owed money to others in the city that still needed to be paid off. He began selling himself to other customers at the casino and the hotel, always hoping that Abdul would come back to him one day. Then he heard that Abdul had been seen around the city wearing smart new clothes, telling everybody he was going to England, a job waiting for him with a big pay packet. He'd come back someday and tell everyone about it. The rumours in the casino were that he was going to England with m'Lord. Maurice had never heard from him again.

It took many years, but Maurice got himself back on a financial even keel, but it had come at a cost. His wife of thirty years had left him. He'd become unwell, finally diagnosed as being HIV positive. The doctors now said he had terminal cancer and had little time left in this world. So far, he'd proved them wrong by two years, but part of him wished he hadn't. He didn't really know why he was bothering to stay alive. The only thing Maurice was trying to stay alive for now was to wait until Abdul came home, so he could pay his respects to the boy he loved and had sold into slavery.

"So, Maurice hasn't led us to any great drug gang or conspiracy, he was just a sad man who loved a boy and lost him and who then disappeared.

"But again, Marie, I reuse an old analogy. Maurice was an avenue we had to go down. A leaf we had to turn. We've done that and the man's gone from 'possibly being involved in the death of Abdul' to, in my mind anyway, the 'not involved'. Each time we turn these leaves we learn more about our victim and the lives of those around him. In the end, it will build us a complete picture of our victim's life and eventually give us a reason for why he died. We'll find who did this and if he, or she, is still alive we'll bring them to justice. If nothing else, Marie, we'll send that body home here to Narbonne for his mother and his lovers."

"May I ask, what was in the envelope that you left at reception?"

"It was DCI Craven's number, I left instructions that if we'd not returned to the hotel by six p.m. this evening, they should open the envelope, if they did the letter said to call the number on the paper and tell him we needed help and gave the last address we were at. So I'm just bloody glad the car didn't break down while we were out. Now, Marie, I don't know about you, but I really don't feel like going to Madame Mehemet's this evening and having to talk about her boy. I could do with a few hours off. So, would you put on your most apologetic voice and phone her? Tell her something important came up and we can't make it, but will be in touch soon. I'm off for a shower, then a lie down, then we'll go out for dinner, just the two of us, on our own."

CHAPTER NINE

Lancaster walked beside Vidêt in the warmth of the evening. Across the square and down side streets till they got to the canal footpath. They continued alongside the canal, crossing over at a different bridge, coming out into yet another cobbled courtyard. On one side of the courtyard was a restaurant, large white parasols giving shade to partially-filled tables gathered beneath. Around the central square, large, white-painted wooden planters, in which big evergreen olive and orange trees grew, gave the space a definitive Mediterranean feel.

On the righthand side of the square was a long red brick wall. A pair of huge terracotta pots containing trimmed olive trees denoted an entrance, between them, an arched, open doorway, beside which was a restaurant sign and framed menu. Approaching the doorway, they saw a delightful tree-filled garden, a dozen or so tables scattered beneath. Through the branches of the trees, strings of coloured light bulbs illuminated the scene, giving a touch of the fairy garden. The decision was made instantly and the pair strolled inside. The waiter confirmed they had a table for two. He had them seated within seconds, menus in hands, the first Ricard's on ice on the way.

The couple had spoken little since Lancaster woke from his afternoon sleep. When he awoke, Vidêt had been reclining on one of the loungers on the balcony, sunglasses on, fast asleep. He'd left her there and taken another shower to wake himself up. He'd dressed in a clean, short-sleeved shirt and a pair of lightweight chinos, feeling an evening meal warranted something more than shorts. The espadrilles went well with the chinos, however, so were retained. When Vidêt had dressed and come out onto the balcony to join him she'd appeared wearing a stunning, simple, black, short, cotton dress that set off her tanned legs and arms. She'd sat on one of the balcony chairs and pulled on a pair of black, plain, strappy, high heeled sandals which, whether by accident or design, allowed her tattoo to be framed by the gap in the strapping, drawing your eye straight to it. Lancaster was pleased to find that, despite his initial thoughts when she'd appeared on the balcony, she did, of course, look stunning. Tonight, he was so frustrated by the events of the day and this whole case in particular, and he had so many thoughts and ideas wallowing around in his head that he found he'd no improper thoughts towards his colleague this evening whatsoever. He just wanted to eat. Well maybe eat and think. Well maybe eat, think and drink. But he would have to go steady on the latter.

The two detectives sat quietly, sipping at the cold pastis. The dappled shade under the trees, cool and mesmerising as the evening breeze gently moved the leaves, making shadows dance and flicker. It was still light, so the effect of all the strings of lights hanging above and about them was not being fully felt. Nevertheless, it was an idyllic little spot to eat.

Eventually, just after their starters arrived and the waiter wished them bonn appétit, Vidêt broke the silence.

"I have to ask, sir, what are your thoughts now about this southern connection?"

Lancaster had been deep in thought for the last ten minutes. He finished the mouthful of Salade Niçoise, swallowed and took a sip from the chilled glass of rosé he'd poured from the pitcher on the table.

"Well, my thoughts are, when we get back to Plymouth, DCI Craven is not going to be a happy bunny. Between you and me, I think he was convinced the Stottard family was tied up in drugs. When I gave him the links of one dead body, the family connections, with not only the home of our victim. but also the last place he was known to have worked, he was virtually rubbing his hands with glee. He'd no problem at all with us coming down here and busting not only some drug cartel, but also the high and mighty Stottard family. When I go home and tell him it's been about a whole series of gay romances, he'll be pretty pissed off. It will, of course, be my fault for coming up with such a daft idea and it'll be me who'll have to carry the can."

"But we have found out more by coming here than we ever knew before, sir," Vidêt said in support.

"Can we keep it to Christian names, Marie, just for the duration? It makes this visit feel more like a holiday, I haven't had a holiday in years. God knows when I'll get the chance to take another one so let's drop the sir and stick to the David, OK?"

"Two weeks ago," Vidêt said, taking a sip from her glass,

"we had a bog body that nobody knew existed. We now know he was not ancient. We know he was murdered and when. We know his name. His mother. Where he lived, where he worked. We know he was gay. Which is more than his mother knew. We know, and have met, at least two of his former lovers. Also, we know for a fact it was Sir Philip who took Abdul to England. We have a direct link between him and the victim, whereas before, the link was circumstantial speculation, a purchase of a belt from a tailor. We go back to England with more flesh on this boy's bones than he had when he was dug up out of that bog. All we have to do is find out what went wrong between Abdul and his new lover and, did it get him killed?"

Lancaster had finished his salad. He sat back, took another sip of rosé and caught the droplet of condensation that dripped from the glass with his serviette before it landed on his chinos. He thought for a moment. He liked this woman. She was too smart to be a sergeant. She was, of course, right, he'd been wallowing in the mire of despair, caused by not being capable of fulfilling his bosses wish. Coming home with the big one under his belt. But Vidêt was correct, they'd found out a lot. Just not what had been wanted? Either way, it was a lot, and it would never have come to them if they'd stayed at home.

"You're right, Marie. You're definitely right. We've found out a lot. We've also found that the shining light of the Mehemet family was not, in fact, quite so bloody squeaky clean as his mother would have everyone believe. We know he lied to his parents, albeit by default, not telling them he was gay. Without a doubt, he was leading a double life one his parents had no idea he was living. He deserted his first lover.

Left him believing that one day they'd share an apartment, that they'd be back together, despite the fact Abdul appeared to have moved on to someone else. We also know he blackmailed his next lover, Maurice, kept taking money from him until the next new man in his life appeared, Sir Philip. If he tried that same trick when he got to England there's a chance Sir Philip, or people around him with interests at stake, had him taken care of. There's also a chance that, despite her protesting shock and surprise at finding her husband was gay, maybe Lady Pamela knew all along. If Abdul had started threatening their orderly lives with a touch of blackmail, maybe she'd had him topped. So, despite not finding any links to organised crime and drugs trafficking, we've put the Stottards and Abdul in a much closer proximity and more completely linked than they were previously. We know from Abdul's history he probably made enemies with ease, now we need to get home and pick up the trail there. Somebody knows Sir Philip brought Abdul into the country. I think we need to be talking to those people who were around Sir Philip at the time."

"Where are you thinking of going with this next then?"

It has always been like this, Lancaster thought. Time and time again whatever he was working on, whether it was as a child building model planes or as a student working on an essay. He'd reach a point where none of it made any sense. There'd come this same moment, where he couldn't work out what the point of it all was. He'd be ready to call it quits, walk away; set fire to the half-built plane, screw up the paper work, stick it in the bin. Give up on the case and tell Craven it wasn't going to happen. But he'd always been able to put whatever it was down, step away, leave it for five minutes, a day, a week and then, in that space of no pressure once you'd given up, a clarity returned. The picture reformed. The instructions came clear and a new direction would metamorphose before his very eyes.

"I'll tell you where we're going with this, Marie," he said with sudden new conviction. "Tomorrow before we get on the plane, leaving as little time as possible for him to think about it, I will put through a call to Craven. I intend being brief, keep him engaged. I shan't lie, I'll tell him as little as possible as obviously it would be too dangerous to tell him too much over the phone, wouldn't it? But I intend to tell him the truth. We've a definitive link between the lord and the victim, can't go into detail. That should keep him engaged for the moment, at least. I'll inform him that when we land at Bristol, we plan to hire a car and drive straight to London. We'll book into a cheap hotel, then we intend to visit some old friends of the man in question to gain more information. When we're done, we'll drive back to Bristol, pick up our car and head for home."

"Why do we not just take our car?"

"Congestion charges, young Marie. If it clocks up with the Met or Traffic that a car registered to Devon & Cornwall Constabulary is trundling around in central London, they're going to want to know why nobody asked them first."

"Ah, cunning. Who do you plan to visit first?"

"First, Marie... I haven't got a clue," Lancaster replied, as the waiter arrived to clear away the debris from the finished starters. Lancaster tapped the pitcher to ask for a refill. "But we've plenty of time tomorrow plus time on the plane and in a hotel Friday night to do research. We need to find his old

Etonian friends, though I suspect they'll close ranks when they know the police are sniffing around one of their old boys. It's still worth trying. There must be something in the gossip columns from back then. Some journalist that had an inclination of His Lordship's inclinations. I think we'll just go straight to his old home at Dolphin Court and see who remembers him. See if anybody has any fond memories they'd like to share. Ah, brilliant! I see steak and chips on the horizon, I suddenly feel starving again." He was up and running on all four cylinders again, possibly even six.

"Will we still take a look at the Stottard chateau?"

"I think so. I don't think we'll get anything from it, but I'm nosy. We know Abdul moved there before going to England. I think it would be fair to actually go and see the place. At least we'll have a mental picture of his last footfall before he left for the UK. If there's nobody about, we might get a couple of exterior shots for the file. Then we can drop the car off and still have time before our flight leaves late afternoon."

The pair finished their meal with nothing more than casual chitchat about their lives outside of the day-to-day police work they were involved in. Vidêt spoke of a Breton dance group she went to in Liskeard, by coincidence, twinned with the town of Quimperlé, not far from her home. The dance group practiced the dances from her homeland of Brittany and played music from the bands she knew back there. From time to time, she returned to Benodet or at least the area around there. She went mainly for the Fest-noz. The Breton festivals filled with local music and dance where people of all ages joined hands and danced the circle dances of the region together late into the night. She had to explain all of this to Lancaster in detail as he'd no idea that Brittany considered itself to be a state in its own right and part of France as secondary. It had its own traditions, dance, music, even language, similar to that of the Cornish. She'd identified herself with the Cornish people as soon as she'd arrived in Plymouth, moving quickly to the other side of the river Tamar to a flat in Torpoint, admittedly still within eyesight of Plymouth, a quick ferry ride away across the river. She was still in Cornwall, it felt more like home.

Lancaster spoke of his music collection. Surprised that Marie had heard of many of the bands he listened to. The Eagles, Steeley Dan, Marshall Tucker and Lynyrd Skynyrd. Most of his musical taste was inherited from his parent's. When growing up, the house had been filled with his parent's friends and there was always music being played. It was never the kind of house where the kids were hidden away whilst grown-ups played. He'd always been encouraged to meet grown-ups on his own level. He'd joined in. Been included in conversations around politics, music, art and literature from an early age, so it was the era of their music he reacted to, loved the most. He spoke of his joy of walking; he loved the moors, the coastal footpaths. All-in-all he gloried in the South West countryside in all its forms. It was a walker's paradise.

The two finished their meal with a brandy before the walk home. Lancaster thinking what a stunningly simple restaurant that had been, and what a perfect meal with good company and conversation. He realised just how much he'd missed something as simple as a good meal shared with a friend, rather than lunch to discuss a case. Although they'd talked of the case, Lancaster felt it had been constructive, valuable, fed into by both sides. The most enjoyable part of the evening had been finding out so much of his partner's life, her likes and dislikes. Though coming from different cultures, they did in fact have much more in common than he'd first believed. They strolled down the side street, away from the brightly lit square, emerging onto the canal side by the bridge.

"It's no good, I'm just not used to wearing heels. It has been a long time. These are coming off. I would rather walk in bare feet." Vidêt plonked herself down on a bench and started undoing the straps of her sandals. She had the first one off and was working on the second when Lancaster spotted the three figures emerging from the deep shadow of trees at the corner of the street. Initially, he wasn't unduly concerned, he could see they were teenagers, all wearing hoodies. One riding a little stunt bike. It looked OK when he was standing, but when he sat on the saddle, he looked ridiculous. It was when he saw them huddle in a little three-way group to talk, that the hairs on the back of his head began the customary tingle of fight or flight mode kicking in.

"Marie, don't look down the canal side," Lancaster said, then watched as she automatically did so. "I think we're about to get mugged by three kids."

"Bugger!" Vidêt said. Which, when said with a strong French accent, did, in fact, make Lancaster laugh. Just then, the three youths made their move and arrived beside them at the bench. The one on the bike hopping it from side to side annoyingly. The biggest one of them spoke first.

"Allo," he said, smiling, whilst his annoying friend hopped

about on his mini bike. "English?" he asked.

"Non. Je suis Breton," Vidêt interjected before Lancaster could speak. Finishing the unstrapping of her second sandal she stood. "Quel est problèm?

"Oh, Bretton." With that, all three giggled like the schoolboys they were. "Vous-avez de l'argent Breton, bitch," the big lad said, raising a laugh from the other two.

What happened next took Lancaster by surprise. With a click, the big lad produced a switchblade knife that shone briefly in the dim glow of the streetlights but, before he had time to use it, Vidêt swung her sandals at him, using the straps to hold onto. Then, more by accident than design, she managed to catch the knife first time in the straps and ripped it from his grasp, leaving him empty handed, a silly look on his face. The blade dropped to the floor with a cheap-sounding clatter. At the same time, Vidêt swung her bare leg upwards. Her foot connected with the big lad's groin, which took all the wind from his sails. He went down on his knees like a brick through water and stayed on his knees, gasping for breath. No longer the big man of the group. Lancaster spotted the other standing lad drop to his knees in search of the knife, but a sideways kick to the face from Lancaster hit hard. The boy screamed and held onto his bleeding nose. Meanwhile, bike boy was disappearing in the opposite direction, peddling as fast as his legs could manage on a bike that was two sizes too small.

"We'd better get out of here before we draw more attention," Lancaster said. He picked up the knife with the corner of his shirt so as not to leave any prints, just in case it should ever be used again, then threw it sidewise into the canal where it sank out of sight beneath the dark, murky water. Leaving the two lads on their knees, sobbing, the pair started to run across the bridge. As they did so, Lancaster instinctively reached out and grabbed hold of Vidêt's hand, they both started to laugh as the adrenaline cooled and flight kicked in. The pair ran over the bridge still holding hands, along the canal towards their own square, not stopping until they arrived under the plane trees, still laughing hysterically, still holding hands. People on the tables nearest them turned to see what the commotion was, but immediately returned to their food once they saw it was just two young lovers laughing together. After all, this was France. It was a natural occurrence.

As the pair stopped to catch their breath in the shadow cast by the trees in the square, Lancaster instinctively pulled Vidêt toward him and kissed her full on the lips. In an instant response, Vidêt wrapped her other arm around his neck and returned his kiss with ardour and an intensity neither of them had expected. After a heated moment, Lancaster broke off the kiss and looked down at her.

"Marie... I'm so sorry—" he began to say.

Vidêt put her finger across his lips and said, "Ssh." Then, still holding tight to his hand she walked towards the hotel. They picked up the key from reception and went up the stairs to their room, Vidêt holding onto Lancaster's hand all the time. He allowed it, it felt warm, natural, and sensual. He knew they shouldn't be doing this, whatever 'this' was going to be, but he was in a dreamlike state. He couldn't let go of her hand, didn't want her to release his. She unlocked the door and they entered. With the curtains at the balcony doors still wide open the room was lit by dappled streetlight coming in from the square, filtered by the leafy canopy. Without turning on the light, Vidêt lead Lancaster to the bed and without any kind of resistance from him, pushed him gently backwards onto it. Then, placing her knees either side of him, she leant forward and the two kissed again, only this time, gently... at first.

A couple of hours later, Vidêt came out of the bathroom to find Lancaster sitting on the balcony wrapped in a blanket, drinking a glass of cold water. Another stood on the table waiting for her. Vidêt grabbed the bathrobe and wrapped this around her as the air now held a chill. Lancaster looked at her. Her short black hair in disarray, a flush of colour to her face. She'd curled up in the chair, wrapping the robe around her body, her tanned legs still protruded and hanging off the seat, the tan shining in the street lights. He knew he had to say something, but didn't want to break the spell they'd been under for the last couple of hours. They'd made love several times. Something Lancaster didn't think was ever going to be possible again. They'd made love gently, slowly, sensually. In tune with each other. They'd made love passionately, rampant and rough. He could feel the sting of the bites on his shoulder as testament to this, he'd enjoyed it nevertheless. Still, he knew something had to be said.

"Marie—" he started in a serious voice.

"David, let me speak first. Please," Vidêt said, cutting him off quickly. "We said yesterday that we are both grown-ups. We have both been there before and both come home with the T-shirts. I do not make friends easily. When we are back in

Plymouth, I am a foreign girl in a foreign land, I have been too busy doing my job to meet many people in England. Those that I have are mainly on the force, to be honest I would rather leave them at the station, present company the exception. You know me well enough to know that I speak my mind and say it out loud, which is probably one of the reasons I am still a sergeant. Well, that and the fact that I am, of course, French and female and they don't want to promote me over an Englishman. But all that said... I have not had sex with anybody for over a year. This evening we drank a lot of wine. We drank several brandies and nearly got mugged. All-in-all, I think that after an evening like that, having sex cannot be as bad as lying in the gutter with a knife wound and no wallet. If I was going to have sex with somebody, I would rather it had been with you than anybody else, but there is no commitment. We work together, I trust you. We have each other's backs... but that is where it ends. I say nothing, you say nothing... that... is where it ends... OK?"

Lancaster smiled. "You do realise that what I've done is a sackable offence for a senior officer?"

"Which bit of what we did?" Vidêt said, pretending to be serious. "The kissing, the undressing, the biting, or the—"

"Stop it, Marie," Lancaster said with a laugh. "This is serious."

"David, no, it is not. Tomorrow, we fly back to England. I go back to calling you sir. Neither of us needs to write up a report. We don't need bullet points, we don't need to present a spreadsheet or a graph back at the office. Though personally, I think it would have scored quite high on a graph, even if I say so myself."

Lancaster laughed at this last comment.

"David, we are both away from the office in unusual circumstances and let us just be honest, we both needed tonight. I, for one, have absolutely no regrets, none whatsoever. Now I must go to bed, it's late. Will you stay out here and slash your wrists or will you come to bed also?"

Lancaster looked up at her as she stood, holding out her hand to him. She was, yet again, quite right. They'd both needed that and they were both adults. What's more... the night was still young...

The following morning, they rose and took it in turn to shower and dress, Lancaster was pleased to feel there appeared no change in their relationship. Vidêt had showered first. When he emerged and got dressed for the day he found her on the balcony again, dressed in the jeans shorts and T-shirt of the previous day, sitting crossed legged on one of the chairs scrolling through her iPad and making a list in her notebook. He realised she was researching Sir Philip's social circle of friends, trying to find some of his old Etonian school chums. She'd also tracked down a separate short list of residents at Dolphin Court who were resident in the block at the same time as Sir Philip prior to his death, who were still in residence now. Lancaster was impressed. He was also impressed, and suitably pleased, to find there was no mention of last night whatsoever. No cuddles, hugs, kisses or holding of hands. He was pleased about this. Also, slightly disappointed. He'd enjoyed last night immensely.

He'd had the occasional drunken free-for-all that had sated his sexual appetite temporarily, but nothing of the intensity of last night's couplings. However, they'd both agreed last night that this was a one-off and wouldn't be mentioned again, though Lancaster was pretty sure they also both knew that at some stage in the future the one-off could well become a two-off, maybe even a three. The pair had to vacate the room by eleven a.m. and planned to lunch in Salles-d'Aude on the way to Béziers. They packed. Double-checked the whole room between them, to make sure they'd left nothing. Just to be on the safe side, they also used the towels to clean down everywhere, removing their fingerprints. Lancaster felt they should take no chances in case anything cropped up in the future. It was better to be safe than sorry and it didn't take them long. They signed out, handed in the key, reclaimed the car from the underground carpark and headed out of the city, both with an unmentioned twinge of sadness at departure. They'd completely enjoyed this short break away from Plymouth and the office.

The drive out of the city into the vineyard areas was easy, they joined the A9 in the direction of Béziers and the airport. They took a slip road off quite early as the Stottard's country home was tucked into vineyard-covered land to the West of Salles-d'Aude, very near the big wine producer, Chateau Pech-Celeyran, but there didn't appear to be a simple way to get to it other than through the back lanes. The Stottard chateau itself was almost within the town of Salles-d'Aude. When it had been built it would have most certainly stood out proud and visible, and alone. Square on to the world, surrounded by its own vineyards, now long since traded away. It was perched on the edge of the town, partially surrounded by trees. Lancaster knew from accessing satellite imagery, (*There is no privacy in the world anymore,* he'd thought) that within the enclosing walls the complex had several large estate buildings. A large garden with an assortment of mature trees as testament to the age of construction, and a very large swimming pool. The satnav got them virtually to the gates. It was easy enough after that to find the place. It was the house you couldn't see. Surrounded by a six-foot high, red brick wall. They drove right past the place once, just to see if there were any gaps in the armour, but none could be seen from the car. They'd have to get out and scout around to find a weak point.

On the second pass, they had a chance to look down the short drive and through the large, ornate, wrought iron double gates to get the only semi-clear view they could find. Lancaster suggested Vidêt park just off the road in a space beyond the house. Pop the bonnet and pretend the car was broken down. At least, speaking French, she could explain away a broken-down car to any suspecting passer-by. He was going to have a quick scout round the perimeter wall to see if he could get a view inside or a sense of the security around the place. Mainly for nosiness' sake, if truth be told. Within fifteen minutes, he was back at the car. He'd skirted down one side of the wall, turned the corner along the long back wall. He'd watched for a while to see if there was anyone about. Seeing no movement, he'd quickly travelled the full length of the rear wall until the next right angle to turn back up towards the road when he realised that this was as far as he was going to get. Running down the full length of this wall, from the road, then continuing off into the distance of the woodland was a drainage ditch. Three feet deep, five feet wide, and full of brown, scummy water. Between it and the wall was a dense undergrowth of bramble and nettles. He'd turned back and returned to the car with no visible signs of access to the property to be seen, other than the main gates.

"I have an idea," Vidêt said. "Why don't we just drive up to the gates, ask for directions or water or something? At least we will get a look inside the actual gateway."

"Well done, Marie," Lancaster replied and parodying an old TV programme he still laughed at, followed it with, "I wondered when somebody would think of that."

Lancaster dropped the bonnet and Vidêt drove them straight up to the gates, stopping just short of them.

"May I suggest you leave this to me, sir?" she said with a smile.

She jumped out of the car and walked right up to the gates. Beside the gate was a large brass bell pull which she pulled with relish. The sound of a tinkling bell heard just inside the gateway; she waited. She was getting ready to pull it again when she heard the sound of footfall on gravel. A middle-aged man wearing traditional garb of the French working man, blue overalls, appeared inside the gate. Vidêt had a brief conversation with him, the man pointed back down the road in the direction of the way they'd come. It was obvious from the sign language that he was giving her instructions of some sort. She obviously asked him something, then pointed back at Lancaster sitting in the car. Lancaster waved at him casually. Vidêt returned to the car, reached inside and popped the bonnet again.

"The nice man at the gate has given us proper directions

to the Chateau Pech-Celeyran vineyards, darling, we appear to be at the wrong house. Quelle surprise. Also, he will find a container for us to have some water for our overheating car. What a nice man, yes?"

Lancaster had to smile. He remembered passing the sign for Chateau Pech-Celeyran a couple of miles back, getting lost would be an obvious excuse for stopping here for directions. Lancaster got out and pretended to open the water cap, knowing full well it was too hot to be doing anything of the kind. Meanwhile, the friendly worker reappeared in the gateway carrying a watering can, presumably filled with water. Vidêt explained the motor was still too hot to take the cap off the radiator, and as it was so hot in the car, would it be possible to come inside the gateway, sit out of the sun for a couple of minutes till the engine cooled? The friendly, blue-overalled workman was only too happy to oblige. He ushered them inside where, on their left-hand side, stood a small cottage, its back wall formed from the estate's brick wall. It had windows to either side in the gable wall along with several windows to the front, facing into the garden. The cottage had probably been a gatekeeper's home in the days when there would have been carriages trundling into the courtyard. The roof of this single-storey cottage overhung the front of the building, extended out by at least ten feet, forming a covered veranda. To the front, a wooden table and several sturdy chairs, to which their new friend drew their attention, asking them to sit. Lancaster got the feeling the guy was glad to have somebody to talk to.

A circular driveway formed just inside the gate, curled around a neatly cut semi-circular lawn, on one side of which stood a large cedar tree. Its lower branches removed so the girth of the trunk could be seen in all its glory, also to give height for vehicles to pass underneath and pull up at the front of the house. The chateau itself was built in the classic style of the South of France. Not huge, but built with classic proportions and style. Large centrally placed front doors accessed the ground floor. Three windows to either side, themselves framed by deep blue, painted wooden shutters. The first floor was larger than the ground floor, which supported a blue-painted balcony that ran right the way around the whole building as far as Lancaster could see. Again, the wooden rails were painted the same blue and matched by the shutters for the first-floor windows. There was a second floor, but most of this and its accompanying windows were constructed within the roof-space, complete with little pitched, red tile roofs. Again, these windows were shuttered using the same blue-painted shuttering. Lancaster sat looking at the front of the building across the lawn. It was an impressive place to be a holiday home, he hoped it was used often; it needed to be.

"C'est magnifique le chateau," Lancaster said in his best French accent, looking to Vidêt to continue.

Vidêt broke into conversation with the man and he readily replied. Soon the two were chatting away like old friends. After a while, the man stood up and gestured for them to follow and they headed off for a guided tour of the grounds. To the right of the drive and opposite the huge cedar tree there was a blue-painted wooden door which gave them access to the main formal parts of the rear garden. It was beautiful. A pair of well-manicured lawns ran either side of a gravel pathway that stretched from the large rear patio all the way down the garden to a stepped down area that housed the big swimming pool Lancaster had seen on the satellite image. At one end of the pool was a large, open-fronted summer house come eating area and what looked to be changing rooms or toilets. At the far end of the pool, a large rose garden filled with flowers, the scent from which wafted to where they stood. Beyond the pool the wooded part of the garden began. This continued all the way back to the outer walls of the estate.

Lancaster made signs that he was going back to top up the water and told Vidêt to keep chatting. He went back out of the garden gate onto the lawn at the front of the house. He used his phone to grab photos of the house before heading out of the gate to pour away water from the can. Vidêt stayed in the garden for some ten minutes or so, chatting, before once again returning to the car. They both thanked the man profusely then, returning the watering can, gave a friendly wave and drove away. They drove into Salles-d'Aude to get back onto the A9, choosing to stop for lunch in a little roadside eatery on the edge of town. The carpark was full. In France, always a sign of a good menu and a good meal. They opted to sit at an outside table on a terrace set to the side of the restaurant away from the road. They ordered from a simple lunch menu and Vidêt gave Lancaster a blow-by-blow account of her conversation with the workman.

"The guy was Andre. He looks after the house and grounds, a handyman-cum-gardener. He has apparently worked for the owners, an English family called the Stottards for many years. They are a very nice family, but the husband has long since died and things are not quite the same. Apparently, when he was alive there were often people staying at the house. Sir Philip was an English lord. He used to have parties at the house often. Sometimes, his wife and the two boys would come down on their own and spend the summer. Occasionally, the whole family with friends, but often just His Lordship and his group of special friends. Then the staff were all sent home, the guests would look after themselves. But, according to Andre, he had to come up a few times to fix the pool pumps when there was one of His Lordship's parties going on, and at this Andre had tapped the side of his nose, the French sign for a secret. This was accompanied with a laugh and a double-shouldered Gaelic shrug. 'Mais, pas de problem,' the man had said. Since Sir Philip had passed, it had been the wife Lady Pamela and the boys who came for their holidays, now even that had changed but it had gotten busier. Now it was sometimes just Madame, sometimes a son and his wife then during August the whole family arrived for three or four weeks. Lady Pamela, both sons, their wives, children, sometimes friends as well. The pool was always needing maintenance. Madame Pamela always wanted the gardens to look perfect, just in case she arrived. So, Andre had given them nothing they did not already know. But it was worth the visit just to put a picture in their minds for when they were back in the office in the UK.

"I have to say, when I walked around that garden, when we got to go inside the gate and your friend Andre was generous enough to start showing us around, my gut feeling didn't lead me to think the place was or had ever been being used for anything illegal. If Andre had been standing in that gateway built like a proverbial brick-shithouse and kept the gate locked, told us both to bugger off, it may have raised suspicions. But to have worked there for so long and not bat an eyelid at letting us in does not to me speak of dope dealing or slave trading. Craven's not going to like it, but that's that. I'm more convinced than ever that whatever triggered the murder of Abdul happened once he got to the UK. It wasn't a foregone conclusion once he'd been offered a job; it wasn't part of a great plan that the boy would go to England and die. That being the case, we've narrowed our suspects. Number one: It's a member of the family, Sir Philip or Lady Pamela. She talks a good talk and proclaims all innocence but then she's a magistrate and knows a thing or two about keeping a straight face. The kids may not even have known anything about their father's secret life or lovers and anyway, they were both too young at the time."

"Children have murdered before," Vidêt pointed out.

"That's true, Marie, but how would they have driven Abdul out onto the moor? They'd have been fourteen, fifteen at the time. And, before you suggest it, yes, Abdul could've driven all three, but then once they killed him, how did they drive back? I can't see it. No, it's not the kids. Number two: It'll turn out to be a close associate, a member of the business team, a shareholder or a 'Mr Fix-It' who didn't want Abdul threatening the family fortunes. Number three: There's just a chance that, after his arrival in England as Sir Philip's plaything, our boy Abdul did what he'd done several times previously, found a new man from Sir Philip's group of friends. He then got killed because of jealousy or failed blackmail. Either way, our next line of enquiry begins in the UK."

They finished lunch then continued their journey to the airport. An hour later, they'd dropped off the car, off loaded baggage at check-in and were sitting in the departure lounge of the little provincial airport waiting for their flight. Lancaster, as promised, used this waiting time to put in his call to DCI Craven. As he thought, Craven spent as little time on the phone as possible, but was keen for them to pursue any line of enquiry that might put the Stottards in the frame. Lancaster avoided having to mention anything at all about what they had or had not discovered in France so he'd not had to tell lies. Lancaster was confident that somewhere down the line they would, at the end of the day, manage to close this case. Find out who'd committed the deed itself. The question was going to be, was the perpetrator still in the land of the living? Or had they found Abdul's body too late and missed their opportunity to nail the murderer all together?

Their flight home was uneventful. This time, both detectives slept, waking only as the captain told them they were due to land. The crawl through customs and passport control took twice as long as their arrival in France. Once they retrieved their luggage, they still had to arrange to extend their parking space for another couple of days and allowing for the fact that England was an hour behind the South of France, it was almost dark when they finally got to the car hire location. Half an hour later, however, they were on the road in yet another VW. At least this time the steering wheel was on the right side of the car and instead of air-con they had the heater on. Lancaster wished he hadn't put his sweat-shirt so deep in his luggage.

Vidêt was doing the driving and Lancaster was using the map he'd purchased at the car hire to locate a suitable place for an overnight stopover. Lancaster didn't want to go right into London tonight. It would be too busy and hectic after three days in the South of France. His brain couldn't cope with the thought of it let alone actually doing it. His plan was to find a hotel to stop at for the night just outside the perimeter. Get some sleep, grab breakfast, head into the city once rush-hour was over, making straight for Dolphin Court on the Thames Embankment. He voiced his plan to Vidêt who thought about it for a few minutes before putting forward her own idea.

"Sir, if I may make a suggestion?"

"Please do."

"Well, if we stop for an overnight at Bracknell," she continued, pleased to feel they'd dropped back into normal roles. There appeared to be no sign of change in their relationship. Maybe the broken protocol of their night of passion could be ignored. Though, secretly, she was not altogether sure she wanted it to be. "Then we will be just outside of the expensive boundary. We could book in for two nights, then travel into the city by train. Then we wouldn't have to worry about one-way systems, no parking areas, the hassle of trying to drive around London. I lived there long enough to find my way around on the tube. If we go into town from Bracknell we go into Waterloo Station. Pimlico Underground Station is not far from the embankment, that's only a couple of tube stops from Waterloo. Or, we could stay above ground and get a taxi."

"So what you're saying is, we could've brought our own car," Lancaster replied with a smile.

"Sorry," she said without looking at him, but then, with a smile, she followed it with, "I was wondering when you would think of it... sir."

Lancaster used his phone to find a chain hotel on the outskirts of Bracknell. He phoned ahead and booked a double with single beds, aware of a snigger from the driving seat as he did so. He booked a table for two in the restaurant for eight p.m., giving themselves a good hour and a half to finish the journey. Lancaster then surprised Vidêt by keying in the hotel post code into the sat-nav. Then rolled the seat back, dozing until Vidêt swung the car into the hotel carpark. Booking in was quick. Lancaster thought it ironic that he'd found it harder to get the young, foreign receptionist to understand what he was saying than it had been in the hotel in Narbonne, nevertheless, their room was warm, clean, functional and came complete with the requested twin beds. The pair were unpacking when Lancaster's mobile rang. Caller ID flagged up as Rover.

"Rover, what can I do for you, mate?"

"I rang the office earlier this week, they said you were out of the country till today. I presumed work related! I didn't want to call your mobile, I can't afford it, anyway, I presume you're back at base by now?"

"Actually, Rover, no, but don't panic. We're back in the UK but on the road to another line of enquiry. What were you after anyway?"

"I've made an important discovery, well, I think it's important, anyway. You may think otherwise. I wasn't happy with those facial tattoos. Nobody in the tattoo world had ever seen anything like it, or even vaguely like it. So I decided to take a better look. I used the digital camera to take macro shots of each symbol. Then pieced it back together on the wall screen in the same form they are on the face. What you see is an eyeopener. The shapes are exactly the same size and format, in fact they are the same font..."

"Sorry... what do you mean by 'font'?"

"I am pretty certain they're not symbols. I think they're letters."

"What... as in, actual letters?" Lancaster asked with incredulity.

"Well, yes. Actual letters, as in 'Times New Roman' to be exact. Once you have them all blown up on the big screen, it's bloody obvious. What I did was then take macro photos of some fonts, get them to the same scale, then superimpose them over the originals. They are definitely 'Times New Roman' lettering. It gets better. I'm pretty certain they're not tattoos. I think somehow the letters have been stamped into the skin. Again, once you have the letters blown up on the skin you can see that. Similar to the scar across the body's back, you know, the straight line between the shoulder blades? When you get the facial letters blown up you see they have the same disfigurement along the edges. The puckering skin, as if they'd been tears, and the tanning and sediment had opened them up. Made them swell, absorbing the colour from the peat before they'd a chance to heal. Which isn't surprising, if they were done just prior to the corpse going into the bog. They would've been raw, open scars. But once the body got into the tanning fluid, they'd never have the chance to form any scarring tissue, so they just sat there open, absorbing the peaty water for years until we took him out of the mire. By then they looked like tattoos."

"Can you work out what letters they are?" Lancaster asked.

"Well duh! It took a while because they didn't make any sense. They appeared to be letters in reverse, back to front. It wasn't until I flipped the photos that I could see what they were. Basically, the letters form the word ALL then there's a space, followed by the letter Y. On the second line we have DEAVO. The letter D was what we thought was a half or crescent moon, but once you have the letter blown up you can see that the back of the D has hardly made a mark, but when you zoom in you can just make out the faint outline of the back of the letter. Of course, when we first looked at these marks, we were all thinking the body was ancient, it wasn't difficult to imagine a full moon symbol, then, at the other end of the symbols the other shape then became an obvious crescent moon. In a minute, I'll text you the letters and put them in the exact places as they sit on his face. At first, I thought it could be a Latin inscription, but when you get the chance to come and have a look, you'll see what I mean. I think they're part of some other writing, but only the letters on those parts of what ever hit him across the face have left an impression in the skin."

"Have you got any theories, Rover?"

"Only that I reckon the damage I told you the side of the face and skull had sustained. Well, that damage and these letters are connected. I'm sure of it. I reckon he was smacked across the side of the head with something very solid, a manhole cover or some-such that had letters engraved on it. He was hit with such force that the skin virtually got squeezed into the engraving marks. Then, the sharp edges of the engraved letters left their mark on the flesh of the boy's face. As the skin started to swell and bruise as a result of the surface trauma he was plunged into the bog. Nature and tanning fluid did the rest."

"Rover, you're a bloody star. We'll be back home Saturday or Sunday night. I'll get back in touch then and come and have a look, but thanks for this anyway."

"No prob's, mate. I'll text you the lettering in a minute. Enjoy yourself wherever you are."

Lancaster rang off and was relaying this information to Vidêt when Rover's text arrived. It had been laid out on the screen just as it was on the face.

ALL Y
DEAVO

Set out like that it was obviously lettering, but setting it up on end and reversing the letters and, taking the back, straight edge of the D and the central bars from the A and the E was as good a reason as any for not spotting it sooner. All Lancaster had to do was work out what the inscription had said. At the moment, he'd no ideas. Absolutely none at all. If he did, he was certain it wouldn't give him any directions to his killer. He didn't think he'd ever get that lucky. Twenty-odd years had gone by since the crime had been committed. The likelihood of whatever piece of heavy, engraved object still being around was almost nil. He made a mental note to get somebody with a metal detector out to the bog when they got back, just in case the weapon was sitting in the bottom of the mire having sunk deeper due to its weight.

Lancaster and Vidêt went to the dining room for their evening meal. The choice was OK, but it wasn't France. The dining room was OK, but it wasn't outdoors and warm. But the wine was good. They shared a bottle of Barbera that warmed them both. The intensity, the passion and the late night of the previous day in France had taken its toll on the two detectives. They returned to their room, went through the teeth-cleaning routine and climbed into separate beds with no hint of irony or temptation. Both fast asleep within minutes. The following morning, after a 'Full English' breakfast, (it was funny how, whilst in France, Lancaster loved tearing open fresh, buttery croissants, filling them with jam for breakfast accompanied by coffee, but then walking into the restaurant and catching his first whiff of bacon and eggs had him 'on it like a bonnet', as they said in Plymouth) they drove to the station carpark, parked and then grabbed a couple of hugely-expensive Rover tickets. As they jumped on the train for London's Waterloo Station, the cost made Lancaster think that they could probably have a got a taxi into London for less. An hour or so later, they were standing under the big clock on the platform with a thousand other people, re-grouping, looking for the underground sign. Shortly after, Vidêt led them down to the underground, 'the Tube'. The part of the journey Lancaster had been dreading. Being underground, not in control, was an aspect he didn't like to contemplate. He had to breathe deep, remember it would be over soon. A bit like the dentist, but without the pain.

Vidêt was a natural, which surprised Lancaster. He'd thought she was a Breton seaside girl at heart, but she'd mastered this underground business whilst based here during her stint with the Met Police. It took a couple of line changes, but within thirty minutes they were coming up for air (of a sort) at Pimlico Station, a stone's throw from the Thames Embankment. A short walk and they were opposite the massive red brick and grey concrete structure that was Dolphin Square. Built in the mid-1930s, between two world wars, Dolphin Square was a series of luxury flats and apartments. The whole square edifice surrounded a private garden for tenants' only, with mature trees, formal gardens, paved walkways and water features. It had an underground carpark, a restaurant, and an indoor swimming pool. This place reeked of money. At various stages of its life the Garden Square had courted controversy and developed legends.

It had been home to at least ten Lords of the Realm. Seventy different members of Parliament, members of MI5 and MI6, along with famous topless models and several spies, one of whom was arrested whilst still in his flat. Inquiries here by police during previous years had included a disproven paedophile ring, a prostitution racket running 'escorts' out of luxury apartments and, a cell of Russian spies and double agents. The fact that Lord Stottard had a home here, was a closet gay and had imported gay young men from other parts of Europe, possibly even the world, didn't surprise him one little bit. What Lancaster wanted to know was, was this part of some bigger picture? A male prostitution racket, some kind of import/ export of gay sex? If so, had it all gone wrong for Abdul? Worse still, not just Abdul. Were there other bodies buried around the countryside still to be unearthed, the residue of some sordid sex game or club?

They walked the outer perimeter until they found the main entrance where they knew there'd be a doorman. Similar to a hotel, the apartment block not only had its own gardeners and maintenance men, but a team of doormen and lobby assistants, there to answer any request, field unwanted visitors. Lancaster made the decision to dive straight in and use his warrant card to get some answers. He wanted to spend as little time in the city as need be and get back on the road to Devon ASAP. Having found the imposing entrance doors, he pressed the bell and was instantly answered through the speaker system.

"Good morning, sir, what may I do for you?" the voice in the wall said, politely.

Lancaster looked up, saw the camera that had identified him as a 'sir'. He pulled out his warrant card, Vidêt did likewise. They held them up toward the camera as Lancaster replied, "Good morning. Detective Inspector Lancaster and Detective Sergeant Vidêt. I'm sorry to trouble you, but I wanted some background information with regards a previous tenant here and wondered if we could pop inside for a chat with you for a minute? A name's cropped up in the course of an enquiry we're currently involved in. We thought you'd be the right person to seek out."

"May I ask who you wish information about, sir?" the voice said from the wall.

"I would prefer not to bandy names about in range of the public's hearing, if that's all the same to you," Lancaster replied, still smiling at the camera.

There was a buzz from the door. Lancaster pushed his

way in, followed by Vidêt. At the end of a marble-floored hallway, filled with potted palms, stood an impressive dark wood counter, behind which stood a middle-aged gentleman wearing a pinstripe suit, sporting a bowler hat. Lancaster couldn't help but think the guy just looked so out of place in this day and age. He looked like something from an episode of Hercule Poirot, but you have to go with the flow and not antagonise. He calmly walked up to the counter and held out his hand. The pinstriped gent held out his and they shook. Initial contact made, Lancaster held up his warrant card, but not long enough for the man to be able to read the Devon & Cornwall section, but hopefully see the star and the photo.

Lancaster flipped open his notebook, appeared to quickly read something from it before saying to the pinstripe man, "I just want to check that I've found the right man, your name is?" He said smiling at the man behind the counter.

"Greeves, sir. Peter Greeves," Pinstripe replied.

"Brilliant, got the right man. I was told, Peter, that you'd been working here for quite a while, would that be correct?"

"Well yes, sir, that would be correct. I started here over twenty years ago under the previous doorman, Mr Barkis. I started here as a junior doorman and runner and have been employed here ever since."

"That's what I was told," Lancaster said with a broad smile. "That's why I was pointed in your direction. The man who sees all and knows all. Would that be right, or is there somebody else I should be talking to?"

"Oh, I don't think you would find anybody else who knows as much as I, sir," Pinstripe replied proudly.

"Good, well what we have to ask about is just a touch delicate. We're making enquiries about a missing boy," Lancaster started, feeling it might make Mr Greeves more sympathetic if he was helping find somebody who was missing. "This lad was a good friend of Sir Philip Stottard who resided in the block. Lady Pamela is very keen for us to find out anything we can about this lad and his friendship with her husband but, obviously, she wants to keep it on the old QT. I'm sure you know what I mean. You look like you're a man of the world. I'm sure you must have known Sir Philip."

"Indeed I did, sir, a fine gentleman he was too. We were very sad when he died, very sad indeed. Always gave us runners and doormen a gift at Christmas. Always remembered our birthdays. A fine gentleman, despite everything."

"Well in this day and age being gay wouldn't bother anybody would it?" Lancaster said, feeling he had to talk about the elephant in the room. "But I bet you chaps guarded his secret life for him with the efficiency of your profession. I know Lady Pamela is still grateful to this day."

"It is part of our job, sir. Be observant, stay shtum. Between you and I, there are people here who would have us out on our ear in an instant if they thought we were talking out of turn. That's why they pay so much to live here. It's a safe place, they're well looked after, night and day."

"Let me show you a picture," Lancaster said, calling up Abdul's picture on his phone, "See if you have any memory of the lad. Obviously, this lad went missing twenty-odd years ago so I don't expect much, but I know damn well that if anybody can remember a face, it'll be you." Lancaster showed the artist impression to him.

"Well, of course I recognise the lad. That's young Abdul. What's he done to his face? Where's he been all these years?"

Lancaster was stunned into silence. He never for one moment expected to have Abdul identified so quickly. He was using the picture as an opener to find out more about Sir Philip.

"So obviously you remember him?" Lancaster stated.

"Well yes, he stayed with Sir Philip at his flat. I think Sir Philip had adopted him or some such. Obviously, he didn't discuss the boy with us other than introductions. Told us we were to offer him all the services available to tenants. We were to keep an eye out for him as he was new to London. Well, that was no surprise to us. The boy spoke some English, but most of the time he gabbled in French. Funny lad. Always smartly dressed, looked a proper toff most of the time; very sad that episode was, very sad."

"What do you mean by that, Peter?"

"Sir Philip looked after that boy, bought him lots of clothes. Always coming back here loaded up with bags. That's why the boy always looked so smart, without a doubt, Sir Philip liked the boy. Treated him like one of his own really. But... I shouldn't tell you this really... but I don't think Lady Pamela was keen on him."

"What makes you say that?"

"Lady Pamela arrived here one day," Peter continued. "You probably already know that most of the time this place was just used by Sir Philip. Lady Pamela preferred Devon where they had another place. Sir Philip used this as his London base.

It was near the office you see, he used to have clients here for meetings. He'd tell us so-and-so would be expected at such-and-such time and we'd show them across to Sir Philip's place. Well, one day, as I said, Lady Pamela arrived with no key. We let her in. Apparently, she'd been up in town, shopping with friends and her train had been cancelled. She came over here to stopover for the night. I mean it wasn't unusual, she'd been here lots of times. Well, she went on over to the flat and Stephen, one of our runners, was over there on the next floor delivering a parcel. He heard them shouting from the next floor up. They had a right two-and-eight, they did. I don't know what was said, but according to young Stephen it was all about young Abdul. He heard her say some terrible things about him and Sir Philip. She picked up her bags and got me to phone for a taxi. Stayed at the Belmont instead. Must have upset her, mind, because she only ever came back here after he died. Came with the boys to go through the flat. Luckily the boys have kept the flat on, they often stay there now when they're in town."

"Was that what you meant by being very sad?" Lancaster asked.

"Well not just that," Peter continued. "The thing was, about a month later, Sir Philip said he was going to Devon for a visit and could we do the usual and water his orchids. He had quite a collection. All over the flat they were; it was like a jungle in there. We could spend hours watering the things, still, a job's a job. Anyway, he went off to Devon, Abdul went with him. We helped carry the cases to the car. It was a hot day, I remember that much. To put it politely we sweated buckets taking all those cases down to the carpark. I know we shouldn't laugh; I don't even know why we found it so funny, but young Abdul was wearing a pair of pinstripe shorts, he looked like he was going off to school," Peter said with a laugh. "Stephen and I struggled to keep a straight face, but that boy was so proud of his shorts."

"So, what was sad about that then, Peter?" asked Lancaster.

"I was getting to that, sir. The point was, we never saw the boy again. When Sir Philip came back a couple of weeks later, he looked white as a sheet. Didn't look well; face all drawn, not well at all. When I asked if Abdul would be coming back, Sir Philip put me in my place. Very unusual for him, took me by surprise I can tell you. Actually, it upset me for days. He told me to remember I was a doorman. The comings and goings of guests and tenants had nothing to do with me. He apologised a couple of weeks later, said he hadn't been feeling well at the time, but I didn't want to ask him about Abdul again and he was never mentioned. We never saw him again, but, and this is the sad part, Sir Philip was never the same again. He always looked sad. Stayed in the flat on his own most of the time. One time he phoned down, said he was expecting somebody and would we show him up when he arrived. That chap turned out to be a detective. I mean, we wouldn't have known but for the fact that when he rang the bell, he announced himself as Brian Peachy, private investigator, to see Sir Philip. Well, there wasn't much 'private' about that, was there? Anyway, he came and went on and off for a couple of months, then he stopped coming as well. It seemed to me that when Abdul left, His Lordship left us as well, although it was ten years or more before he had his heart attack. But I reckon he went downhill from the day that boy went."

Lancaster turned to Vidêt and gave her the look. She replied with a nod and a flick of her phone that told him she'd recorded the whole conversation. Lancaster thought this interview had probably netted all they were going to get. He thanked Peter, told him he'd been a great help. Peter saw them both out and they waved as he closed the door behind them. The two detectives walked around the corner back into Pimlico, where they found a little tree-filled park with some sunny placed benches and regrouped.

"I have him," Vidêt said, looking at her phone. "Brian Peachy Detective Agency. He is still in business, he's in World's End."

"Where?" Lancaster asked incredulously.

"World's End," Vidêt replied with a smile. "It's at the western end of the King's Road in Chelsea. It would appear Peachy has an office there."

They walked out of the square and headed back across the road towards the tube station just as a black cab pulled up, offloading two young ladies in business attire. Lancaster grabbed hold of the open door of the cab before they could close it, ushered Vidêt inside before the seats had time to cool. She gave the driver the directions for the World's End Pub, King's Road. Lancaster jumped inside and slammed the door before there could be any discussion. He'd had enough of the underground for one day.

The traffic around King's Road was horrendous. It took nearly an hour to get from Pimlico to the bottom of King's

Road. Before they'd reached the pub, Lancaster told the driver to pull over, saying they'd walk the rest of the way. He paid and thought to himself that they could have hired a car for less. They walked the last part of King's Road and quickly found the pub, which these days was now a 'gastro experience bar'. Lancaster wondered if they still served beer. They realised the address they had for Peachy was just across the street from the pub and up a side alley. They crossed King's Road, walked up the alleyway until they got to 28B Delforth House and stepped up to the imposing blue painted door, beside which were a series of individual name tags and bell pushes. Peachy Detective Agency was the third button down. Vidêt pressed and waited, ear close to the speaker. Seconds passed before a woman's voice was heard through the grille.

"Peachy Detective Agency, can I help you?"

Vidêt thought that was an odd thing to ask, as they wouldn't have pressed the button if they didn't want some kind of help.

"Is it possible to speak with Mr Peachy, please?" Vidêt asked.

"Can I ask what it's in connection with?" the voice asked.

"Of course you can, but I don't intend discussing it with you," Vidêt replied. "Just tell him he has two visitors, Detective Inspector Lancaster and me, Detective Sergeant Vidêt. We would rather not be having this conversation through an intercom." She turned to find Lancaster smiling broadly.

"What?" she asked.

"Nothing, I was just admiring your forcefulness."

Before she could reply, the buzzer went.

The voice said, "Second floor, name's on the door."

The door opened, they pushed in and climbed the neatly kept stairs to the second floor and found the agency door as named. The detectives knocked and entered without waiting for a reply. Despite the 1960s decoration of the stairwell outside, the office they entered was a completely different, modern, chrome and leather-furnished room. Carpeted and pot-planted, with a reception desk behind which sat a smart suited young lady with hair stacked on her head in a bun and a pair of bright orange rimmed glasses.

"Sorry to keep you chatting on the doorstep," she said. "We get rough sleepers who pretend to be clients then hide in the basement when we unlock the door. So we keep them talking for a bit. They don't appear to like that and tend to move on. It's a bloody pain really, but hey-ho. What can we do for you?"

"We've an ongoing enquiry we're working on," Lancaster said. "During the course of this enquiry, Mr Peachy's name came up and we'd like to have an informal chat with him to see if he can help us in any way."

"I'll see if he can fit you in. He doesn't actually have anybody with him at the moment, please take a seat," she said, pointing to the shiny leather and chrome armchairs. Walking to one of the office doors, she knocked and entered. Neither detective sat, both preferring to stand. Seconds later, the smart lady reemerged. "Mr Peachy will see you now."

The detectives crossed the room and entered the office. Mr Peachy was a man in his sixties, at a guess, though well built, had a full head of hair and a penchant for gold jewellery. He looked like he worked out every day. He was smart suited, clean shoed. He stood as they walked in and smiling, held out his hand.

"Good morning, detectives, I am intrigued. What can I do for you both?"

CHAPTER TEN

Mr Peachy was not what Lancaster had been expecting. During his time with the police, he'd met several private investigators. He'd never been impressed. He could quite understand why somebody would want to use one though. Throughout the UK there were, sadly, many people looking for solutions to the mystery of lost loved ones. At the start, they're keen to help and expect the same from the police, but sometimes you come up against a brick wall. There's no visible, obvious solution to a disappearance. Then those people who have money hire a private investigator. If you don't have the money then you sit, wait and hope. The thing about private investigators, Lancaster always thought, was that they didn't make any money if they just walked out the door and solved the case straight away. It stands to reason they'll want to stretch it out, but there's a balance to be struck. They need to make it last long enough that it pays, but quick enough that the client is pleased to tell all their friends how good you are. You need the endorsement, not the negative.

If it's a good detective the joy of the trade is, you can push the boundaries of legality and good taste. Only a private detective would turn up at a funeral, as Lancaster once observed, then start surreptitiously questioning all the friends and family of the deceased as the casket was lowered into the ground. Lancaster heard a story from DCI Craven about finding a guy they'd been interested in for a vicious assault, but couldn't for the life of them make anything stick. No witnesses (too frightened). No physical evidence at the scene (other members of the biker gang had washed the whole place down after the assault). The victim recognised no one, despite the fact he knew who the perpetrator was. He'd been pulled from the street and a hood put over his head the entire time. But then the victim's father had called in a private detective from Exeter. An ex-Royal Marine with friends still in service. DCI Craven received a written confession two days later and the accused was found in a dockyard storeroom with both his feet nail-gunned to the floor. There were times when Lancaster wished he had that leeway. But then again, he was grateful he didn't.

He thought, as he shook the man's proffered hand, that Brian Peachy, for some reason, looked honest. He looked the kind of man who did the job because he wanted to solve crimes. Lancaster couldn't believe he was thinking this. But the man had a face you could trust.

"Good morning, Mr Peachy. Your secretary probably told you, my name's Detective Inspector Lancaster, this is my colleague, Detective Sergeant Vidêt. We're in the middle of an enquiry regarding a missing person, your name came up during research. I was hoping you might be able to help us iron out a couple of things."

"I am more than happy to help if I can, but without wishing

to offend, may I see your warrant cards?"

With a smile, Lancaster offered his up and Vidêt did likewise. Lancaster knew what was coming next.

"Devon & Cornwall?" Peachy said. "You're a long way off your patch? What enquiry brings you all the way up here?"

"We're looking into what was a missing person," Lancaster replied, deciding honesty was going to be the best policy here, and probably the quickest way to get a result. "You were contracted some years ago by Sir Philip Stottard. We wondered, as the client is now deceased, would you be willing to discuss exactly what work you were doing for him?"

"Stottard. Bloody hell, that goes back a bit. That must be at least twenty years ago. Hang on, you said a missing person that was... are you saying you've found... Abdul?"

Lancaster looked at Vidêt. "Is there any chance of a coffee, Mr Peachy? I think we've a lot to discuss."

Mr Peachy went on to explain his contract with Sir Philip. In June of 1999, a date confirmed when the secretary arrived with three cups of coffee, a jug of milk, a delightful little pink pig, who's back opened to reveal sugar and, an old brown cardboard file containing the details of work carried out on Sir Philip's behalf. Peachy had visited Sir Philip at Dolphin Square. Sir Philip wanted him to do three things.

One: Search for a young French North African. Early twenties. Abdul Mehemet. He may have been frequenting gay bars or clubs within London or possibly Devon. As a final resort he could've returned to Narbonne in the South of France.

Two: Search for, locate and follow another gentleman. Piers

Ward. A man in his early 30s, at the time. Possibly frequenting the same clubs within London, possibly in the company of Abdul. If so, report back.

And Three: Ensure no mention of it should ever reach any one else whatsoever, especially the media in any of its forms.

He was to report weekly and solely to His Lordship. No other member of his staff or family.

"Who was Piers Ward?" Lancaster had asked.

"He was an old Etonian school friend," Peachy replied. "It didn't take long to track him down. I don't think he was hiding. He was a right tosser, but vicious. He'd long blond hair, held back in one of those bloody Alice bands. Bloke looked like a tart. He spent a lot of time mincing around gay clubs in Soho, snorting coke, picking up rent boys. Getting pissed, beating them up, paying them off then sending for the chauffeur to come and pick him up. By the way, I presume you already know that Sir Philip himself was, you know... gay?"

Lancaster nodded. "I don't think it's a secret anymore, his wife told us."

"Ah the delightful Lady Pamela. A great looker at the time, but she was a right cow. I made a mistake there. I was told she was in France, so I went down to your part of the world for a sniff round. She caught me in the garden talking to the staff and the builders. They were having a load of building work done at the time. Well, she came into the garden and asked me outright who I was. So I thought I'd pull rank. I said I was working for her husband and she told me, excuse my French, she told me to fuck off or she'd set the hounds on me. Very nice."

"What about this Piers bloke? Where did he fit in?"

286

Brian Peachy went on to tell them what his gut feeling was. Reading between the lines, His Lordship thought young Abdul had buggered off with his mate Piers.

"Sir Philip had brought young Abdul over from France. Then, six or eight months later, he just buggered off. Well, or he disappeared, depends on who you asked at the time. It was strange, I mean, I don't confess to know much about gay relationships, but if I didn't know better, I'd say Sir Philip loved the boy. I know, weird isn't it? He was genuinely upset, gutted about the boy disappearing like that. He didn't think Abdul would've done that. But then, when I asked him if Abdul had access to his own funds, he confessed he'd been paying the boy on a regular basis. I got the wrong end of the stick there and jumped to the conclusion the lad was a rent boy. That didn't go down well I can tell you; Sir Philip was down my throat like a G & T on a Friday night. No, he said, although he purchased all the lads' clothes, gave him treats and pocket money. Turns out, before he disappeared, His Lordship confessed he'd been paying the lad for his silence. Never said how much, or how often, and I never got the chance to eyeball his personal account details to find out. But Abdul was definitely blackmailing His Lordship."

"Did you ever manage to make any connection with Abdul and this Piers bloke?" Lancaster asked.

"Oh yes. No two ways about it. I flashed the boy's photo around the clubs and came up trumps. Lots of people recognised the lad. I mean, he was a pretty boy. People had seen him with Piers in at least three of the gay bars in town. Piers wasn't a guy many people liked much. I mean, they hung around him because they all liked to suck cash from him, but they all cleared out when he started getting stoned or pissed. He was too dangerous to hang around with for long."

"Just out of interest, do you still have the photo of Abdul?"

Peachy dipped into his brown folder and extracted a 6" X 5" photo showing Abdul in an artistic, semi-naked pose. Sitting sideways on, looking at the camera, his chin resting on the palm of one hand, his elbow on the arm of the chair he was sitting in. He was smiling at the camera, or the cameraman. As Peachy had said, he was a pretty boy. Smooth, shiny, unblemished, copper brown skin. Masses of tight, black curly hair above a broad, deep forehead and not a mark on his face. He looked happy, confident, but with a coquettish look about his smile and pose, he was enjoying himself. Lancaster realised this was the first actual photo he'd seen of their victim. Maybe if they'd gone to Madame Mehemet's home for the offered meal in Narbonne she would've got the photos out. But to date, the only picture they had was the artist's impression. Here was a picture of the real person in happier times. Before somebody chose to commit murder and sink him on Dartmoor. Lancaster asked if they could have a copy of the photo for their records. This request was granted.

It led Peachy to ask the obvious question, "If you think you've found Abdul, why haven't you got a photo?"

Lancaster pulled out his phone, scrolled and showed Peachy the artist's impression.

"Sadly, we haven't found Abdul alive, but we've found his remains. We've constructed this picture based on the body we have in pathology. Our artist has done the rest."

"Bloody hell," Peachy said, looking at the phone. "Did he join some kind of cult? What's with all the tattoos?"

"Well we're still working on the case at the moment so I'm afraid I can't say."

"I've got to ask though," Peachy said, handing the phone back. "Did you find his body up here in the 'smoke' or down there in the 'sticks'?"

"His body was found near Plymouth," Lancaster replied, not wanting to give too much away. "That's why we're conducting the enquiry. In fact, I'm surprised you didn't see the picture we posted in the newspapers a couple of weeks ago?"

"Never read em, don't get time, they're too bloody depressing."

"So, can I ask, how did you conclude your case for Sir Philip?"

"Well, I drew a complete blank. After about three months work, I couldn't find a bloody thing. The boy had disappeared without trace. I finished up giving the man a complete dossier of where we'd looked. Who and where we'd tracked, who we'd talked to. Sir Philip had last seen the boy down in Devon. He'd had a party down at the estate there. He couldn't nail down an exact day or time when he last saw him, but narrowed it to within a couple of days during the early part of May 1999. I don't know what went on at these parties, but I got the feeling it was a bit of a free-for-all and there may have been some drug use... you know what I'm saying... so he couldn't be more exact than that. At some stage, he looked for Abdul and he was gone, along with several other members of the group. He presumed the boy had deserted him, come back up the city with the crowd. When he got back up here, Abdul wasn't around. Sir Philip phoned around his cronies, they all claimed they'd no idea where Abdul was. He waited for a while expecting him to turn up when he needed money, but he never showed. That's when he called me. Obviously, he couldn't go to the Old Bill, he didn't want to flag up the fact that he'd brought a French tourist into the country, took him to a private party and lost him. Like I said, I couldn't find a bloody thing. I think he was worried that if he didn't find out who the boy was with, he wouldn't know who he was talking to. So, it was a bit of 'better the devil you know'. I can tell you Lady Pamela had nothing to do with any of it. Well, if she did, it wasn't directly. Despite the fact that I would've loved to have found out she was involved. But one of the reasons he had the party down in Devon was, that, at the time, she was in the South of France with the boys. As for Piers, well, apart from finding out he'd been seen with Abdul a couple of times, I just couldn't find evidence of him and the boy being together after the party. I had a PI in France have a sniff round back home, but apart from finding out the boy had left a bloody good job and a couple of boyfriends, it appeared that once he'd left France for England, he never contacted anybody from Narbonne again. I mean, what kind of bloke doesn't call his mum eh, I ask you."

"So, were you confident that Piers had nothing to do with the disappearance?"

"I never said that. I just couldn't find anyone who saw him or the boy leave the party. Now what you've got to remember is they were all a bunch of 'hooray henry's', old school, you know? Not many would speak to me, anyway. On the whole, when I asked around it was like looking for a missing shovel in a pikey caravan park. Nobody had seen anybody, doing anything, anywhere, at any time 'old chap'. To be honest, someone could've cut him up with a handsaw in the library and stuck him in binbags and still no one would've said anything. I had to tell Stottard I'd drawn a complete blank. Funny enough, he didn't really appear too pissed off. He did appear impressed by the detail of the work I'd done. In fact, I was a one-man band up till then, but after I handed him the dossier he paid me off big time, more than my invoice. Later, he sent various acquaintances to me for work, then they sent other friends. I did pre-nuptial investigations, tracked down lost loved ones, did surveillance prior to divorce proceedings, even got paid very well, thank you very much, for finding and stealing back a bloody great big Borzoi bitch that'd been stolen to order by some dodgy Albanians. So as you can see, even though I didn't find Abdul, my whole business was sort of built on his back, so to speak."

"Do you know if this Piers Ward is still alive?" Lancaster asked, ever hopeful.

"Funny enough, I know for a fact he is. He's been on the TV of late. He's involved in property development, building the luxury flats by Battersea Park. They've pissed off the locals over the water big time, chopping down a load of trees in the park, pretending they'd some sort of disease. Obviously, it's all bollocks. They wanted to open up the view to the river. Hopefully, they'll get shafted on that one. Anyway, if there's anything else I can help you with please just ask, but I've another client due in a couple of minutes, so if we're done?"

"Mr Peachy, you've been very helpful. You've certainly filled in some blank spaces for us. We may be back in touch."

"If nothing else," Peachy replied, "let me know the full story when you've closed it? I was always sorry I couldn't find the lad. It's strange, but I haven't had a contract since then that I haven't been able to bring to a conclusion, but that case got my business up on its feet, yet it's the only one I couldn't close. Weird, isn't it?"

Fifteen minutes later, Vidêt and Lancaster were sitting in a wine bar round the corner, eating paninis and drinking tea, mainly because the wine bar didn't warrant the title. The list was short, all extortionately overpriced, as was the Panini but then needs must; it was lunch time. Vidêt had sourced an address for Piers Ward and looked up London news headlines to find the story behind the Battersea Park debacle. This gave them a company name, which led to a company address and contact details. Vidêt had to trawl deeper to find any kind of close, personal numbers for Piers, but find them she did. Lancaster was flicking off the last bits of crust of the slightly burnt surface of the brie and lettuce panini from the legs of his chinos when she handed him a home address and landline number for Ward's Cadogan Street residence just off Sloane Square, top of the Kings Road and, the email, landline and mobile for his office in Victoria.

"I think he should be on our list of suspects until proven otherwise sir, don't you?" Vidêt suggested.

"I certainly do, Marie. He sounds like the sort of bloke who wouldn't be pleased if somebody tried to take the piss. I think he'd be capable of teaching Abdul a lesson if he thought he needed it. So yes, he goes on the list until we get a chance to take him back off."

Lancaster worked the list in reverse order, trying the mobile number given for office use. It went straight to answerphone. Lancaster left a simple, precise message for Mr Ward to contact him ASAP. Next, he used the office landline. The phone rang for a few seconds before the system cut in. He was offered options and numbers. Construction: Line One, Design: Line two etcetera. Lancaster stayed on until somebody decided to pick up. He asked to speak with Piers Ward and was told he wasn't available. Lancaster told the voice it was important he speak with the voice's supervisor immediately. The voice had never had this before and panicked. A moment later, a female voice came on the line and told him the same thing. Mr Ward was a very busy man and not available to take calls, could she be of assistance?

"OK," Lancaster replied, "this is what I suggest you do. Contact Mr Ward. Inform him that Detective Inspector Lancaster needs to discuss an urgent matter with him. It involves the late Sir Philip Stottard and a murder. I'm in London for today, and today only. I need to speak with him today as after tomorrow the issue will no longer be under our control. Did you get all that? And if you're not high enough up the pecking order, you need to speak to someone in a higher paygrade right away. Is that clear enough for you?"

Apparently, it was. Lancaster left his mobile number with her then rang off. He ordered another two cups of tea and they waited.

"Do you think he will call, sir?"

"Oh I know he will, Marie. If he's innocent he'll be intrigued as to the connection between Sir Philip and a murder. If he's guilty, he'll want to know how much we know. If he's a clever little bunny he'll trace me back to Devon & Cornwall Police. And, guilty or innocent, he'll want to know what I am doing up here in London wanting to speak to him. So yes, I think he'll call."

Just as the fresh cups, milk jug and a little china tea-pot arrived, Lancaster's mobile went.

"Detective Inspector Lancaster speaking," he said, being ever hopeful.

"Good afternoon, Detective Inspector," a woman's voice replied. "Janine Kyle here, Mr Ward's PA. Obviously, Mr Ward is very busy at the moment. Is there anything I can do for you? I understand the issue is urgent."

"Well, it's very kind of you to call, Ms. Kyle, but the answer is no. There's nothing you can do for me. Obviously Mr Ward doesn't understand that the issue is in fact, very urgent. As I've said to various members of staff along the way, I need to speak to Mr Ward personally. An intermediary isn't going to work, besides, were you working for Mr Ward twenty years ago?"

"Well... no, I wasn't."

"Then you won't have a clue about anything I wish to discuss with him," Lancaster continued. "Just repeat to him for me, will you, that I need to speak with him about the late Sir Philip Stottard and a murdered young man called Abdul Mehemet. I need to speak with him today whilst I'm in London, tomorrow will be too late."

"Just one moment," she replied.

Lancaster knew the man himself was standing next to her, attempting to avoid the call. It was only a matter of time before curiosity or annoyance got the better of him. He was right.

"DI Lancaster, Piers Ward here. What exactly is all this about?" a well-spoken man's voice said down the phone.

"Good afternoon, Mr Ward. I think I've explained several times what this is all about. I need to have an informal, off the record conversation with you, about you and Abdul Mehemet's relationship with the late Sir Philip Stottard and, the subsequent murder of Abdul. Now, we can have this conversation over an unsecured landline or you could spare me half an hour for a face-to-face chat. At the moment, I'm sitting in a wine bar near the World's End pub, I'm in easy reach of your office or your home. I wouldn't recommend you coming to the wine bar, it's rubbish, but if you wish to meet somewhere more to your liking, I'm sure I can find it."

There was a silent pause from the other end of the phone and Lancaster let it lengthen. He'd dropped the match, he just needed to see if it would catch and burn.

"At present, I'm at my home address," Ward said. "Have you got a pen and paper, I can give it to you?"

The fire had caught and was burning nicely.

"No need, Mr Ward, I already have it. Shall I come now?"

The answer was in the affirmative. Lancaster paid for lunch and neglected to tip. The two detectives got back onto the King's Road, hailed the first black cab that came along, giving Ward's address and telling him they were in a hurry. Lancaster offered an extra tenner if they could get there sooner rather than later. They sat back and let the cabby do his stuff. After a couple of hundred yards, the cab veered off down a left-hand side street, shot to the end, turned a sharp right then thundered along the road before turning left again. He did this repeatedly. Ducking and diving in and out of side streets and back alleys, all the time avoiding the traffic jam that was the King's Road in full flow, getting ever closer to their goal.

"When we get there, you know the drill," Lancaster said. "If you can do it without causing a stir, see if you can get it all down on your phone. I don't intend to stay long. Just pump him for facts, un-nerve him a little, see what shakes loose. If he's involved, I think he'll try and do exactly the same. He'll want to see how much we know then sit back and think about it before he commits himself to take any kind of action."

Six minutes, and a hairy ride through the side streets of Chelsea later, they pulled up outside the residence of Piers Ward, as annotated by the brass plaque on the short gate pillar. Lancaster paid off the cab driver and tipped him the extra tenner as promised. Before they reached the front door it was opened by a young, very efficient-looking lady wearing black-rimmed glasses and smart clothes.

"Detective Inspector Lancaster," said the official welcome. "Janine Kyle," she said holding out her hand in welcome. "Do come in."

"Good afternoon, Ms. Kyle," Lancaster returned. "This is DS Vidêt."

They were ushered into a large, comfortable, well-furnished room overlooking the street. Ms. Kyle offered them drinks, they both refused. There was only so much tea somebody could drink. They were ushered to plush leather armchairs and told that Mr Ward would be with them shortly. So they sat. Lancaster knew what was going on. Ward was elsewhere in the building frantically doing research, he might even be waiting for the arrival of his solicitor if he'd anything to hide. Vidêt took out her phone and notebook, putting them side by side on the coffee table, giving Lancaster a nod to show she knew what she was doing. Seconds later the sound of footsteps in the hallway preceded the grand entrance of Piers Ward.

"Lancaster?" The man said, thrusting out his hand. "Piers Ward, and this is?" he asked, looking at Vidêt as if she could be a problem.

"Detective Sergeant Vidêt, sir," she said standing, holding out her hand which Piers Ward ignored, so she sat back down again. Lancaster noted that as she did so she switched on her phone, but to his detriment, Ward didn't notice. He was making a deliberate show of ignoring her presence.

"At the risk of repeating myself, Lancaster," Ward said. "What exactly do you want of me?"

Lancaster decided he'd no more time for pussy-footing around so waded straight in with some facts. Just to show the man that at the moment a lot of the known facts were already in the marketplace.

"Mr Ward. During the years 1998 and 1999, you were known to be frequenting a series of specific bars and clubs in Soho, often in the company of Sir Philip Stottard. Later, Sir Philip brought a young French National named as Abdul Mehemet to London. You were seen entering these same clubs with Abdul, but not necessarily accompanied by Sir Philip.

In the spring of 1999, you were in attendance with both Sir Philip and Abdul, at a house party at the Stottard family estate in Devon. During the course of that weekend, you were seen in close company with Abdul, (this was a lie, Lancaster thought he would chuck it in anyway) and at some stage before the party officially ended, both you and Abdul left the house. Sometime later, you were seen back at the clubs in London, but without Abdul. So, I have two questions for you, Mr Ward. Firstly, what was your relationship with Abdul Mehemet? Secondly, if you both left the party together, do you have any idea as to how, why and who murdered Abdul?"

Piers Ward stood and stared at Lancaster. He appeared to be trying desperately to think of something to say. His lips were moving, but nothing was coming out. Lancaster was reminded of an angel fish he had as a child. It used to look out at him from the glass tank, bulbous eyes staring straight at him. As with Ward, the mouth opened and closed soundlessly. Eventually, the child Lancaster became convinced the fish was mouthing 'Help' and he was compelled to take it back to the shop and return it to its friends. Ward did look as if the colour had drained from his face, for a horrible moment Lancaster thought he might be having a stroke. Then the man got his second wind. Regained his voice.

"Are you seriously telling me, Lancaster," Ward blustered, "that you've come here, all the way from your green and pleasant little land of Devon... and yes, I know where you've come from, Inspector. I've done my homework and I'm presuming that you have permission to be in an area where the Metropolitan Police hold sway. You've come up here to accuse me of being involved in the murder of somebody I hardly ever met or knew. How dare you come into my home and accuse me of this. I had no idea whatsoever that the chap was dead. I shall call my solicitor before this conversation goes any further."

It was at this point that Ward appeared to run out of steam. He could for a moment think of nothing more to say. Lancaster saw the outburst for what it was. Bluff and bravado. A smokescreen to give the man time to recall a forgotten past. Remind himself of things he thought had been put to bed, a carefree youth. Before he could have a chance to explode again Lancaster dived back in. He didn't like this man. He didn't like what he stood for and was not about to stand here and be lectured to by a blustering buffoon.

"Mr Ward. If you wish to telephone your solicitor, then do feel free. I think you'll find, if you think back to what I've asked of you, at no stage did I ever accuse you of anything not supported by fact. Fact: we have witnesses, they've told us what clubs, when and who with. Not an accusation but fact. Fact: I have witnesses who put you at many of the functions given by Sir Philip, including the one given in early May of 1999. Not an accusation but a supportable fact. Fact: I have spoken only today, to a witness who says that you and several other members of the Devon house party, left that party early and at the same time as Abdul Mehemet. So again, not accusation but fact. And what I actually said to you was, what was your relationship with Abdul Mehemet, and as you both appear to have left the party together, do you have any idea as to how, why and who murdered Abdul? So, you see, I was actually asking for your help in this matter. At no time did I ever accuse you of anything. Finally, as regards the jurisdiction of the Metropolitan Police, I am well aware of the courtesies required when operating in another forces area. My colleague and I have the permission of my direct superiors to come to London to conduct an enquiry and source information that relates to that enquiry. Only at such time as I may need to make an official arrest do I then need to inform the Met. Then, and only then. Now, shall we sit down and have a polite, informal conversation about the points I've asked for your assistance with, or do we need to await your solicitor?"

Lancaster was surprised to find that a man of Ward's stature and temperament could fade so quickly. He'd been expecting another outburst of bluster but the man simply sat down and pressed the button of an intercom, beside his slightly grander chair than theirs. A second or two later, Ms. Kyle entered the room, whereupon Ward asked her to pour him a brandy and offered likewise to the two detectives. They declined. Lancaster thought that the least you would expect from an Eton education would be the ability to pour one's own brandy, but then again... maybe having a servant do it summed it all up. Ms. Kyle left the room. Ward spoke.

"You say Abdul has been murdered, Inspector. May I ask how and when?"

"He was murdered in 1999, but I am not prepared to say how at this moment in time." Lancaster realised the blusterous outburst had actually been the result of shock. A forced reaction to news that Abdul had been found dead. In fact, murdered.

"It would appear," Lancaster continued, "based on the

timescale we're working on, that Abdul was murdered on or around the time of Sir Philip's party in Devon. The one you attended, Mr Ward. His body was taken onto Dartmoor and buried, where it lay until accidently being discovered a couple of weeks ago. So you can see, you were amongst the very last people to have seen Abdul Mehemet alive. So, I ask again, please, what was your relationship with these two men?"

Piers Ward took a sip of brandy, stared at Lancaster, appeared to make a decision. He tossed the brandy down the back of his throat before replacing the crystal glass back on the table and sitting back into his chair.

"You asked about relationships, Inspector," Ward began. "Well, Pip, Sir Philip, that is, and I went to school together, at prep, then Eton. We became good friends, I mean, you know... very good friends, if you get my drift... well anyway, our friendship continued after we both left school. Pip always wanted to keep parts of our friendship a secret. Family commitments, honour and all that. Absolute tosh, obviously, but that was the way he wanted it so I went along with it on the whole. I mean, we weren't joined at the hip, so to speak, he had family commitments, I didn't... you know... it was the eighties, then the nineties. There was an awful lot of fun to be had... clubs, music... As you know, I wasn't short of a shilling so I made the most of it. Pip and I got together when we could, well, actually Pip and I got together when he wanted, but that was OK really. I certainly wasn't going short, I can tell you. I mean, we managed to keep our relationship alive and secret for years, then he came back one day from one of his trips down to Salles-d'Aude, they've a holiday home down there.

Well, he comes back and tells me he's, wait for it, tells me he's fallen in love. I said, 'Pip, that's just bloody tosh. You're a gay married man with children and more money than you know what to do with, what's the bloody point of falling in love? The world is yours, you silly sod.' But he was adamant. He was planning to bring this young boy over here. Hide him from his wife and family, as if that was going to work for long. I mean, she might have pretended she had no idea what Pip was up to when in town, but I think her blind eye was more a matter of dark glasses for convenience. She knew what side her bread was buttered on, I can tell you. She liked being lady of the manor down in the sticks, you know, 'big fish, small pond', that sort of thing. Swanning around being Lady Muck, telling everybody that hubby was busy in the city all week. I'll say he was busy! Anyway, one day he just turns up at the club with this pretty black French boy in tow, he was like some kind of mascot. I mean, Pip didn't actually have the boy on a leash or anything, but he always kept him close by, almost with an arm hovering across a shoulder saying keep-off, don't touch. Bloody pathetic to watch. I mean, the boy was too old for anyone to be shouting pedo at Pip, but then Pip, let's be honest, he was far too old to be wandering around the clubs with this young boy. It was unseemly, I can tell you. People were talking. Anyway, young Abdul took a shine to me, I mean, it was understandable, really. Pip was a lovely chap, but bloody hell he was boring. I mean, he was more conservative than Margaret Thatcher and it wasn't surprising the boy got bored quickly. I took him to a couple of clubs with me when Pip wasn't looking, he was a bit of a naughty boy really, I had to keep an eye on him. Give him a moment and he'd be chatting up anything in tight jeans. Couldn't keep him off the dance floor either. I mean, to be honest, he was eye candy, it was like walking around with your own pet model, he tended to draw attention wherever he went, especially with that adorable French accent. A lovely boy..."

Lancaster was aware that Ward had dropped into deep reminiscence, picturing a time where he was young and carefree. A time when the darkness of the AIDs epidemic was not fully upon the UK club world. It was a shadow rising in the west. Warning videos appearing on the television. Icebergs floating through a sea of fear. But nobody thought it would happen to them. The club music scene was one of stroboscopic sounds, pulsing rhythms chosen to bring an audience to an ecstasy-ridden fever pitch. Not conducive to acceptance of death as a result of an evening's liaison. Gay or otherwise.

"The thing about young Abdul," Ward continued, "was that he was such a likeable chap. He was pretty. Athletic, lithe, bubbled over with a love of life. He was like a bloody puppy. Always so inquisitive, what's this? How does that work? Who's that? But he was a bit of a useless bugger when it came to social niceties. He just thought we all had money and he had so little, it was a bit like monopoly, really. He would just ask for it. He had no idea just how incorrect his attitude was, it made him quite a few enemies, I can tell you. I'm bloody certain he was blackmailing Pip. I mean, that was the thing about the boy, he didn't understand it was blackmail. You know, saying things like, 'Well if I can't have any more money I might have to go and ask somebody else, they'll want to know where I have been, who I've been with', you know the sort of thing.

Silly little bugger. I know I handed over the odd wedge here and there under the threat of 'I might have to tell Pip what a naughty man you are', silly bugger."

"Did you actually have an affair with Abdul?" Lancaster asked.

Ward laughed. "An affair? How quaint. You've led a sheltered life down there in Devon, haven't you, Inspector? No, of course we didn't have an affair. We had sex, Inspector. It wasn't an affair, it was unadulterated, rampant 'rumpy-pumpy' whenever we got the chance, that was normally whenever Pip was down in Devon keeping up the family image. I warned him. 'Pip, old chum,' I said, 'you can't leave a house pet on its own, it'll rip up the furniture, make a bloody mess then get itself into trouble,' but he took no notice. Carried on regardless. Every time he returned, he'd take the boy out shopping in town. New suits, shiny shoes, do you know we all thought it looked like he was kitting him out for school. Sad, really. Bordering on the pathetic."

"So, when you left the party in Devon," Lancaster asked, "did you give Abdul a ride back up to town?"

"No, I bloody well did not," Ward returned quickly. "As the man is now dead, Pip, I mean, it'll do no one harm to tell you what actually happened. It's not something I'm particularly proud of. In fact, to this day, it saddens me to recall the event. I'd been indulging in some casual use of cocaine during the Saturday, maybe the Friday, to be honest, it doesn't really matter what day, but I'd indulged, let's just leave it at that. I was feeling a little smashed and also just a little pissed off at Pip and his puppy. At some stage, when Pip trotted off upstairs for a nap, young Abdul accosted me, started flirting outrageously. I thought, well, why not? So, we trotted off to the garden and found our way to the big greenhouse. Well, one thing led to another and the two of us were in full swing, so to speak, when the door scrapes open and in walks Pip... I feel terrible even now, just thinking about it. Pip just stared at us. He looked horrified, tearful. I tried to make light of it, said it was just a bit of fun, then Pip did an extraordinary thing. He slapped me around the face. Seriously, slapped me across the side of my face! I was broken. I mean, we'd been together for years and he slapped me. Well, I pulled up my trousers, grabbed my jacket and walked out, there and then. Went straight to my room, packed and left. Didn't speak to anyone, certainly didn't give anyone a lift back up to town, Inspector. When I left, the only two people who were in that greenhouse were Pip and Abdul."

"At what stage did you realise that Abdul had gone missing?"

"Well, when I got back up to town, I left it a couple of weeks for the dust to settle. Then, I tried phoning Pip to apologise. Try and makes things right, but he wouldn't take my calls. I went round a couple of the old haunts, see who knew what, but none of the crowd knew anything other than that Pip had called a halt to the party earlier than people thought it would end. Nobody was told why, they were just told the party's over, bugger off the lot of you. To be honest, it wasn't the best of Pip's parties, several of the crowd had already left on the Saturday for pastures new. Nobody mentioned Abdul, missing or not, which I took to be a good sign. I mean, there was no gossip about what had happened so I just presumed it would settle and be fine given time. Then at some stage, can't remember when, probably late May, early June, I suppose, a few of the chaps said there'd been some guy in and out of the clubs asking about Abdul and me so I thought... well, actually, I thought Pip was being a bit naughty. So, I called him up. Turned out it was him that had set the dogs on me. He thought Abdul was with me! I put him straight. I told him the last time I saw the boy was in that bloody greenhouse... and sadly that was also the last time that Pip and I spoke."

"So, you've no idea what happened to Abdul?" Lancaster asked.

"Absolutely none, Inspector. Cross my heart and all that. I've absolutely no idea whatsoever. When he didn't turn up at any of the clubs or with any of the crowd, I just presumed he'd run out of people to fleece and buggered off back to France."

"You said earlier that Abdul made a lot of enemies. Was there anybody in particular he offended that you can remember?"

"Inspector, when I said he made enemies, in our circle of friends it just meant you didn't get invited to parties. You wouldn't get offered a drink or get included in a social gathering. They were all gay, Inspector, not bloody gangsters. Seriously, I cannot for one moment think of anyone who would've wanted to kill the stupid boy. Although... there is just one possibility. There were a couple of the crowd, a separate little clique really, they were into bondage, a bit of... BDSM. The boy was always wanting to play new games. I think he'd been repressed in his home town, when he got over here it was like a child in a candy store, a bit of an eye-opener for him. I mean to say, I left that party, as I said, straight after the incident in the greenhouse. It's possible Abdul may have separated from Pip, got involved with somebody else. There's just a possibility that something went wrong during some frolic or other, maybe something got out of hand? I can tell you no more, Inspector. Honestly. I didn't know the group and it was certainly not my thing. Not my thing at all. It was only a sort of word of mouth... thing. I don't even know who was in and who was out, but I was definitely out, not my scene at all. I tell you what though, just a thought... there was an artist who came to a few of Pip's gatherings. He was from down your neck of the woods. Lived not far from Pip's place. Had a workshop and gallery at Totnes. I'm bloody sure he was in the group, always dressed in leather and stuff. Can't remember if he was at that party though, he might have been, it was a big place, some of those weekend parties had stuff going on all over the house... What was his bloody name? Second generation Polish chap. Dad flew Spitfires during the war and stayed here after it finished. Lived in a community for Poles... bloody hell, what was the chap's name? Stefan, Stefan... Pelchek... that's the chap. Stefan Pelchek, used to do portraits of the guys, you know arty, but flirty. Yes... that's the chap."

"You've been very helpful, Mr Ward," Lancaster said. "I may have other questions for you later, may I contact you?"

Ward opened a silver box on the table and handed Lancaster a simple card with name and mobile on it. "Of course you can, Inspector. I'd absolutely nothing to do with the boy's death... I hate the thought that the young idiot has died, needlessly, and been buried for so long... He wasn't a bad lad, just a fish out of water really. He should never have been enticed out of his own little pond. He came here and trusted everyone and paid

307

with his life. It's tragic, Inspector, tragic... Will you please let me know if you solve this?"

The two detectives left Piers Ward in a pensive mood, sitting in his armchair, a second glass of brandy clasped in his hand. There'd been a change in the man. All attempts of bluster and bravado gone. Replaced by memories of times gone by. Missed opportunities and the passing of friends. The detectives had arrived and Ward was in attack mode. The detectives had left and he was sunk in a deep melancholic frame of mind, a bottomless sadness had swept over him, set fast for the rest of the day.

Vidêt and Lancaster walked out onto the King's Road and hailed a cab for Waterloo Station. In the cab, Vidêt confirmed she'd managed to record the entire interview, transcribing it would wait until she was back at base. They both agreed a full discussion regarding the events should wait until they were back in their hotel. It was late afternoon, but it felt like it had been a hard-fought day. They struck lucky at the station. Within fifteen minutes of the taxi dropping them off, they were sitting on a train heading out of the city, ahead of the evening rush hour. Lancaster stared out of the window and watched in silence as the city passed by. He was depressed.

There were no two ways about it. This case had originally stirred his professional interest. He'd felt an injustice had been done to a young man some twenty years ago and he was disgusted by it. Disgusted by the way the murder and interment had been carried out with such disregard for humanity. Disgusted that a young French national could've left his home and disappeared, yet no one appeared to care. Disgusted that the brotherhood of the gay community, so often victimised and abused themselves, who'd fought to be recognised for who they were, had lost one of their own. Yet no one had noticed. Except the man who appeared to have loved him most and lost him.

Lancaster was most disgusted with himself. *He'd misread this case right from day one.* He thought. Originally, he'd been too easily convinced the victim was a farmer's son, unloved and abused. Then it became obvious that it was a random murder carried out by the very same unloved son. Then, even more obvious, the boy had been murdered callously by the landed gentry who may or may not have been dabbling in the world of drug exportation, who'd used their wealth and power to entice a young boy away from his home and ultimately, to his death. Lancaster watched the tower blocks, side streets, flyovers, parks and traffic all pass by outside the glass window, occasionally interspersed by his own reflection. A reflection he didn't want to see. Whenever it appeared, it showed a lonely man sitting in a railway carriage with no idea where to go next.

He knew the obvious answer. Back to Totnes and this artist Stefan Pelchek, but why? Why bother? They'd followed up so many leads in this enquiry, everyone had led them to another. None of them had led to a killer. They'd all led to sad, lost individuals, all just waiting, reminiscing about a time gone by. All fixated by one single short era in their lives, one that had ended just as suddenly as it had begun. None of them able to move on. They were left stranded in stasis, no chance of release. Now Lancaster felt he'd been drawn into this select few. He was trapped in this perpetual state of excitement and interview. Followed by excitement and interview, followed by excitement and interview, yet he felt no closer to solving this crime. Somehow, it had infected him. He was becoming another of the desperate individuals for whom this boy's disappearance had brought nothing but sadness.

Lancaster had met with depression before. Twice he'd fought the creeping onset of this mental affliction, twice he'd lost. He'd 'walked with the black dog' at his side and suffered for it. He'd been ridiculed for being weak-willed and pathetic. Lancaster would never forgive those that had treated him that way; never forgive or forget. He'd sought help and recovered from the first bout, which had arrived without warning, unannounced. It arrived like a dark cloud coming in over the horizon, blotting out the sun, bringing him to tears whilst walking on the moors. It was a strange experience and it had frightened him. He'd managed to shake it off for a couple of days, until it crept back again. This time, it had stayed. He'd felt lost, alone, pointless and scared whilst still with a group of people that he knew. It had made no sense to him. For a short while, he'd thought he was going mad. Which frightened him even more. For months he'd been unable to tell anyone, but eventually his then girlfriend, later his wife, noticed the change in him and eventually persuaded him to discuss his feelings, which led to an appointment with a sympathetic GP, who immediately signed him off work. Put him on sleeping tablets, anti-depressants and a course of counselling. That had helped. But the counsellor had told him, 'You're never cured of depression, you just learn to recognise its arrival and prepare for it'. She'd also told him not to be afraid. Depression was a bloody nuisance, but you could learn to float on the surface. That way you don't drown, you survive. You have a chance to reach the shore and walk away. You could meet the black dog of despair, but you had to learn to put a collar and lead on the damn thing, tell it you're not ready for a walk; he must sit and wait until you're prepared to go along.

Lancaster had applied his dyspraxic mind to this process and did research. Planning ways to avoid going under the surface of despair, and he'd survived. Walked away. His second bout had occurred not long after the death of his wife. Triggered by the shock of her death, the complete pointlessness of it all. Despite the fact that he could hear that black dog scratching at the door, he couldn't find the collar and lead. Eventually, it broke in and haunted him. 'Walkies, walkies' it kept saying. Hour after bloody hour. It was weeks before he'd been able to go back to his GP, who once again threw him the lifeline of the anti-depressants. His lifejacket, which kept him afloat until he could swim to shore, walk away again with the 'dog' back on its lead.

As the afternoon sunshine streamed in through the width of the window it did little to lift his mood. He turned his head away from yet another glimpse of his reflection and looked across the table to where Vidêt was sitting, also staring through the window. She had her phone in her hand and her earpieces plugged in. Lancaster saw, under the rim of her dark glasses, a damp, thin line ran down her face, terminating in a small, crystal-clear teardrop resting on her cheek. He leant across the table and touched her hand.

"Marie, what's wrong?"

She flinched, only for a second, when he touched her. "I'm sorry, sir," she replied, turning off her phone, pulling the plugs from her ears. "It's just all so sad. All these people, all finding love and losing it. Even Lady Pamela! You would think she had the perfect life but she lost her husband, twice. Abdul... he left a mother and a trail of broken men behind him in France all still sitting there waiting for him to return. Then he came here and did it all again. Ward, he loved Stottard, but couldn't have him, then even worse, he lost him. Lost him twice. Once to Abdul, once to a heart attack. But he can't forget or move on, despite all that forced bluster he was just a sad man who had lost the love of his life. It's just so tragic and I know you will say that all murder is tragic, but this one to me just feels different; it's just left me feeling very sad."

Lancaster took hold of her hand in both of his and squeezed it gently. "Marie, there's no shame in feeling sad about this case, part of the reason you're here, in England and working with me is that you're sensitive. This isn't just a job for you. You've an empathy, not just for the people damaged by these crimes that we investigate but an empathy for all victims. You and I are special, I don't mean that in any kind of royal, God-like way, we're not superhuman or anything, but we're both different to those around us. Either by accident of birth or by events in our lives, we're not like the average cop. That's not to say there is anything necessarily wrong with the other cops but we are without doubt... different. DCI Craven knows this and understands it. I don't know why, he just does, that's why he put us together. That's why we work well as a team. You pick up the bits I miss, you feel the vibes that I don't. You keep me on track and think of things that I hadn't. But we both feel the pain of these people. It infects us like a disease, at some time we both need to cry and become emotionally attached to our victims. It drives us. It makes us more determined to succeed. I feel the same, but what it's reminded me is this. We owe it to all those people left behind. The mother, the lovers, whoever, we owe it to them to not drown in this despair... we need to rise above it and solve this bloody crime, for everybody's sake."

"You're right," Vidêt replied, taking off her sunglasses and wiping her eyes with a tissue. "But, with respect, sir, what I actually need is a drink."

An hour later they were sitting in the hotel bar, two large glasses of a subtle French Malbec in hand. Lancaster had 'put the dog to bed', for now. His conversation with Vidêt on the train had made him realise that now was not a good time to succumb to despair. He could hardly lecture Vidêt on what their roles should be and how they should conduct themselves if he slumped now. The dog would have to wait; it had been told, it might get a walk once this case was over but not before. They booked an early table for dinner and went up to their room to shower, change and recap the events of the day. It had been busy. All of it influential in where they went next. Put together, it became an accumulator filling in the pieces of the puzzle. Colouring in the picture.

When Lancaster came out of the bathroom to get changed for dinner Vidêt was lying on her bed going through her notebook, her earphones plugged into her phone. She was jotting down headings and bullet points in preparation for future paperwork. She didn't look up when he got changed and when he was finished, he sat on the edge of his bed and tapped her duvet to get her attention. Vidêt pulled her earpieces out, switched off her phone, turned part way toward him.

"I have googled this artist, Stefan Pelcheck," she said. "He still has a studio in Totnes. He runs art classes, sells works. He's written books about controversial artists and runs exhibitions. His paintings are shit, but that's just my opinion. Somebody is buying them and they are not cheap. So, I have an address ready for when we get home, unless of course you have other people for us to see while we are here?"

"I think we've done London. I don't think there's anything more to be gained from trawling old haunts talking to old men. If we're to believe Ward, and I'm inclined to, once his bluster had been deflated there was an honesty about his sadness. So yes, I'm inclined to believe that when he left that party Abdul was still alive. Now, unless Stottard constructed an elaborate double bluff by pretending that Abdul had gone missing, then getting a private detective to investigate and go look for him. Then, accusing Ward of going off with the boy and spending years pretending he was broken hearted, I just can't see it. So, I for one don't think that he killed the boy in a fit of rage at finding him in the arms of another man. Ward's suggestion that maybe Abdul had somehow gotten himself involved in something that he couldn't get out of and accidently got killed, well that does require a bit of looking into. We know from everyone we've spoken to so far that Abdul liked to try new things and meet new people. So, what if he and Sir Philip had a big falling out over finding him with Ward? Sir Philip goes off in a huff. Abdul's still up for it, goes off, finds a room

314

in the giant candy store where a dose of BDSM is going on, then gets invited to join in. Abdul thinks to himself this looks like fun, all the leather and straps and the like. But it turns out it's not fun. By then, it's too late. There's some kind of event. Abdul accidently gets strangled or knocked out. The other participants panic. They don't want to tell Sir Philip they've killed his boyfriend, so somebody takes his body out onto the moors and buries him in the bog. What do you think?"

"I think it's completely feasible. But I am a bit un-nerved by how you know so much about the BDSM thing," she said with a smile. "But, apart from that, it sounds very feasible. So far there could have been the possibility that somebody Abdul had blackmailed could have had it done but it would appear that all those who Abdul had approached were only too willing and able to give him money. So that does not appear to be motive for his death. The possibility that it was an accidental killing is a good candidate. Therefore, the only conclusion for us as a next step is to interview Stefan Pelchek. If for no other reason than that he was at that party and may have seen something, or he may be able to name others who did. I have had one other thought though, sir, if I may?"

"Of course, Marie, what is it?"

"Well, I think we should double check Lady Pamela's alibi. When you showed her the artist impression when we were at her house, she immediately said she hadn't seen the boy. Yet according to the doorman at Dolphin Square, Lady Pamela had an argument with her husband about Abdul, so she must have known him even though the facial markings were a later addition. I mean, we all agree that Abdul has striking features and I can't believe she wouldn't recognise him. After all, it caused the break-up of her marriage so maybe she arranged to have him killed while he was down in Devon for the party. It was just a thought."

"But a bloody good one, Marie. I hadn't thought of that, well spotted."

"Ah, you disappoint me, sir," she said with a laugh. "I expected you to say, 'Well done, Pike, I wondered when you would think of that'."

Despite these moments of humour, both detectives felt affected by this case, and dinner, though enjoyable, was accompanied by too much alcohol and was a subdued affair. Neither of them could shake of this melancholic cloud, even the final brandy hadn't lifted their spirits. When Lancaster came out of the bathroom, Vidêt was curled up in her bed with the duvet up to her shoulders. Lancaster turned out the bedside light and nestled into the crisp clean sheets, pulling the cover up around his chin. His momentary inner smile at the comfort of the bed suddenly evaporated by the knowledge that the black dog of depression was still there, curled beside him on the floor. Tomorrow, he'd fight back; he'd awake with a new sense of purpose. But for now, he needed sleep.

He'd just drifted off when there was a voice by his ear.

"David?" Vidêt said gently. "I'm sorry, but... may I share your bed? I just can't shake off this sadness. I just want someone to hold for the night, I'm sorry."

Even in the semi-darkness of the room Lancaster could see the tracks of tears and the shiny droplets on her face. He knew what this was like. The night time loneliness; compounded by the case in hand. Lancaster pulled back the duvet without saying a word and let her in, kissed her forehead and put an arm around her shoulders where she snuggled her head against his chest. He felt the chill of a teardrop drip against his skin. There she stayed, until they woke in the morning, Lancaster with an arm that appeared to be completely dead. They stirred awake at the same time,

Vidêt lifted her head to look at him. "Thank you," was all she said. She kissed him briefly on the lips, turned and slipped quickly from the bed and straight into the bathroom. Moments later, he heard the sound of the shower. It was the start of a new day. Lancaster was determined the 'dog' would get no walk today. If it did, it would walk four paces behind.

The pair dressed, packed, and closed the door behind them. They left their luggage with reception, then headed for an early breakfast in the dining room. Lancaster paid and they were out on the road within an hour of getting up. Vidêt was driving as they retraced their route back down the motorway to Bristol Airport to pick up their car. The one they didn't need to have left behind, but never mind. Just over five hours after the last bit of bacon had been swallowed, they were approaching the turning for Totnes from the A38. Lancaster had decided they'd get this over and done with today. Either this man was going to be of use to them, or he wasn't. He didn't intend to wait another day to find out which it would be. They took the turn. A short time later, they found the turning to the converted farm buildings that housed the little artists collective. There was a pottery with a shop. A basketwork outlet, woven willow shopping baskets hanging from the rafters, reed baskets on the outside wall. Next to that, the gallery and studio of the artist, Stefan Pelchek.

Having parked in the adjoining carpark, they opened the door to the studio and walked straight 'in. Inside the room, the walls were hung with a vast selection of paintings. One whole wall was signed as 'Works by Resident Artist, Stefan Pelchek'. Without the sign it would have been easy for the two detectives to have known the work was by Pelchek. Most of the oil paintings were of naked or semi-naked young men, though there were two paintings of semi-naked women. The brush strokes were bold and sweeping and despite Vidêt's comment of the previous day, Lancaster thought several of the works were, in fact, quite striking. He wouldn't want them on his wall, but he could see why some people would. However, one would probably be enough.

A woman in her forties with masses of curly red hair popped her head round a door at the end of the gallery.

"Are you looking for Stefan?"

"Actually yes, we've driven quite a way—" Lancaster said, but didn't get a chance to continue.

"Oh of course," the woman replied. "You're quite late! We thought you weren't coming, but Stefan was expecting you. Please, go straight up," she finished, pointing to a wide wooden stairway leading to the loft space above.

The two detectives did as they were asked. Realising there'd been a case of mistaken identity, but making the most of it. When they arrived at the top of the stairs you could see the former barn's detail. The upper floor, once a hay loft, was a long room with huge exposed timber rafters, whitewashed walls. The floorboards, nearly a foot wide, curved and dipped through years of use and the effects of the seasons. Around the walls, on the floors, leaning up against the walls were dozens of finished and unfinished pieces of artwork, or 'shite', as Vidêt would say. Everywhere there were sweeps and swirls of oil paints on canvas, all depicting nakedness. Buttocks, breasts and various other body parts were all on display around the length of the room. It was an assault on the senses. Sitting in the middle of the room on a short sofa, itself resting atop a wooden dais, was a naked young man, legs curled up on the seat, one leg resting over one arm of the seat. His body was draped in a purple sheet and in a half circle around him were a series of chairs and easels at which a half dozen artists were busy attempting to capture his every shape, shadow and form.

"Ah, my late arrivals," the man in the oil and paint covered trousers said. "Susan and Peter, if I remember rightly. You are about an hour late, but welcome anyway. I know the traffic's been awful, dears, but let me get you seated and painting right away."

"Actually, I think there's been a mistake, Mr Pelchek," Lancaster said, holding up his warrant card. "I'm Detective Inspector Lancaster of the Devon and Cornwall Constabulary and this is my colleague Detective Sergeant Vidêt. We'd like to have a quick chat with you, if we may?"

Stefan Pelchek looked surprised, then quickly regained his composure.

"I'm very sorry, Detectives, but as you can see, I've a class and I'm very busy. I'm afraid you'll have to see my secretary downstairs and make an appointment. What exactly did you want to see me about?"

"We wanted to discuss a party you attended at Sir Philip Stottard's home near here in May 1999," Lancaster said, watching for the man's reaction.

The reaction was swift. He wiped his brushes on a cloth attached to his belt, turned to the class. "Ladies and gentlemen, it's time for a break, please, put down your brushes and if you head downstairs Madeline will pop the kettle on." At this point he leant to one side and shouted down the stairwell. "Maddy, they're coming down for early coffee, pop the kettle on, my love, will you? And get the biscuits out."

Stefan Pelchek took the two detectives to the other end of the room where a partition wall separated a small office space.

"1999. My God, what on earth do you want to drag that all up for? That was bloody years ago, a completely different life all together. It was all legal, between consenting adults, and in the privacy of somebody's home. I should say, somebody very influential at the time. Who on earth has dragged all this up again now? I cannot for one moment think anybody is making any accusations or complaints. I just don't believe it. I don't believe it."

"Well, Mr Pelchek, maybe it's probably best if you give us your side of the story," Lancaster said, looking to Vidêt to see if her phone was out and ready. Of course it was. He gave her a brief smile and continued, "It's always best to have a full account from as many sides as possible so please, just tell us yours."

Stefan Pelchek went on to tell them what had happened on that afternoon at Sir Philip's residence. In the 1990s,

Pelchek had been part of the gay BDSM scene, attending gatherings and private parties all over the country. During that period, he'd been a student at Plymouth Art College and managed to get part-time work as a male model. He did it less for the money, but more in the hopes it might open a door into fashion design. It had been his bondage-inspired clothing designs and accessories from college that had opened a different door, however. A door that led to him being invited to BDSM parties. Once through that door, he revelled in the excitement, the exotic, erotic nature of the games that were held and the alternative acts of sex being performed. For him, it had all been new and inspiring, if sometimes a little painful. Sometimes even just a little frightening. He enjoyed meeting with like-minded people, not just gay, but alternative people on the fringes of society, people out on the edge.

The party that May weekend back in 1999 had been the second one held at the Stottard home. The first one had been OK, but not well attended. It lacked the numbers to make it buzz. Different people took over different rooms within the house and cliques had formed. The BDSM group had gathered in the dairy larder, a large room attached to the kitchens. It was handy and fitted the bill to a T. It had a tiled floor that was easy to clean. It had meat and game hooks hanging from the rafters, a ready supply of water on tap and slate-covered work surfaces. All in all, an ideal setup for them, so by the time of the second party Stefan and his friends had bagged the room. Word spread through their little community and just about every gay BDSM follower had turned up. In fact, there were too many to use the room at the same time so they'd drawn lots as to who'd use it first.

Stefan had drawn a second-place ticket but didn't mind, it just built the expectation and excitement. During the waiting period he indulged in drinking as much of Sir Philip's wine as possible. By the time the second group got their turn, they were, in Stefan's words, 'gagging for it'. There were virtually no holds barred. A sexual free for all. It was halfway through the afternoon when a latecomer joined the throng. The young lad appeared to be up for anything and joined in with some of the lighter fetish stuff being performed. He became fascinated watching a guy and his partner who were indulging in bondage and whipping. Everyone had their own recognised 'cave' or 'break' words, used when the pain got too much or you'd had enough. At some point, the newcomer said he wanted to have a go on the hook. Well, by this time, almost everybody in the room was either in a state of extreme sexual arousal, stoned, in recovery or thoroughly pissed. So, the guy took his clothes off and somebody tied him to the hook by straps around his wrists and they took it in turns to whip him with a riding crop. It did all get a bit 'Lord of the Flies'. People were laughing, the guy was crying and kept shouting stop, stop. People just kept taking it in turns with the whip. Stefan started to get a bit worried, as by this time the guy's back was bleeding badly and he was sobbing his heart out, though he had stopped shouting. Stefan managed to get people to stop and asked the boy what his 'cave' word was and had he had enough, through his sobs he said his word was 'stop'.

Well, they took him down off the hook to tend his wounds and Stefan told him never to choose the word 'stop' again as a 'cave' word. It just wasn't the done thing. Stefan offered to find somebody to take him home or get a taxi, but he said no, he was OK. He just wanted to go to his room as he was staying over. Stefan and another guy helped him up to his bedroom on the second floor and he assured them he was OK. He just wanted to bathe and sleep, so that was where they left him. That was the last time they saw him. Stefan Pelchek wasn't invited to stay over, he wasn't part of the inner sanctum. So, he left later that evening and never thought anymore about him really until today.

"And you're telling me, that the last time you saw him he was definitely still alive?"

"Good God, yes!" Pelchek replied quickly, looking shocked. "Of course he was still alive, what the bloody hell do you think I am? I mean he was obviously hurt and upset, but dead? No way! When did he die? I don't believe it. It was all such a long time ago. How?"

Lancaster got his phone out and scrolled through till he found the photo he'd taken of the picture of Abdul that Brian Peachy had given them.

"Was this the man you helped to bed, Mr Pelchek?"

Pelchek took the phone from Lancaster and stared at the screen.

"Nope. Never seen this guy before, who is he? Anyway, this guy's black. The chap I was talking about was a tall skinny blond guy, I think he said his name was Patrick."

Lancaster left the loft looking like a thunder cloud, Vidêt in hot pursuit. They returned to the car and got in. Lancaster slamming the car door as he did so.

"If I go down one more bloody wrong alleyway," he said out loud to Vidêt, "I swear I'm liable to kill someone myself just so that I know who did it. I'm growing tired of all these false leads, Marie. Very tired indeed."

"But, sir, you know how this process works; you've told me often enough. Every person we have spoken to in the course of this enquiry has told us more about our victim and his life. We are filling in the detail, putting the flesh back on the bones—"

"Don't you dare fire my own cliché's back at me, Marie," Lancaster snapped back in reply, regretting the riposte instantly, but unable to apologise. "That's the last thing I need at the moment. We may well have told the story of this boy's sad life and crossed paths with those he met along the way, but so far none of us have the slightest idea of the two crucial elements to this whole enquiry. A: Why was he murdered? And B: Who was responsible for his death? It doesn't appear to be drug related, which would have pleased the boss no end. It doesn't appear to be revenge, or a result of a blackmailed lover or even a non-blackmailed lover, come to that. And now it doesn't even appear that he fell in with a sadistic cult or leather clad, whip wielding bloody fetish group or some such and got himself killed accidently. We've been on this enquiry for two weeks now and I don't feel any closer to solving the bloody case than when we started. You're right, and I'm sorry I snapped at you, we do know much more about Abdul and his short, sad little life than we ever knew before. We even know things we can't tell his mother. But those two crucial final points are evading me, out of reach, and I bloody well know that any moment now Craven will be on the phone all excited, wanting to know when he can book a TV crew and arrest somebody from the Stottard family. Better still, all of them. Between you and me, Marie, at this moment in time I've not got the foggiest idea where to turn next. I'm in the dark. It's been a long day and its Sunday, let's just head for home and call it quits for this afternoon. In the morning, you can write up all the notes from our interviews and I can start going over everything we have. See if we've missed something or somebody. But I've a bad feeling the answer is just going to be a resounding 'no'."

"Can I remind you, sir, with respect, we still have to speak with Lady Pamela about the discrepancies in her story with regards knowing Abdul."

"Very true, Marie, but I don't think I'm in the right frame of mind at the moment. I think we both need to be sharp and, on the ball, when we go to question her again. She'll keep for another day. No, for now let's just go home and get a good night's sleep."

CHAPTER ELEVEN

Lancaster ended his Sunday with a brain-clearing run. Jogging from his flat, arriving at the slip-way at Admiral's Hard in time to catch the little Cremyll Ferry across the river Tamar, landing him five minutes later on the opposite side of the river in Cornwall, at the entrance to the wooded landscape of Mount Edgcumbe. Lancaster often jogged around the estate. He'd jogged it in the snow. Jogged it in the teeth of a south-westerly gale and jogged it as today, on a gloriously warm, sunny evening. It made no difference to him. There were wooded paths through the dappled shade of tree covered trackways. There were tracks that ran along the coastline, giving stunning views across the sea. He could run up over the parkland to the tops of the hills behind Edgcumbe House. Running helped Lancaster clear the head. He often did it when the brain had a log-jam or, when he'd a lot on his mind. At the moment, he had both and couldn't separate them. Lancaster had two things troubling him, well, three, if you counted the looming cloud of depression he was fighting to keep at bay.

The first and most obvious problem was not being able to read this case. He was extremely concerned that he'd, unusually for him, put all his eggs in one basket on several occasions during the course of this enquiry. They'd come out as an omelette every time. Lancaster couldn't understand how he'd fallen into that trap. He was always telling Marie, 'Never set your sights on the first course of action'. Follow it, obviously, but always presume there was more to come. Keep your options open. He was confident they'd turned over every leaf they'd come across, but was worried that somewhere down the line he'd misread something they'd found, or had been told. Tomorrow he'd go through it all again, just to double check.

The second, most unsettling problem, was what to do about his feelings for Marie? He'd often looked at her when they were working. He couldn't help but notice she was good looking and had a nice figure, he was, after all, a male; it was built into the psyche to observe these things. He'd often noticed the lithe way she moved, the way she took stairs two at a time and never missed a breath. He liked the fact that she shared his sense of humour, though he doubted she understood it. He knew she was good at the job; he'd never had to tell her something twice. She picked things up in an instant and remembered them for next time, better still, she wasn't frightened to put forward points of view. He admired that from a professional standpoint, but he also liked it in a woman. He knew where he stood with people like that, he hated sycophants. But the few days and nights in France had broken the mould of the inspector/sergeant relationship. The cat was out of the bag, there was going to be no way he'd get the damn thing back in there without a fight. He'd broken the golden rule of a working relationship. He'd mixed business with immense pleasure and didn't know what to do about it. Worse still, he wasn't even sure he wanted to change anything about it at all. Should he go with it, see where it led?

He'd chosen his run for the day to be up to the Edgcumbe Folly, the mock ruin that sat on top of the hill. It was a hard run if you pushed it, which was what Lancaster wanted today. He wanted to feel the burn in the legs, the rasp in the throat when he tried to breathe. The only sound to be heard should be his struggle for breath, the blood coursing through the body. He set his stopwatch and broke into a full-on sprint as soon as he got through the gates, into the park proper. On the lower section he overtook several casual joggers and, without missing a stride, managed to avoid several dog walkers. He pushed hard until his lungs were burning, his throat felt raw. He didn't break stride until he reached the folly and, even then, ran round it three times for good measure. Eventually, he settled and stopped on the south east side of the folly and lay on the grass doing his usual leg stretches and twists to ease the body back into normality.

He sat up, resting his back against the wall to take in the view, checked his stopwatch, he'd done the run in sixteen minutes. Sixteen minutes... it had felt like an hour. He'd time to rest before going back down. The view back across the bay to the east, towards Plymouth Hoe was incredible whatever the weather but, in the sunshine, it was a joy. Sitting out in the bay, just inside the long breakwater were several warships sitting at anchor along with a massive fleet auxiliary vessel. Around these, several yachts in full sail curved round the bay, heading for open water, into the English Channel. He could see, even from where he sat, people out for a stroll on the Hoe, and why not?

Lancaster was contemplating the return jog when the mobile in his backpack rang. He contemplated ignoring it, but always gave in. Seconds later, it was out of the bag and in his hand. He didn't look at the screen, he knew it was going to be DCI Craven and he really wasn't in the mood to talk to him yet. He hit the answer tab and put the phone to his ear and kept it simple.

"Hello," he said, laying his head back against the warm stone of the folly wall.

"Good evening, sir," Vidêt said, much to Lancaster's surprise. "Am I disturbing you?"

Lancaster thought to himself, *if only you knew just how much.*

"No, Marie, not at all," he lied, "what can I do for you?"

"I know it was a long day, but could we meet up for a chat?"

"Of course, where are you?"

"I'm still at home at Torpoint, but I can jump on a ferry."

"I've a better idea. I'm at the Mount Edgcumbe Folly at the moment, just a touch sweaty from a run, how about you meet me at the Edgcumbe Arms in about fifteen minutes? I can buy you a beer."

"That being the case, make it twenty and I'll get a taxi."

"Twenty beers sounds like a lot, Marie," Lancaster laughed.

Vidêt laughed in return. "I meant I shall see you in twenty minutes."

Lancaster sat back to think things through. *Bloody hell. Now what do I do? So much for running her out of my mind. She just went and jumped straight back in.* He got up, took a swig from his water bottle, using the rest of the bottle to wash the sweat from his armpits, drying himself with his shirt. He kept a fresh T-shirt in his bag for the journey home, but for now he'd jog back down topless and change when he got to the pub. Even this course of action had left Lancaster thinking, *why? How could he stop this process? He wouldn't have changed his shirt for Craven! Why do it for Vidêt? Bloody hell...*

Lancaster was sitting alone, his clean T-shirt on, outside the busy pub at a table overlooking the Tamar River when the taxi arrived. Vidêt jumped out, paid the driver, slung a shoulder bag around her neck and walked across the grass to join him. Lancaster was acutely aware that in the past they'd meet in the office, sometimes go for a meal after work and discuss cases. However, in all that time he wasn't aware of ever taking any notice of what his colleague was wearing, never. Now, since spending time with her in France, away from the offices he was becoming obsessed with what she would be wearing as civilian clothing. Tonight was no exception. She was wearing the same bejewelled flipflops. Her tanned legs were met at thigh level by a pale denim skirt and she was wearing a loose white cotton shirt over the top with a neat leather belt clinching it at the waist. Her short black hair had an appealing, slightly scruffy unkemptness about it, as if coming out was an unplanned event. Sitting atop her hair were the obligatory sunglasses. He greeted her and offered her a beer or a cider. She opted for a cider. Lancaster popped into the bar, returning with a pint of Old Rosie in a chilled glass.

"Cheers," Lancaster said, clinking glasses. "Now, what did you want to see me about?"

"This is completely off the record and just between us, sir. But I wanted to get this, as you say over here... I wanted to get something off of my chest. Since we got back from France, I've noticed you have been withdrawn, a little off with me. OK, it may be my role as your sergeant to be your punching bag, but I think it has more to do with what happened in Narbonne and us breaking the rules. I wanted to tell you something and hope it will help you to understand me a little better."

Lancaster went to speak, and Vidêt put her hand up to stop him.

"Please, sir. I have thought about this a lot and I need to say it. When I was home in France, from when I was a child until I left school, started my service as a police cadet, I was physically abused by my father. Never sexually, you understand, always physical. He beat all of us. Me, my mother, my brother, until my brother ran away. I have not seen him since that day. My mother had gotten so used to the beatings she almost expected them; it became almost a ritual for her. But not for me. It just made me angry, I hated him and still do, but I was never strong enough to be able to stand against him. Until I joined the police. It was then that I told him, if he ever touched me or my mother again, I would see him in court and my fellow officers would see him in an alley one night. My mother wouldn't leave him; she still lives with him now, as far as I know. I don't know if he beats her or not, I have no idea anymore. But I escaped. But it left me with a great feeling of mistrust of men. I kept them at arm's length, they were not to be trusted. They could be vicious and dangerous, but in the force I learnt self-defence. I have always tried to keep fit, always tried to be better than the men I worked with. More to prove to myself than to prove anything to men. I was promoted early as a detective because I was good, but when I was stationed in Brest my boss there kept asking me out. I always said no, mainly because I didn't like him, but also, I didn't trust him, I was right not to. One night, we were supposed to be on a stakeout of a dealers flat and my boss tried to rape me. It didn't last long... he ended up on his knees in a lot of pain. I said I would not report him, but that wasn't the last of it. He started spreading rumours that he'd had me... My colleagues started to treat me differently; others tried to ask me out, they thought I was going to be the station bed-maiden. They got pissed off when I told them no, that's when I got posted to England. What happened when I was co-opted into the Met is another story, but what I am trying to get over to you, sir... is that with you I feel different."

She stopped for a moment and sipped at her drink before continuing.

"You are not like other men. You never once attempted to flirt with me or make suggestive comments. You accepted me from the moment I arrived in Plymouth and was assigned to you. You treated me as an individual, not as a woman. You asked me what my thoughts were on whatever case we worked on. You never mocked or made me feel insecure, never made me feel I must keep my guard up. That night in Narbonne was spontaneous. Instant. I let my guard down because I wanted to. Just because I don't trust men doesn't mean I am going to live the life of a nun. I enjoy sex, I am just very, very choosey about who I share my body with. That night in Narbonne was one of those nights. I trusted you. I shared my body with you because I wanted to. Not for a promotion, not to prove anything, simply because on that night I wanted you, I thought you enjoyed that night because you wanted me as well. No complications, no politics, no hidden agenda. I don't want to get married. I don't want to cause any trouble, I don't intend to go telling anybody else about it. I won't accuse you of pulling rank or spreading gossip, that's not because I am ashamed or sorry or even frightened of you, it's just that my life is just that, my life. It's private and it's mine. So... I am sorry if somehow you are upset by what we did. Sorry if you wish it hadn't happened, but it did, so please don't be changed by what happened in Narbonne. Don't make me regret putting my trust in you that night and blank me out. Don't be angry. But if you regret it and you need me to leave then I will. There... that's about it... I just needed to get that said."

Lancaster reached across the table and took Vidêt's hand. "You've got it all wrong, Marie," he said. "There are so many things going on at this one moment in time, I struggle sometimes to keep them organised and separate. You know I'm different, my brain's wired differently to other people. I look at life in a different way to most. I've always been an outsider. I struggle with the whole male macho business and have never been 'part of the team'. For a long while that worried me. But for many years now I've found I'm proud of being different, proud of not fitting in. When I met my wife, she understood that and rolled with it, made space for it. I loved her for that. When I lost her, I spent a lot of time being angry. Angry with everyone and everything. Angry at her for allowing me to trust her and let her into my weird world, then letting me marry her... and then leaving me. I subconsciously made the decision not to put my faith in a woman again. When you arrived, you posed no threat. You pushed no buttons and you're right, I sensed there was no hidden agenda. You were just here for the job. You wanted to learn and solve cases. We make a team. It took a while, but I began to trust you, I could bounce ideas off of you and you'd respond. Many detectives don't want their subordinates to realise when they're stumbling in the dark, they want them to think they're in control. They've a plan, they know where they're going next. With you I don't need to do that, but there's something else about me you don't know, and this is where I show my trust in you, Marie... I've suffered several times with depression. It creeps up and it hits me from time to time. There is no rhyme nor reason to its arrival and it arrives when I least need it or expect it. I've learnt over the years to keep a full-blown attack at bay, but it still affects me, still affects my moods... There's one looming in the background for me at the moment; it's been hovering for days now and one of the side effects is it clouds my judgement, makes me a hard person to be around. It also makes it harder to keep things separated and at the moment it's impinging on my ability to solve this bloody case..."

Lancaster immediately noticed the look of rejection appearing in Vidêt's face and realised she was getting the wrong message. "But the one piece of judgement, the one decision that I've absolutely no regrets or doubts about is that night of trust together in Narbonne. You're right, it was spontaneous, instant, but also simply brilliant and beautiful. It was erotic and slightly dangerous, and I've not felt that in tune with another person for years. I loved every moment of it... and I don't want it to have been the last time we share a bed together. I don't think either of us at the moment want to dive into a full-on relationship, but I certainly don't want to lose you from my life, Marie, either professionally or personally."

A broad smile spread across Vidêt's face and she gave Lancaster's hand a squeeze.

"I'm so pleased we understand each other better, I was worried we had messed up our working relationship and our personal life at the same time. You've put my mind at ease, but now you must go."

Lancaster was confused. "Why don't we have another drink first?"

"That would be nice, sir," she said, pointing at the slipway. "But it's 9:40 and I am pretty sure that's the last ferry back and neither of us have a car..."

As Lancaster grabbed his bag and stood to run for the ferry, Vidêt stood and turned his face to her and kissed him gently on the lips. "Thank you, sir, I will see you in the morning."

Lancaster went to go, but instinctively turned back, wrapped an arm around her shoulders and pulled her to him, returning the kiss. He gave her one last look then ran for the ferry, jumping across the gap and into the boat as it pulled away from the slipway. He watched her standing on the grass. He'd surprised himself. It wasn't until he'd found himself saying all that, that he realised it was actually what he wanted. Tomorrow wouldn't just be the start of another day, a new week. But possibly the start of a whole other life.

Lancaster arrived in the office at eight o'clock the following morning. He was bright, alert and ready to take another look over this whole case. He'd left the black dog at home. For today, at least. Vidêt was already at her desk, earphones in, playing back the recordings of the various interviews they'd carried out, typing them up onto pro-forma statement sheets ready for printout. There was a lot to catch up on, starting in France and going right through to their last, inconclusive conversation with Stefan Pelchek. Playing back the interviews made in France was a surprisingly enjoyable experience, despite the sometimes sad and depressing content. She could pick out background noises of people drinking coffee in the sunshine. The audible sound of plane tree leaves, rustling in the breeze of a Narbonne square and the occasional screaming sounds of a swift flypast. She heard the sounds of crickets in the southern sun and picked out the scraping song of the first of the cicadas singing in the trees around the pool at the villa. She'd never realised just how much you could get from background noise.

Vidêt's plan was to keep her nose to the grindstone. Not stop until all statements were on a hard drive and printed for the file. She knew as well as her boss did that sometime soon DCI Craven would be calling for an update, and if nothing else, a cardboard file packed full of statements and interviews always appeared to impress the man. She wanted Lancaster to be ready for him. She didn't want what had developed between them since they left for France to impinge in anyway on the practicalities of their work. If anything, she wanted it to have a positive effect, which was why she'd started at seven o'clock that morning. Lancaster arrived at her desk just after eight o'clock with a takeaway cup of coffee for her. She stopped her phone and pulled out her earplugs.

"Good morning, sir, and thank you... for the coffee," she said with a slightly impish smile.

"Not a problem... Vidêt," he replied, smiling back in return. "So, if you're OK cracking on with the notes I intend going back over everything we've covered so far. If it's not being a pain can you print out each statement as you finish them, then I can add them to my pile and read back through them again? If I find anything untoward or anything I think could be important I'll give you a shout and see what you think, is that OK?"

"That's fine, sir, I can print you off the first three already."

They smiled at each other and Lancaster went off to the white board to update some facts. He thought there was a new atmosphere in this office, and in this relationship. And he liked it.

Vidêt arrived at his desk every thirty minutes or so, depositing another set of interview notes. Lancaster put them at the bottom of his stack and kept on reading. He'd gone right back to the beginning. He'd read the notes they'd made during the initial autopsy at the path lab and gone back through all of Rover's comments and notes. He'd gone over all the communications and conversations he'd had with the tailor shop, Hyams. Lancaster spent a long while going back over his interview with Lady Stottard and Vidêt was right. Pamela definitely looked at the photo and went out of her way to state she'd never seen Abdul before. That certainly needed clarification now they'd a proper photograph of him, rather than an artist's impression. He also glanced through the notes Vidêt had made from the chat they'd had with the gardener at Lady Pamela's old house at Totnes. That made Lancaster think: they'd got quite a lot out of the gardener at the villa in France. It was all circumstantial background information, but it had filled in a lot of detail and had in fact clarified a number of points. *Maybe*, Lancaster thought, *heading back to see Lady Pamela and having a stroll around the main garden again to find that gardener might also pull in a bit more information about life at the 'big house'.* He made a mental note to add that to his to-do list.

Lancaster began ploughing his way through the material from Narbonne. There was nothing bright and sunny about these interviews other than the memories. He did think they made for interesting reading. The sad stories relayed by Abdul's first friendship with Christopher, then his affair with Maurice were just that, sad stories of love and betrayal. But no other names or details magically appeared before his eyes. No missed clues or inferences. They were just a series of sad, lost love affairs. A life cut short. Finally, he worked his way through the London interviews. These had given him more than he was expecting. They hadn't solved the case, but they'd almost filled in the detail of Abdul's short life in the bright lights of London. Lancaster had been convinced, as they thundered through Chelsea in the back of the black cab, that they were on the way to speak with the murderer, and he'd be contacting the Met for assistance by mid-afternoon and making an arrest.

Yet, once again, Abdul had left behind, indirectly, yet another broken heart. Another sad man left drowning in the wake of Abdul's cruise through the gay community.

Lancaster checked his watch. He was wondering why his stomach was rumbling, when he realised it was two o'clock. He looked across the room to where Vidêt was still typing, earphones plugged in. Lancaster headed to the canteen, picked up a couple of rolls and two mugs of tea, then wandered back to the office. Walking back in, he was disappointed to see, standing in front of the whiteboard next to Vidêt, the unmistakable form of DCI Craven being talked through the items on the board by Marie. They both turned as he walked through the door. The look on Vidêt's face said 'sorry', though there was nothing to be sorry about.

"Bomber," the big man said, holding out his hand in greeting. "Looking tanned at our expense I see, and you read my mind, I was gagging for a cup of tea."

Lancaster handed over one of the mugs to Craven and handed the other to Vidêt along with one of the rolls.

"Are we all up to date, Vidêt?" Lancaster said, looking optimistic.

"Yes, sir. Folder is on your desk, it's all backed up on the data base. If it's OK, may I pop to the canteen for lunch?" She made a tactical retreat.

"Right then Bomber, what have you got for me? Worryingly, I don't sense from your board any sign of an arrest coming up any time soon. So, what have we found out? I don't see much sign of the Stottards on the board either. So, what was the trip to France all about? I can't believe it was a jolly, but I was hoping you'd come back with more than just a tan and an expense sheet."

Lancaster filled him in, telling him straight away why there was no sign of the Stottard family being on the board. His fear of prying eyes and masonic links within the rest of the station being his prime concern. He then followed that with all they'd found out to date, précising as best as possible, but trying to give as much new information as he could to show that although they'd not solved the case by going to France, they'd certainly found out more about their victim and his life. That had enabled them to, sadly, cross any involvement with drugs completely off the list. The trip to France had also categorically confirmed the fact that it was Sir Philip that brought the boy to England. That then led them into the gay community in London and introduced more characters and it appeared the arrival of Abdul was then the catalyst for the collapse of the Stottard marriage. But as DCI Craven pointed out, after Lancaster had finished his report, all the file actually contained was a long list of people who hadn't killed Abdul. As this was in fact a murder enquiry, the answer they were all searching for simply wasn't there. Craven's last question was as to where Lancaster expected to go next in his search for the truth about this crime.

"Well, sir," Lancaster replied, knowing just how weak this was going to sound. "There are two lines of enquiry I want to follow up. The first is a discrepancy we've found in the interview with Lady Stottard, who claimed she'd never seen Abdul before when we showed her the artist impression. However, we now know this to be untrue, so why did she lie? Secondly, we want to interview the gardeners at Boldean, the old Stottard family home. We feel they may well have information that could lead us in the right direction."

DCI Craven stood and looked at Lancaster. Several moments passed before Craven spoke.

"So basically, Bomber, you have nothing. Nothing at all. Would that be a correct assumption? You've been on this for over two weeks. You've spent a chunk of my annual budget on a jolly for two to the South of France and we don't appear to be any nearer finding the culprit. Being gay is no longer a crime. Being separated from your husband is not a crime, though the amount my ex-wife takes from me every week, it bloody well should be. To be honest, Bomber, I have to say I'm a touch disappointed. I give you these weird ones because I know the way your brain works. The other DI's don't have the patience for picking these things apart, they know there's no glory in it. But my feeling is always that if it's a crime, it needs solving. Every time some bastard commits any kind of crime and is allowed to get away with it, we've failed, they've won. I don't like that, but sometimes you just have to know when you're beat. Austerity bites, Bomber, my son, austerity bites. The buggers up top will tell you it doesn't make a difference, we should be able to manage with less money, still get the job done. But you and I both know that's bollocks. Some days you just have to know you've spent enough time and money on something and you call it a day."

Lancaster looked at the man. He liked his boss, but some days he just didn't get it. He turned and walked back to his desk, picked up the by now, thick manila folder and walked back to DCI Craven and put it into his hands.

"With all due respect, sir," Lancaster replied to Craven's monologue, "I have to disagree with your reading of the case. You can't say we have nothing. Two weeks ago, we had a three-thousand-year-old bog body. Now we know his name, how old he was, where he was born, what date he died, how he died and how he lived. We know he was gay. Not even his mother knew that. We know who brought him into the country and when. We know when he came to Devon and, where he was directly before he was murdered. So, from a standing start of a three-thousand-year-old bog body two weeks ago to today... well, I reckon we have a lot. I'm sorry if you don't think so. Now all we have to do is find out who killed him on that Saturday in May 1999 and why. Then, we're done. Sorry, sir, with respect... again, many other DI's would've just left it as a bog body and walked away. I'll shut up now."

"Bomber, I honestly don't know why I put up with you. You and I both know you're a nutter, but somehow you always get the job done... I tell you what we do, my son. You and Frenchie have got one more week on this. I want this closed, either way, by next Monday morning at this same time. Then we release the body, get it shipped back home to Mum, is that understood? If nothing else, the boy deserves that, anyway, it looks better to be able to say, 'we repatriated the body' rather than us having to cremate somebody and send home his ashes."

"Yes, sir, of course, and thank you again," Lancaster replied.

"Bomber, don't grovel son, it's unseemly," Craven answered. With that, he left the office.

Vidêt walked in shortly after.

"So how did that go, sir?" she asked with a quizzical look.

"We've got until next Monday to solve it. So, what do you reckon?"

Vidêt didn't have an answer.

†

By close of day, all interviews were filed and stored online. Vidêt and Lancaster had shared the process of going back through all the interview notes to cross-reference the decision that Lancaster had come to. They both agreed that they'd missed nobody or anything. They could see no other avenue that would account for the murder of Abdul. There had to be something that either happened on that Saturday back in 1999 that would account for his death, or the only other alternative at this moment was the involvement of Lady Pamela. Did she have Abdul taken out by persons unknown? The only way to find that out was to attempt to get a slip-up from the lady herself, which Lancaster thought highly unlikely. Or, they find a witness who saw something out of place on that day or either side of that day. Somebody who's face didn't fit. Somebody who, like Abdul, stood out from the crowd, then attempt to identify that individual after an absence of twenty-one years, by next Monday. Simple.

Lancaster finished the day by putting a call through to Lady Pamela. She didn't answer, so he left a short message asking her to call. Five minutes later she did just that, the husky voice Lancaster thought she'd cultivated just for moments like these came on the line.

"Detective Inspector, what a pleasant surprise. What can I

do for you?"

He explained he wanted to run a couple of things by her and was she by any chance available at any time the following morning. An appointment was made for the next day, nine o'clock. Lancaster couldn't help but think of all the people they'd met so far during the course of this enquiry, tangling with Lady Pamela was the most dangerous. The detectives had found the day's process of typing up and going over all the statements and interviews twice a tiring exercise, but it needed doing. They were confident it had served its purpose. In line with their promise to each other to keep their affair an arrangement of convenience, they went separate ways for an early night and a plan to meet up first thing in the morning at the office before the drive to Totnes.

Unusually for a Devon summer, the next day was sunny. It wasn't too hot, just bright and blue skied. Vidêt was again at the wheel. The journey to Totnes took longer than normal on account of the continuous convoys of tractors and trailers they got held up behind. They arrived in good time and spent a couple of minutes in the car planning their course of action. Vidêt agreed that, should Lady Pamela decide she wanted to discuss the intimate details of her previous life in private, then she was happy to drop out of the interview and wait in the car. After they were done here, if it proved, as Lancaster thought it would, to be inconclusive, they'd continue up the drive and make a formal visit to the main house to speak with the garden staff.

The housekeeper answered the door, ushering them into the lounge where a well-dressed Lady Pamela stood waiting for them, coffee at the ready.

"Good morning, detectives, coffee?"

They said yes. The housekeeper poured before withdrawing with a polite nod to Her Ladyship.

"Now, what can I do for you this time?" she said, sitting back in her chair.

"I'm trying to finalise a chain of events, Lady Pamela," Lancaster began, noticing straight away that he wasn't reprimanded and told to call her Pamela. "If it's not being too invasive of your privacy, can I ask exactly when and where your final breakup with your husband occurred? Was it down here at the manor or was it at Dolphin Square?"

Lady Pamela looked shocked at the question. "My God, Inspector, you really are a dog with a bone. Do you never let go once you get your teeth in? Why does this matter now? It was a long time ago. My husband is now deceased, even that was a long time ago. I cannot see what this could possibly bring to any enquiry you might be involved in."

"It's relevant, Lady Pamela," Lancaster replied. "Because I've a witness that puts you inside your husband's apartment arguing over a man your husband was with at the time. You then left the apartment and stayed overnight at a hotel, and if that was what caused the breakup, then that's relevant to my timescale. If there was another reason for the breakup then it must have happened whilst both of you were staying down here at the Manor and that would give me something else to follow up. It's as simple as that."

"Man! A man. Detective Inspector, he wasn't with a bloody man," she replied angrily. "When I walked in, he was with a damn boy." She took a sideways look at Vidêt. "I suppose there are no secrets between you two anyway, but it's something I

345

would much rather forget, it was disgusting," she continued. "When the doorman let me into the apartment there was no sign of Philip. I knew he was home because the doorman had told me so. So, like any normal wife would, I just walked straight into the bedroom to use the ensuite and there he was. Naked, on the bed, on his knees, bent over the backside of a boy, well, a young man, but it doesn't really matter. It was disgusting, how could he? I mean, we'd been married for years. I knew he had another life up in London, but it never came between us. But I never, ever thought it was spent with men. Good God, man, we had two children together! What was I going to tell them? So yes, I did leave the apartment and went and stayed at a hotel and yes, it was the cause of the breakup, I was disgusted. I could hardly bear to be in the same house as him, let alone the same room. As I told you, soon after that I took the boys out of school, we went to the chateaux and spent the rest of the year there. Any other conversations were conducted over the telephone. By the time we came back to the UK later that year the deal was done. I had very little say in any of it. I was given the gatehouse to live in. Philip had already got contractors in and they'd started on the conversion work. He'd also made a considerable number of estate staff redundant which, and pardon my French," she said, looking at Vidêt, "pissed me off considerably. Many of them had been on the estate for years, sons of fathers' etcetera. Philip was a complete arse about it. Said we needed to cut the wage bill if the manor was going to give an income. What an absolute bastard."

Lancaster opened his folder, removed the naked, artistic photo of Abdul from it. He passed it to Lady Stottard, adding, "Do you recognise this person?"

Lady Pamela took the photo from him, looked at it only for a moment before saying, "I'm sure you showed a similar picture the last time you came, Inspector, only the one you showed had tattoos. I seem to remember that I told you then, the answer is no. I do not know this man. So apart from him obviously being the very same person whom you had plastered over the newspapers, who the hell is he?"

"He is the man your husband was in bed with, Lady Pamela." Lancaster watched for her reaction. "And you still say you don't know him?"

She looked again at the photograph. Again at Lancaster. Returned her gaze to the photo.

"My God. He had better skin than me. He was a pretty boy before he had his face tattooed. Why do people do that? I mean, there's nothing wrong with body art... but never the face, surely?"

"And you still maintain you don't recognise him?" Lancaster asked again.

"Inspector Lancaster. I walked in on my husband and this person, or so you say. All I ever saw was his buttocks, and before you ask, Inspector, I knew it was a male because my husband was in the process of playing with his genitals. Most of the rest of him was covered by the body of my late husband. I never bothered to look at his face and anyway it was buried in the pillows. The pillows I'd chosen from Harrods! All I could ever remember was the sight of my husband, naked, with another man. I don't remember any formal introductions being made. I left the room and Philip came after me. We argued in the hallway, I picked up my bag and left. At no time did I ever see this boy's face and to this day all I can ever picture from that day was the raw, blatant, carnal nakedness of two men on the bed together, and being the prude that I am, that memory still haunts and disgusts me."

"You never saw this boy here at the estate with your husband or anybody else?" Lancaster asked, knowing he was clutching at straws.

Lady Stottard handed back the photograph looked Lancaster straight in the eyes and said simply, "No... Now was there anything else, Inspector? I have a busy day."

"Many thanks for your time, Lady Stottard," Lancaster replied, pocketing the photo and thinking to himself that he couldn't imagine she'd be putting on that husky 'come hither' voice again if he ever phoned.

Lancaster and Vidêt sat in the car, despondent. That, in all honesty, had been Lancaster's last real card. Even if Lady Stottard had arranged the murder, and Lancaster didn't really think she had, he'd no way to directly connect her to Abdul's death. As Craven would say, he had nothing. He'd run out of characters, had nowhere else to turn. At this moment, he could find no more. They'd been down every alleyway, checked every side street, and had found nothing. They'd filled in detail. Coloured in the picture. Put together the jigsaw and it all fitted. But there were bits missing. The very bits that showed the murderer and told them the reason why. Lancaster knew in his heart they hadn't missed anything. He knew nobody had slipped through their net. Whoever committed the crime had to be random? Abdul must have just been in the wrong place at the wrong time. For Lancaster that was no consolation, it was still an unsolved murder. He couldn't imagine what he was going to say to Madame Mehemet.

"I know this won't make it feel any better, sir, but I don't think we could have tried any harder. In the hands of another team, they would still be looking for a name."

"Well, you're definitely right about one thing, Marie, it doesn't make me feel any better. Start the car. Let's go up the drive to the main house. If nothing else, we can have a nice chat with the old gardeners."

Vidêt got to the top of the main drive and parked in the designated parking zone. *Obviously not a leftover from when the manor was a private residence,* Lancaster thought. The two detectives were approaching the main door when around the corner came the same gardener they'd seen when they visited previously.

"Gardens ain't open," the man said. "Them's not open again till next month, tis in the yeller book."

Lancaster and Vidêt both pulled out their warrant cards at the same time in a coordinated movement that looked like it had been choreographed for the occasion.

"DI Lancaster, DS Vidêt, Plymouth CID. I wondered if you might be able to help us. Can I ask how long you've worked here?"

"You were here on open day. You'm never said you's police," the man said.

"Well, actually, when we were here for your open day we came as visitors to look at the gardens. Now, can I ask again, how long have you worked here?"

"Man and boy," he replied. "Started here soon as I left school. I wuz fifeteen. Did'n wanna work nowhere else, me dad and me granfer all worked here, see."

"If it's not a rude question, are they still alive?"

"Granfer went years ago, Dad's still alive. Lives here with me and me missus in the old cottage. He's bin with us ever since he was made redundant and lost his house."

"So you must have been working here when Lord and Lady Stottard split up," Lancaster said.

"Bloody tragic. Us didn't see that coming, I can tell yer. One minute everythin was fine n' dandy then bugger me them's had a big fallin out gone separate ways."

The man, Peter Baylis, went on to tell them how it had been a lovely place to work up until then. There'd been five gardeners, plus casual estate workers when needed. There were four staff in the main house; including the cook, Mrs Jenks who, according to the gardener, in time-honoured fashion, 'made bloody good cakes'. Every year, they'd have a summer garden party for staff and families and the tradesfolk the estate used. Every Christmas, a church service, then a kid's party. The Stottards were the last of the old school, before accountants got their noses in the trough. The bottom dropped out of the local community when the pair had split up. Everyone was shocked. Everything changed overnight; there was a meeting of all staff in the courtyard one morning. Lady Pamela told everyone there and then that the two of them were going their separate ways, but everybody should keep doing their jobs until told otherwise. Then Her Ladyship packed up, she and the boys left for the South of France for the summer. Just as the estate was settling back down again, His Lordship arrived with a load of blokes in suits for a couple of days. Before he left to go back to London, he called all the staff together again and told them there were going to be some changes at the estate. Sir Philip told them Her Ladyship would be moving into the gatehouse on her return from France. The main house was going to be leased out. Converted to become private retirement flats. Some of the staff would be made redundant or take early retirement packages. The estate manager would be staying on to manage all the estate woodlands and the gardens, but all the farms would be rented out or sold. Existing tenants of estate premises would be given the option to buy, which was going to be difficult as most staff were poorly paid in the first place. You got your tithe cottage instead of a chunk of your salary, most estate folk understood that and were fine with it. But the chances of being able to raise enough money to buy your cottage when you'd just lost your job were virtually nil. That's how the gardener ended up having his father, Godfrey Baylis, living with him and his wife.

"Did the staff at the manor all know why the couple had split up?" Lancaster had asked.

Apparently not. No one was ever told. Most people just thought Lady Pamela might have had a bit on the side, some fancy man and got found out. It would've been understandable, the gardener had said. Sir Philip spent so much of his time elsewhere, Scotland, London, out in the Caribbean. Nobody would have cared less if she'd had another bloke though, they were all just pleased she spent her time down here with the boys. It made the place feel lived in. The boys were always in and out of the garden or the woods.

"Had any of the staff heard the rumour that maybe Sir Philip was gay?" Lancaster asked tentatively.

At this, the gardener laughed.

"What you mean, rumour? Rumour... you'm hav'in a bloody larfe, corse he were queer, us all no'de that. Didn't fuss us. He use ta have these parties. Bugger, there was blokes mincing bout all over the place. Weren't no trouble to us, them left us alone, wim left them alone. They were harmless enough. Don't think Her Ladyship knew though. Him always had his parties when her was off in France or some-such with the boys."

Apparently, according to the gardener, he was often at the manor alone when the wife was away, with just his old friend from school, Piers Ward. ("Now ee wuz defnitly queer.") They'd stay in bed half the day then play croquet on the lawn all afternoon. If it was wet, they'd be in the billiards room all day drinking brandy.

Vidêt had pulled out her phone and scrolled through it whilst the gardener was telling them all this until she found the semi-naked photo of Abdul. She handed it to Lancaster.

"Just out of interest," Lancaster asked, taking the phone from her and showing the man the picture, "did you ever see this young man around the place at all?"

"Yes," the man replied, looking at the phone. "That looks like Abdul. He come down here a couple of times with Sir Philip. Funny a'nuff, when my old man seen 'im first, him reckon'd he wuz a bad omen. I said to him, 'Why'd ja reckon that? Coz him's black', he said, no. Colour don't mean nuthi'n. Tis coz His Lordship look like him's in luv, and bugger me he wuz bloody right. No sooner him's on the scene than that's when the whole place went to 'hell in a handcart', if you get my meanin'. Don't know how or why, but dad wuz bloody right. I thought when I first seen him His Lordship had adopted him or some'in. He only looked like a boy, second time he come here he looked even more like it. He was poncing around here in a pair of pinstripe bloody shorts that looked to bloody long for 'im, tween you an me, him looked a right twat."

"Can you by any chance remember what time of year that was?" Lancaster asked, on the off-chance.

"Bugger, twuz a long time ago, can't remember that far back."

"I know it's a lot to ask, but would it be possible to have a chat with your dad, Mr Baylis? He sounds like he was a bright spark, would I be right?"

"He still is. Him's eighty-three but still got all the marbles rattlin around in there, bloody shame they made him redundant all that time ago. He still had lots to give, now he helps out for free cos he don't like sittin on his arse all day doin nuthin. My missus loves the old bugger."

"So, what do you think? Do you think we could just have a quick chat with him? He may remember Abdul as well and he might just be able to give us some more information."

"What's this all about then?

"Well Abdul's mother's been looking for him," Lancaster replied, not exactly lying. "It appears he's been missing for over twenty years. We've been trying to piece together his movements."

"That's sad. Well, Dad might like a chance to chat about old times. I can take you over to the cottage, I know he's in, coz I seen him jus' now by the back porch sittin' in the sun on the bench smoking his pipe. My missus won't let 'im smoke it in the house"

The gardener left his wheelbarrow and led them through a gate, then on through the almost fully planted vegetable garden. Rows of young French beans in orderly lines, rows

353

of cabbage plants nestled under netting and, a beautiful collection of tripod-tied bamboo canes, the twining tendrils of runner beans already a third of the way up the framework. The gardener led them towards yet another gate in the imposing wall at the far end of the plot.

"I just had a thought," the gardener said, coming to a halt just before the gate. "I can tell you what time of year twas' when us seen him, I mean, young Abdul. Must ave bin in May, dunno what year mind, but had to ave bin May, cos I remember; I just planted out the runner beans and Sir Philip came in the garden, said us could all go home early and to stay away till the Monday, he wuz avin a party. I always plants'em in May, in'that a thing, juz came to me, yep, had to be in May."

They continued toward a row of cottages. Lancaster could see the one with the garden bench outside resting neatly against the wall. However, there was no sign of anyone sitting in the sunshine. The gardener led them to the back door of the cottage, opened it and called out. A male voice called from somewhere inside and the three of them walked into the house. They went through the kitchen and pushed open a door, entering a large living room swept by sunlight, beaming in through a bay-window. Sitting on one of the armchairs, watching the television, was an elderly gentleman wearing a pair of heavy brown cord trousers, an open necked pale blue shirt and tartan slippers. Mr Baylis looked every bit of his eighty-three years. His face furrowed, lined and bronzed, like a work of art. His hands huge, out of scale with the rest of his body. Lancaster was reminded of a mole, sitting there with earth moving hands at rest on the arms of the chair. He looked like a man who'd had a hard life. Physical and mental, though on his head a full mound of silvery grey hair hung long down around his shirt collar, making him look like an ageing rock star. The man looked up when they walked into the room, immediately reaching for the remote and turning the television off.

"Dad, these people are detectives from Plymouth. They wanna word with you bout Sir Philip's young friend from way back, you remember? That black boy, Abdul."

Lancaster and Vidêt had displayed their warrant cards to the elderly gent and Lancaster had passed Vidêt's phone to the man to show him the artistic, semi-naked photo of Abdul. He was preparing to pose the first of his questions when he was taken by surprise by what happened next. The ageing Godfrey Baylis took the phone from him, stared at the picture on the screen. Then started to sob. Gently at first, so gently that Lancaster thought the man was laughing. Then as he looked, the man's tears began rolling down the wrinkles of his face, like a flash flood in a ravine. The sobs became more uncontrollable until the man's whole body was racked by them. His body began to shake in time to the sobbing. Lancaster was afraid they'd triggered some kind of fit, but then Peter Baylis knelt beside his father's chair. His own face turned white, a look of complete shock swept across it. The boy obviously had no idea what had just happened to his father.

"Dad, what's wrong? What is it? Shall I get the doctor or sum'it?" he said looking concerned. Peter went to take the phone from his father to give to Lancaster, but Godfrey Baylis wouldn't let it out of his hands. He just kept crying. Rocking back and forth in his chair, big teardrops falling onto his trousers, forming damp markings on the material. It had never occurred to Lancaster that the old man may be senile, even possibly suffering from some form of dementia. Peter hadn't mentioned it when he'd asked to speak with him but he couldn't imagine he was going to be able to get much information out of the poor sobbing man sitting before him, clasping Vidêt's phone in his hands.

"Do you want me to call in medical assistance?" Lancaster asked.

"I dun'know what's wrong with'im," Peter Baylis said. "I ain't sin im like this before."

The old man sobbed for a little longer before making a conscious effort to hold back his tears. Peter handed his father a handkerchief to wipe his nose, as the old man did so he looked up at the two detectives. He stared at them for a little moment, as if working out who they were, then spoke directly to them.

"I knew this would happen sometime," the old man said through his tears, whilst looking at Lancaster. After a long deep breath he continued, "I knew you'd find me in the end, given time. I knew he wouldn't stay buried for ever. Knew it'd all come out one day. It's hung round my bloody neck for twenty-odd years. Hung there like a millstone. Getting heavier every day till some days I can hardly lift me head up. It's followed me round like a bloody cloud. Every time I look up there it is, just hanging there. I got to get rid of it. I gotta tell someone. Clear the air before I meet me maker, he's bin tappin' on my shoulder a few times of late. When I sin his face in the paper a cuple a weeks ago I knew him soon' as I sin 'im. Knew someone was gonna come lookin."

The aged Godfrey Baylis told his story. Finally allowing pent up words and memories of a twenty-one-year-old secret to be released, to spill out as an act of cleansing.

As the present gardener Peter had done, Godfrey had followed his father, Cecil, into the trade of horticulture. Coming into the gardens of the manor house first as a 'pot boy' at the age of fifteen. Washing, sorting and stacking away the flowerpots used for raising plants around the greenhouses. He'd begun working under his father Cecil as a child, but was never paid. His father, Cecil, served in the First World War, but had gone in late as his skills were needed at home working the land and the woodlands. It wasn't until so much cannon fodder was laid beneath the mud of the front lines that skill on the land suddenly became less important than standing in front of enemy machine guns, providing more targets in the 'war to end all wars.' He survived, returned to the land and his job at the manor. The rural tranquillity, the growing of flowers and vegetables, helped ease the painful memories, lay the ghosts of fallen comrades. Gave him the peace and breathing space to father three sons, Godfrey being the only one still alive. Godfrey could remember the Second World War. The one that came despite the 'war to end all wars.' He remembered as a child, the old Stottards, Sir Philip's parents, being moved into the gatehouse lodge when the main house was taken over by the Americans. First, used to house officers and those of a higher rank while the woodlands filled with tents and weaponry. Tanks, jeeps, lorries all destined for departure the following year from Dartmouth, Salcombe, Brixham, heading for the D-Day landings. Then, after the June invasion of Europe, for a brief moment in time there was emptiness and peace, but only for a moment. Soon, the house became a hospital for returning waves of wounded, of which there were many.

After the war years, Godfrey became a full member of the

garden staff. He honed his skills watching and listening to his father and going to the nearby agricultural college to study all the new techniques, becoming the first member of the Baylis family to ever gain any actual qualifications in the trade of gardening. As the years went by Godfrey had slowly taken over the reins from his father. He'd fallen in love with Clarice, the daughter of the estate's head forester and the pair married after a short courtship. A year later, Clarice had given birth to baby Peter, just over a year after that, she gave birth to a daughter, Daisy. Following the sudden death of his father from a heart attack they'd moved this new Baylis generation into the old family cottage. His mother had died many years prior to the death of Cecil so the old home held many memories for him. It felt like a safe place to bring up his family. His new role as head gardener came easily to Godfrey. He was ready to move the gardens into a new age. It didn't take long before he'd managed to earn himself a considerable reputation amongst the other gardeners and 'allotmenteers' of the area. Entering plants, vegetables and fruit in the name of Boldean Manor at all the local agricultural shows. Bringing home cups and certificates to prove he was the best at it for miles around. He'd even been featured a couple of times on the local television channel as part of their gardening series and for a brief moment, had held high hopes of becoming a TV gardener just like old Percy Thrower or the new guy on the block, Geoffrey Hamilton, but it was not to be.

Life had settled into a steady rhythm of the seasons. Sowing seeds, planting out plants, nurturing them to bear fruit, then harvesting whatever crop it was. Clearing away, tidying up, then starting all over again. Godfrey was happy with his lot.

His wife often said it would be nice to take young Peter and Daisy for a holiday. A seaside holiday. So they could swim and play on the sand in the sun. So Godfrey used to take them down to Torquay and leave them for the day to have their holiday, then he'd go down at the end of the working day and pick them up again. He told her he couldn't leave the garden to go with them, there was too much to do.

After the old Lord Stottard died, the young son, Philip, inherited the estate. The place stepped up a gear. Sir Philip wanted the estate run on the new wave of 'organic' principles. Godfrey had to get a different set of books to read to get the hang of these new ideas. He loved the challenge. He loved finding out new techniques, new ways of doing things. Saw it as improving his skills, making himself a better gardener.

Sir Philip had arrived with his new fiancé, Pamela. Everyone loved her. She was beautiful, funny, just a little bit saucy, and soon had all the old boys on the estate falling over themselves to please her. She'd come from the Channel Islands and had French ancestry or so they said. After the huge wedding held in marquees on the manicured lawns beside the manor house, attended by all the great and good of the area and even further afield, the couple settled into the manor. They had the whole place redecorated and brightened up with new furnishings. Lady Pamela took a great interest in the running of the estate, in particular, the kitchen garden. She wanted fresh-cut flowers in most rooms three times a week. She wanted the whole of the main staircase garlanded with evergreen foliage and berries for Christmas; a time when the house was full, with guests and staff gathered at the bottom of the stairs in the main hallway for the Christmas carol service before the children's party in the afternoon. Godfrey remembered it as a rich and wonderful period in his life. He felt he was at the top of his game. He was respected not only by other gardeners, but by the estate staff and more importantly, by the Stottard family. They came to him for advice on what to plant, where and when, and to find what new cut-flower had become all the rage. A must have for vases and pots around the house.

This glorious époque, however, didn't last. Godfrey's wife Clarice and their daughter Daisy were both killed in a tragic accident when a tree fell across the bus they were travelling in on the way to Newton Abbot during a summer storm. Godfrey could still remember holding his hat in his hands as he stood beside Peter at the grave side, the day of the burial. Held it so tight he'd left marks in the material of the rim, still there to this day. Lady Pamela and Sir Philip had both been supportive, given both the men, Peter and Godfrey, time off to recover. But apart from the official meetings with the coroner and the day of the funeral, neither had taken any time away from work. It was summer, there was too much to do or all the work done during the spring would go to waste. Clarice and Daisy would have understood, besides, both men could either have sat at home thinking about their loss or been at work thinking about their loss. They both knew were they'd rather be.

That was just the start of the down turn in the life of the estate. Before long Sir Philip started spending more time in London and, in late summer and autumn, up to Scotland overseeing the other estate and its shooting season. 'A profitable resource, an important networking location', Sir Philip had said. From time to time, His Lordship would arrive at the manor whilst Lady Pamela was away. When he did, he was always accompanied by a small group of gentlemen. They took over the house for a weekend here, a weekend there. On those occasions, all staff were sent home, given the weekend off.

Godfrey's problem was, His Lordship didn't really understand the labours of the garden. You couldn't just go home and ignore the place. There was watering to be done. Fruit and vegetables to be harvested. Seedlings to be moved out of the propagator onto the benches, plants pricked out or potted on. Then there were those that needed to go into the ground before they became pot bound. Godfrey used to sneak into the walled garden via the rear gate. Check there was nobody around, then quietly go about his business whilst keeping his head down and his ears peeled to ensure he wasn't found out. It was during the course of some of these covert operations that Godfrey got a pretty good idea what sort of weekend parties were actually going on at the manor. He picked up snippets of conversation over the garden wall. Heard the sounds of 'male engagement' and once, had even had to hide for over an hour as two of the manor's male guests were 'at it' in the greenhouse. An hour that Godfrey wished he could no longer hear in his head, but there it was, still.

And then, along came Abdul. Godfrey knew he was trouble with a capital T as soon as Sir Philip introduced him and that had been a warning there and then. He'd never introduced any other guest other than his old friend Piers Ward. Godfrey took an instant dislike to the boy. Hated the way he'd 'swan about', as if he already owned the place. Hated the way the boy would fuss and frolic around Sir Philip like some lamb around its mother. He was like a puppy, always running around, looking in places he had no need to. Godfrey even found him in the potting shed one day, apparently playing hide and seek with Sir Philip. Hide and seek, Godfrey had said, grown men playing hide and seek, whatever bloody next! He'd told the boy he shouldn't be in there, there were things that could get damaged. Abdul had told him point blank that 'm'Lord' said he could go anywhere. He didn't need permission from a servant. That hadn't been the end of the matter. Abdul had obviously gone running to Sir Philip with tales of wrongdoing, because the next day he was called up to Sir Philip's study and given a rollicking. The first and only time that Sir Philip had ever spoken to him that way; it was like being back at school. Humiliating and had upset him greatly. It wasn't long after that that Lady Pamela arrived for a couple of weeks break and summoned them all to her to announce that she and Sir Philip were splitting up, going their separate ways. Then she'd packed her things, picked up the boys from school and disappeared off to France for the rest of the year, leaving the estate with a quiet, subdued air. The following month, the bottom fell out of Godfrey's world.

Sir Philip announced that, on her return from France, Lady Pamela would be moving to the gatehouse lodge. The manor was to be converted into private apartments and flats to provide income for the estate as a whole. There'd also need to be cutbacks. This involved making many estate staff redundant. Some of them given notice of eviction from their homes at the same time, these included Godfrey. He was going to have to leave the home he'd lived in all his life. The home where he'd been born. The home where he'd raised his family, the place where his wife's and daughter's bodies had lain, awaiting their funerals. Worse still, after working for the

Stottard family for sixty years, he was to lose his job. The only reason he had for getting up in the morning. His passion, his life other than his son Peter. His only reason for living and only source of income. Godfrey had been shellshocked, devastated. Not certain what life was to hold for him now. Then Sir Philip had called him into his study and he'd been told.

"Godfrey," Sir Philip had said, "after all these years of splendid service to all of us in the Stottard family and the Boldean Estate, I wanted to give you this special gift as a mark of our respect and love for all that you've done."

"And he gave me a spade," Godfrey said, the glint of tears forming in the corners of his eyes. Memories still raw. "A bloody spade. If I wern't goin' to be working in the garden, what bloody use was a spade. I knew why I was gowin. Bloody Abdul. Cos I pissed 'im off, him got me to losing me job."

Peter was to take over as head gardener. Godfrey would have time to find somewhere else to live. As luck and love would have it, his son Peter only took a second to tell him they'd make space for him in their home. He'd have to move into the cottage his son had moved into when he'd gotten married and started his own family. As if that wasn't bad enough, Sir Philip had then told everybody they could all go home for the rest of the week and the weekend as he was having one of his parties, people would be arriving. So with one breath he'd ripped the heart right out of the estate, with the next, he was telling them all he was having a party. None of them could understand it. But Godfrey had other plans for the weekend. Peter had planted out all the runner beans that week and Godfrey had decided it was time to get the French beans planted around their frames and get the kale plants in the ground. He might be losing his job, but work went on. And that was how it had happened.

He'd gotten all the kale plants in the ground and watered by close of play on the Friday with no interruptions. Saturday, there'd been a lot of comings and goings around the main house. He'd kept clear for the morning until it settled down. After lunch, he'd listened at the gate and it all sounded quiet so he'd gone into the potting shed, entered through the greenhouses, to get string to run around the canes prior to planting the beans. Then he'd heard the scrape of the greenhouse door on the floor, accompanied by giggling and laughter. He'd recognised the voices straight away. The public-school voice of Piers Ward and the African French voice of Abdul. He'd waited to hear Sir Philip, but never heard him. Then the sounds of the two men giggling, removing each other's clothes. Things became heated. He heard the men engaged in passionate kissing, the sounds of deep breathing. He was wondering how long he was going to have to wait until he could escape, when he heard the scrape of the door on the slabs once again followed by exclamations of surprise and shock. It was obvious to Godfrey what was happening. Sir Philip had stumbled into the lovemaking between his old best friend and his new lover. He couldn't see what was happening, but whatever it was shocked Sir Philip. He kept saying, 'how could you, how could you'. He heard Piers tell Sir Philip it was nothing. Just a bit of fun. Then he heard the sound of a hard slap.

He couldn't tell at first who'd hit who, but then recognised Pier's sounds of pain and upset. The sounds of clothes being grabbed and the door opening again. He presumed somebody had left. Then he heard the whining voice of Abdul. "Oh, m'Lord, don't be silly, it was just fun."

He heard Sir Philip crying, saying, "How could you, Abdul, I love you."

Then Abdul, making light of it. "Don't be a silly Billy, m'Lord."

Godfrey felt sick to his stomach. Then he heard the door opening, the sobbing voice of Sir Philip fading as he left the greenhouse.

Godfrey stepped out of the potting shed to find Abdul kneeling on the floor, naked, gathering up his clothes. He'd looked up when Godfrey appeared from the next room and started giggling. He'd wagged a finger at Godfrey, said he was a 'naughty servant listening at doorways', he'd have to tell the master he'd been listening. Godfrey didn't know why he'd done it. Maybe it was the boy calling him a servant. Kneeling there in the dirt of the greenhouse floor, his body naked and shiny with sweat. Maybe because this boy held more sway with Sir Philip than all of Godfrey's sixty-odd years of service. Maybe it was because he found him guilty of destroying this family, this estate. Laying waste to generations of history and hard work. Trampling over the graves and bodies of family members gone before. Or maybe it was hearing the hurt in Sir Philip's voice as he'd walked away. The next thing Godfrey remembered was picking up the spade from on top of the bench where it lay, and slapping it, hard, into the side of the stupid boy's smiling face as he knelt with his back to Godfrey. That would stop him from giggling. It wasn't until the boy was lying on the floor, apparently dead, that Godfrey realised the enormity of what he'd done. He'd taken a life. He'd started to cry then and he'd cried inside for the last twenty-one years.

After a moment or two, Godfrey had snapped out of it. He'd had the realisation of the magnitude and consequences of what he'd just done. He'd go to prison. His son would lose his job, the family disgraced, lose their home, security. On top of that, Sir Philip would hate him. He had to get a grip of the situation, work fast. He left Abdul's body on the greenhouse floor and locked the door on his way out. He got his van, reversed it back against the gate, recovered Abdul's body and clothes into the back of the van. Dumped potting compost over the blood spilt on the paving slabs. Next, he had to think of somewhere to get rid of the body. First, he thought of the river Dart that flowed not far from the manor, but it would be discovered too quickly. It would be best if the body was never discovered at all. He was driving out of Totnes, heading for the A38 and Cornwall when he had the brainwave. Dartmoor. Miles of it, rolling away on the horizon to his right. Then the thoughts crystalized. He'd visited a farm once, near Princetown, to buy live geese to raise for the Christmas dinner at the manor. It was a wild and desolate place and the geese had all been wandering free around the farm, puddling about in a marshy area with a pond near the farmhouse.

Thirty minutes later, he was parked next to the big old stone barns where he'd gone to get the geese. He'd gotten out of the van, stood listening for sounds or sight of any farmer or worker. He'd a plan to ask if they still raised geese, could he put in an order if questioned. However, he could see and hear nobody. There were no vehicles about. Godfrey felt he'd struck lucky, maybe it was a market day. Either way, it was too good an opportunity to be missed. He'd reversed his van all the way down a trackway to where he'd once walked to choose his geese. He opened up the van doors, was about to lift the body out when it gave a groan. It took Godfrey by surprise, but there was no going back. Whatever happened next, he was in trouble. If Abdul regained consciousness, he would tell all. The whole family would be doomed. Godfrey had taken the belt from the boy's shorts that were in the back of the van and ripped of the buckle. He used it to tie the boy's arms behind his back. He'd thrown the body over his shoulder, grabbed his spade in case he had to bury the body and went through the gate towards the bog at the far side of the field. It was as he put the body down on the wet ground that Abdul had sprung to life. He couldn't talk properly, the initial smack with the spade had damaged the side of his face, but he started making a horrible, guttural, screaming noise.

Godfrey had to partly drag him out into the flooded, boggy part of the marsh until he himself was up to his knees and starting to sink, feeling the under-surface of the peaty bog starting to give way under his feet. Then Abdul had realised what was about to happen and struggled to his knees, but Godfrey knew what had to be done if his family were going to survive. Using the blade of the spade, he pushed it into the middle of the boy's back, right between the shoulder blades, then using just his body weight and the strength of fifty years of digging, Godfrey had pushed the body through the weeds that clothed the surface, forced it under the green slime and mossy plants until it was right out of sight under the brown liquid that now floated on the top.

At first, there had been some movement from the body, but it quickly stopped. By the time Godfrey was certain that

Abdul was no more, he was almost up to his waist in the mire, the body deep beneath him. He withdrew his spade and waded back out from the bog. Looked around and could see nobody but the rooks in the sycamore trees in the little woodland at the bottom of the field. He walked back to the van, threw the spade in the back, climbed in and drove home, throwing Abdul's clothes out of the window of the van bit by bit as he crossed the moorland. Arriving back home he managed to get changed and washed his new spade without anybody seeing, then still had time to string the canes and plant out the beans before tea time. Since then, he'd seen that boy's face every day when he woke; seen the look of fear in his eyes just before he'd pushed him under. Heard that horrible whining he'd made. But it was done and there was no way back.

Lancaster and Vidêt had sat spellbound for the last hour, listening to this man's story. It sounded farfetched, like an episode of some period drama, but at the same time, it all fitted. The timing of the discovery in the greenhouse. Piers Ward. The belt. The access to the farm and the mark across the shoulder blade. It all made sense, but for one thing.

"What did you make the marks on the face with?" Lancaster asked.

"What you mean? What marks?" Godfrey said.

Vidêt called up the picture from her phone showing the artist's impression and handed it to the man who looked at it and stared.

"I dunno what them is," he said.

"I don't suppose you still have the spade?" Lancaster asked.

"Course I still have the spade, tis only thing them ever give me. T'iz hung on the back of the door."

Vidêt went to the door where the man had pointed. Sure enough, a wooden handled, shiny, stainless steel, immaculate spade hung on a hook at the back of the door. She handed it to Lancaster. He looked at it. He didn't know much about garden tools, but it looked impressive, probably expensive. He weighed it in his hands. Certainly, with a little strength behind it, it could be a formidable weapon. He turned it over, looked at the back of the blade. On the rear of the bright shiny spade, in capital letters was an inscription:

FOR GODFREY BAYLIS.
FOR
ALL YOUR
ENDEAVOURS.

Lancaster studied it in detail. He took Vidêt's phone and the picture of the artist's impression showing the markings on Abdul's face. He froze the screen so it wouldn't flip the picture, then turned the screen till it was on its side. Realisation hit him.

If you smacked the boy across the side of his face hard enough with this engraved weapon, the sharp edges of the then fresh engraving would've left an indelible mark on the boy's soft skin, ready for the peaty water to impregnate the new, open scarring, slowly tanning it. Turning it over the years into a tattoo. When the letters had been stamped only the very flat back of the blade would have hit hard. All you would read were the letters:

ALL Y
DEAVO

Only in reverse, a mirror image on the boy's face. The text would be stood on end, just as Rover had suggested. Lose the back of the D, that gave you a half-moon at one end and the O, a full moon at the other. Losing the middle arm from inside the A's, gave you two arrow or spear points with the V and the Y pointing in alternate directions. The rest of them all certainly looked like 'Ogham Finger' writing he'd seen on the British Museum website. Lancaster realised he was holding the murder weapon used on Abdul, and sitting opposite was his murderer; an eighty-three-year-old disgruntled gardener, Godfrey Baylis.

Thirty minutes later and they'd called in the nearest uniformed officers in a police car. They took the now silent Godfrey away in the direction of Plymouth and their office interview room. Under arrest for the murder of Abdul Mehemet. Lancaster had no doubt whatsoever that they had their man. The person they felt most sorry for in this unfolding story was Godfrey's son, Peter. He'd been in total shock all the time his father had been speaking. It was all a complete revelation to him. He simply had absolutely no idea that his father had committed this horrible crime all those years ago. He could hardly remember the young Abdul. He could remember seeing him around, twenty-odd years ago, but he hadn't really made much of an impression. He'd just thought the guy was like an overgrown child. Lancaster told Peter he'd keep in touch, keep him informed as to what would happen to his father, and suggested the family prepare themselves for when the story broke.

As the two detectives walked back through the garden

towards their car, Lancaster suddenly started laughing. He tried to suppress it, feeling it inappropriate. Vidêt turned to look at him. His laughter then turned into a full blown, hysterical bout of laughter until he was bent double, hands on his knees. Vidêt couldn't help but think this was in very bad taste.

"What on earth do you find that is so funny?" Vidêt asked, looking at him slightly aghast.

Lancaster stopped his laughter, then reduced it to a smile. "I'm so sorry, Marie. I know, it's in very bad taste. But have you heard of the board game, Cluedo?"

"Of course. We have it in France."

"Well, I can't believe it. Here we are at the Cluedo country house, and it turns out our victim was murdered by the gardener. In the greenhouse with the spade. No drugs involvement. No angry blackmail victim or their operative. No broken-hearted lover, no fetish game that went wrong. Just the disgruntled gardener in the greenhouse... with a spade." With that he started laughing again, stopping only when they were in the car heading towards Plymouth.

By close of play that day, Godfrey Baylis had supplied a full written confession and had been charged with the murder and disposal of the body of Abdul Mehemet in May of 1999. He was to be confined for the moment in the cells at the station. It would be up to the Crown Prosecution Service to decide whether the eighty-three-year-old gardener was fit and able to stand trial. As far as Lancaster was concerned, the case was closed. Done and dusted. There were loose ends to tie up. They needed to contact Madame Mehemet and bring her up to speed, and they'd promised to contact various lovers he'd been with over his short life. Then there was the simple task of getting the body released and repatriated back to Narbonne. He decided that would be a job for Vidêt and it would all wait until the morning. But now, again, they'd missed lunch. It was time to eat.

EPILOGUE

The sun was hot on Lancaster's back. He and Marie stood in the Mehemet family plot, in a cemetery on the outskirts of Narbonne, watching the urn filled with Abdul Mehemet's ashes being laid to rest. The marble shrine had been next to a similar shrine that held the ashes of his late father, and one day, hold the pot containing the ashes of his mother. Today, despite the incredible heat of a southern French summer bearing down on them, and accompanied by the incessant, deafening sound of the cicadas in the trees surrounding the cemetery, Madame Mehemet was standing next to them, clothed from head to foot in black. Standing with them, but a step to one side, his old school friend and lover, Christopher. On trying to contact Maurice Durand they'd been saddened to hear, but not unduly surprised, that he'd since died. Only a couple of weeks after they'd interviewed him. To date, Lancaster hadn't found it necessary to tell Madame Mehemet the full story of her son's life and death. He felt no need to destroy her illusions of a good son trying to better himself, who'd gone to England only to be in the wrong place at the wrong time, to be murdered by an enraged gardener. So not having Maurice there did in fact make life just a little easier. There was slightly less to explain.

Having his old school friend attend was of course only natural.

Lancaster had been surprised when DCI Craven had told them he wanted the body to be accompanied back to France but Craven was adamant. The murder had been committed on his patch, on his watch, and he wouldn't stand for it. It didn't matter to Craven that the Stottards couldn't be implicated and that no great drugs bust had ensued. It was only right that this young lad, who'd believed that England was going to turn his life around, should receive the best return journey, accompanied by the two detectives who'd solved it. They should make sure that anybody that could be told, should know that this son of France had come home and that the crime had been solved by British detectives; the ones who'd listened.

The pair had booked into the same hotel as before and were catching a flight back home the next afternoon, from the much larger Carcassonne airport to the north. After the brief funeral service and drinks back at the family home of Madame Mehemet, an afternoon nap and an evening meal in the square. Apart from sleep, there was little else on their minds. No pressure to perform on either side; it was a relaxed and trusting relationship and they got their taxi back to Carcassonne the following morning and flew home.

Two days later, and the two detectives were standing by the remains of the now almost dry, grass-covered bog at the bottom of Whiddons Farm. They were there to fulfil a promise to Madame Mehemet to lay a special wreath of olive sprigs, Rosmarinus and the flowers of the iris, all plants of Algeria and ones that her son had often bought for her as a bouquet to remind her of the land where she'd been born.

They'd seen no sign of the farmer, Pete Claypole, when they arrived. In fact, the whole place had looked deserted. There were no animals in sight either. They'd presumed the stock had been taken to higher ground for the summer. Lancaster had informed the park ranger, Brian, of their intentions that day out of professional courtesy. They'd reached the bottom of the trackway leading to the lower meadow when the sound of another vehicle coming down the farm driveway alerted them to his arrival.

Once the detectives were standing inside the walled field waiting for Brian to join them, Lancaster was struck by the complete, natural silence held within this space. Yes, there were sounds. The leaves of the sycamore trees rustling in the breeze. The distant 'caw caw' of the rooks from the rookery, now no longer at roost, but working their way through the piles of sheep droppings across the moorland in the distance in search of food and, the mesmeric and hypnotic sound of trickling, skipping water, playing out tunes over the stones as the perennial waters of the mire continued to work their way down the drainage gulley to empty into the now beautiful pond created at the lower end of the meadow, around which grass and sedge had naturalised and spread, already making it look as if it had been there for ever. Dotted amongst the grasses were clumps of common buttercup and a fine leaved dandelion, flower heads moving and jostling in the breeze. Giant hawker dragonflies and smaller peacock-coloured damsels skirted the water's surface. Lancaster couldn't help but think, *if there was any truth in Madame Mehemet's belief. That the spirit of a person resided where they'd died. Then there couldn't be a better place on earth for Abdul Mehemet to reside. This water meadow was about as close to rural perfection and total tranquillity as you could get.*

Lancaster unwrapped the bouquet they'd brought. He didn't intend leaving any manmade product, plastic or rubber bands here in this little bit of perfection. He was about to lay the wreath when they were joined by Brian, holding hands with Alison. The pair walked through the gateway together and joined them by the old mire; nothing secret or hidden about their relationship now.

"Morning," Brian said to the detectives. "We hoped you wouldn't mind us joining you for this little ceremony. We sort of felt we were quite involved in this young boy's story. It was a big turning point for us."

"Not at all, it's nice that you could both find the time," The 'both' just left hanging in the air.

"Well, as you've probably noticed," Brian replied, holding tight to Alison's hand and picking up on the 'both' whilst it still hung, and dealing with it straight away, "I've separated from my wife. Alison and I are together as a couple now. We plan to take over the lease of this farm now Claypole's moved to another on the lowlands. He's under the impression there are better subsidies to be had than farming up here on the moor. Alison and I are in talks with the Parks Authority about creating an education centre up here. We plan to convert the old barns into a hostel for school groups to stay over. We intend working with the team at the university to uncover some of the hut circles dotted around this place and investigate the archaeology. Then put a whole package together teaching people about the ancient history of this valley and its ecosystems. Ali and I intend to move into the farmhouse once Claypole's finished shifting his rubbish, which shouldn't be too long now. We hope you won't mind, but we're having a piece of Dartmoor granite cut and carved with Abdul Mehemet's name and dates inscribed on it in memorial. We plan to set it into the wall, near to where we found him. I don't think we should hide what happened here, we just don't think he should be forgotten."

Lancaster said he agreed and liked the idea, to let him know when it was done and they'd both come out to see it put in place. He also offered to chip in to cover the cost. Abdul Mehemet's case had been a turning point in his life as well. Both he and Marie were now in a more regular, though still casual, relationship. Lancaster was convinced that, terrifyingly, the relationship was growing stronger by the day. At some stage, he thought, *a commitment might have to be made. He'd cross that bridge when he came to it.*

But for now, the case of Abdul Mehemet was finally closed.

WITH THANKS TO...

'Ludlow' Jane & Nigel, Lin, Paul, Greg, Matt & Julian, who gave me encouragement, constructive criticism and lots of support. And many thanks to the team at Cranthorpe Millner, for giving me the chance to get this story between the covers and out onto the shelves.